The pain in Savrinor couldn't drag in enough air and his head spun with nausea. But through the miasma he realized what Vordegh meant, what he intended to do, and suddenly the more formidable sickness of terror washed over him. Sweet gods, not this – they couldn't do to him what they had done to Iselia . . . he wouldn't be able to endure it, wouldn't be able to withstand the horror and the pain and the monstrous assaults on his mind –

He struggled against choking constriction to find his voice, and suddenly it came in a frantic surge. 'You know I am innocent of this charge! I'm no traitor – you know it, you of all men know it!' Dizziness flowed over him again in a hot, raging wave and his legs gave way. He sagged to the floor, and through blurred eyes stared beseechingly, agonizingly at Vordegh. 'It's a travesty . . .' The strength had gone from his voice and it was no more than a cracking whisper. 'I can't submit to this . . . I *can't!*'

Vordegh looked down at the foot of the block, at the thing that crouched there. 'Bring him,' he said.

A soft, wet sound came from the monstrosity's throat and, slowly but with repulsive purpose, it began to move. Savrinor saw it and his eyes started wildly. 'Ah, no . . .'

Then the pain hit him for the third time, and his protest turned into a cry of shock as a huge force seemed to erupt from within him, punching the breath from his lungs, blinding him with a black starburst. He heard Andraia shriek, but the weight under his ribs was crushing him and he couldn't move, couldn't reach out to her – he felt himself collapsing, felt the cold marble of the floor under him, and his hands clawed for purchase. *Get away from it* – he had to get away from the thing that was crawling towards him, for if it once reached him and touched him, he would lose his sanity –

BY THE SAME AUTHOR

Mirage

The Star Shadow Trilogy
(Prequel to The Time Master Trilogy)

Star Ascendant
Eclipse
Moonset

The Time Master Trilogy
The Initiate
The Outcast
The Master

The Chaos Gate Trilogy
(Sequel to the Time Master Trilogy)

The Deceiver
The Pretender
The Avenger

The Indigo Series

Nemesis
Inferno
Infanta
Nocturne
Troika
Avatar
Revenant
Aisling

Voyager

LOUISE COOPER

Moonset

The Star Shadow Trilogy Book III

HarperCollins*Publishers*

Voyager
An Imprint of HarperCollins*Publishers*
77–85 Fulham Palace Road,
Hammersmith, London W6 8JB

A Paperback Original 1995

1 3 5 7 9 8 6 4 2

A catalogue record for this book
is available from the British Library

ISBN 0 586 21725 8

Set in Linotron Sabon by
Rowland Phototypesetting Ltd
Bury St Edmunds, Suffolk

Printed in Great Britain by
HarperCollinsManufacturing Glasgow

This trilogy is warmly and appreciatively dedicated to June Hall, who, with her guidance, insight and acumen, showed a directionless ditherer that she should stick to her guns . . . and by so doing, brought Tarod and Yandros unequivocally back to life!

CHAPTER I

The first thing he was aware of as he regained consciousness was a stunning headache that had its root at the back of his skull and spread forward to clamp like an iron vice over his temples. In the early confusion of waking he believed for a few moments that he was in Magus Pirane's citadel once more, snatched by her sorcery out of the mayhem of the uprising and now recovering from what the rebels had done to him. But that was in the past now; this was something else . . . a second blow to his head, but not inflicted by any enraged mob. He didn't know who had hit him this time. He had been in the corridor outside the dining hall, talking to Savrinor – no, *arguing*, though he couldn't recall why – when with no warning there had been a violent impact that knocked him senseless. And afterwards, he had dreamed . . .

Then something cold and crawling and sick took hold of him as his mind, and with it his memory, cleared at last. *Not a dream.* Iselia's secret, the deception he had helped her to maintain since the night she came to the Star Peninsula, was known. And Savrinor had been about to go to the magi –

Benetan Liss's eyes snapped open, and with a shout of horror and denial he sat bolt upright in his bed.

'Captain Liss!' A woman's voice cut across his and a figure flurried at him, hands pressing him back. 'Lie *down*, Captain!' The room was dimly lit, curtains shut against the night, and for a moment he didn't know who the woman could be. She smelled of herbs and something sharper, acrid; then in the glow from the fire burning in

I

the hearth he recognized the round face of Kitrir, the herb-aller who tended minor injuries and illnesses in the castle.

'Still, now, be still.' Kitrir's tone dropped and, oblivious to his confused attempts to protest, she began to examine his skull with a firm, expert hand. 'The blow drew blood; you must have struck against a sharp edge, and I don't want that cut to be re-opened.' She peered closer. 'Hmm, well, no more damage done, it seems . . . How did you come by this, Captain? An accident?'

He drew breath, but before he could speak another voice interposed sharply.

'Captain Liss slipped, herballer, nothing more. As you say, an accident.'

The answer Benetan had been about to give died on his tongue and he turned his head, ignoring Kitrir's renewed admonishments. A figure was sitting in a chair, away from the fire, in shadow. But he knew her voice, and even in the dimness there was a gleam of fire and copper in her hair.

He said, 'Andraia . . . ?'

Andraia, who had been his lover for two years before the split provoked by their last and most vicious quarrel, didn't answer him but instead rose to her feet and came to stand at the foot of the bed. As she moved into the light he saw that her face was very pale, her eyes red-rimmed, and her expression had a hard, bitter edge. She gazed at him for a few moments, then – deliberately it seemed – turned away and addressed Kitrir again. 'If you've done all you can, herballer, I will thank you to leave us.' A pause. 'If you please.'

Kitrir didn't like the order, but she knew she was in no position to argue with someone of Andraia's rank. She made a small bow. 'As you wish, madam. But the captain shouldn't be allowed to exert himself in any way until –'

'I'll see he stays where he is, and you may call on him again in the morning.' Andraia's tone was unrelenting, and Kitrir departed, though with obvious reluctance. As the door closed behind her Benetan struggled upright again. Though he knew there were a hundred other things he should have said, only one subject goaded him, and he asked desperately, 'What hour is it?'

Andraia turned the key in the lock. She glanced at him again, still with that alien expression. Then she walked back towards the fire.

'Andraia! Andraia, *please* – I have to know!'

She looked over her shoulder. 'Why?' Her voice was flat, indifferent.

'You know why! Gods, I tried to explain; I tried –'

'Oh, you remember that, do you?' Her eyes glinted angrily as she turned her back on him again.

'Of course I remember! I was trying to make Savrinor understand; I was trying to make you *both* understand, and then something hit me and –'

'I hit you.' She said it without any emotion whatever. 'With a wine flagon.'

'With a . . .' He stared. 'Andraia, why did you *do* it? I only wanted you to listen to me, to *see* –'

Suddenly, violently, she rounded on him. 'I *see*, Benetan Liss! I see exactly what you are, and what you've done, and –'

A knock at the door interrupted her. Andraia's tirade snapped off in mid-sentence; she glared at the door for a moment as though it were something lethal, then went to answer the knock. Benetan heard an exchange of whispers, a key grating, then the door opened. Someone slipped silently into the room, walked to the bed, looked down, and Benetan's eyes narrowed furiously as he recognized his visitor.

'You spineless hypocrite – what in the Seven Hells are you doing here?'

'Be quiet, Benetan, and stop behaving like a damned fool!' Savrinor, the castle's senior historian, pocketed the key that Andraia had given him and sat down on the bed.

He wasn't his usual immaculate self; his long, fair hair was ragged and his silk shirt wet, as though he had been out in the snow without a coat. His face was dead-white, haggard, and his pale eyes held a nightmarish look that for once wasn't induced by narcotics.

'One word from you about my behaviour tonight and I'll pick up your own knife and cut your throat where you lie!' he said quietly but savagely. 'I've spent the past hour trying to save your skin, and I think I might have succeeded; so if you feel anything towards me at this moment, it should be gratitude!'

Benetan stared back, horrified. 'What have you done? *Where's Iselia?*'

'I've done what I had to do. And Iselia's whereabouts are none of your concern – or they won't be from now on, if you've a single grain of sense left in your head.' Savrinor's eyes narrowed. 'Forget her, Benetan. You've no other choice.'

'No!' Benetan flung the blankets back and tried to struggle out of the bed, but pain shot through his skull like fire and with a gasp he fell back, shutting his eyes in an effort to stem physical and mental agony. For a few seconds he couldn't breathe, but at last the thumping in his head receded a little, and he dragged air into his lungs before opening his eyes once more and looking at Savrinor with impotent hatred.

'You degenerate *serpent*.' He tried to swallow, found he had no saliva. 'You went to the magi, didn't you? You betrayed her!'

'*Betrayed* her?' Savrinor repeated the word incredulously. 'In the sacred name of our Lord Yandros, she's a heretic! Don't you understand that even now? She has rendered her soul to the demons of Order, she grovels at the feet of that evil monstrosity Aeoris – she has committed an act of *treason*!' He stood up, loathing warping his expression. 'Do you know where the First Magus found her, Benetan? In his own chambers, in the innermost sanctum!'

'I don't believe that!'

'Believe what you please; it makes no difference to the facts! She had a knife in her hand, and she tried to use it on Lord Vordegh.'

Benetan made an ugly, inchoate sound and covered his eyes. Iselia was dead. He couldn't doubt it now; not if she had fallen into Vordegh's hands.

'No . . .' he whispered. 'Oh no, oh no, no . . .' A racking breath sawed in his throat. 'She told me there was nothing more to it . . . she told me that they'd simply leave, go; she *promised* . . .'

'Then she lied.' Savrinor didn't unbend, though if Benetan had had the wit to look for it he would have seen a pain to match his own in the historian's eyes. 'She duped you, just as she duped me for so long. And now she may have condemned you with her.'

Benetan didn't care about that, couldn't even assimilate it; he was crying, and though he knew it was both foolish and futile the tears wouldn't stop. Savrinor watched him for a few moments, then with a sigh that hovered uneasily between embarrassment and anger he stood up and thrust one hand into a pocket, pulling out a small twist of paper. He turned to Andraia, who was standing a little way behind him, mute and miserable.

'Mix this in a cup of something – wine, beer, it doesn't matter. It'll calm him down, and relieve his headache more efficiently than any of Kitrir's third-rate nostrums. He's going to need a clear head if he's to keep it at all.'

She looked back at the historian, and her eyes glittered. 'He still loves her. Even now, knowing what she is.' Suddenly something within her seemed to fold in on itself; she went to him and pressed her face against his shoulder, biting at the knuckles of a clenched fist. '*How can he?*'

Savrinor stroked her hair. 'I know,' he said. 'I know.'

Benetan still loved Iselia, and Andraia still loved Benetan, and he himself ... but in truth he no longer knew with any certainty what he felt; those waters were too deep and too turbulent for anything to be clear any more. 'Oh, gods,' he added desolately, 'This is an unholy tangle.'

Andraia straightened, sniffing and wiping ineffectually at her eyes. 'I'm sorry.' She was making great efforts to control her voice, force out the tremor. 'I didn't mean to ...' She shook her head, knowing he understood and that there was no need to say more, and stepped back. 'I'll mix the powder.' She took it from him and walked away.

Between them they made Benetan drink the concoction, and when it had gone down Savrinor sat on the bed once more and turned the younger man forcibly to face him.

'Now, you're to listen to me, and you're to take heed,' he said tautly. 'Whatever the rights and wrongs of this abysmal episode – and I'm not going to get into another argument about it, there isn't time – you're in danger, and I may be the only person in the castle who can help you.'

Benetan's lip curled, though he still felt too weak to express himself more forcefully. 'Do you think I give a white curse for your help, after what you've done?'

'You should, if you want to stay alive.' Savrinor hunched his shoulders restively. 'It would have been better for all concerned if the First Magus had simply killed her where she stood, but as it is –'

'What?' Benetan sat bolt upright. 'What do you mean, *if* he'd killed her? Are you saying she isn't ...'

'Dead?' When he couldn't bring himself to utter the word, Savrinor voiced it for him. 'No, she isn't dead.' He saw the spark of hope that lit in Benetan's eyes; it disgusted him, and goaded him into speaking more explicitly than he might otherwise have done. 'She has been taken to the Marble Hall, where I imagine at this moment Physician-Magus Croin is patching together what's left of her sanity

6

and preparing her for the discomfort, shall we say, of interrogation.'

Benetan said, chokingly, 'Gods —'

'The gods aren't involved in it.' Savrinor's eyes glinted malevolently. 'Yet. But under the circumstances you might be well advised to consider what you'll have to say when they *do* become involved — either to Magus Croin, or to our Lord Yandros.'

'Me?' Benetan's face blanched.

'Yes, you!' Savrinor's tone was shot through with anger once more. 'Don't you realize what I'm trying to tell you? As yet the magi know only the bare bones of this story, but that won't pertain for long. Croin is a master of his art, and with the First Magus standing at his shoulder he'll stint nothing whatever. Iselia will tell them *everything* — including the identity of her husband, and the name of the man who conspired, innocently or otherwise, to bring him to the castle!' He paused. '*Now* do you understand?'

Benetan did — but it meant nothing to him. All he could think of was Iselia. A prisoner, her allegiance known, taken to the Marble Hall and given into the appalling care of Croin . . .

'If she told you what she planned,' Savrinor said, 'she'll confess it. She won't be able to stop herself. *Did* she tell you, Benetan? Did you know where she had gone, and what she intended to do?'

'No! I knew nothing about it! If I had, I would —' And he stopped as an inner voice asked: *What would you have done, Benetan Liss? If she had confided it all to you, told you that she and Kaldar meant to strike a blow against the magi, even against Chaos itself . . . would you have stopped her?* He covered his face again as grief swamped him and with it an appalling confusion of memories. Memories of the atrocities he had witnessed, committed in the name of Chaos by the gods' own avatars; memories of his desperate pleas to Yandros to intervene and stop the

7

carnage, to which there had been no answer. And the memory of a barren island, and kindly people, and the serene face of Aeoris, highest Lord of Order, a god in exile holding out the hand of friendship to a man he should have hated and reviled. For twelve years Benetan had served Chaos faithfully, had never questioned its ways or the ways of the magi who interpreted its laws. The horrors he had seen had shaken his conviction but had not shattered it; even Aeoris had not shattered it, for Benetan had also looked on the face of Yandros of Chaos and knew what it was to be held in his favour. But this . . .

Savrinor spoke again, softly. 'I've done what I can, Benetan. I've told Magus Pirane that I believe you to be the victim of a clever deception, just as I was.' He smiled, but the smile had no trace of amusement. 'I even took the risk of reminding her that your red-haired friend was resourceful enough to deceive Lord Vordegh himself. But although the lady magus accepted my point . . . or appeared to . . . simply swearing to your innocence might not be enough to redeem you.' Suddenly he leaned forward, his eyes intent. 'You *must* clear yourself, and the only way to do it is to prove to the magi, unequivocally, where your fealty lies! Even now the Chaos riders are being mustered to go after Tarkran; you must be ready to lead them, to –'

He was interrupted. 'Kaldar hasn't been caught?'

'Seven Hells, does that *please* you?' Savrinor shouted. 'Benetan –' He took a grip on himself and his voice dropped. 'Benetan, for all the gods' sakes try to comprehend! You're no devotee of that foul cult, you're as loyal to Chaos as . . .' Then the words faded and died as he saw what was in Benetan's eyes. Savrinor had been about to say, *as loyal to Chaos as I am*, but suddenly his certainty was sliding away into a void, and it horrified him.

He said sharply, 'You *are* loyal! I know you are, and that hasn't changed; it can't have changed! You know the truth; you know what's right – *Yandros!*' He jumped like a startled cat as suddenly a fist hammered on the door.

'Captain Liss!' A man's loud voice sounded from the corridor outside. 'Captain Liss, are you there?'

Savrinor jerked round, staring at the door, and Andraia, who had returned to her chair in the shadows, got quickly to her feet.

'It's Averel.' Benetan had recognized his senior sergeant's tones and he frowned, nonplussed by the others' reaction.

'Yes.' Savrinor gave him an unfathomable look, and in that look he seemed to have aged ten years. He drew Andraia's key from his pocket and held it out to her. 'Open the door and let the sergeant in. We might as well get it over with.'

Sergeant Averel came into the room, and three more Chaos riders followed him. They were in full regalia; black clothes, silver accoutrements, circlets with the Seven-Rayed Star of Chaos glinting harshly over their brows. All were fully armed . . . and a sick feeling took hold of Benetan as he saw, clipped to Averel's left shoulder, a heavy silver flash adorned with seven quartz pendants. As the Chaos riders' leader Benetan wore two such emblems on his own shoulders, the badges of his rank. And he knew that under only a single circumstance could one such badge be carried by another man – if the magi had placed that man in temporary command.

'Captain Liss.' Averel's voice sounded strained and he didn't – or couldn't – meet Benetan's eyes but fixed his gaze above the bed. 'By order of First Magus Vordegh, you are relieved of duty. You are to be . . .' He swallowed. 'You are to be placed under arrest and detained in a fitting manner, to await further investigation in the matter of the captured heretic.' A muscle in his neck worked convulsively and his shoulders sagged a little, though he still didn't look at Benetan. 'I'm sorry, Captain . . .'

'Oh, gods.' Savrinor rose and crossed the room to where

Andraia stood rigid. He saw the horror and disbelief on her face, saw that her self-control was a brittle stem which could snap at any moment, and his arm went round her, drawing her towards him. 'Hush,' he said as her mouth began to quiver. 'Hush, now. It's all right, they're not going to harm him.' He hadn't expected this; he had hoped that his own intercession with Pirane might have been enough to make it unnecessary. Clearly, though, Pirane had been unable to sway the First Magus. 'Let them do what they must, Andraia. It won't come to anything, I'm sure of it.' He looked up. Benetan was climbing out of bed, assisted by one of the riders. He looked bemused.

Then Averel turned to face Savrinor.

'Master Savrinor.' He made the Chaos riders' salute; it was a long-ingrained habit when addressing anyone of high rank. But his tone gave away the truth, and Savrinor felt as if the blood were draining out of him. 'Master Savrinor, by command of First Magus Vordegh you also are under arrest.'

There was a sharp silence. Eventually, Savrinor broke it. 'To await further investigation . . . ?'

'No, sir. There is a formal charge against you.'

Savrinor stared at him. His face had turned grey and it was some while before he could find his voice again. 'What charge?' he asked very quietly.

Averel looked miserable. 'Treason, sir.'

For several seconds Savrinor continued to stare, but Averel's burly figure no longer registered in his brain. All he knew was a reeling, helpless terror, as though some vast force had coiled itself around him and was crushing him, slowly, inexorably and without hope of reprieve. Treason . . . it wasn't possible, for it wasn't *true!* He was no traitor and the First Magus knew that he wasn't.

But then the First Magus also harboured a deep, abiding dislike for him; a dislike which had been seeking an outlet for a long, long time . . .

Suddenly Andraia swung round, placing herself between him and the sergeant, and her voice shrilled out. 'This is preposterous – it's a mistake, it *must* be a mistake! Savrinor isn't a traitor!'

'I'm sorry, madam, truly I am,' Averel said desperately, 'but the First Magus –'

'*The First Magus can go to –*'

'Andraia, no.' Savrinor gripped her arm, silencing her before she could damn them both. 'Don't make matters worse.'

'But it's unjust!' She ignored Benetan's sudden caustic bark of laughter, for she had forgotten the circumstances of their last and most savage quarrel, in Magus Pirane's citadel after the abortive uprising. 'The gods have no servant more loyal than Savrinor, and they know it even if Lord Vordegh doesn't!' She whirled again, snatching herself free from Savrinor's grasp, and her eyes burned wildly. 'Savrinor, tell him, make him understand!' Savrinor shook his head. Her outburst had in one sense been his saving grace, for it had broken the paralysis of blind terror that had threatened to overwhelm him. The terror was still there; oh yes, it was still *there* and nothing would dislodge or lessen it. But he was in control. Iron control, granite control. He *had* to be.

'My love.' He used the term of endearment deliberately, felt her hands take hold of his in response and was grateful for it. 'It will be all right. I promise you. If the First Magus believes I've done wrong, he'll soon see that there's no evidence.' His tongue touched his lower lip and it felt like old, dry parchment. 'Speak to Lady Pirane. Be sure that she knows what's afoot.' He glanced in Benetan's direction. 'For both our sakes.'

'I'll do more than that! I'll appeal to –'

'No.' He knew what she was about to say and didn't want her to utter it. It would be a profanity, a negation of a principle that he refused to break. 'No, Andraia. It's too trivial, and the gods owe no debt to either of us. You know that.'

Sergeant Averel cleared his throat noisily. 'I beg pardon, sir. But if you please . . .'

His face devoid of colour and his mind dulled to resignation by dread, Savrinor nodded. 'I quite understand, Sergeant. And I appreciate that this is nothing personal against me or your captain. You're simply obeying the First Magus, as we all must.' He kissed Andraia; she tried to hold on to him but he wouldn't allow it. One swift look towards her mirror, a reflex he couldn't break even now; with a lingering vestige of self-respect he smoothed a hand over his hair. 'Very well, Sergeant Averel. I'm not altogether familiar with procedure in these circumstances, but I presume you'll lead on?'

The party left, Averel and one of the riders flanking Benetan, the other two walking beside Savrinor. Benetan hadn't uttered a word since the sergeant's arrival, and he didn't look back at Andraia. Nor did Savrinor look back, but that, Andraia knew, was for her sake rather than for his own.

The sound of the door closing was, to her churning senses, like a distant and threatening rumble of thunder. She stayed motionless for a long time afterwards, afraid that if she moved, the frail threads that held her together would break. Then suddenly the nature of her fear changed and she knew that she *must* move, must get away from this room, Benetan's room, with its memories and its terrible associations.

A low, unhappy sound tried to bubble up in her throat, and savagely she forced it back. Then she wrenched the door open and ran, out into the corridor, away towards the sanctuary of her own chamber. And as she ran, she prayed, an anguished litany not to Yandros but to his brother-lord, who once had granted her a privilege that few mortal women could ever know.

'Lord Tarod, please help me! Oh, Lord Tarod, if you remember me as you did once before, and if you care for those who love you, please help me now!'

CHAPTER II

The sky split open as though cracked by a titanic hammer-blow, and searing black light blasted across the landscape, twisting the contours of the mile-high rock formations into new and impossible distortions. Far in the distance something screeched in a frenzy of joy, and the sound mutated into a wild squall that drove horizontally over and past the stack where the seven had gathered. '*Prayers!*' Yandros's molten eyes followed the progress of the squall, then he turned his head to look at the translucent rock at his feet, down through the sheer drop into howling nothing. 'I am not interested in *prayers!* If we answered every individual plea, every petty supplication, we'd be dragged down under a weight of purposeless trivia between one sunset and the next, and what would that achieve? *Nothing* – save for a pallid and enfeebled world, filled with pallid and enfeebled mortals incapable of asking each other the time of day without our sanction!' Lightning spat violently overhead, making the rocks sing back an echo, and the greatest Chaos lord glared at his brother with barely-suppressed fury. '*Damn* you, Tarod! You began this; you see it through – I've far more urgent matters on my mind!'

Tarod's black hair snapped in the wind that had risen again in response to Yandros's anger, and his eyes, green and unfathomable, closed momentarily as he inclined his head. Ostensibly he seemed to have acknowledged and accepted the reprimand, but when he looked up again Yandros knew that his mind was focused on something beyond the boundaries of the Chaos realm.

'This state of affairs doesn't sit any more easily on my

shoulders than it does on yours,' Yandros continued less ferociously. 'You know my view of First Magus Vordegh — and Savrinor of all mortals doesn't deserve such treatment; he's one of the very few whose devotion to Chaos *isn't* in doubt. But the issue goes far deeper than the fate of one man, or a hundred, or a hundred thousand. It strikes directly at *us*.' His eyes changed from gold to crimson. 'Or it could well threaten to.'

All six of his brother Chaos lords watched him in silence as he began to pace. Yandros was aware that he had their full attention now. 'Two mortals,' he said. 'Only two; but between them they drew an impenetrable curtain over the magi's eyes, and almost succeeded in gaining control of the wand which links us to the Chaos Gate. But for Savrinor, helped by the young woman Tarod has been favouring' — he flicked a sharp glance in Tarod's direction — 'and who now appears by a complicated chain of events to have become something more than a friend to Savrinor, they would have succeeded. Succeeded, in the face of all the magi's knowledge and power — indeed, in the face of all *our* knowledge and power.' He stopped and turned to face them all. 'Theoretically, that is not possible. But theory appears to have been found wanting; instead we are faced with some very unpalatable *facts*. And from those facts I can draw only one conclusion. Contrary to my own convictions — and yes, for a long time I dismissed the possibility; but now I'm prepared to admit I was wrong — the forces of Order are at work again.'

On the vast horizon light shivered suddenly, and a deep, slow vibration began to pulse in the rock beneath their feet. One of Yandros's brothers moved restlessly; there was a scent of the sea as his hair swung, and a gaunt, graceful hand, silver-tipped, flung the grey-green curtain of it back. 'And not only in their own realm,' he said, his voice quiet but lethal. 'They couldn't have broken the strictures we set upon them after our last encounter.' A smile, and the promise of insanity flickered in his eyes. 'Even Aeoris isn't capable of that.'

'No, he isn't.' Yandros returned the smile briefly. 'Yet for all our powers, the seal between Order's realm and the mortal world has never been entirely perfect. Aeoris, as you say, could not breach it – but from the other side it might be a different matter.'

'It would take sorcery of a level known only to the magi to break through.'

'Indeed. And that's why I assumed – erroneously, it now seems – that they and we would have been aware of any such untoward activity and could crush it.' Yandros frowned at the sky, which was changing colour and darkening. The vibration hesitated, then began again more forcefully. 'The magi have always taken care to ensure that any mortal with the potential to become such a sorcerer is nurtured and trained at the Star Peninsula, but it appears that someone has slipped through their net. And that same someone has learned enough to conceal their intent, and even their existence, from all scrutiny. Including ours.'

A fourth Chaos lord, black-haired as Tarod but with a gracious serenity that contrasted sharply with Tarod's volatile edge, spoke up. 'If that's so, Yandros, then the magi have been negligent.'

'In one sense, perhaps. But the magi aren't omnipotent, and I'd be a rank hypocrite if I censured them for failings which we ourselves share.' Yandros laughed ironically, aware that he had aired this matter before, and recently. 'If we had the ability to see all that takes place in their world, and were capable of reading the minds and hearts of all mortals to the marrow and beyond, life would be a great deal easier for us; although I'll admit that it would also be a great deal less interesting. But we don't have that power, despite what many of our worshippers may like to believe. And if a mortal sorcerer has succeeded in making contact with the forces of Order, then I've no doubt that

Aeoris remembers enough of his old tricks to be able to shield that person, and his followers, from discovery. That, at least in potential, is a dangerous situation.'

Tarod couldn't keep silent any longer. 'Which is precisely why I feel we should set the magi aside and intervene directly!'

His brother's unquiet gaze turned on him. 'And by so doing, overturn all the principles and watchwords by which we stand. I've told you before, Tarod, and I'll tell you again – I will *not* countenance that! What would we become, if we took to controlling our followers and dictating their every move? That's Order's way, not ours, and if –' he broke off, realizing that the argument was all too familiar. Overhead, a twisting vortex appeared in the sky and began to suck the black light into itself, draining the landscape of colour and perspective.

'We can no longer trust the magi,' Tarod said quietly.

Yandros drew a vivid, coruscating cloak around himself and stared moodily into the middle distance. Shadows moved in his fiery golden hair. 'If by that you mean that we can no longer trust First Magus Vordegh, then I have no choice but to agree with you. His mania is such, now, that he's become obsessed with these personal grudges of his and will go to any lengths to pursue them.' He glanced over his shoulder. 'Savrinor being a case in point, and even that young fool Benetan Liss, though I'm less sure of him.'

'And for the sake of personal grudges, he's losing sight of the greater objective,' Tarod said. 'Meting out random punishments, using this latest development as an excuse to strike at Savrinor, while the real enemy continues to run free. As you said yourself, the attempt to steal the wand almost succeeded – what will they achieve next time? Vordegh should be removed!'

'I've considered removing him. Believe me, I've considered it very seriously indeed. But I still say it would be a betrayal of our principles.'

'He's also turning the ordinary people against the magi, and against us,' Tarod persisted. 'These edicts –'

'Yes, I *know*. I've seen some of the monstrosities he's created to do his work for him, and I like them no more than you do. But he hasn't called directly on us. He has used only his own powers, and his own imagination.' His gaze raked his brother briefly. 'That, as I recall, was your complaint the last time we discussed this; the fact that what Vordegh was perpetrating was carried out in our name. It's no longer true.'

'And therefore you won't stop him.'

'Precisely.' Yandros turned fully to face him at last. 'How can I? My nature – the nature of us all – is Chaos, and one of the great paradoxes of Chaos is that, in all fundamental matters, we are constant.' The corners of his mouth twitched, but without humour. 'Aeoris would bend his own rules without blinking, if it suited his purpose to do so. His only interest is in preserving Order's inexorable progress,' his lips had a cynical curve now, 'and if the parameters needed to maintain that progress should change, he will change them and think nothing of it. We view the course of existence, mortal or otherwise, differently. And another word for our view is freedom.'

Tarod realised that the two of them now stood alone on the rock stack, and he sighed. Their brothers knew that this was an old argument between himself and Yandros, and one which had never been resolved to either's satisfaction. They knew, too, that Yandros's link with and affection for Tarod had an extra dimension, inexplicable but substantial, and, acknowledging it without rancour, they had silently withdrawn.

He raised his left hand, upturned, palm open. The landscape melted and faded into a soft dusk shot through with a rosy hint like a sunset's afterglow. Quiet swept over them; suddenly there were silent, flowing walls of water where the harsh rocks had been, and they stood in a richly – and mortally – furnished room.

Yandros looked assessingly at the new surroundings. 'You know me too well,' he said.

'As well as I know myself.'

'Yes, and that's half the problem, isn't it?' Yandros walked across the room and sank down onto a couch, resting his head against its piled cushions. 'Very well. I understand you, and you understand me, and we both know that in this one matter our views are not in harmony. I won't try to persuade you that I'm right and you're wrong, for I don't even know if that's the truth.' He looked at the undulating wall; a window appeared, and beyond the window was mayhem. 'If that scene reflects my mood and my doubts, so be it. This is in the magi's hands, and it is for me, ultimately, to decide whether or not it shall remain so. I have made my decision, and for all our sakes I won't change it. The magi must resolve and defeat this threat unaided.'

'The threat of Order, or the threat of Vordegh?'

Yandros's eyes narrowed; outside, bands of dark, murky colour began to wheel across the screaming sky. 'Both.'

There was a long pause. Then Tarod said carefully, 'Would you at least consider our . . . advising them?'

Abruptly the pulsing vibration returned with a new and deadly emphasis. 'If by that you mean delivering a warning of where Vordegh's road might lead,' Yandros replied, 'yes, I might consider it. But we would do no more than advise. We *can* do no more than that, Tarod. Vordegh is their responsibility. And as for the threat that Order might pose . . . well, you know the truth as well as I do, however unpalatable it might be. Order's realm is beyond our ability to penetrate, and if they have established a foothold in the mortal world, that, too, is shielded from our scrutiny. Our natures are inimical; we can't touch them, we can't stop them . . . we can't even overlook them, or whoever is working on their behalf. Only the magi have that power.'

'And Savrinor?' Tarod asked.

'Ah, the discussion comes full turn again. Savrinor . . . well, from what I know of him, he's skilled enough to talk or inveigle his way out of most predicaments.'

'He might fail on this occasion.'

'Yes . . . That wouldn't please me. But I'm not sure that even Vordegh is *quite* mad enough, yet, to forget all else in the pursuit of one man who has committed no crime.' Then Yandros looked up at his brother. 'I will, however, bear your misgivings in mind, and if the Lady Andraia's heartfelt prayer should need an answer then I might contemplate breaking with our precedent.' He hesitated, then raised a finger warningly. 'But I don't want you taking matters into your own hands. You know my views about liaisons with mortals; they're a pleasurable diversion but they shouldn't be carried too far.'

Tarod nodded, masking a smile. 'I understand. And thank you.'

'Don't thank me; I've made no promises.' Yandros reclined more comfortably then glanced up. The ceiling of the room Tarod had created faded, exposing a sky that had darkened to a grim spectrum of browns and purples and blood-reds. At a silent command from Yandros the walls of the room turned from water into fire.

'We'll watch,' he said, and his silver eyes reflected the fire's gory light. 'But no more than that, Tarod. Not yet.'

The north wind was howling like a soul in torment, and no matter how hard he strove, Kaldar couldn't shut the noise of it out of his mind. Though the cave was deep enough in the mountain flank to protect him from the bitter world outside, it couldn't shield him from that abysmal, elemental voice but only magnified it until he felt his head would burst apart.

He *had* to get his will back under control. The fire wasn't burning properly, and with only scant dregs of carbon-fuel to feed it, and those wet when he gathered them, he needed *power* if it wasn't to fail altogether. And he had to have the fire. Without it, he would be helpless.

Cross-legged on the cold floor, Kaldar rocked himself violently back and forth, striving to force his mind to focus on the energy-raising chant. His teeth chattered as his lips formed the words, and the sound of the blizzard was driving a swathe through his concentration, raising unwanted images that he struggled to blot out. Iselia in the magi's hands, her secret betrayed, captured before she could flee the castle. His own narrow escape through the Maze and into the uninhabited mountain ranges . . . Gods, if only he hadn't agreed to *wait* for her; if only he'd taken the risk, gone in through those black gates, searched for her and used sorcery, if necessary, to try to bring her out . . . But the time for self-recrimination was past; he had put himself through that torment with ferocious thoroughness and to go over the ground again would achieve nothing. There might still be a chance to save her. And *nothing* must stop him from fixing his entire being on that.

A brighter tongue of flame licked suddenly in the sullen, failing fire, and there was a sharp hiss of trapped gases escaping as one of the pieces of fuel split in two. Kaldar's blue eyes focused intently on the flame, and the whispered chant became more urgent. His skin was beginning to tingle, not with heat but with a charge of energy that rose from deep within his psyche. Yes, *yes* – the rigorous discipline he had instilled in himself over the years was coming to his aid, and the power was rising. Now: *will* the flame to grow . . .

A violent exhalation punched from him as abruptly the fire leaped into vivid life. Light flared across the cave floor and danced on the walls, and Kaldar scrabbled on hands and knees to snatch up the small pack which was all he had carried with him when he and Benetan left the White Isle. The mind-expanding incense was there, carefully stowed under his spare clothes, and he pulled it out, measuring seven grains into his palm.

He was, he knew, taking a terrible risk. He didn't believe that the magi were able to trace the destination of anyone who had left the Star Peninsula through the Maze, but he was also aware that that belief could well be wrong. If it was, there was every chance that the Chaos riders had already been despatched in pursuit of him and were even now combing the mountain pass, closing in. And if the magi had called something out of Chaos itself to help the riders in their search, then at the first scent of sorcery those monstrosities would have him. He should have set an astral sentinel, something that would warn him of their approach in time for him to escape, but to do so would have drained too much of his strength as well as using up precious time. Whatever the dangers, he must act without any delay and pray that his gods had enough power to shield him and his work from discovery.

The incense grains sizzled as he dropped them into the fire's heart, and a sharp, heady smell assailed Kaldar's nostrils. He breathed in deeply, drawing the pungent scent into his lungs, into his brain. Then he closed his eyes, forcing himself not to fight the giddiness that always preceded this ritual, and felt his senses begin to distort. The cave walls – he couldn't see them now but he could sense them – seemed to slide away into a vast, echoing emptiness; heat and cold pulsed through him in regular, alternating waves, and he was no longer aware of the rock surface under his body.

Abruptly, forcefully, he felt the side-slip out of normal consciousness. His eyes flicked open, staring into the smoke, seeing only the smoke, and his mind projected the call of Order's innermost coterie.

Brothers of Aeoris. Sisters of Aeoris. The night is silent but the day brings a flash of lightning. Hear me and answer. Hear me and answer.

As the silent message went out, Kaldar's inner eye formed an image of the long-house on Summer Isle, where he knew that Simbrian and his fellow sorcerers kept vigil, constantly alert for any telepathic contact from the mainland. For a moment he feared that his skill would not be great enough to project the call over such an enormous distance, but reminded himself fiercely that physical proximity could have no bearing. All he needed was the will. Only the *will*.

Simbrian. Simbrian Tarkran. Hear me, Simbrian, and answer. Hear Kaldar. Hear Kaldar. Over and over again he flung the plea across the planes and dimensions of his mind. And at last, hazily, a shape began to materialise in the smoke of the fire. It grew more coherent, taking on form as the smoke curled, and the outlines of a face appeared as Kaldar's mind felt the clear, cool and powerful touch of an answering consciousness.

Simbrian . . . ? But the question faltered, for the face in the smoke wasn't Simbrian Tarkran's. A *woman's* face – Fear shot through Kaldar and almost snapped the mental link as he thought of the magi. But the other mind held on to his, and in his head he heard a familiar voice.

Kaldar. It's all right, Kaldar. Simbrian has asked me to answer. I have the gift.

Nanithe? Kaldar could barely believe it. *I didn't know – I didn't realize –*

None of us realized. But when our Lord Aeoris gave me back my power of speech, the other gift was simply . . . there.

Kaldar felt the eager warmth that accompanied that statement, and hope surged agonizingly in him. If Aeoris had the power to grant such a boon to Nanithe, then . . .

Urgency filled his mind. *Nanithe, listen! I need help – I must have help! Iselia – she – we tried to – but –* And suddenly the whole story poured from his consciousness, flooding through the link and into Nanithe's mind. *I don't know what's become of her; whether she's alive or dead,* he finished desperately. *But if the magi put her to torture –*

Suddenly a new sensation cut across his turmoil and he felt a second presence taking hold of him, calming him.

Kaldar. It was Simbrian himself. *What can we do?*

He didn't know. That was the worst of it; he didn't *know,* and the strain and terror of that cracked like a whiplash as it communicated itself to Simbrian.

Wait, the sorcerer said. *Try to stay in control of your mind, Kaldar. Try to hold on. We can do nothing directly, but our Lord Aeoris might have enough power, now, to help her. If she is still alive, then there's still a chance!*

Misery swelled in Kaldar's soul. *She's in Chaos's stronghold. Even Lord Aeoris hasn't the strength to prevail against that!*

Nonetheless, there might be a way. Order's power is growing, and growing fast. Our gods are close to breaking through into the mortal world in full force, and only the wand of Chaos holds them back now. At the very least I believe that Lord Aeoris will be able to keep you hidden from the magi, and he might even be able to grant Iselia some measure of protection.

But if he can't – Kaldar interjected.

Kaldar, don't lose hope! Listen to me – I will make contact with our gods, and I'll appeal directly to them. Wherever you are . . . The smoke coiled, and for a moment the sorcerer's bearded face was superimposed over Nanithe's. *Ah, yes, I see where you are . . . you must do nothing, make no move, and above all don't even think of trying to go back to the castle. Stay in hiding, shield yourself as best you can, and wait.* Simbrian paused. *I know how hard that will be, but you must do it. Do you understand me?*

I understand, Kaldar said. *And if it's Iselia's only hope, I'll do as you say.*

He felt warmth suffuse him, warmth and sympathy, and in it was an iron core that gave him strength. *Be ready for our call,* Simbrian said. Then, abruptly, *Kaldar . . . there's one thing I must know. Did Benetan Liss betray you?*

Did he? Amid all the mayhem in his mind Kaldar hadn't considered that question, but now the possibility stabbed him like a thin, lethal blade in the back. Twelve years of indoctrination; twelve years serving the magi, serving Chaos – it would be more than enough to corrupt anyone; and in the past, in their youth, he had never trusted Benetan.

But that was before their mutual love for Iselia had changed them both . . .

He said: *No.*

A sound like a sigh reverberated in his head. *Then we didn't misjudge him. In all this misery perhaps that's one small thing to be thankful for. Aeoris protect you, Kaldar. We'll speak again before long. And . . . we'll all pray for her.*

As Kaldar's image wavered in the smoke, the girl who crouched before the smouldering fire reached out in a sudden, impulsive gesture, as though trying to clasp and comfort him across the vast distance that separated them. But Kaldar's face was fading, and her hands closed on nothing as it vanished altogether.

Another hand took hers, drawing her back, and as the telepathic link snapped Nanithe jolted out of the semitrance. Her body sagged, and Simbrian slid a supporting, comforting arm about her.

'He's gone.' The sorcerer's voice was soft.

The girl shuddered, then uttered a sharp gasp and blinked her dark eyes rapidly as the last of the spell lost its hold. Simbrian nodded to the older woman at his side;

leaning forward she cast a handful of leaves onto the small fire, and as the smoke changed colour and the last of the incense dissipated she rose to her feet and crossed the floor to open the shutters at the windows. Daylight flowed in, and at last Simbrian felt Nanithe relax in his arms.

'If only there was something we could *do*,' Nanithe said unsteadily. 'He's so far away, Simbrian. And I feel so helpless.'

'I know, my love, I know.' Simbrian rocked her gently back and forth. 'But though we haven't enough power to help Kaldar and Iselia, our gods may be able to succeed where we would fail.'

Nanithe shivered. 'We should have tried to persuade him to come back to us. He's too close to those demons – I fear they'll find him, and then . . . ' She couldn't bring herself to express her thoughts any further.

Shammana Oskia Mantrel had opened the last of the shutters, and she came quietly back to kneel down once more beside the couple. 'Nanithe, there is no living soul in this world or any other who could persuade Kaldar to leave his hideaway and come south again. I doubt if even our Lord Aeoris himself could change his mind.'

'Shammana's right, love.' Simbrian sighed. 'And if there's any hope of saving Iselia, it's better that Kaldar does stay where he is.'

'But the First Magus won't let matters rest!' Nanithe protested. 'He'll hunt Kaldar down, and destroy him as well as his wife!'

'He knows the dangers, Nanithe; better, perhaps than we do. But he *must* take the risk; he *needs* to take the risk for Iselia's sake. I can't fault him for that.' Over Nanithe's bowed head Simbrian's gaze met Shammana's, and the sorcerer added, 'If the woman *I* loved were in the magi's hands I'd feel just as he does.'

Shammana understood, for in these last few days she had been the closest witness of all to the deep affinity which

26

had taken root and flowered between Simbrian and her own surrogate daughter. Since the monstrous desecration of her mind and body by a band of brigands that had robbed Nanithe of speech and, almost, of sanity, Shammana had been her only friend and protector. She had cared fiercely and lovingly for the girl for three years, until their final flight to join the followers of Order and become a part of their greater family on Summer Isle. She had seen the first signs of an attachment soon after their arrival; but for all Simbrian's loving patience Nanithe had been a little afraid, and, unable as she was to express her feelings in words, felt herself unworthy of him. But Aeoris had changed that. Shammana still felt echoes of the huge emotion that had overtaken her when the great lord of Order had healed Nanithe's damaged mind and restored the voice she had so cruelly lost; and for Simbrian that gesture of compassion had been a greater boon than perhaps even Aeoris knew. For with the healing Nanithe had burgeoned, and the love that she had been afraid and ashamed to show was at last able to find its expression. For all the great gulf in their ages, the match between Nanithe and Simbrian was a true melding of souls.

Then the cloud came back to Shammana's mind as she thought again of Kaldar. She hoped with all her heart that Aeoris would have the power to help him and his wife as he had helped Nanithe. But for all that had been achieved, for all Order's growing strength and influence, the last barrier remained, and while Chaos still controlled the gateway between this world and the dimensions of the gods, that barrier could not be breached. Kaldar's and Iselia's bid to steal the wand of Chaos had ended in disaster and Shammana could see no hope for a second attempt. But without the wand, the key to the gateway, Aeoris couldn't break Chaos's stranglehold.

Simbrian was standing now, and he caught Nanithe's hands, lifting her to her feet beside him. For perhaps a minute he looked into the heart of the quietly smoking fire, then at last he nodded slowly, as though acknowledging some inner thought, and raised his head.

'Shammana, we must go back to the White Isle. Those of us who made the first journey – we must return.'

Shammana stared steadily at him. The barren, volcanic island that lay between Summer Isle and the mainland was the one place in all the world where Order's full powers could be focused without fear of discovery. There Aeoris's followers had performed the great ritual that opened the way to their gods; there Aeoris himself had gained the strength to manifest in the mortal realm. And there Kaldar's bid to reach Iselia, and through her the wand of Chaos, had begun.

Her voice was quiet as she said, 'It's come to that?'

'I think it has. I think it must. I told Kaldar that I'd appeal to our gods to help Iselia, but if she is to be saved – if she *can* be saved – I believe it will take more than even our Lord Aeoris can achieve from his own realm. We must take a greater step, Shammana. With or without the wand of Chaos, we must try to break the last of the barriers and call our gods fully into this world.'

Shammana felt a deep, atavistic shiver rack her. 'But that will mean revealing what we are and what we have achieved to the powers of Chaos . . .'

'Yes. But I can see no other choice for us now.' Simbrian paused. 'You and I both know that it can't be long before Kaldar is hunted down and caught – and in breaking him, Chaos will break us all.'

'They might already have done so,' Shammana said sombrely. 'If they *have* tortured Iselia' – with one hand she formed the circle sign of Order, expressing a silent but heartfelt plea that she was wrong – 'then they will have stripped her mind of everything she can tell them about us.'

'Which is little enough, thankfully.' Simbrian saw her

face tighten in shock and quickly added, 'Shammana, don't mistake me; I'm not saying that her suffering means any the less because of that – it doesn't, and I'll do *anything* within my power to save her. But she can't betray our whereabouts, or our numbers, because she doesn't know them. And what she does know will be of little use to those devils at the castle . . . but for one thing.'

'The truth about Kaldar,' Shammana said bleakly.

'Yes. Once he is in their hands, that will be the end of everything.' Simbrian paused. 'He might have the power to withstand what the magi are capable of doing to him, but Yandros is another matter; and from Kaldar, Yandros will be led directly to us. We can't stand by and wait for that to happen.' His big shoulders hunched and he hugged Nanithe closer, as though trying to protect her from his own sudden vision of a grisly future. 'Whatever the odds against us, I think we must mount our challenge to Chaos – before Chaos comes looking for us.'

CHAPTER III

Pastel mists curled and drifted about First Magus Vordegh's motionless figure as he stood gazing thoughtfully into the obscure dimensions of the Marble Hall. The shadows that of late had gathered around him wherever he went were quiescent, shrouding his handsome, ascetic face and masking the expression in his calm brown eyes. But the two magi who stood a little way off, watching and waiting, felt the psychic echoes of his satisfaction and a little of his intent, and the look that passed between them reflected the depth of their shared disquiet.

The Hall's silence seemed profound in contrast to what had preceded it. But the grim, unearthly things that Vordegh had allowed, briefly, to enter the mortal world and taste the prey he offered had returned to their own dimensions now. They were replete; his purpose was served. He had all that the captive could give him. And he was pleased.

At last the First Magus moved. Behind him, vague in the Hall's refracting light, the seven ancient statues of the gods towered like sentinels; he turned to face them, then walked slowly and deliberately to where a block of wood, like an altar but with a very different purpose, was set into the Hall's mosaic floor. One deviant creature – a creation of his own – still remained, crouching on the floor at the block's head. At his approach it stirred and uttered an abhorrent grunting sound; he made a slight gesture and it settled once more.

Vordegh looked down at the block and at the unconscious human flotsam spreadeagled on its surface. 'She has put us to some trouble,' he said, 'but it has been worthwhile. I commend you, Croin. Your skill, as ever, is exemplary. And Pirane; your assistance has been most useful.'

Physician-Magus Croin glanced up uneasily from the implements which he was now packing neatly away and inclined his head in acknowledgement. Pirane, however, made no move. Her silver-tinged face was expressionless.

Vordegh continued meditatively, 'So, now we must consider the substance of what we have learned. We know the true identity of the supposed informer whom Captain Liss brought to the castle, and the origin of the psychic shield that enabled him to pass the tests we set him. We also know the names of the heretic leader and his closest cohorts, though not the location of their hiding place. That, however, can be rectified simply enough.' He paused reflectively. 'The demons of Order must be naive in the extreme to have used a child like this for the task they attempted. But then she is clearly of little value; she has small knowledge and even smaller skill. Her husband,' his lips curved faintly, scornfully as he used the term, 'will furnish us with a great deal more when he returns to the castle. When we have what he can give us, the eradicating of Order's ambitions, and its followers, will be a small task.'

Croin put away the last of his instruments and closed his bag with a small sound that echoed before the mists swallowed it. 'We should waste no time in pursuing Alvaray, First Magus,' he said. 'Do you wish me to begin preparations?'

'Oh, no.' The reply surprised Croin. Then Vordegh looked up. 'Pursuit will be quite unnecessary. From what the girl has revealed of Alvaray's nature it's obvious that he won't rest until he has made a suicidal attempt to rescue her. Why should we trouble ourselves searching for him when he intends to return to us of his own volition? We shall wait for him. And while we wait, we can attend to some unfinished business – the question of the guilt, or otherwise, of those other individuals who are implicated in this affair.'

A shadow moved in Pirane's strange eyes. 'I still feel, First Magus, that the confession we have heard may not be entirely reliable.' She nodded towards the block. 'The girl has personal grudges, and to accept her word without further investigation could be –' she hesitated, touched her tongue to her lips, '– deceptive.'

Vordegh smiled, not amicably. 'And *I* feel, Pirane, that you would be making a grave mistake if you allowed your own partialities to cloud your judgement. The girl tells us that Captain Liss was entirely ignorant of her own and Alvaray's intentions, but she has also confessed to an old acquaintance with the captain. That cannot be overlooked. And the fact that there also appears to be an elaborate and ambiguous entanglement between the captain and the other two people in question is obviously significant in the light of what we have heard. It is the merest justice to grant all concerned an opportunity to explain their involvement in further detail.'

The argument was twisted, and Pirane knew that another motive lay behind it. 'But to embroil Andraia –'

'She embroiled herself by coming to you.'

'She came only to tell me the little that she knows, and to ask my advice,' Pirane insisted. 'She looks on me as a friend.' *But then she also looks on Savrinor as a friend,* she thought, *And with the heretic's claims to endorse Vordegh's own prejudice, that could be enough to condemn her.*

She added helplessly, 'I am certain Andraia is innocent of any misdeed.'

'Then she has nothing to fear.'

Pirane sighed. 'Of course. Of course. But –'

'Innocence is its own defence, Pirane, and I wish only to discover the truth.' Vordegh turned to regard her tranquilly. 'As, I am sure, do you.'

'Of course, Lord Vordegh.' Pirane knew she was losing the argument, yet she had to make one more effort. 'But it is possible that the girl has embroidered her confession with some tales which are *not* true. She knows that it was Savrinor who alerted us to her perfidy – that in itself would be reason enough for her to wish to strike back at him.'

'And, I would have thought, at Captain Liss. After all, has Savrinor not insisted that the captain is as loyal a servant to Chaos as he is himself?' Vordegh saw that she couldn't refute the point and added with a mildness that didn't deceive her for a moment, 'If that's so, then for the girl to try to ruin one without the other would not be rational. I think we have had the truth from her, and must look elsewhere – and in one particular direction – for our liars.'

The skin around Pirane's eyes and mouth tightened, but she was aware now that to pursue the issue any further would be futile. Vordegh had made his decision, for his own reasons, and would believe no more and no less than suited his purpose.

He was waiting for a response; there was only one she could give, and she made a small, helpless gesture of acquiescence. 'Of course, First Magus. As you say.'

Satisfied, Vordegh nodded. 'Then, in pursuit of the truth which we all wish to ascertain, the Lady Andraia may also be confined pending our investigation.' He paused thoughtfully for a few moments. 'A day or two for them all to consider and reflect will be enough, I think. Then we shall bring them to the Marble Hall and hear what they have to say.'

A muscle worked in Pirane's throat. 'All of them, First Magus?'

'All of them.' For the second time Vordegh smiled at her, and the smile was sanguine. 'You need not worry, yet, about your protégée; or for that matter about her former paramour. They, I think, are lesser players, and I doubt

33

that it will prove necessary to put them to any rigorous test. I believe we can learn enough from Master Savrinor to avoid further unpleasantness. In the meantime, I will send word to Chaos of what we have unearthed.' He glanced at the block, then towards Croin. 'And as for this creature . . . I want her to survive for a while yet. Presumably you can ensure that she does?'

'For as long as our purposes require, First Magus, yes.' Croin came to join him. 'She is in a state of extreme shock, and shock can kill under some circumstances; but I can restore enough of her mind to ensure that that doesn't happen. And her body is relatively unimpaired.' He eyed Vordegh obliquely.

'Good. I don't wish to lose the bait before our quarry has attempted to take it. Do whatever is necessary, and have her conscious and ready to be brought back to the Marble Hall at my order.'

'You will wish to question her again, First Magus?'

'No, no; I need nothing else from her.' The First Magus's eyes held contentment. 'But when our other interviews are conducted, her presence will serve as a salutary and timely lesson on the consequences of treachery.'

By the time he learned that Andraia had also been arrested, Savrinor felt too ill to show any outward reaction. But inwardly, it almost broke him.

From the windowless underground room in which he had been confined he could sense nothing of the outside world, but his mind and body told him that the sun had risen and set once since his incarceration began. It was easy enough to judge; he was well acquainted with the cravings of narcotic withdrawal and knew to a matter of minutes how much time passed between each stage. If only his escort had allowed him to collect a phial or two from his cupboard before locking him in here, this cold, shivering sweat could have been avoided; even now one dose of a relatively innocuous concoction would enable him to restore the precarious balance that he had successfully maintained for so many years. But the First Magus's order had been explicit. No detours, no privileges. And it needed little intelligence or insight to know why . . . or, now, to understand what lay behind this latest development.

Two Chaos riders – different men, whose names he couldn't recall in his present state – brought him the news of Andraia's imprisonment, and a short while later they returned. He was, they said, to be questioned; but though they were respectful they were also uncommunicative, refusing to answer when he demanded to know where he was to be taken and who was to be his interrogator. Savrinor felt too sick and exhausted to argue with them, and walked passively and a little unsteadily out into the narrow passage beyond his cell and away towards the courtyard. They emerged into overcast darkness; no snow tonight but there was a bitter wind blowing, carrying the restless and ominous roar of a high tide far below the castle stack. Savrinor judged that it was around second moonrise; the castle was unlit, and as they began to cross the black flagstones he shivered with cold. Then abruptly he realised where the riders were taking him, and the shivering took on a new dimension that brought him to a standstill.

'*Yandros* . . .' His whisper was carried away by the wind.

One of the riders took hold of his arm. 'If you please, sir.' He sounded ill at ease and out of his depth; little wonder, Savrinor thought . . .

'Yes,' he said aloud. 'Yes, I understand.' A vestige of pride struggled to the surface and he shook the man's hand off, brushing his sleeve as though to brush away something he didn't want to acknowledge. 'I'll walk unaided, thank you.'

Along the colonnaded walkway, through the low door at the end and onto the flight of stairs that spiralled downwards into the castle's foundations. *Gods, this route was so familiar* . . . but this time it didn't end in the silent, deserted library. Another door, half hidden behind ranks of bookshelves. A passage, peculiarly symmetrical, illuminated by a faint silver-grey glow that had no visible source. The riders were nervous now, he sensed it, palpable as a scent to a hunting – or hunted – animal. They were both junior men; doubtless they had never set foot here before. Probably had never so much as entered the library; probably they couldn't even *read* . . . Savrinor shut his eyes against a wave of dizziness as he was led onwards; his skin was beginning to prickle and burn and he felt disorientated. *Great Yandros, he couldn't lose what was left of his wits now. Not now, when he was about to need wit as he'd never needed it before.*

Then, quaveringly, a familiar voice spoke his name.

Savrinor's eyes opened. They were approaching the door, the dull, metallic door that led to the Marble Hall. And, flanked by more uniformed riders, Andraia and Benetan were waiting for them.

Andraia's face was blotchy with crying and the vitality and beauty had bled from her, leaving her gaunt. Shocked and dismayed, Savrinor shook off his own escort's attempt to restrain him and stumbled towards her.

'They told me –' For once in his life he was inarticulate as his hands closed over hers, gripping them hard. 'It's *insane!* Lord Vordegh can't possibly believe that you had any part in this!'

She shook her head helplessly, and pulled one hand free to touch his face. 'You look ill.'

Savrinor almost said, *I'll survive*, but he was no longer sure of that. 'I'm well enough.'

Benetan, who was watching silently, flicked him a searing look that combined unhappiness and bitter disgust. Though he had stonily affected to ignore them both, the exchange between the historian and Andraia had renewed his own misery and terror for Iselia with a vengeance. Their

36

obvious intimacy was like a deliberate barb, and he wished
he had a blade in his hand – sword, knife, it didn't matter;
anything that he might use to cut through Savrinor's perfidious heart in revenge for what he had done. In a part of
his mind that he refused to heed, he knew that the desire
wasn't rational; Savrinor had acted out of devotion to the
gods, and only a few months ago Benetan himself would
have done no less, without pause and without question.
But that had been before Vordegh's depravities had
destroyed his faith and trust in the magi; before Yandros's
continuing indifference had turned reverence to anger –
and before Iselia had come to the castle . . .

He didn't know what had become of her. All he did
know was that but for Savrinor she would have been long
gone from the castle, safe with Kaldar, safe with her
friends. Benetan didn't care that she had deceived him, and
no longer cared what crime she had been trying to commit
when she was caught. All he could think of, all he had
been able to think of since his own arrest, was the torment
she was suffering at Vordegh's hands, and anguish had
reduced him to an exhausted, impotent shell.

One of the riders spoke up quietly. 'Captain. We must go
in.' He met Benetan's gaze uncomfortably. 'I'm sorry . . .'

Benetan's shoulders slumped and he made an acquiescent gesture. 'Yes. Yes, of course.' One more glance in
Savrinor's direction, but suddenly he was too weary for
the contempt he felt to have any meaning. He just wanted
this to be over.

The metallic door opened at a touch, and they entered
the Marble Hall. As they advanced into the drifting mists
the sound of their multiple footfalls created strange, hush-
ing echoes that to Benetan's overwrought imagination
sounded like distantly whispering voices. He could sense
fear like smoke in the air; looking over his shoulder he saw
Andraia's lips moving and suspected she was praying. In
one sense he envied her her faith, in another he despised

her for it. Savrinor, though, seemed to be beyond such efforts; he needed help now, walking unsteadily with the riders supporting his arms, and staring at the floor in front of his feet. His face was expressionless.

Vordegh was waiting for them. He stood, as ever, in his wreath of restless shadows, and as the party drew nearer to him Benetan felt – or rather sensed, for this was too subtle for physical awareness – a deep, regular throbbing, permeating the shifting air of the Hall and pulsing subliminally through the mosaic of the floor. Its inexorable rhythm seemed to drag his own heartbeat down, slowing it to a painful thudding under his ribs, and he found suddenly that he could barely breathe.

The First Magus exuded an aura of patience as he stood watching them approaching. Behind him two more figures were visible in the mist now, and something within Benetan curdled. Pirane, as well as Croin? What had *she* to do with this? Then Vordegh spoke, and at the soft, cold and utterly pitiless sound of his voice all thoughts of Pirane were snuffed out.

'Leave.' He spoke to the escort of Chaos riders, and with a formal salute they released their captives, took two precise paces backwards, then turned and departed. Savrinor tried to turn his head to watch them go, but dizziness hit him again and he abandoned the effort.

'Master Savrinor. Captain Liss. Lady Andraia.' The First Magus pronounced their names with great and deliberate precision. He was holding the wand of Chaos, and as he stroked it reflexively, dark, strange colours moved within the wand's depths. 'It is possible that any or all of you are guilty of conspiring with the heretic followers of Order, and of assisting two such heretics in a conspiracy against Chaos.' He paused. 'Do any of you wish to confirm or deny this?'

Andraia made a small, inarticulate sound; Vordegh's gaze snapped to her. 'Yes, Lady Andraia?'

From a reserve of courage that he hadn't known he possessed Savrinor found his voice. 'She is innocent of any charge, my lord!'

'Indeed.' Vordegh still watched Andraia. 'I'm afraid your gallantry doesn't entirely convince, Master Savrinor. I would expect you to champion the woman who currently indulges your carnal appetites, just as you championed her predecessor for so long.'

Sickly colour flared in Savrinor's cheeks. 'My lord, that is unjust –' Breath failed him; he coughed unhealthily and Vordegh's lip curled with disdain.

'Your indulgences in other directions also seem to have taken their toll of your faculties, Master Savrinor,' he said. 'A failing which does little to enhance your credibility. And in the light of the evidence against you –'

'Evidence?' Savrinor's voice went up sharply, nervously.

'I would prefer not to be interrupted a second time.' Vordegh's gaze held him and Savrinor began to shake. 'Evidence. Enough to condemn you as a traitor to the gods, unless you are able to disprove it beyond doubt.'

The historian's mouth worked and he stared at the First Magus in disbelief. Vordegh, ignoring him, continued.

'The nature of your transgression, Master Savrinor, has been revealed freely and without the need for coercion. That, I think, is evidence enough.' The emphasis he now meticulously placed on the word *evidence* was chilling.

Pirane shifted uneasily; unseen by the First Magus, Croin gave her a warning shake of his head. And Savrinor, feeling that his world was collapsing under his feet, said slowly and hollowly, 'There is no valid evidence against me, my lord. There cannot be, for I know that I am not a traitor!'

Vordegh contemplated that for a few moments. 'Well,' he said at last, 'we shall see.' He raised one hand, beckoned, then pivoted and walked slowly towards the altar. His three prisoners stood motionless and after a moment the First Magus looked back. 'Approach. All of you.'

They couldn't disobey him. One by one they moved, Benetan leading. He was aware that Andraia had surreptitiously drawn closer to Savrinor and the historian's arm was around her, but this time their attachment didn't stab his emotions as it had done before. His gaze was drawn unwillingly to the block, still indistinct in the mist, and to the faces of Pirane and Croin standing near it. A shape, swathed in a cloak or wrap of some kind, was lying on the block. He couldn't look. *Dared* not look.

By the block's head something shifted, snatched his attention. Vordegh's sentinel, the monstrosity he had created, still crouched on the floor, quiescent and waiting, and as he saw it Benetan swung aside, a shocked sound choking from his throat. It wasn't even a creation of Chaos. He knew Yandros's demons; he had ridden with them, controlled them, guided them in their work, and never, *never* had he encountered anything so foul as this! Vordegh must have invented it from the perverted depths of his own mind to help him in his task, and Benetan's gorge rose as he thought of what such a loathsome abhorrence could be capable of . . . 'There's no need to fear it, Captain Liss,' Vordegh said serenely. 'It is entirely under my command, and will not interfere with you unless I should order it to do so.'

Though Benetan knew it could have no intelligence, the thing on the floor answered with an abysmal, satisfied noise. Vordegh's calm voice sounded almost as obscene. 'Look at the block, if you please.'

Benetan didn't move a muscle.

'Kindly obey me, Captain,' Vordegh said tranquilly.

He had no choice. His foot scraped loudly on the marble floor as he turned, and he looked.

Iselia's face stared back at him. She was conscious – he knew that instantly, on a terrible, primal level – but her mouth was slack, saliva running over her jaw, and her tongue protruded, bruised black where she had bitten into it over and over again. Her teeth were stained with blood. Her eyes, the whites turned to crimson and the pupils shrunk to tiny black pinpoints, stared madly, insensately into his, not recognizing him, not recognizing anything, unable to acknowledge reality in any form.

Benetan made a terrible sound and tried to shrink back, but Vordegh's detached voice stilled him before he could move.

'Unwrap the cloak, Captain. I would prefer you to understand the full consequences of transgression against the gods.'

He couldn't disobey the command; he couldn't fight Vordegh's will. One hand moved, slowly, fearfully, lifting the cloak's folds aside to reveal the body beneath.

Benetan had seen cruelty and hideousness before; he had seen death, mutilation, the results of sorcerous torture, and as a Chaos rider it had been easy to shut such things from his mind; the magi's drugs, and the frenzied changes they induced, had made it easy. But he had no such protection now. And *this* . . . Iselia was naked, and every inch of her skin was patterned with fine scars where blood had been drawn from her, drop by tiny drop, to feed the horrors that had come to strip her mind of its secrets. And Croin's knife had just been the beginning of it; across her body – on her neck, her breasts, her thighs – the marks of unhuman hands glittered with a pulsing nacre where the things had touched and squeezed and crushed and burned their stigmata into her flesh. She could no longer move her limbs; they were twisted into appalling contortions, beyond any control. And Vordegh's own unholy pet had had its role to play, for in the numbing moment when he looked at her Benetan had seen, between her thighs, the torn and bloody aftermath of an abominable violation.

They must have kept her conscious through it all. For the image of her face, her drooling mouth and mad eyes – an image now stamped indelibly on his brain – told

Benetan that she had experienced every moment of her ordeal and that her mind was re-living it still, over and over in insane, ceaseless procession.

For a moment that seemed eternal he couldn't move, couldn't react. Then suddenly the thrall snapped and his legs gave way under him. He sagged to his knees, covering his face with both hands, and tears streamed down his face, spilling between his fingers, soaking the long strands of his hair. *It wasn't true, this was a dream, a nightmare; he would wake at any moment and it wouldn't have happened, it wouldn't be TRUE . . .*

The First Magus stared down at him disdainfully and said, 'You really are a fool, Captain Liss. But perhaps that is all you are; a fool who allowed himself to be deceived by others. We shall investigate the truth of that a little later; at present, however, I have more urgent concerns.' He looked up, and his gaze rested on Savrinor. 'And greater imperatives.'

Savrinor and Andraia had both seen Iselia's mutilated body, and now Savrinor stood rigid, his face bloodless, while Andraia clung to him, eyes tightly shut as she struggled to control the revulsion crushing in on her mind. Vordegh's gaze locked with the historian's, and panic began to take hold in Savrinor's pale eyes as he realized what the First Magus's words portended.

He freed himself from Andraia's grasp, took a step back.

'Stay where you are, Master Savrinor. *If* you please.'

A force from outside him rooted Savrinor where he stood. Sweat beaded his face. Vordegh continued to gaze at him.

'I have the girl's confession, Master Savrinor.' The soft, implacable voice seemed to penetrate deep through his skull. 'She has told me many things about you. Things which I did not know, and which cast a new and revealing light upon . . . shall we say, your *interests*.' An old, deadly loathing burned in his eyes, a scorn and a repugnance which at last had found an outlet, and he continued with soft and terrible malignance: 'I name you a traitor, Master Savrinor. And by the testimony given freely to me by Iselia Darrow Alvaray, I name you a *heretic!*'

CHAPTER IV

'It is a lie.' White-faced, Savrinor held the First Magus's accusing stare with all the courage and dignity he could muster, but shock had reduced his voice to a whisper. 'Every word of that accusation, Lord Vordegh – it is a *lie!*'

Tension was building to a suffocating level in the Marble Hall. As Vordegh disclosed the details of Iselia's confession Andraia had tried to speak up in protest, but Pirane had intervened to silence her, knowing that one ill-chosen word could be catastrophic. She now held Andraia by one arm, while Croin, eyes closed, stood near Benetan, who had raised his head, hands falling away to his sides as he stared numbly, bemusedly, at the tableau of Vordegh and his victim. No one among the watchers dared speak.

'A lie.' The First Magus stroked his own chin thoughtfully. 'I see.' His gaze didn't leave Savrinor's face and his expression didn't change. He was quite calm, quite implacable. And, Savrinor knew with a certainty that made him feel sick to the pit of his stomach, entirely beyond reason. 'You claim, then, that my own and Magus Croin's abilities are wanting in some way? That our sorcery has failed to elicit the truth – that we are not *competent?*'

'No!' Sweat broke out anew on Savrinor's face. 'That is not what I mean!'

'It is what you imply.'

Sweet gods, every word he said was being twisted – '*No,* my lord!' Savrinor protested desperately. His ribcage heaved and a leaden pain went through him. 'I mean only that – that as well as revealing the truth to you, as she could only do' – he flung an involuntary glance towards the block where Iselia lay, and felt his stomach rebel – 'she has also invented lies about me! You said yourself, my lord, she *volunteered* that part of her testimony without . . .' He swallowed. 'Without persuasion.'

'Because she wanted revenge on you?'

'Yes!'

'Why should she want that, Master Savrinor? You were her benefactor. Her protector. And her very *intimate* friend.' Vordegh gave the word "intimate" an exquisitely contemptuous edge. 'So intimate, it seems, that when you discovered the nature of the secrets she was keeping, you promised not to reveal them . . . for a price.'

What little colour had been left in Savrinor's face bled away, leaving him looking like a corpse. 'That is not true! I had no knowledge –'

Vordegh ignored him, continuing relentlessly. 'You exacted your price in full, did you not, Master Savrinor? You initiated her into your private world of squalid indulgence; you kept her as your own plaything, to gratify your degenerate tastes, and while she continued to submit without protest you preserved her secret. Favours granted for favours given . . . until, that is, you grew bored with what she had to offer and turned your attentions elsewhere.' He aimed a scathing glance in Andraia's direction; she started to say something but Pirane's hand tightened on her arm and the magus whispered, '*No, child! Keep silent, for his sake and your own!*'

'And when you had a new diversion to entertain you,' Vordegh went on urbanely, 'it occurred to you that this woman's continuing presence might no longer be in your best interests. So you decided – perhaps with others and perhaps not; this is something we shall ascertain in due course –' now his look swept from Andraia to Benetan, 'to remove her from the arena by exposing her as the heretic she is, and at the same time raise yourself higher in your masters' esteem.' He paused. 'Is that not the truth of it, Master Savrinor?'

Savrinor couldn't answer. The accusation was so monstrous and so colossally distorted that he couldn't fight it by any rational means. Anything he might say or do was irrelevant, for it would all be swept aside on the tide of Vordegh's rising zeal to see him damned. This was what the First Magus had been looking for. One mistake, one blot on an unblemished record; a long-awaited chance to be rid of a man he despised. And now Iselia had provided that chance. He should have known, Savrinor told himself bitterly; should have anticipated. It wouldn't matter to Vordegh that the tale Iselia had spun was unsubstantiated and so implausible that a child could have torn the logic of it to shreds. Logic had no place in the First Magus's vindictive mind. Iselia had told him what he wanted to hear, and that – as she must have known – was enough.

'Have you nothing to say, Master Savrinor?' Vordegh asked, his voice ominously soft.

Savrinor looked away. He had *tried*. He had said it all, again and again, protesting his innocence until his head rang with the words and his body ached with exhaustion. He had pleaded for reason, for justice, for *sanity*; but there was none to be found. At the last, Iselia had twisted the knife, and now there was nothing and no one left with the power to help him.

Without warning the leaden pain came back, and with it a rush of giddying nausea. Savrinor's mind began to swim; he couldn't think, couldn't even *breathe*. If he had one of his phials, just one, just an especial one, he would be so sorely tempted now to swallow its contents and let it hurl him into oblivion, and it wouldn't matter any more, because he was lost.

He swayed suddenly and perilously on his feet and, as though from an enormous distance, heard Andraia's voice rise shrilly.

'He's ill! Lord Vordegh, please –'

Pirane said, 'No, Andraia!' and the First Magus turned to regard the stricken girl mildly.

'Your concern is admirable, Lady Andraia, but I would recommend that you reserve it for yourself rather than squandering it where it is of no value.' He paused until he was sure that she had taken in his implication, then turned slowly and regarded the wooden block for a few moments. 'Master Savrinor is well enough to be questioned more thoroughly. And it will be interesting to see what else he has to tell us that we do not already know.' He nodded to Croin. 'Lift the girl down.'

The pain in Savrinor's chest was passing, though he still couldn't drag in enough air and his head spun with nausea. But through the miasma he realized what Vordegh meant, what he intended to do, and suddenly the more formidable sickness of terror washed over him. Sweet gods, not this — they couldn't do to him what they had done to Iselia . . . he wouldn't be able to endure it, wouldn't be able to with-stand the horror and the pain and the monstrous assaults on his mind —

He struggled against choking constriction to find his voice, and suddenly it came in a frantic surge. 'You know I am innocent of this charge! I'm no traitor — you know it, you of all men know it!' Dizziness flowed over him again in a hot, raging wave and his legs gave way. He sagged to the floor, and through blurred eyes stared beseechingly, agonizingly at Vordegh. 'It's a travesty . . .' The strength had gone from his voice and it was no more than a cracking whisper. 'I can't submit to this . . . I *can't!*'

Vordegh looked down at the foot of the block, at the thing that crouched there. 'Bring him,' he said.

A soft, wet sound came from the monstrosity's throat and, slowly but with repulsive purpose, it began to move. Savrinor saw it and his eyes started wildly. 'Ah, no . . .'

Then the pain hit him for the third time, and his protest turned into a cry of shock as a huge force seemed to erupt

47

from within him, punching the breath from his lungs, blinding him with a black starburst. He heard Andraia shriek, but the weight under his ribs was crushing him and he couldn't move, couldn't reach out to her – he felt himself collapsing, felt the cold marble of the floor under him, and his hands clawed for purchase. *Get away from it* – he had to get away from the thing that was crawling towards him, for if it once reached him and touched him, he would lose his sanity –

'Yandros . . .' He struggled to utter the god's name, clasping desperately for the only hope of salvation there was left. He could hear other voices now but he didn't know whose they were or what they were saying; all that mattered was to get away. But heat and cold were washing through him in vast, suffocating waves and he couldn't *move* –

Then suddenly, flailing, his mind caught hold of an incoherent thread. There was a prayer, an old, old prayer – he had learned it as a child but had never used it, for no one ever used it and perhaps no one had ever dared to. One of the highest and most ancient litanies; an invocation to the great lord of Chaos to aid a mortal soul in the last extremity of torment. To utter it without impeccable cause was a sacrilege that could have no reprieve, but this was no sacrilege, no blasphemy; the gods *knew* he was faithful –

'Yandros . . .' Savrinor's eyes were tight-shut as he fought to break free from the stranglehold that pain and terror had on his throat. He could hear Vordegh's creation approaching, slithering, nearer . . . 'Yandros . . . *high lord of Chaos . . . bringer of the day and silent watcher of the night . . .*' His voice was failing him; he tried to cough to clear it, but couldn't. '. . . *Yandros, whose hand has shaped the destiny of us all . . . I call upon you now, in my time of ultimate need . . .*'

The shadows that cloaked Vordegh flared violently outwards as he heard and recognized the words of the litany. His face and posture grew very still.

'Master Savrinor.' The soft warning cut through Savrinor's halting invocation. Savrinor opened his eyes. The monstrosity was less than three feet away from him. '. . . *in my time of ultimate need . . . and I entreat you, beloved Yandros, to hear me and to know that . . . I speak with truth and I speak with honour and I speak with the voice that is the voice of Chaos; to – to call damnation on my enemies and grant to me . . .*'

Vordegh took a single pace towards the historian. He raised his hand, and the wand of Chaos glared into livid brilliance. 'Curb your tongue, Master Savrinor. This is sacrilege, and I will give you no second warning.'

He took another step forward, slow, deliberate. Savrinor raised his head, met the pitiless stare with a challenge of his own. There was madness in Vordegh's eyes, but Savrinor was beyond caring. He drew breath . . .

'Yandros!' In the roiling, burning darkness Tarod's call set vast echoes clashing and yelling through the Chaos realm, and the black-haired lord spun round, searching for his brother. '*Yandros!*'

The darkness ripped apart and shattered, and Yandros paced out of its ruins to stand beside him. Lightning shivered in the burning cloak he wore, and his eyes were turbulent.

'That madman –' He looked into the vortex that had sprung into being as Savrinor's desperate plea rang out.

'You hear the prayer?' Thunder bawled in the wake of Tarod's rage.

'Yes.' Flames were catching light in Yandros's hair. 'I hear it.'

'Then you know who has invoked it, and why! We must *answer*, Yandros! Vordegh knows the truth about Savrinor – this is an outrage beyond tolerance!'

Far away, an eerie, terrible howling rang through the dimension, and overhead the sky bled dark, lethal colours that began to move like the spokes of a gargantuan wheel.

The vortex darkened, pulsed. Yandros said, '*If he dares –* '

'*Grant to me, sweet Yandros, your help and your relief in my extremity . . .*' Savrinor wanted to shout the words to the Marble Hall's invisible ceiling, but he had no strength to shout, and the pain was washing over him again. He saw Vordegh raise the wand – Yandros and Tarod exchanged one look. A fearsome charge of power cracked between them, and Yandros said, 'Unlock the Gate!'

'*. . . For I am true and I am steadfast; my heart and soul are the heart and soul of Chaos . . .*'

The wand turned white-hot. Fire flooded down Vordegh's arm, and an answering fire lit in his eyes. For one instant the power raged around him, and Pirane cried out, 'Lord Vordegh –'

'*. . . and with my last breath and my last strength I will speak the names of the seven great lords and all their legions, and in their names –*'

Vordegh struck.

The bolt of energy hit Savrinor and flung him twenty feet across the floor. Momentarily the light from the bolt blotted out the agitating mists. Then it vanished, and the mists began to settle again.

Vordegh lowered the wand. His face was perfectly composed and he paid not the smallest heed to the four people who stared at him in shock. Then with a violent movement Andraia broke free from Pirane's hold and ran across the floor. Her action snapped the thrall; ignoring Croin, who tried to call her back, Pirane went after the girl. Andraia had fallen to her knees beside Savrinor; hope flared in her face as she saw that he was unmarked, and she was trying to lift him when, gently but emphatically, Pirane pushed her clutching hands aside. Andraia froze, and the rustle of the magus's gown as she dropped to a crouch seemed suddenly deafening.

Pirane's examination took perhaps half a minute. Then she rose to her feet.

'He is dead.' The mist lent soft echoes to her voice as it carried back to where the others stood. There was no expression in her tone. Then she raised a hand to her face and her fingers traced a sign of the deepest reverence. 'Yandros give sanctuary to his soul.'

Behind the immobile figures of Vordegh and Croin, Benetan stared through the mist at the place where Savrinor lay. In the shock of the power-blast he had flung himself to the floor; an instinctive, protective reflex that in retrospect seemed foolish as well as futile; but now, slowly and unsteadily, he rose to his feet. Savrinor, *dead*? He couldn't fully comprehend it; couldn't assimilate the twist of sheer insanity that had turned the historian so swiftly from the magi's own advocate, the betrayer of Iselia, to a man accused of heresy beside her and paying the ultimate price. Vordegh knew that Savrinor was faithful to Chaos. No man could have been *more* faithful; it was Savrinor's unwavering devotion to the gods, and what he had done for their sake, that had turned Benetan's own feelings of friendship to feelings of hatred. Less than an hour ago he himself had been ready to kill Savrinor, and would have taken satisfaction from it – but if he was to die, he should have died for a valid reason. This was wrong. This was *deranged*.

In the quiet that had fallen he could hear Andraia crying, an ugly, racking sound that went on and on as she knelt over Savrinor's corpse. Between sobs she was choking out a flood of words – he couldn't be sure what they were – and her voice was starting to rise as she repeated them over and again with increasing fervour.

Then, shocking them all, Vordegh spoke.

'Remove the girl.' The command was directed at Pirane, and the First Magus gestured emphatically with the hand that held the wand. 'Take her out of the Hall and detain her.'

Pirane's eyes glittered angrily; she had recognized the plea Andraia was repeating, and the emotion that moved her. 'Lord Vordegh, she is in prayer! I will not –'

Vordegh's attendant shadows seethed. 'I said, remove her. And send servants to deal with those remains in the proper manner.' He stroked his thumb over the wand. 'I won't repeat my command a third time, Pirane.'

The magus hesitated – then suddenly Andraia's voice rose up. 'He was right . . .' Her face was ugly with grief. 'He said this was a travesty, and he was *right!* You know he was loyal and true; and yet you – you –' She drew a great, racking breath. 'This is an injustice! Oh, dear gods, *it is an injustice!*'

In the Chaos realm the Warp was screaming into full flood, and under the mayhem of lightning Tarod's eyes lit with venom. He looked at Yandros –

'Yes,' Yandros said ferociously. 'You have my leave!'

Before him, the vortex split –

The blast of power as the Chaos Gate opened rocked the Marble Hall. Black light smashed upwards from the mosaic circle, and a massive concussion tore the mists apart. Pirane was thrown forward; Vordegh, facing her, reeled back with a bellow of shock, and as he fought to regain his balance his hand came up in an enraged impulse –

'*You would think to use the wand against me?*'

The voice shattered into every mind with the force and fury of a Warp, and a glacial wind ripped through the Hall as Tarod stalked out of the Gate. Shards tore from the tower of black light and fused with his hair and flying cloak, and a silver aura burned blindingly around him, turning his face to a stark, malevolent mask. Vordegh had frozen in mid-movement, his arm still upraised; Tarod's eyes focused on the wand, then narrowed slightly, and the First Magus recoiled as the wand was snatched from his hand and spun away into the mist. There was a small, metallic sound, an unnerving contrast to the violence of a few moments before, as it fell to the floor somewhere in the distance.

Tarod's glittering emerald stare held on Vordegh's face for a moment longer. Then with an abrupt movement he turned, darkness smoking around him, and walked back to where Savrinor's body lay. Andraia was still crouching over the historian but she had raised her head, seen the Chaos lord's arrival. Her face was desolate and her eyes sunken and despairing as she stared at him. Tarod stopped a few paces away and, seen only by Andraia, his look changed.

'Lord Tarod . . .' She started to rise, hesitated – then suddenly lurched upright, ran to him and fell to her knees. 'Oh, my lord, my lord –'

Tarod reached down, took hold of her shoulders, raised her to her feet. Then he turned to face Vordegh and said, calmly but with such menace that Andraia shuddered and stepped back a pace from him, 'What is your justification for this, First Magus?'

Pirane and Croin had both made ritual obeisance; Vordegh, however, remained upright, though his posture was formal and conveyed respect if not absolute subservience.

'My lord.' He had regained his composure and was now under fearsome self-control. 'Historian Savrinor has proved a traitor to Chaos.'

Andraia cried, 'That isn't –' but a slight movement of Tarod's hand silenced her.

'I find that unlikely, Vordegh.'

Vordegh made a complaisant gesture. 'As did I, my lord. But the evidence against him was hard to refute. It was my

53

intention to test him – in the accepted ways – and disentangle truth from fiction. Unfortunately, Savrinor resisted. I was obliged to restrain him, but . . .' he shook his head eloquently, 'it appears that he was not capable of withstanding the force that proved necessary. His heart, I believe, had been damaged by his level of self-indulgence over the years, and –'

'I am aware of the nature of Savrinor's indulgences.' Now Tarod's tone was becoming extremely dangerous, and it was obvious that he didn't give Vordegh's claim an iota of credence. 'And chief among them, as you are well aware, is – or rather *was* – his unswerving and profound devotion to his gods.'

Vordegh drew himself up. 'With respect, sir –'

'*Respect?*' The word snapped out so venomously that the First Magus rocked back on his heels. 'I think, Vordegh, that your definition of respect and mine are not entirely in accord! And not for the first time . . . or must I remind you more rigorously of our previous interview?'

Pirane and Croin, who knew nothing of that, exchanged a sharp glance. Vordegh, however, was undaunted. 'We have the testimony of the heretic girl,' he countered. 'She gratified Savrinor's lusts, and in return he conspired to shield her from discovery.'

'Lord Tarod, that isn't true!' Andraia started forward again. 'Savrinor didn't know what she was!'

Vordegh's mouth curved in a chilly smile that had a measure of patient sorrow in it. 'My lord, whilst no man could fault the Lady Andraia's compassion, I should perhaps point out that her championing of Savrinor does not altogether convince. She was, after all . . .' He allowed the sentence to tail off, making a delicate gesture that implied reluctance to speak too explicitly.

Tarod's aura flickered with darker colours and his face took on a very sinister edge. 'She was what?' he prompted softly.

Vordegh's mouth pursed. 'How the lady chooses to conduct her life is entirely her concern,' he said carefully. 'But the loyalties of a woman who distributes her favours intemperately to one suitor after another are, as I dare to think you will agree, questionable at best.'

Tarod knew suddenly that his temper was not going to hold. His long-standing dislike of the First Magus was flowering into loathing, and this, on the heels of the outrage of Savrinor's death, had goaded him beyond forbearance.

'That is a grave slur, Vordegh,' he said ominously. 'And not only on the Lady Andraia.' Very deliberately he caught hold of the girl's hands, drawing her to his side, then turned, lowered his face to hers and kissed her in a way that left none of the watchers in any doubt whatever of the kiss's significance.

Benetan felt as though something had decayed inside him. He had watched this newest turn of events as if the entire experience were a dream, his mind too dazed with bewilderment, fear and misery to make sense of anything. The horror of Iselia's torture, the First Magus's vindictiveness which had led to Savrinor's violent end, the arrival of one of Chaos's own great lords in their midst . . . he couldn't assimilate, couldn't react, couldn't *feel*. All emotion had shut down, as though something within his soul had given up the ghost and died. But Tarod's gesture, and Andraia's reaction, brought reality home to him with a violent impact. As if turning her attentions to Savrinor wasn't enough, she had also given herself to this entity, this creature – the knowledge brought shock and sickness in a devastating rush, and he uttered an inchoate sound of protest. Tarod heard; his head turned quickly and he spared Benetan one raking yet almost pitying look. Then, gently, he allowed Andraia to draw away from him and focused his stare on the First Magus once more.

Vordegh stood motionless. His skin had taken on an unhealthy tinge and his cold sanguinity had slipped,

revealing something that came close to fear in his eyes. 'I
. . . I did not . . .'

'You did not know.' Tarod's voice was soft. 'Of course
not; I hardly think that I'm under any obligation to
acquaint you with the details of my every visit to this
world.' He paused. 'But how very easy it is for one small
piece of ignorance to lead a man into revealing his true
nature. Isn't that so, First Magus?'

Vordegh didn't answer, and with a latent psychic instinct
Andraia felt the spark of the Chaos lord's anger turning
to flame. She tried to pull away, but Tarod didn't let her
go. His face was changing, losing its semblance of humanity, and a shock jolted through her as suddenly his touch
seemed to burn like fire –

One gesture. Tarod's fury was honing to a fine, lethal
edge that he no longer had any wish to control. *One
instant's demonstration of what he truly was, and the
power he commanded, and this mad upstart would learn
an indelible lesson* –

And Yandros's authority cut violently through the rising
havoc in his brother's mind –

TAROD! ENOUGH!

From the direction of the Gate came an unearthly howl
that snapped violently into silence as Yandros stepped
through the portal. He moved with easy, feline grace, his
gold hair catching the light from the mists and refracting
it into prisms of every colour in the spectrum. His slanting
eyes were the indigo-black of a starless and moonless sky.
Andraia turned, saw him and instantly and reverently
dropped to one knee, and over her bowed head Yandros
gave Tarod an affectionate yet warning smile before sur-
veying the rigid tableau of mortals before him. Everything
in the Marble Hall was suddenly very still. Croin had made
a bow of deepest homage, Benetan had hidden his face
in his hands; even Vordegh, now, had abased himself in
deference to the greatest lord of Chaos. Only Pirane had

56

made no movement yet, but as Yandros's gaze turned to her, she curtsied to the floor.

'My dear Pirane.' Yandros smiled again and moved to take her hand, lifting her fingers to his lips. Then he sighed and looked at Savrinor's body. 'This is not a happy state of affairs.' *And you, Tarod,* he added silently, *were about to make the tangle far worse than I wish it to be! Keep a curb on your temper from now on.*

'For our good Savrinor to end like this . . .' He released Pirane, paced across the floor and stood over the corpse. 'Unfortunate, Vordegh. *Very* unfortunate.' His head came up and his eyes turned crimson. 'I am not pleased.'

Vordegh rose slowly to his feet. He might have argued his case with Tarod; Yandros was another matter, and he was well aware of what it could mean to anger the highest of the gods. A muscle in his throat worked as he said, 'Lord Yandros, it was not my intention to –'

'To kill him, no. I am prepared to accept that.' Yandros's expression, however, made it clear that he didn't believe it for one moment. Silence fell again as he walked towards the altar block, taking his time. Passing near to Benetan he gave the young man a long, meditative look but didn't otherwise acknowledge his presence. Then he stopped. Vordegh's unholy creation had crawled back to its station and Yandros's mouth expressed faint distaste; he made a negligent gesture and the thing winked out of existence. ' "Tested in the accepted ways" – I quote your own words, First Magus.' Iselia was still conscious, though there was not a spark of reason in her eyes; she twitched violently but made no sound as Yandros traced a finger lightly over her face. 'Your methods may serve well enough to wring the truth from one of Aeoris's deviant servants, but they are *not* appropriate for a mortal of Savrinor's merit.' Yandros turned. 'Your action, Vordegh, was ill-judged and unnecessary. Savrinor was innocent of any charge of treason. And

57

I do not like to see servants whose qualities I cherish annihilated for the sake of a *mistake*.'

'My lord,' Vordegh's voice wasn't quite steady. 'If I could reverse that mistake . . .'

'I'm sure that your desire to make amends is genuine.' Yandros's look was sardonic. 'But it is, of course, beyond even your capabilities to restore the dead to life.' His eyes turned dark grey, and arctic. 'Power of that order has only one source in this world.'

Pivoting with a flicker of fire, he returned to where Savrinor lay. Andraia had moved away from Tarod and was crouched on the floor, eyes introverted, cradling the historian's head and shoulders and stroking his hair slowly, mechanically, as though trying to convince herself that he was merely asleep. She looked up as Yandros approached, and a taut edge coloured the misery in her expression.

Yandros smiled kindly at her, then shook his head as she made to move aside. She stayed still, watching his face, and the Chaos lord knelt beside the body. He touched Savrinor's heart, once. A shock seemed to ripple through the Marble Hall . . .

Savrinor's eyelids quivered, and air rattled in his throat. He drew breath – then a convulsion shot through him, and as though something had struck him a physical blow he jolted to a sitting position, reeling back against Andraia and shaking his head giddily. An oath formed on his tongue – and choked off as he found himself staring into Yandros's eyes.

Fire and ice went through him with devastating force and one hand jerked convulsively out to clamp on Andraia's. '*Lord Yandros* . . . '

Yandros gave the stunned historian a private, conspiratorial look that also conveyed more than a hint of amusement. 'It was merely a small favour, Savrinor. I think you know your worth to us.' Savrinor was trying to rise now, trying to make obeisance, and a long-fingered hand touched

58

his arm, restraining him. 'No, no; that isn't necessary. And you're weak; you will be for a while yet.' Yandros stood up and turned to Andraia. 'Look after him. I think you of all mortals can be entrusted with that responsibility.'

'Th-thank you . . .' It was so inadequate, so *impossibly* inadequate an expression of her feelings and her gratitude for what he had done, but Andraia could find no better words. 'Oh, Lord Yandros, thank you!'

'If you wish to thank anyone, thank my brother. He had his own reasons for persuading me to intervene.' Yandros's strange eyes focused briefly on Tarod, then he added lightly but pointedly, 'And I suspect he is already aware of your gratitude.'

He left them sitting on the mosaic floor, gazing dazedly after him, and returned to where Vordegh stood erect and tense before the altar block.

'First Magus.' Yandros's voice was cool, but there was an underlying note in it that warned Vordegh to pay very close attention. 'A word of advice. I believe that in your heart you know as well as I do that Savrinor is entirely innocent of all the charges laid against him, and that the same applies to his lady. Clearly the heretic girl had her own reasons for wishing to make false accusations, and while I cannot but commend your zeal in pursuit of those who would set themselves against Chaos, I think in this instance your dedication has been misapplied.' The mists of the Hall pulsed abruptly. 'Would you not agree?'

Vordegh bowed his head. 'As you say, Lord Yandros.'

The Chaos lord paced to the block and looked down at it. 'Then we understand each other. Do whatever you will – indeed, whatever is necessary – to flush out and destroy the nest of vipers that spawned this girl and her consort. But ensure that from now on you search only in directions that will yield a worthwhile harvest.' He glanced over his shoulder at the First Magus, with the air of a lazy but predatory cat. 'I'm sure you take my meaning.'

Vordegh did, and Yandros saw confirmation of it in his eyes. 'Very well,' he said. 'Then our business here is done.'

The First Magus drew back respectfully as he started to move towards the Chaos Gate. Then, unexpectedly, a new voice spoke up.

'Lord Yandros . . .'

Benetan had taken a step forward. He was sweating profusely, but with a great effort he held Yandros's penetrating gaze as the Chaos lord turned to look at him.

'Captain Liss.' Yandros's lips quirked. 'And sober this time, I see. I had overlooked your involvement in this.'

Benetan sensed the implicit foreboding in those words, but it was too late to retract. He had to speak. Had to *plead*.

'My lord, I beg of you . . .' His fists clenched at his sides; involuntarily he looked towards the block –

'Ah, no,' Yandros interrupted quietly. 'I think, Captain, that that would not be wise.'

His eyes were steady, and Benetan's hopes turned to ash. The compassion that had moved Yandros to show such benevolence to Savrinor and Andraia was gone, and the eldritch features now held only cruelty; abiding, unwavering, steadfast. Cruelty, and disdain.

'I don't intend to probe your part in this, Captain Liss,' Yandros continued. Tarod had crossed the floor silently to join him, and Benetan felt the dark lord's gaze stinging his soul. 'That is for your mortal masters to ascertain as they see fit. But there will be no quarter for her, and nor will she be allowed the release of death for some while to come. If you are what you have claimed to be for the past twelve years, you'll be content with that.'

Benetan's face was arid as he watched them walk away. He saw the eerie black column of the Chaos Gate pulse with shimmering energy as they reached it, but he alone did not bow or kneel as they departed. Something within him had been snuffed out; something that had been a part of his life for as long as he could remember. Faith. He had no other word for it. The flame of his faith in Chaos, his faith in the gods, had been guttering long before this grim night began: now, finally, it was dead. And he knew that nothing would rekindle it.

The Warp was gone, and in a hard, brazen sky seven titanic prisms hurled spears of blinding light down to the horizon as they turned slowly and relentlessly on their axes. Tatters of a fine, soft darkness blew away like smoke on the breeze as the last traces of the Gate vanished, and Yandros sighed.

'These personal vendettas of Vordegh's are getting out of hand.' Flame glinted in his eyes for a moment, then they quieted as the last of his anger dissipated. 'Let's hope that this latest episode will also be the last.'

'Perhaps,' Tarod said, 'you should have spoken privately to Pirane.'

Yandros hesitated, then shook his head. 'No. I was tempted . . . oh yes, for all you might think, I was *sorely* tempted. Vordegh seems to have lost all sense of proportion; I honestly believe that the chance to break Savrinor was more important to him than anything else he gleaned from the heretic girl.'

'Which in itself was little enough.'

'True. She is a very minor pawn; what she had to reveal won't go far towards wiping out this contamination.'

'We could put her to our own form of testing.'

Yandros shook his head. 'No. For all his defects I can't fault Vordegh as a sorcerer; he's extracted everything she could give. And that's another reason why I still hold to what I said, Tarod. Vordegh is better qualified than any of the other magi to succeed in rooting out these heretics and putting an end to any ambitions Aeoris and his pallid scum may have in the mortal world. Provided he concentrates solely on that from now on, we'll leave matters as

61

they are. He's been given fair warning. I shall wait to see if he has the wisdom to heed it.'

Tarod let it go at that; he wasn't in a mood to reanimate the old argument. 'Your boon to Savrinor drove the point home, I suspect,' he said.

'That had nothing to do with Vordegh. It was a whim, no more.'

Tarod smiled obliquely. 'And one which you haven't chosen to indulge for a century or two. I wonder what made you break with habit?'

Yandros shrugged. 'Blame yourself, if you must insist on looking for a reason. As I said to Andraia, you persuaded me to intervene in the first place.'

'Then you allowed me to repay a small debt to her, and I thank you for that.'

'A debt?' Yandros turned and regarded him in mild surprise. 'You entertain some strange notions at times.'

'Possibly. But her heart has already been broken once, and it would have been a greater unkindness to let it happen a second time.'

That, Yandros thought, was ambiguous to say the least. 'You're referring to Benetan Liss, of course?'

'Of course.' Tarod's face was inscrutable.

For some moments Yandros continued to gaze thoughtfully at him. Then he laughed, shortly and sharply. 'Sometimes, Tarod, I wonder if your visits to the mortal world are beginning to have an untoward effect on you.'

There was wry amusement in Tarod's eyes as he watched his brother walk away, and softly, unheard by Yandros, he said, 'No more untoward, I think, than yours have on the mortals themselves.'

CHAPTER V

Sergeant Averel – or rather Captain Averel, though he felt uneasily that it would take him a long time to become accustomed to his new rank – had given strict orders that the heretic girl's removal from the Marble Hall should be carried out by senior riders, hardened to such tasks. But someone had slipped up, and when Averel found Lotro hunched in a corner of the stable block shortly before dawn, face miserable and eyes staring blankly at nothing, it didn't take long to discover the cause of his distress.

'She were still *alive*.' Lotro's voice shook woefully when at last Averel had coaxed him out of his paralysis and extracted the whole unhappy story. 'Twas what struck me so 'ard, sir. All broken-like, and cuts all over her and other things . . . other things . . . and her eyes staring and staring, like she were looking into the Seven Hells and – and still *alive!*' He covered his face with his hands and his indrawn breath broke in a sob.

Averel made a ferocious mental note to find out who had been so witless as to assign this gangling, impressionable junior to such a detail, and shook Lotro's arm gently but firmly in a way intended to convey sympathy. 'I know, boy, I know. I've seen it myself, many a time. I know what it's like.'

'But . . . but I din't think they'd *do* such things to people!' Lotro protested helplessly. 'Not like that. Not like *that*. And when we put her in the cell, laid her down – I tried best's I knew how to be gentle, sir, but 'twasn't gentling would do her any good – her eyes, they – they *looked* at me, right at me, and I thought . . . I thought . . . she d'want to die. Thass all she d'want. And twas like she were asking me . . . begging me . . .' He looked up suddenly, tears streaking his stricken face. 'But they ant going to let her die, sir, thass what I hear. They ant going to let her.'

Averel stared at the floor between his own feet. 'She's a heretic, Lotro. She's given her soul to the demons of Order. You know that, don't you?'

'Es, I know, sir. But she be human too. An' she were so nice, and so pretty . . .'

Averel knew that Lotro had been a little infatuated with Master Savrinor's protégée, and had warned him more than once in the past not to entertain any hopeful notions about her. The girl, he knew, had been a concubine as well as a servant, and there were rumours circulating now about some three-way involvement with Captain Liss into the bargain. Averel didn't know the truth of it and probably never would, but it all added up to an unholy mess.

'They're saying,' Lotro went on hollowly, 'as Capun Liss be heretic, too.' His head turned. 'It ant true, Sarn't? Not Capun Liss?'

'I don't know the answer to that any more than you do, boy. All I do know is that he's locked up under guard and can't be seen by anyone who hasn't had permission from the First Magus.' Averel paused. 'And he's not Captain Liss any more; you'd better remember that. I'm your captain now.' Then he relented a little. 'Doesn't matter if you still call him Captain in my hearing, but there are some others might not be so tolerant.'

Lotro looked blank. 'What should I call en, then, sir? I cann't think of en 'cept as Capun.'

You might as well call him a dead man . . . but Averel kept that grim thought to himself. 'Best stick to "sir"; that way you won't offend anybody. Not that you're likely to see him at all.'

'No. S'pose not.' Then Lotro shuddered. 'Will they . . .' he swallowed. 'Will they do same to him, sir? Same as to her?'

Averel only shrugged. In truth he had no idea what would become of the captain; all he knew for certain was that he was in dire trouble over the unmasking of the heretic girl, and that the story was a good deal more complicated than anyone had yet told him. Rumour was flying; but then rumour always did, and sorting fact from fiction wasn't easy. One story said that Captain Liss had helped the heretic's accomplice to escape, while another tale was circulating about great Yandros in person bringing Historian Savrinor back from the dead after the captain had murdered him. Then there was Secretary Qenever's daughter, who had been the captain's woman for two years past; she was said to be embroiled in it somewhere. And now the First Magus had shut himself away in the east spire and was refusing to see anyone, not even the most senior magi. That had given rise to the latest and, to Averel with his new responsibilities, most disturbing rumour: that Lord Vordegh had plans which would involve the Chaos riders in an operation the like of which hadn't been seen in living memory.

He sighed audibly. 'Like I said, Lotro, I don't know what's true and what's false in all this. And there's only one piece of advice I can give you. Don't question it, any of it. Just do the work you're supposed to do and don't even *think* about things that aren't your concern.'

'But –'

'No. You're half-fledged; you haven't even had a year's experience here yet, so you listen to me and you take notice. Whatever happens to Captain Liss, there's nothing we can do to change it for good or bad. Whether he's guilty or innocent, the magi will find out, and how they do it isn't for us to say. They know best, Lotro, and they'll do what's best. You remember that, and keep hold of it.' He stood up, giving the youth an avuncular if faintly awkward pat on the shoulder. 'All right now, are you?'

Lotro looked up at him uncertainly. 'Yes, Sarn – Capun. Reckon so . . . if tis as you say.'

'It is. Now; daylight's growing and you're supposed to be on duty. What are you detailed to this morning?'

'Horses, sir. Training if it don't snow, just exercise if it do.'

That would be strenuous enough to drive out the phantoms, Averel thought. 'Well then, best make yourself presentable and be ready.' Then he added a parting shot which he hoped would drive his message home once and for all. 'As for the girl, you give thanks that she didn't look too kindly on you, because if she had, you'd probably be in the same straits as Captain Liss by now.'

Lotro got to his feet and saluted automatically as Averel walked away, but as he lowered his arm again there was a hint of rebellion in his dark eyes . . . and the sparking of an idea. As yet it was by no means fully formed, and Lotro wasn't the quickest of thinkers. But during his short time as a Chaos rider he had become fiercely and loyally devoted to Captain Liss, and this new state of affairs disturbed him deeply. Maybe, as Serg – as *Captain* Averel said, he shouldn't think about things that weren't his concern. But Captain Liss *was* his concern. Lotro couldn't believe he was a heretic, for heretics hated the gods and that was evil. Captain Liss wasn't evil. And Lotro didn't want to see him suffer as that poor, pretty girl had suffered. It would be *wrong*.

When they carried her back to her cell, the girl had said something to him. Well, in truth not to *him*; not to anyone in fact, for Lotro didn't think she was even aware of the riders' presence. But he had heard what she said clearly enough, and as she whispered it there had been a tiny glimmer of sanity struggling through the derangement in her eyes. She had said: '*Benet . . . tell him. Tell him . . .*'

The words were lodged unshakeably in Lotro's memory, and now the slow fires of determination were kindling in his mind and wouldn't be extinguished. *Tell him.* Lotro didn't know what it was she wanted Captain Liss to be told, and he wasn't sure, yet, how he might find out. But somehow, by one means or another, he was resolved to do something to *help*.

Savrinor was standing with his back to the window, watching as the two servants he had commandeered removed the final items from the heap stacked in the middle of the floor. Though his face was very calm it was also very white, and his eyes had an introverted look. The last objects were gathered up; one of the servants looked to him for permission to depart and he gave a curt nod. As the door shut behind the pair's departing backs Savrinor left his position with a sudden, fierce movement and paced to the middle of the floor. Then, halting, he raked the room with an intent gaze and said, 'That's all. There's nothing remaining now. Nothing of her *taint*.'

He started to pace again, and as he passed the chair where Andraia was sitting she rose and caught hold of his hand. His skin was chilled; shock, Magus Croin had said, and hardly to be wondered at under the circumstances. But the feverish, almost manic energy that had gripped him all through the day was showing no signs of abating, and she sensed that he was walking a very sharp and hazardous knife-edge, and keeping his equilibrium only with the greatest difficulty.

'Savrinor, sit down,' she urged him. 'You're still weak; you've not recovered yet and you won't recover while you go on like this. Remember what Magus Croin told you; you *must* rest.'

'I can't.' But he had stopped pacing, and didn't reject the arm that she put around his shoulders. 'Not yet. Not yet.'

She could feel that he was trembling. 'At least let me get you some wine.'

He considered that for a moment, then laughed. The laugh recalled the old, familiar Savrinor, but there was a new note in it that disturbed her. 'Have I ever been known to refuse?'

She ventured a smile. 'You haven't touched a glass all day. Nor eaten a morsel.'

'Haven't I?' He seemed surprised, as though he couldn't remember. 'Perhaps not.' Suddenly the trembling surged into a violent shiver. 'Gods, it's so *cold* . . .'

'Come. Come to the hearth.' He had originally refused to order a fire to be set and lit in the room, and she was thankful now that she had overruled him. The flames were burning brightly, casting a hot light that kept the gathering evening shadows at bay, and she was relieved when Savrinor allowed her to lead him to where a low, comfortable couch was set before the blaze. He stood staring at the flames while she poured wine, took the proffered glass from her with grave but distracted courtesy and sipped at it, though clearly hardly aware of what he was doing. His eyes seemed to be focused on nothing now, and he was shivering again.

Andraia went quietly into his bedroom and found a long robe trimmed with grey fur. She brought it back, draped it around his shoulders, then interposed herself between him and the visions that moved so silently and invisibly before his gaze.

'Savrinor.' Her voice was gentle as she took the glass from him, set it aside and made him sit down at last. 'You *must* try to rest.' She sank onto the couch beside him, hesitated, then: 'For my sake if not for your own. I lost you once . . . I don't want to lose you again.'

He turned his head quickly and fixed her with a curious, uncertain and almost – though it seemed strange, so strange in him – defenceless look. Then abruptly he leaned towards

68

her and, for the first time since they had left the Marble Hall together, drew her close to him. He didn't speak, but there was a tight urgency in the way he held her and Andraia sensed a need in him for something that was beyond his ability to express. And perhaps beyond the ability of any living soul, she thought, as the memory of what had taken place lit clear and acute in her mind once more.

All day she had watched, physically close yet mentally distanced, as Savrinor tried to find an anchor in the turmoil of his mind. She knew he was exhausted, yet he had refused to rest, refused to eat, seeking, it seemed, a kind of refuge in tense and constant activity that at times only just stopped short of violence. On their return he had gone to his cabinet, and whatever it was that he took from it had brought, briefly, a kind of stability, or at least its semblance. With sharp, controlled efficiency he had scoured his rooms for Iselia's belongings; to be burned or otherwise disposed of, he said, but not under any circumstances to be re-used by anyone. That had awakened a painful shard of memory as Andraia recalled giving similar instructions to her own servant when ridding herself of all that might remind her of Benetan, but she had said nothing, only silently helped him in the task of tracking down every last item. Then when all were found and ready for removal Savrinor had turned to his work-table, tidying, cataloguing, tidying again, sheaves of paper stacked and neatened and put away with every edge perfectly aligned, pens and ink and all the other trappings of his profession straightened, rearranged, straightened again with obsessively precise accuracy, refusing to stop, refusing to be satisfied even when there was no more that any man could have done.

And every few minutes he would cross to the window and stand motionless, staring out at the courtyard, with a look that combined deep anger and deep fear in his eyes.

Once, Andraia had thought that perhaps her presence was an intrusion and had quietly made to leave. But he saw her move towards the door and his head came up and he had said, 'No. Stay, please.' So after that she had sat near the fire, knowing she could do nothing more to help and wondering uneasily as she watched him what his haunted, introverted eyes were seeing. She would never ask him any questions, just as she knew he would never ask her about her own experiences. But she knew that what had happened had changed him irrevocably.

And she, too, had changed, for she had discovered a truth about herself, and one that she was finding hard to assimilate. She didn't yet know whether her grief when Savrinor died – she had to use the word, had to acknowledge the fact that he had *died* – whether her grief had truly been for him or merely a railing against the monstrous injustice that had led to his death. She didn't know how deep her feelings for him ran; in so many ways she still hardly knew him. But last night, when Yandros had restored Savrinor's life, something had awoken within Andraia – a devotion so intense that her entire being ached with it; a new and abiding devotion to the gods that surpassed any other emotion she had ever known ... even, she acknowledged, the emotions that her brief liaison with Tarod had aroused. And with that change had come a revelation of another kind. She understood, now, the true nature of Savrinor's fidelity, for it had possessed her soul just as it possessed his. And, whatever else there might or might not be between them now or in the future, the bonds forged by that shared knowledge could never be broken.

She felt his hands slide away from her suddenly and he leaned back, closing his eyes and pinching the bridge of his nose between thumb and forefinger. Another shiver racked him, and Andraia said softly, 'Please, Savrinor, won't you try to sleep now?'

He shook his head. 'No.'

She sighed. 'Why are you goading yourself like this? It's

as if . . . I don't know; almost as if you're *afraid* to sleep.'

Savrinor's eyes opened and he gave her a look that was quite unfathomable. 'When *you* sleep, Andraia, how often do you dream?' he asked.

She thought about that. 'Often enough, I suppose. Though I can rarely recall my dreams when I wake.'

'I dream every night, and I always recall them.' He exhaled tautly. 'There is a drug that can suppress the memories, but it also damages the heart and I'm not about to take that risk a second time. So yes, I am afraid to sleep tonight. Afraid of what I might have to re-live. Not the memory of Lord Yandros – I'll never forget that, *never*; nor ever want to. But the rest . . .' His gaze darted quickly, uneasily towards the window, then with an effort he seemed to bring some dark thought under control and reached out for her hand. 'You understand.'

She said, 'Yes. I believe I do. But Savrinor, the First Magus can't strike back at you. Whatever his feelings, however great his anger, he won't *dare*.'

'I know. Rationally, I know. But rationality isn't proving to be a great deal of help to me at the moment.' Abruptly, startling her, Savrinor got to his feet, threw the fur-trimmed robe off his shoulders and paced across the room. Reaching the window he hacked the curtain aside and stared out into the gathering dark. 'What is he *planning*? What will he *do*? That's the question spinning around and around in my head, and I can't find an answer that doesn't horrify me.'

From here the east spire wasn't visible, but Andraia knew that at the top of that giddying height a light would be burning, bleak and cold and indomitable, as the First Magus continued his solitary deliberations. After the departure of the two Chaos lords, Vordegh had been the first to leave the Marble Hall, but although he showed not the smallest outward sign of emotion, or indeed reaction of any kind, Andraia had heard his quietly ominous orders to Pirane and Croin. He would go immediately to the spire, he said, and until he emerged he was not to be disturbed or interrupted under any circumstance whatever. As for his erstwhile prisoners . . . Andraia could hear his voice in her mind now, and it sent a squirming chill through her. 'The heretic and the rider' – Vordegh hadn't even dignified Iselia or Benetan with names – 'shall be returned to their cells, to await further judgement.' Then the First Magus had paused, turned his head and subjected her and Savrinor to a long stare before adding, 'I have no further interest in the historian or his concubine.'

And his eyes, as they met Andraia's, had given the utter lie to it.

She rose and went to join Savrinor at the window. 'He *can't* harm either of us, Savrinor,' she insisted urgently, gripping his shoulder and refusing to acknowledge the fact that she was trying to convince herself as much as him. 'Not even Vordegh would defy Lord Yandros.'

Savrinor flinched at her touch, as though the hand was someone else's. Then he said: 'That's what I'm trying to make myself believe. But I'm no longer certain that I can.' Then before she could say anything he suddenly swung to face her. 'Didn't you read the signs? Oh, Vordegh bowed to Lord Yandros's will – of course he did; what other choice did he have? But he didn't *accept*. Not in his –' He hesitated, and gave a curt, acid laugh. 'I was about to say in his heart, but somehow I doubt if the First Magus has such an attribute, or understands the concept of it. He didn't accept. And he is an extremely clever man – I won't go through the charade of affecting modesty; it takes a very high degree of intelligence to recognise its own match, and so I of all people am in a position to *know* how clever he is.' He started to pace again, walking towards his work-table. 'In some areas Vordegh is a genius; that's how he rose to be our overlord in the first place. And I can't outwit him.' He reached the table, snatched up a handful of papers and stared at them. 'When it comes to strategy and intrigue I can run rings around virtually everyone in the castle, and have done. But Vordegh's the exception. And if he wants to take revenge on me, or you, or both of us, then unless Lord Yandros is watching over us throughout every moment of every day — and I don't think either of us is *quite* so inane as to think the gods have nothing better to do — then Vordegh will find a way to take that revenge, in one form or in another.' For a few moments longer he continued to stare at the papers, then with a sudden, vicious movement flung them across the room. They hit the wall and flew in all directions like a small but violent snowstorm, and as they fluttered to the floor Savrinor looked at Andraia. The intense, bitter anger and fear was burning afresh in his eyes. 'So, to return again to a question you asked me a while ago, that is another reason why I have no intention of allowing myself to sleep tonight.'

Andraia didn't want to acknowledge the truth of what he was saying, or even the possibility that it *could* be true. But the denial forming in her mind withered on her tongue before she could voice it as she remembered Vordegh's clash with Tarod in the Marble Hall. Savrinor knew nothing of that, for she hadn't told him, but Andraia was well aware of how close matters had come to an outright confrontation between the Chaos lord and the First Magus. Tarod, of course, could have annihilated Vordegh in an instant, and she suspected that only Yandros's last-minute intervention had stopped him from doing so. Yet until the very moment when Yandros appeared, Vordegh had continued to defend his actions in the face of Tarod's rising fury. It had been subtle, it had been respectful; but it had been a form of defiance.

Savrinor had subsided onto the chair which, in his earlier obsessive tidying, he had ranged neatly beside the table. His elbows rested on the table top and he had hidden his face in his hands. Andraia, her thoughts churning like a storm-tide, began to move towards him; she was three steps from the table when his voice halted her.

'He's insane.' It was a flat, quiet statement, muffled by his hands. 'Sweet gods, I've never had the courage to say it aloud before; I've been too afraid that something would hear me and carry word of it back to him. But I don't think I care now, not after what we went through last night. Vordegh's insane. And I fear what his insanity might lead to.' He lowered his hands then and laid them palms downward on the table, gazing at them as though they were alien things. 'Call me a spineless coward if you like, I won't argue with you − but I fear it to the pit of my soul.'

Andraia stood watching him. Instinctively she wanted to offer reassurance and comfort, but in truth what he had said had only served to augment her own growing disquiet. She still didn't believe that Vordegh would openly defy the clear command Yandros had given him; but, as Savrinor implied, there were many ways of taking revenge. And the ugly memory of the look in the First Magus's eyes before he left the Marble Hall last night was enough to turn confidence into deep doubt.

She let her breath out in a sigh that sounded loud in the quiet room. Then she turned, walked back to the hearth and stood beside the table.

'I'm going to pour us both another glass of wine,' she said composedly. 'Come and drink it, and sit with me.'

For a few seconds she thought he wouldn't consent; but then, without a word, he rose from the chair and came to join her. The wine splashed into the glasses − her hand only shook a little and she didn't spill any − and when they were both settled on the couch she laid the discarded robe on his shoulders again and nestled under it, close to him.

'Don't let me dream,' she said.

Savrinor didn't speak, but his fingers twined in her hair,

74

giving her the answer she needed. He knew that someone else was haunting her thoughts, someone who was in far greater danger than they were, and that she was fighting to keep his name and his plight from her mind. And another face was haunting him. *Empty eyes. A drooling mouth. The abysmal helplessness of a mind that had cracked . . .* But his love for her was dead now, and there was no room for pity, even for memory's sake.

They drank the wine in silence, and when the glasses were empty Andraia rested her head on Savrinor's shoulder. She tried to keep her eyes open but her tiredness was too great, and within a few minutes she was asleep. Savrinor was beyond sleep now, he sensed it and was grateful. Tomorrow, perhaps, he would find the courage to rest. But not yet.

Time passed. Once, in her sleep, Andraia tensed anguishedly and called out a name, and tears ran from beneath her closed eyelids. Savrinor gently woke her, whispered some foolish words to her and almost succeeded in making her smile before she drifted away again. As she relaxed and her head drooped once more, he continued to watch her, his expression barren but his mind ranging, thinking. He knew the First Magus too well to have any doubts on the matter of Benetan's fate, and he had also judged Andraia's emotions too astutely to be deceived by the indifference she had tried so hard to pretend to through the day. Whether Benetan himself still had any feeling for her was a question he didn't care to probe, for even now Benetan stubbornly clung to the infatuation with Iselia which had led him into disaster. But when Vordegh had taken his reprisal, as he would, Savrinor believed that Andraia's mask would crack; and he didn't want that to happen. There must be a better solution. A kinder solution.

Andraia's breathing was quieter now, shallow and even as she sank deeper into sleep. Carefully, not wanting to disturb her, Savrinor eased a cramped arm into a more comfortable position. Then he settled again, staring into the glowing heart of the fire and trying not to see images in the embers as he waited for dawn to come.

CHAPTER VI

From a reserve of guile which he wasn't even consciously aware that he possessed, Lotro managed to get himself assigned to the collecting and serving of Benetan's morning meal the following day without Captain Averel being any the wiser. Although he had been with the Chaos riders for only a year, there were others more junior still in the ranks, and one of them proved easy enough to intimidate into exchanging duties at short notice without any reference to his superior officers.

Averel was safely asleep in his bed and out of the way when Lotro went to the kitchen for Benetan's breakfast-tray an hour after sunrise. The kitchen servants kept him waiting and the food when it finally came was already going cold, but Lotro made no comment, only took the tray and, balancing it carefully, set off back towards the stables and the cellars beneath where his erstwhile captain was confined.

He took a short cut across the courtyard, going carefully because of the hard-packed snow and ice underfoot, and was so intent on his chosen path that the sound of a voice addressing him almost made him skid in shock.

'You are Lotro, I believe?'

Lotro wobbled, regained his balance, looked round – and blanched.

'Sir –' Something close to panic filled him as he realized that he couldn't salute without dropping the tray, and in a desperate attempt to convey respect by other means he snapped to attention and stared fixedly ahead. He had had only a momentary glimpse of the man who addressed him, but the image of pale eyes with the glitter of haunted fatigue in them stayed sharp in his inner vision.

'Walk on to the stables.' The command was quietly authoritative and Lotro obeyed, moving stiffly and feeling sweat slick his hands despite the bitter cold. He pushed the stable door open with one elbow and would have stood back to let his companion precede him, but an impatient gesture urged him on. The hard daylight turned to gloom, and as the door shut behind them the cutting wind gave way to stillness and the warm smell of horses.

Savrinor made sure that the latch was secure, then leaned his back against the door. Lotro still didn't dare to meet his eyes but stood shaking, wondering what in all the Seven Hells was going to happen to him. He had always been terrified of Master Savrinor, and the historian's apparent return from the dead had heaped a considerable amount of new fuel on that fire. Savrinor was aware of Lotro's discomfiture but was in no mood either to reassure him or to play on it as he might have done under other circumstances. Benetan had thought highly of the youth's potential, and had trusted him. That, at the moment, was the only relevant factor.

He said, 'That tray. I presume it's intended for someone?'

Lotro swallowed. ''Tis for Capun Liss, sir.' Then belatedly he remembered Averel's warning. 'That is — well — he ant Capun now, but —' Another swallow. ''Tis hard to break the habit, like, sir.'

'I imagine it is.' Savrinor's tone gave nothing away and Lotro sweated anew. 'And where is *ex*-Captain Liss being held?'

'In cellar, sir. Leastways . . . till . . .'

'Until the First Magus in his wisdom and justice decides how best to extract the truth — or a convenient version of it — from him.' But the vitriolic comment was clearly lost on Lotro, and Savrinor didn't pursue it any further. Glancing sidelong and speculatively towards the door that led to the

78

cellars, he asked, 'Have you been attending to Benetan's needs since his imprisonment?'

Lotro's face registered real dismay now and he tried to dissemble. 'Not 'xactly attending, as you might say, sir, but . . . well . . . that is, you see . . .'

'For our Lord Yandros's sake, boy, either you have or you haven't!' Savrinor snapped. 'Which is it?'

Too frightened to lie, Lotro stammered, 'Well, sir, truth is . . . I ant properly supposed to be seeing en at all, like. But I talked the proper guard into changing duties with me. Sarn't – I mean, Capun Averel – thass what I've to call en now, beggin' pardon – Capun Averel don't know as I've done it, and he won't be best pleased if so he find out.' He gave Savrinor a look in which hope and despair mingled. 'I hope you'll not tellen, sir, I hope that with all my heart!'

Savrinor smiled cynically. 'I'll not tell him unless you give me good reason to do so. Why were you so anxious to take on this duty?'

Lotro's expression grew evasive. ''Tis . . . personal, like.'

'You forget, Lotro, that Benetan and I have been friends for a long time.' Then Savrinor saw the youth's changing expression and his eyes narrowed shrewdly. 'Oh, I see. You've heard the rumour that he killed me, have you? And you think, therefore, that I'm looking for some devious way of taking revenge on him. Well, you may take my word that that story has no foundation; the truth is considerably more squalid and has nothing whatever to do with Benetan Liss.' But Lotro's reaction had provided Savrinor with the confirmation he needed. The youth was faithful. And his fidelity went deeper than habit or pragmatism dictated.

'I think,' he said, 'that I understand your reasoning, Lotro. You are loyal to your former captain; you look on him as your friend as well as your superior officer. Thus you are concerned for his welfare, and because of that concern you wish to ensure that he is being treated well and justly.'

Lotro stared down at his own feet. 'Thass true, sir, right enough.'

'And therefore you've changed duties without Captain Averel's knowledge or permission, so that you might see for yourself how Benetan is faring and if there is anything you can do to help him.'

The young rider flushed. 'Es, sir.'

'Very well. Then there is something you can do to help Captain Liss. You can take him a message.'

Lotro raised his head and regarded Savrinor curiously. 'A message, sir? From you?'

'From me. It's very simple – and it is also very private.' Savrinor's eyes turned stone-hard. 'If you ever divulge what I am about to say, or even the fact that I said it, to any living soul other than Captain Liss, your remains will be lying at the foot of the castle stack in time for the next tide to carry them into oblivion. Do I make myself clear?'

Lotro eyed him sidelong, frightened but also a little angry that his integrity had been called into question. 'I won't give nothing away, sir!'

The hint of indignation in his tone satisfied Savrinor. 'Good,' he said. 'Then tell Benetan this – he has no future in the castle; that is a fact, and one that can't be changed. Therefore he must make a simple choice: find a means of saving his own neck, or wait patiently for death.'

Lotro blanched. '*Death*, sir? But – but –' His mouth worked, then suddenly the words came in a rush. 'I know what they're sayin', sir – that Capun Liss be heretic, that he's betrayed the gods and magi and all of us – but I don't believe en, sir! I don't! Capun Liss ent an evil man, he wouldn't do such things as they say!'

'I'm inclined to agree with you.' Savrinor's eyes were still arctic. 'The First Magus, however, does not.'

'But Capun Liss ant been tried yet, sir! How can First Magus *know*?'

It was a great pity, Savrinor thought, that Lotro wasn't astute enough to grasp the extreme irony of his own words, and he said a little bleakly, 'I assure you, in his own mind the First Magus *does* know. And I don't think it would be wise for either of us to question his decision, do you?' He watched the young rider's face as he spoke, saw that he was beginning to understand, and in a detached way felt pity for him. Disillusionment was never an easy lesson, and when it clashed with innocent idealism the experience was all the harsher.

'It is all a question of justice, Lotro,' he added more gently. 'I believe, as do you, that however great his alleged crime might be, an accused man deserves nothing less. Captain Liss, however, will not receive it within these walls. And you may tell him he has my word on that.'

Lotro knew as well as anyone that when Master Savrinor gave his word it could be trusted, and he nodded miserably. 'I'll tellen that, sir. And . . .' He turned his head, gave Savrinor a peculiarly perceptive look, 'I reckon I see the sense of what you've said. And I thank you.'

Under the circumstances Lotro's gratitude was the last thing Savrinor wanted, and he made an impatiently dismissive gesture. 'I simply believe that there's no point in hiding the truth.' His tone was suddenly curt and he turned away to face the door. 'You'd best be on your way with that unappetizing mess.' Hand on the door-latch he paused. 'And this conversation has never taken place.'

'No, sir. I understand.'

Savrinor was beginning to feel sick; telling himself that he had never been able to stomach the smell of horses, he lifted the latch —

'Sir . . .'

Oh, gods, Savrinor thought. He looked back. 'What is it?'

Lotro was biting his lip, and the look in his eyes betrayed his thoughts – the thoughts Savrinor had dreaded – before he could bring himself to speak. 'Sir, if . . . if Capun Liss ant been given justice, then . . .' He faltered.

'Then?' Savrinor asked, knowing what must come.

'Then . . . what about *her*, sir? For it seem to me that . . .' He blinked rapidly. 'That they could have been kinder.'

An image sprang unbidden into Savrinor's mind, as vivid and as ugly as though he had suddenly been transported back in time, back to the Marble Hall. He focused hard on a pile of hay-bales, fighting the image away, fighting to keep his voice on an even keel. 'You've seen her, have you?'

'I was one of them that took her out of the Hall, sir.'

'Ah.'

'They won't let her die, sir.'

'I know that.' Savrinor had regained his composure now and his tone was sharp. He looked at Lotro. 'And you know what she is, don't you? There's no question about her allegiances; she *is* a traitor to the gods.'

A nod. ''Es, sir.'

'Then she deserves no less than she's received.'

Lotro nodded again, but Savrinor heard him whisper something under his breath. 'What did you say?' he demanded.

The youth blinked again. 'Nothing that d'matter. sir. Only that . . . she were so pretty. I wish they'd let her die now.'

The slam of the stable door was his only answer.

Outside, Savrinor leaned against the black stone wall and drew air between clamped teeth and into his throat. Cold, clean air; and the stone against his back was like solid ice, striking its chill through clothes and skin and deep into his flesh until its bite became a cruel kind of relief.

Damn the boy! Raising ghouls out of memory with his simplistic compassion – Savrinor cursed himself for giving way to the temptation to meddle in this grotesque affair. Better to have left Benetan to rot in the midden he had built for himself, go the way *she* had gone and let that put an end to the whole sordid mess. No one had *asked* him to save the wrongheaded fool from Vordegh's reprisals, and no one would thank him for trying.

But that, he reminded himself, wasn't true; and it brought back to mind the motive which had incited him to throw common sense off the castle stack and stir these grimy waters again. Or one of the motives.

He didn't care to question too closely whether the thought of Andraia's grief if Benetan should die was quite enough in itself to have propelled him into this impetuous course. But there was another goad beyond Andraia, and he had no doubts about that. Briefly, in the stable, the loathing he felt for Iselia had weakened as he remembered what Vordegh had inflicted on her, but now the hard day-light was sweeping the doubts away and restoring his sense of perspective. As he had said to Lotro, it was all a matter of justice. In one sense Benetan was as much Iselia's victim as he himself had been, and the idea that even now she might still bring him to ruin offended Savrinor's principles to their deepest root. He didn't think that Benetan was in league with the heretics, and neither, he believed, did Yandros. The Chaos lord had made it clear that the gods had no further interest in Benetan, and so to play his own small part in undoing the evil that Iselia had brought about was, Savrinor felt, no violation of Yandros's will.

And at the heart of his reasoning was another issue. Yandros had restored Savrinor's life, and Savrinor was neither so arrogant nor so impertinent as to believe that he had been granted that boon for any other reason than to satisfy a sense of justice. Whatever the other considerations, whatever personal emotions might or might not be involved in this, he could not in all conscience do less than follow the example Yandros had set.

He raised his head, looked along the wall of the stable block to where the huge, black bulk of the east spire reared stark against the sky. There was a light in the summit window, a cold, unnatural and unwholesome light, and Savrinor repressed a stabbing shiver that seemed to penetrate beyond the merely physical. Was Vordegh working still at his private savagery, or was he at that window, staring down, watching his domain as a hawk watched potential prey?

Savrinor looked away again, not wanting to know the answer to that question, and set off towards the main wing.

The windowless store-room that served as Benetan's cell was locked and bolted, but a permanent guard would have been a waste of resources and so there was no one to observe Lotro's belated arrival with the food tray. Precariously balancing his burden, together with a lantern he had collected, in one hand, Lotro let himself into the cellar and peered uncertainly into the gloom.

Benetan was lying on the straw palliasse which was the room's only furnishing. He was facing the wall and at first Lotro thought he was asleep, but as he set the tray down on the floor a restless movement of one leg gave the lie to the impression.

Lotro wetted his lips and said, 'Capun Liss?'

Benetan turned over, blinking in the lamplight and staring at him. 'Lotro . . .' He twisted about, sat up stiffly. 'Is it already morning?'

'Sun's up this hour past and more, sir.' Lotro looked back at him, disconcerted less by his scruffy and unshaven appearance than by the hard indifference in his eyes. He pointed to the tray. 'I brought your brakfuss, sir. And a lantern, so's you can have light.'

'You might as well take them back again. I don't want either.'

Lotro frowned uneasily. 'You did ought to have food, sir. Won't do no good to go hungry.'

'It won't do me any good to eat, either. And there's nothing in here that I want to look at.' Benetan hunched his shoulders and leaned back against the damp wall, his expression closed. 'Take them away, Lotro. That's an order.'

The youth regarded him for a few moments. Then he said solemnly, 'Can't take orders from you no more, sir. Capun Averel says so.'

It provoked a response. Benetan looked up quickly and his eyes narrowed. 'Oh. So Averel's promotion has been confirmed, has it?'

'Es, sir. He don't like it any more than I 'spect you do, but there tis. He's our capun now, like, and you're not.'

Well, it was logical. And it told Benetan that First Magus Vordegh had already decided what the outcome of the questioning which he now awaited would be . . . but he didn't care. His fate, merited or otherwise, didn't matter. Nothing mattered any more.

He turned his face away again. 'Then if you won't take my orders, you can leave the food here until it rots.' He paused. 'Averel shouldn't have sent you. I told him I wanted to be attended to only by men with whom I've had little direct dealing.'

'Mebbe so, sir,' Lotro said stoically, 'But Capun Averel didn't send me; in fact he don't know I'm here. I come of my own.' A long hesitation. 'And I've got a message for you, sir.'

Though he told himself he didn't want to hear any message from anyone, Benetan felt a small, irrational flare of anticipation, and before he could stop himself he said, 'Message? From whom?'

'Master Savrinor.'

'*Savrinor?*' Benetan swung round, his face taut and his eyes suddenly furious. 'What is this — some joke at my expense? Who put you up to this, Lotro? *Who?*'

'It ant a joke, sir!' Lotro protested. 'And twasn't no one put me up to un. Master Savrinor come looking for me not minutes since, and he said —'

'I don't want to know what he said.'

Lotro frowned down at the tray. 'Well, sir, s'pose I cann't make you listen if you ent minded to. But there was another message.'

Benetan's temper was fraying fast and he interrupted angrily, 'I don't wish to hear *anything* from, or about, Savrinor, thank you!'

''Tis nothing to do with he, sir, not the other message. Tis from . . . from her.'

Suddenly, Benetan was very still. 'From . . . *her*? You mean . . .'

Lotro nodded. 'I seen her, sir. Yesterday, like, when I had to help carry her out of the Marble Hall. And she tried to speak to me.'

Then, haltingly, he told Benetan everything. Much of it was hard to endure hearing, for Lotro knew little about tact and his simple but painful description of how he had felt when, for one small moment, lucidity had struggled through the agony of madness in Iselia's mind and she had spoken her three broken words nearly undid Benetan's resolve to hear him out. But he steeled himself to listen, saying nothing, and this time made no attempt to silence Lotro when he cautiously broached the subject of Savrinor's message once more. Lotro had memorized the historian's words carefully and repeated them almost verbatim. Then, as Benetan mutely digested them, he added,

'Master Savrinor told me to say another thing to you, sir, from him. He told me, say that tis all a question of justice, and that Capun Liss will not have justice within these walls. "He has my word on that" is what he said.'

What would Savrinor, of all people, know about justice? Benetan asked himself scathingly. But then a whisper of honesty asserted itself through the bitter prejudice. In truth, Savrinor knew a great deal more about it than most, for his treatment at Vordegh's hands had been anything but just. And Benetan remembered his own feelings in the wake of the First Magus's attack – that if Savrinor was to die, he should die for a valid reason.

A valid reason ... Slowly, like the cold pre-dawn glimmer on a bleak horizon, a new feeling began to penetrate the numbness that had shrouded Benetan since being brought out of the Marble Hall. He had told himself that he had nothing left to fight for or even to live for. He couldn't help Iselia – no mortal power could help her now. And with her ruin, his faith in the gods he had served, and the friends he had trusted, was dead. He wanted only to die in his turn, and had been past caring whether his death came at the First Magus's hands or at his own. But Savrinor's message was changing that. It was a goad, and it was breaking through his inertia – though not in the way that Savrinor had intended.

And then there was Iselia's message. *Benet ... tell him.* Lotro had misinterpreted that, thinking that she wanted to convey some word to his captain, but Benetan knew better. Iselia had meant, *tell Kaldar.* For Kaldar, and the powers he served, were her only hope now.

Lotro was hovering anxiously, trying and failing to read the expression on Benetan's face as he waited for a response. At last, he received one.

"'All a question of justice" ... yes, I think perhaps Savrinor is right.' Suddenly, startling the younger man, Benetan got to his feet. 'Lotro, have they caught Kal –' *careful!* a warning inner voice said: '– caught the red-haired heretic yet? The one who escaped?'

Lotro shook his head. 'No, sir. We was expecting to go

out after en, but First Magus said no. He said 'twould be a waste, and there's better ways.'

'What better ways?'

'Don't know for sure, sir, but Sar — Capun Averel d'reckon that she — that is, the girl; that poor — Master Savrinor's —'

'Iselia,' Benetan said tersely. 'Her name is Iselia.'

Lotro nodded. He couldn't bring himself to speak her name; somehow to do so would bring the whole ugliness of her plight too close. 'Es, sir. She's still alive, you see. Still alive. And Capun Averel d'reckon she'll be kept so, to lure the heretic back here . . .' His voice tailed off as he thought again about the cruelty of that, and he frowned unhappily.

Yes, Benetan thought, that was logical; and wasn't it what Yandros in person had ordered? To keep Iselia alive, to prolong her suffering; doubtless that would amuse the Chaos lord, as well as suiting First Magus Vordegh's sadistic nature very well. Memories sharpened suddenly and violently into focus in his mind; Yandros's malevolent face as he scorned the plea to have mercy on Iselia; the contempt in the green eyes of Yandros's brother when the nature of his link with Andraia was made clear; Andraia herself, who had betrayed his trust far more surely and ruthlessly than he had ever betrayed hers. And lastly Savrinor; the schemer, the manipulator, the player of games. Savrinor, to whom Yandros had granted *justice*. But Yandros's view of justice was not Benetan's. And what Savrinor's message had been intended to convey was a very, very far cry from what Benetan had in mind now.

He had been staring towards the door, eyes narrowed, seeing something other than the confines of the cell. Lotro hadn't spoken again for he didn't know what else to say, and abruptly Benetan swung to face him.

'What orders have been given for the riders tonight?' he demanded.

88

'None, sir. Capun Averel d'say we're to wait First Magus's decision, and that won't be till . . .' He stopped and swallowed, chagrined.

'Until my mind has been stripped of its secrets and my sanity destroyed in the process. There's no need to spare my feelings, Lotro; I've seen for myself what the First Magus is capable of.'

Lotro's face was scarlet. 'I didn't want to put it so harsh-like, sir. But then, Master Savrinor did say as there's no point hiding the truth.'

Benetan could just hear Savrinor's cultured voice uttering those words, and his eyes hardened cynically. 'Master Savrinor can be very sanguine when it suits him.'

'Beg pardon, sir?'

'Ah, forget it. I don't want to think about Savrinor.' He scraped his hair back from his face, revolted by the oily, unwashed feel of it. 'If you want to help me, Lotro, you can. You say tonight's likely to be quiet. Is the Maze open?'

''Es, sir, so far's I know.'

'Good; good. Then I want you to go to my room. Make up some pretext; I imagine it won't be locked anyway, for they won't have moved some other poor fool in there yet. Get my ceremonial regalia – belt, gloves, sword and two knives. And the circlet and mask that we wear on sorties; that's the most important thing of all.'

Lotro counted the items off on his fingers. 'But the shoulder-flashes, sir – full regalia means you should have they, but Capun Averel –'

'Averel wears them now; yes, I know. You needn't worry about the flashes, Lotro. But get my fur coat. Don't forget that.'

'Coat. No, sir, I won't forget en.' Lotro paused. 'You want me to fetch en all to you, sir?'

'Yes. But discreetly – and your timing must be good. Someone will be bringing me another meal this evening. I don't know what time that will be –'

'First moonrise, sir, or thereabouts.' Lotro had checked the duty roster.

'Then I want you to arrive half an hour before that. And if you've any care for your own skin, don't let *anyone* else know what you're about!'

'I shann't, sir, certain sure!' Lotro's face was animated now at the thought that he was to achieve something positive for his old leader. 'Half-hour before first moonrise, then.'

'That's right. Oh, and be sure to wear your own regalia. Is that clear?'

'Es, sir . . . though I don't rightly see why.'

'Don't worry, I'll explain to you later.' Benetan gave Lotro a smile that had an odd spark in it. 'Do this for me, and I'll owe you a debt that I won't forget.'

The young man looked at his own boots. 'No need of that, sir.' He looked up again, trustingly. 'I know you're not a heretic, and Master Savrinor knows it too, I reckon. Thass why, like he said, 'tis only proper justice to help.'

Benetan returned the smile. And the lie came so easily as he said, 'Of course I'm no heretic, Lotro. I only wish that the First Magus believed the truth, as you do.'

'I din't hit en too hard, sir. Just 'nough to be sure and to make it look right.'

Shrugging into his fur coat, Benetan looked down at the unconscious young rider lying among the wreckage of tray and food on the cell floor. 'And you're certain he didn't see your face?'

'Es, sir. Tis dark enough in here, and anyways he were turning to shut door behind en, so he had his back to me.' Lotro looked pleased with himself. 'He'll think twas you slammed en, sir, no doubt of that.'

'Good. Then tie his hands – here, use my shirt-belt. The buckle's distinctive and it will be recognized as mine.'

Lotro bent to the task. 'Want me to gag en, sir?'

'No; no need for that. By the time he comes round I'll be away, so he may shout as loudly as he likes. Not that anyone's likely to hear him down here.' Benetan hesitated, then picked up the silver circlet with its ornate half-mask, the last of the items Lotro had brought to him. He hadn't worn it since the night of the old First Magus's death and the gleaning which had started this whole ugly chain of events, and memories seeped unpleasantly into his mind, together with a sensation of crawling revulsion, as he put it on. Hard to believe that he used to be *proud* to wear this . . . but it would serve his purpose just once more, and then he could be rid of it forever.

Lotro gave a final jerk to the knot at the unconscious rider's wrists, then adjusted his own circlet and mask, which had begun to slip sideways. 'All ready, sir, I reckon.'

Benetan nodded, trying not to let his nervousness show. This would be the most dangerous part of the operation, and the last thing he needed was for his own fears to trigger off a like reaction in Lotro. 'Very well.' His voice was crisp. *Belt, gloves, weapons, coat.* Yes, all was as it should be, and the mask made his face unrecognizable. And he had the unconscious rider's amulet. 'Lead on, Lotro,' he said. 'And don't hurry – we don't want to draw attention to ourselves.'

All the way along the passage, up the stairs, through the connecting door to the stables, Benetan's heart was pounding like a hammer under his ribs. In the stables themselves, warm with the dim, shifting presences of the horses, he signed to Lotro to douse the lamp he carried, and the very junior duty-sentry at the far end of the stalls saw only the silhouettes of two masked Chaos riders walking by, intent on business that was no concern of his. He made a hasty salute which Benetan returned with a curt nod, and the two dark figures disappeared through the outside door.

As Lotro shut the door behind them Benetan paused and scanned the courtyard. The castle's grim black walls were ablaze with lit windows at this hour, and the great double doors in the main wing stood open. There were a number of people in the courtyard, braving the bitter cold to take short cuts from one section of the castle to another, but they were mostly servants, who would pay them no heed. He looked up at the sky; it was blank, with the peculiarly flat glow that presaged another heavy snowfall. And at the top of one of the four titanic spires that towered broodingly above the walls, a faint, unearthly light was shimmering in the First Magus's eyrie.

'All right.' Benetan dragged his gaze away from the spire with an effort. 'We cross the courtyard together, as far as the barbican. Then, provided there's no one to see us, open the postern and watch until I've gone through the Maze. Wait perhaps twenty minutes, then point out to someone that my tray-bearer hasn't returned. One of the sergeants will find him soon enough and raise the alarm. And don't forget *not* to lock the postern behind me – we don't want anyone to think I had help.'

'I understand right enough, sir.' Lotro's voice was confident; he had rehearsed his instructions carefully over the past half-hour, and Benetan was satisfied that he could be relied on. Chances were that the rider he had hit wouldn't be made to suffer too greatly for his apparent lapse; but either way a cold streak had awoken in Benetan that put him past caring. Petty justice no longer concerned him. It was a greater, a *far* greater justice that involved him now.

There was ice underfoot as they walked towards the barbican. Melted snow, re-freezing; it didn't bode well for the conditions he would find at his destination, but that couldn't be helped. If he had misjudged, miscalculated, it would still be better to die of exposure than face what Vordegh had in store for him.

The vast shadow of the barbican arch swallowed them. No challenge came, no presence moved in the darkness, and Lotro hastened forward to unbolt the postern gate.

The huge cold of the northern night swept in as the postern swung back, and for a moment Benetan's resolve almost wavered. But exposure *would* be a better death. And a quicker one.

He turned to the tall, young man at his side. 'I *do* owe you a debt, Lotro. But I doubt if I'll ever be in a position to repay it.'

Lotro shuffled his feet. 'That don't matter, Capun. I don't think on en like that.'

Benetan smiled and was glad that the darkness was too intense for Lotro to see the smile's nature. The youth had a kindly honesty that deserved to survive and prosper; though the odds in favour of it, he suspected, were slim.

'Well, for what little it's worth you have my gratitude. And if I can ever repay you, I promise I shall. Goodbye, Lotro. And good luck.'

Frost crunched and crackled as he stepped out onto the sward of the castle stack. The Maze lay ahead, an unfocused and faintly shimmering patch of unreality above an over-lush rectangle of grass. The visualization was clear in Benetan's mind. Barren mountains, starkly white at this time of year, shining like a ghost-land under the night sky. And the twin peaks, with the pass running through them. Kaldar's old hideaway . . .

He looked back once, briefly. Lotro's face was a pale oval in the dark, hovering in the postern and looking small and lost against the vaster, blacker backdrop of the castle wall. Benetan's hand closed round the stolen amulet on its iron chain. It pulsed under his fingers, responding.

He shut his eyes, spoke one word. And the vortex of the Maze opened.

CHAPTER VII

It wasn't a human figure, Benetan told himself. Only a spur of rock ahead of him where the track through the endless pass curved, an inanimate thing given a false semblance of life by the night's turbulent murk. He had made that mistake before, taking delusion for reality, and last time it had almost led him into disaster for he had drawn his knife in readiness to meet an attack, only to find himself, a minute later, holding it by the blade instead of the hilt and staring stupidly at the blood that ran from his hand, through his gauntlet to drip steadily onto the snow.

A rock, then. Nothing more. He tried to blink to clear his vision and confirm it once and for all, but his eyes were too ice-crusted now and the crystals on his lashes were like starbursts, half blinding him as a new and violent snow flurry hurled itself in his face. Then he realized that he had stopped walking. That was dangerous, potentially lethal; must *move*, keep going somehow. He no longer had any awareness of his body at all, the cold and the wind had driven so deep into his bones, but there was still a sharp spark of self-preservation left in him and he had to cling on to that, or the temptation to lie down in the snow would become too great and then that would be an end to it. So easy just to curl up in one of those deep drifts that piled seductively to either side of the track, hemming him in, and let himself go to sleep forever. At least then he would no longer have to listen to the ceaseless, moaning voice of the wind . . .

This time he almost gave in to the lure, and it was only when he realized that he was veering aside and wading thigh-deep into the whiteness that he dragged his mind back from the brink of complete surrender to the elements. This was *insane*. Either he was going to reach his objective – wherever that objective was – or he was going to die. And if he was going to die, it wouldn't be without a fight. Only when he could be certain that he had misjudged Kaldar altogether and he wasn't hiding out in one of his damned caves would he be ready to admit defeat; and even then he wouldn't let the cold kill him. He'd do it himself, take his second knife – he had dropped the first one when that delusion so nearly fooled him – and make a better job of the cut this time. Both wrists; push them together against the blade. Or his jugular vein, if he could make one last effort to force his hand high enough. Perhaps Yandros would give him that strength, help him on his way, and a snort of amusement turned his throat raw as he recalled what had happened in the Marble Hall. Savrinor and his prayer. Aid for a mortal soul in the last extremity of torment. *Yandros, high lord of Chaos, I call upon you now, in my time of ultimate need ...*

Benetan laughed, or thought he did, though he couldn't hear the sound of it above the grim voice of the wind. His legs seemed to have stopped moving again; gritting his teeth and feeling ice crunch in his mouth, he forced himself on another step, then another.

Ahead of him, blacker against the dark, the rock spur moved. And suddenly he realized that he hadn't been deluded after all. It wasn't a rock spur. It *was* human –

Benetan swayed on his feet and almost fell as recognition penetrated the numbness in his brain. Reason tried to tell him that this wasn't possible, but he had enough awareness left to know that reason couldn't be trusted any more. And the figure that had detached itself from the deep shadow where the pass curved wasn't a figment of his imagination.

'Kaldar?' He couldn't even tell if he spoke aloud or only

imagined that he did. Snow smashed against his face but he didn't feel it bite into his unprotected skin. He couldn't feel anything. And maybe the words were only in his head as he croaked, 'Kaldar . . . curse you, don't you owe me a favour after what you did? Don't stand staring like a ghost – help me to *move* . . .'

Kaldar sat cross-legged on the cave floor, his eyes gem-hard as he watched the recumbent form on the opposite side of the fire. Benetan had fallen asleep – or passed out – within minutes of being half led and half carried back to this shelter, and had been in no state to answer any of the questions that Kaldar so desperately needed to ask. Kaldar was no healer but he thought Benetan had suffered no lasting harm from his experience, and in this cave, which he had deliberately chosen because it was small and well protected from the bitter outside air, the fire's heat was more than enough to thaw frozen flesh and clothing. But it couldn't thaw the psychic ice in Kaldar's marrow, and the ordeal of waiting for Benetan to wake was growing harder to endure with each minute.

He got suddenly to his feet, body moving like a pent, coiled spring, and paced across the cave. Six strides from one side to the other; he had counted them so many times since his flight from the Star Peninsula that they haunted his nightmares now. Helpless in the bleak limbo between hope and dread, he had made himself believe that Benetan would come looking for him, and had prepared for that, been ready . . . sweet Aeoris, if he hadn't set up an astral watch, then Benet would have died out there in the snow-storm without ever knowing how close he had come to this hideout. But Benet couldn't have known that, and wasn't the kind of fool to have gambled on such long odds. This had been no careful, premeditated search. Something had goaded him, had suddenly and violently impelled him to leave the safety of the castle and come hunting with an all but non-existent chance of success. It was an insane act, and for one wild moment Kaldar had feared treachery; a lure, perhaps, to trap him into revealing his whereabouts before a full company of Chaos riders arrived to finish what their captain had begun. In that moment he had felt an urge to take Benetan's knife from its sheath and kill him as he slept, and only the certainty that not even the magi could enter the psychic circle he had created around himself without his being aware of it had stayed his hand. Reason had come back then, calming him. Nothing had followed Benetan from the Star Peninsula. He had been driven by another motive entirely.

'Kaldar.'

Kaldar spun round at the sound of his name being spoken. By the fire, face lit harshly by the flames, Benetan was sitting up. 'What's happened?' Kaldar's voice snapped harshly from his throat and he was across the floor in three strides, skirting the fire, dropping to a crouch and gripping the other man's shoulder. 'Benet, tell me, what's *happened?*'

He was shaken off with a movement so violent that he sprawled back on the rock, and before he could recover himself Benetan stood up. He stared at the flames, blindly, and his expression was so stark that the savage flow of words Kaldar had been about to utter shrivelled on his tongue. Then, deliberately, Benetan shrugged off his fur coat. It fell to the floor with a damp, heavy thud; a foot moved, kicking it viciously out of the way, and Benetan's hands went to his belt.

'Benet, what —' Kaldar began.

'No.' The tone stopped him in mid-sentence, and with a savage jerk Benetan unfastened the belt's complex buckle. The star of Chaos. Seven gems for the seven gods . . . His wrist twisted, and he hurled the belt onto the fire.

Slowly Kaldar rose to his feet. He didn't attempt to speak again, but understanding was beginning to dawn and with it a deep, acute sense of horror. Benetan looked at him, briefly, his eyes barren. Then he pulled off the gauntlets with their silver claws. His right hand was crimson, blood running from the glove in sluggish ropes, and there was a spitting and hissing that sullied the quiet when he flung the gauntlets into the flames.

'I lost the circlet and mask somewhere in the pass.' His voice was flat, dead. 'I wish I hadn't. Silver doesn't burn, but I'd have tried. I'd have *tried*.'

He took a step back. The fire had consumed the gloves, already turned them to dry, black leaves, crackling, writhing, falling into ash. The silver talons were indistinguishable from embers now. And the heavier leather of the belt was disintegrating fast in the flames. But the buckle didn't burn. The emblem, his talisman for so many years. Yandros's sigil, refusing to melt, refusing to die; as Yandros refused to let *her* die . . .

'You make a mockery of it all.' Suddenly there was emotion in his words; a terrible, hard emotion that sent a spear of renewed dread through Kaldar as he heard it. 'You demon. You *travesty*.'

Then, as he stared at the symbol of Chaos in its wreath of fire, and remembered Yandros's patrician face and the inhuman detachment in his ever-changing eyes, the last barrier in Benetan's mind crumbled. He dropped to one knee on the rock floor and bowed his head, covering his face with a hand that shook as though from a virulent fever.

'Lord Aeoris . . . I have no power to alter what has been done.' Then his voice broke, and the rage that until this moment had been beyond his ability to feel was suddenly there in him and spilling hotter than any physical flame into his soul. He looked up, his eyes frenzied. 'But if you hear me – if you have the power to hear me now – then I swear to you that while I live, I will stint nothing and I will stop at nothing – and in your name, Aeoris of Order,

I pledge all that I can, and all that I am, to the path that will see Chaos damned and *destroyed!*'

Kaldar felt as though his heart had stopped. His gaze held rigidly on Benetan's figure and he hissed, 'Benet what are you saying? What's happened, to make you . . . to make this . . .'

Benetan drew in a harsh breath, and Kaldar's floundering questions died away. Then Benetan put a clenched fist to his mouth, biting hard into the knuckles. Blood welled; at last the torn hand fell away, and he said softly, 'There will be no justice. Not while they continue to exist. There will be no *justice.*'

Kaldar made a convulsive move forward – and started violently as the fire suddenly blazed up. A column of flame sprang to violent life, twisting towards the roof. And a voice, sibilant, unhuman, filled the cave with echoes.

'You speak the truth, Benetan, and you speak with your heart. I have the power to hear you.'

The flaming column turned white, and at its core two brilliant gold pinpoints appeared. Then the flame metamorphosed into something more cogent, and, swathed in a white cloak in which a snowstorm far more violent than the storm outside seemed to rage and swirl, the figure of Aeoris manifested in the heart of the fire.

Kaldar choked back a shocked oath and fell to one knee. Benetan, though, could only stare up at the lord of Order, his body immobile and his expression frozen. Aeoris gazed back at him, and the golden light in his strange, blank eyes darkened to an intense hue.

'Tell me of it, Benetan,' he said gently.

Benetan covered his face again. He couldn't speak, couldn't bring himself to relate the hideous story, and he shook his head desperately, trying to convey the reason for his inability to answer. Aeoris understood. He stepped forward, and one graceful hand reached out, touching Benetan's brow lightly.

'My friend, look at me.' His voice was filled with sympathy. 'If the words are too painful, don't try to utter them – only open your mind to me, and I will understand.'

A long silence held, broken only by Kaldar's quick, uneasy breathing, while the god and the man held one another's gazes. Then at last Aeoris broke the contact, and Kaldar felt a psychic shock of raw emotion as the lord of Order turned to look at him.

'I'm so sorry, Kaldar.' Aeoris spoke softly, and with such compassion that the words seemed to crush something at the core of Kaldar's being. 'So profoundly sorry.'

Throat tightening, Kaldar heard his own voice as though from a very, very great way off. 'She's dead . . . ?'

'No.' The word froze him. Grief made Aeoris's expression haggard, and he added quietly, 'She is not dead, Kaldar, because the magi won't let her die. They mean to use her to lure you back to the Star Peninsula.'

Kaldar swallowed painfully. 'Have they . . . harmed her?'

Aeoris glanced at Benetan, who looked quickly away, giving Kaldar his answer. And suddenly, violently, Kaldar lost control of his feelings.

'You saw!' He started to scrabble to his feet, turning on Benetan. 'You witnessed it, you know what they've done to her, and you –'

The words cut off as Aeoris caught hold of his wrist, stilling him with a strength that Kaldar couldn't resist. 'Yes, he saw what they did,' the god said quietly. 'And he won't speak of it to you, which I think is as well for you both. But you know, now, why he is here.' Kaldar's violent impulse was already fading, calmed by Aeoris's touch, and reason was struggling to assert itself once more. But the *grief* – he couldn't contain it, couldn't *bear* it, and it spilled from him in a helpless appeal. 'Please,' he whispered. 'Please, Lord Aeoris, is there *nothing* you can do to help her?'

'Kaldar, if I had that power, do you think I wouldn't have used it?' Aeoris's expression matched his own. 'But we're not strong enough.' He released Kaldar's wrist and his golden eyes narrowed broodingly. 'While Chaos still controls that gateway, we *cannot* be strong enough!'

Benetan spoke suddenly. 'Gateway?'

They both looked at him. Benetan's mind was dull, hurting, but the word had cut through him like a small, sharp knife, and Kaldar saw the shades of ugly memory awaken in his look again.

Aeoris said, 'The magi call it the Chaos Gate.' He paused. 'You've seen it?'

'I've seen it.' There was a harsh edge to Benetan's voice. 'And I've seen the beings that come through it, and the depth of their corruption.' He looked up, met Aeoris's gaze with a strange, wild stare. 'Is that what Iselia was trying to do when Vordegh caught her? Was she trying to take the wand that opens the Gate?'

'She was.' Aeoris looked steadily, penetratingly at him.

'I didn't know.' Benetan put a clenched fist to his mouth, the gesture blurring his voice. 'I hadn't *realized*. I've been asking myself, over and over again I've been asking myself why she broke into the First Magus's rooms, what she *wanted* there. It was so reckless, so *crazed* – I thought she must have been making some bid to assassinate him.'

Kaldar sucked air violently, furiously between clenched teeth. 'Do you think I would have let her do anything as insane as *that*?'

'No.' Benetan shook his head. 'No. I see now, I – I understand.' The meeting in the council hall, ensuring Vordegh's absence; it had been the perfect chance for Iselia; indeed, her only chance. And though Benetan didn't yet know what significance the wand of Chaos might have for Order's gods, he knew the level of Iselia's devotion to their cause.

Then, knowing it, he was suddenly bitterly angry in his

turn, and he rounded on Kaldar. 'But if you cared for her safety, if you cared that much, why did you let her do it at all? Why didn't *you* run the risk, and why wasn't it *you* who was caught and tortured?'

'I had no choice!' Kaldar fired back. 'She told me that by the time the magi met, the truth about me would have been discovered. If I hadn't fled the castle they'd have arrested me, and that would have been the end of *everything!*'

Iselia, Benetan remembered, had told him that, tried to convince him that Kaldar had gone at her insistence. He hadn't believed it then and didn't want to believe it now. But before he could voice his feelings Kaldar said savagely, 'Think what you please about me, Benet. It doesn't matter, because I promise you that whatever you think doesn't come within ten bowshots of the contempt I feel for myself!'

'Kaldar.' Aeoris, who had been listening intently but unhappily, spoke suddenly. The sound of his voice startled them both, for in the rising heat of their exchange they had all but forgotten his presence. Silenced, they looked at him.

'Contempt or guilt or any other such emotions are of no value to Iselia now,' the lord of Order said gently but with an undertone that shamed them. 'And personal quarrels are an indulgence which none of us can afford. Benetan; Kaldar's reasons for leaving the castle were valid. And Kaldar; Benetan could not have saved Iselia from capture, for he himself was betrayed before he could take any action.' His golden eyes glittered abruptly, warningly. 'Does that satisfy you both?'

Benetan said indistinctly, 'Forgive me, my lord. I didn't mean to imply . . .' He couldn't find words to express the rest, and made a helpless, negating gesture.

Kaldar looked sidelong at him. 'You were betrayed?'

A nod, but Benetan didn't elaborate. That story could

be told later; better for now that it stayed locked away without an airing to help it fester. Instead, forcing his mind to another tack, he said, 'Vordegh's wand. It's important to . . . to the cause?'

Kaldar didn't notice that he said *the* cause and not *your* cause, but Aeoris did, and the lord of Order's expression underwent a subtle change. 'It's vital, Benetan,' he said. 'For it is the key to Yandros's command of this world. Through the wand, the mortal realm and the realm of Chaos are inextricably linked, and unless we can break that link we will never wield enough power here to challenge Chaos's stranglehold.'

'Break the link . . . you mean, make another attempt to steal the wand?'

'By one means or another, yes. Though it would be no easy task to achieve.'

Silence fell. Somewhere, seemingly a vast way off, the wind was moaning, but Benetan was unaware of it. Under frowning brows his face wore a strange, thoughtful expression, and when Kaldar made to say something Aeoris forestalled him with a warning movement of one hand. At last Benetan looked up once more.

'I could go back.' There was a challenge in his eyes as he met Aeoris's gaze. 'If I approached the castle directly instead of going through the Maze I could get in without alerting anyone. And there are still one or two of my own men I can trust to hide me once I'm inside.' He paused. 'It's possible – just possible – that I might succeed where Iselia failed.'

Kaldar was very still. Aeoris continued to gaze at Benetan and his face was impossible to read. After a few seconds Benetan's mouth twitched bitterly.

'You don't trust me, my lord? No, well; I suppose that's only to be expected. You know what I am; why should you accept my word?' He looked away.

Aeoris turned to regard Kaldar. 'Benetan gives himself

no quarter. You and he are more alike than you realize, Kaldar. And if what he has told me is the whole truth, then you're united now by two allegiances. Your mutual love for Iselia, and your mutual dedication to Chaos's downfall.'

Kaldar's expression tightened and he flicked Benetan a rapid, uncertain look. 'The one I believe. But the other . . .' He met Aeoris's eyes. 'He's had twelve years in that place, my lord, twelve years in Chaos's service. Only days ago he was professing his loyalty to that demon Yandros; and whatever he might say now, I find it hard to credit that he should suddenly have renounced that!' Another look, a glare this time, in Benetan's direction. 'Even for my wife's sake.'

Benetan said something foul under his breath and Aeoris glanced keenly at him before returning his attention to Kaldar. 'I think there's more behind our friend's change of heart than you know, Kaldar. Perhaps he'll tell you the whole story in his own time, but for now I think a more emphatic demonstration will serve to convince you.' The lord of Order raised one hand and made a small, almost careless gesture. Instantly the fire erupted with renewed energy, roaring ceilingwards so that Aeoris stood wreathed in flames that licked at his cloak, at his hair, turning his face to a blazing golden mask. A wave of ferocious heat hit Kaldar and Benetan, as though a furnace door had been hurled open in their faces; they recoiled, scrambling back from the enormous force of it, and Aeoris raised his right hand, holding it, palm upturned, towards Benetan. Fire danced and crackled along his arm and between his fingers, and his gaze turned white-hot.

'Benetan,' he said, 'when I touched your mind, you revealed what you have undergone, and you claim that you have withheld nothing. You also claim that your fealty to Chaos is dead and you're ready to serve me. Prove that claim by taking my hand.' He saw Benetan's shocked expression and smiled relentlessly. 'It will burn you, yes. But in the throes of such pain you will be unable to maintain any deception, and I'll know all that's in your heart. If what you have shown me is the truth, you'll come to no harm. If it is not . . .' A shrug made any further word unnecessary.

Very slowly Benetan stood up. He could feel the flames' heat beating against his face and body, and the thought of drawing near to that devouring force, of touching it, of feeling the agony as it engulfed his arm . . . he couldn't do it. He didn't have the courage; couldn't find the will. Couldn't bring himself to *trust*.

Aeoris waited. Benetan met his gaze with a mute, desperate and miserable appeal, and as the lord of Order saw what was in his mind his smile modulated into a look of such understanding that Benetan felt as though something within him were caving in and crushing his heart.

Aeoris said, gently, 'My friend, I am not Yandros.'

Those cold, slanting, ever-changing eyes, filled with capricious amusement . . . and Yandros's voice, aloof, laconic, as he set the seal on Iselia's fate and in the same breath delivered a malevolent warning . . . Suddenly a wave of heat with another, inner source washed over Benetan. He had shown that memory to Aeoris; shown him every detail of his last encounter with the great Chaos lord and his brother . . . *oh yes, and that one . . .* and the depth of the repugnance that their pitiless disinterest had driven into his soul. But where Yandros would doubtless find enjoyment of another kind in testing a man's mettle, Aeoris had a very different motive. And, if Benetan was ever to trust any power or any living being, human or otherwise, again – and be worthy of trust in his turn – this was perhaps the only chance he would ever have to prove it. He could feel the raw hunger of the fire's heat. He knew what it would do to him and he had never felt pain of that level; never experienced it and couldn't imagine it. But others had been less fortunate. The hostages, innocent of any crime but chosen at random and imprisoned under Vordegh's edict. More than a thousand of them consigned to die by fire. And he had seen one small, pitiful group; he had inspected them in Overlord Tanneler's cell, looked them over and then shrugged his shoulders and turned away and left them to their fate because he had no choice.

Now, though, there was a choice. And, ironically, Savrinor's message reported to him by the faithful Lotro came back to mind. *All a question of justice . . .*

He didn't allow himself time to think any further, nor even time to brace his body or draw breath. The impulse came fast and he grasped at it before reason could intervene. Two rapid paces forward, and with a swordsman's violent but adept movement Benetan thrust his arm into the heart of the fire and reached for Aeoris's outstretched hand.

The bloody glory of sunset had come and gone, and stars glittered remotely in a clear sky above the bowl of the volcanic crater that formed the heart of the White Isle. Simbrian's companions had lit lanterns to relieve the darkness, but the sorcerer himself spoke no word to them, only continued to sit motionless, cross-legged on the rock floor, keeping the vigil he had maintained for the past two days.

Aeoris appeared as the second moon showed its face above the crater wall. There was a change in the nature of his manifestation this time, subtle enough to elude the majority of the humans present but, to Simbrian, a clear indication of the deeper changes taking place in Order's realm. The hard edges of the god's aura were softened, blending more surely with the air around him, and Aeoris himself seemed somehow more corporeal, the impact of his presence far greater. Slowly but surely, Chaos's blockade was weakening.

Aeoris's golden eyes scanned the gathering; that same inner coterie whose great undertaking had breached the barrier and created the first link between Order's realm and the mortal world. Then his gaze rested more intently on Simbrian, who had risen to his feet and stood taut, uneasy, torn between dread and a hope that he dared not allow himself to acknowledge.

Aeoris said quietly, 'There is a chance for her. And for us.'

Simbrian put his hands to his face as the enormous tension within him suddenly and shockingly eased its grip.

Aeoris, understanding, added, 'I'm only sorry that you have had to wait so long for this news, Simbrian.'

'That's of no importance, my lord.' With an effort Simbrian pulled himself together and his hand dropped back to his side as he looked at the god. 'Then she isn't dead?'

'No. But she is in the magi's hands, as we feared, and that can only mean she has little time left. Benetan Liss has told me that they mean to keep her alive, at least for a while. But though her body might survive the torments they have inflicted, her mind is another matter.'

The sorcerer stared at him. 'Benetan Liss?'

A nod; the golden eyes softened momentarily. 'He's with Kaldar now, and he has had a long and bitter story to tell.' An image sprang unbidden into Simbrian's mind then; the bones of Benetan's tale as he had revealed it to the lord of Order. It shocked the sorcerer, but underlying the shock and its accompanying sympathy for Benetan, Aeoris sensed a vestige of doubt. He smiled grimly, and a final image flared before Simbrian's inner vision; the blazing fury of fire, and a hand reaching out, reaching into the flames. Simbrian felt the twist of Benetan's agony, then the rush of healing, and he understood. Aeoris had set the young Chaos rider a harsh test, but he had passed it, and in so doing had proved himself beyond any doubt.

'Then he's one of us now?' He spoke wonderingly, the

words hovering between question and certainty. 'I didn't believe it would happen.'

'None of us believed it, my friend.' Now Aeoris's smile was wry. 'Even I thought that he would never be more than an unwitting pawn in our plans. But the magi have given us the gift of his loyalty and dedication. It was an unintentional gift, but I think it will prove to be more valuable than anyone yet realizes.' He paused. 'To begin with, Benetan has the ability – and the will – to return with Kaldar to the Star Peninsula and complete our unfinished business.'

Simbrian's eyes widened. 'To gain the wand of Chaos? My lord, is there a *chance*?'

'There is. But we must make some changes to our strategy. The original plan, as you know, was that Kaldar and Iselia should bring the wand out of the castle. That might not be possible now, for both Kaldar and Benetan will be forced to enter the castle by stealth rather than openly, and their chances of securing the wand and escaping to safety are too slender for the risk to be taken.'

'Even with the protection you can grant them, my lord?'

'It isn't enough, Simbrian. Not for that. I was able to shield Kaldar's mind from the magi's attempts to probe, but that alone was difficult enough. And for Iselia I could do nothing.' His aura flared lividly. 'Until Order's powers in this world are stronger – which won't happen unless Chaos's link with the Gate is severed – then I can be little more than a bystander.'

The bitterness behind the god's words cut into Simbrian's psyche and he sensed the depth of Aeoris's frustration. After a few moments, though, the turmoil subsided, the golden aura quietened, and Aeoris looked steadily at him once more.

'As I said,' he continued, 'the risks in trying to repeat our stratagem exactly are too great. We have only this chance left to us now; there won't be a third. But there is another way in which Yandros's control over the mortal world might be broken. We could, as we originally intended, gain possession of the wand and use it to bring the Gate in the castle under our own influence as well as that of Chaos. That would give us power to match Yandros and his demon brothers, and enable us to challenge them on equal terms. Or we could achieve the same end by more drastic means.'

'More drastic?' Simbrian's look grew keen.

Aeoris nodded, and a fire-red tinge crept into his glittering eyes. 'By breaking the power of the Gate itself. And that is what Kaldar and Benetan intend to do.'

Once the wand was in their hands, Aeoris told the gathering, the rest was a simple matter. One ritual – the same ritual that the magi used to open the Chaos Gate – would be enough, and Kaldar could perform it easily; Aeoris had given him the form of the rite and he was already memorizing it and preparing himself. Once the Gate was opened, the wand must be broken in half and the two pieces hurled into the portal. The result would be a clash of energies that would create a backlash of power great enough to wreck the portal and in so doing, destroy Chaos's stranglehold on the mortal world.

There would be many attendant dangers, Aeoris said, and the risk of discovery was the least of them. The opening of the Gate would draw Chaos's attention, and Kaldar and Benetan would have seconds, no more, to do what must be done and get out of the Marble Hall. They could be caught in the power-blast as the Gate imploded, or they could be seized as they tried to flee the castle – though that, in the furore that would ensue, was unlikely.

'By then, I think, neither Yandros nor his mortal servants will care a whit for the fate of one Chaos rider and his accomplice,' Aeoris said, and the gold of his eyes took on a strange, cold quality. 'For they will have another and greater force to reckon with. When the Gate is smashed, the last barriers that have held us back will fall with it.' Then the timbre of his voice softened, so that when he spoke again the words were uttered not with drama or passion, but with the contentment of a quiet, savage anticipation: 'And we shall return to this world.'

CHAPTER VIII

'That is the instruction Lord Vordegh issued, Magus Pirane.' Verdice, the First Magus's half-human amanuensis, met Pirane's stare with sanguine detachment. 'For any servant who transgresses, seven of a like category will forfeit their lives.' She blinked once, rapidly, like a snake, and indicated the collection of small, rolled parchments on the table between them. 'I have the document, and others that Lord Vordegh left in my care, if you wish to verify the order.'

Pirane's face grew very cold and still. 'No,' she said. 'I do not.' Verdice wasn't lying – probably wasn't capable of lying – and the sight of the parchments was evidence enough without further examination. Vordegh, it seemed, was determined to ensure that his word remained law during his absence, and it was easy to imagine him sitting in the spire, meticulously writing out this parcel of petty instructions before entrusting them to his servant's keeping. Doubtless he had covered every eventuality his fertile brain could dredge from its depths, and something in Pirane's stomach turned sour with fury.

'The First Magus might care to consider,' she said with a caustic edge, 'that the castle's complement of servants has already been depleted by recent events. To sacrifice seven Chaos riders whilst at the same time requiring them to be at full readiness at a moment's notice will do little for their efficiency.' Her full lips curled unpleasantly. 'Perhaps you would care to convey that message to Lord Vordegh?'

Verdice made a show of compliance, which didn't

convince. 'I would, of course, madam. But Lord Vordegh has left strict instructions that he is not to be disturbed under any circumstances, and I am not in a position to disobey him.' Her eyelids flickered again. 'He anticipates that the magi will deal appropriately with any matters that arise during his absence.'

Pirane looked down at the icy, impassive woman. 'Very well,' she said, her tone curt. 'Then we shall do precisely that.'

She turned, her grey, smoke-like gown swirling around her, and made to depart. Verdice coughed delicately and the magus looked sharply over her shoulder. 'Yes? Is there something else?'

'The executions,' Verdice said, 'are to be carried out publicly. That is Lord Vordegh's instruction.'

For another moment they regarded each other. Then Pirane said, 'Yes. I imagine it is.'

She stalked from the room, leaving Verdice staring impassively at her departing back.

There was a sharply familiar scent in the corridor outside Croin's apartments as Pirane approached. Recognizing it, she didn't knock but opened the door silently and entered.

The apartment was in darkness but for a pinpoint of chill blue light that shone from the inner room. As Pirane approached, a shadow moved behind the light, then abruptly it winked out and Croin's voice spoke in the darkness.

'Come in, Pirane. I've completed my work; for the time being there's no more I can do.'

A lamp flared into life, lighting the physician's thin, lined face and reflecting in the gems of the rings he wore. Pirane glanced at the scrying-glass, silver-framed and its surface almost black with age, that stood on a small table nearby. She raised her eyebrows in query but Croin shook his head.

'I've found nothing. Nor, frankly, did I expect to. If

Captain Liss used the Maze he could be anywhere, and even the higher elementals haven't the wit or the scope to seek out one man among countless thousands in such a short time.' He brushed a speck of dust from the mirror. 'We'll track him down eventually, of course, but we'll need to use more powerful methods. And as our overlord has decreed that the Marble Hall is forbidden to all in his absence, that must wait.' The mirror was clean again; Croin raised his head and met her gaze directly. 'And you, Pirane. How did you fare?'

As yet none of the other magi knew of Benetan's disappearance, and Pirane and Croin had agreed that until they had explored certain avenues the matter wouldn't be made public. Now, Pirane's expression gave the gist of her answer even before she spoke, and Croin knew that the quandary which until now neither had dared to voice in any but the most oblique way was about to come to a head.

'Vordegh has been as thorough as we might have expected,' Pirane said, her voice scathing. 'No message may be conveyed to him, but he has left documents giving full instructions for this or any other eventuality in the care of his tame sentinel. We are required, it seems, to execute seven Chaos riders to atone for the offence of one. Oh, and it's to be a public matter. As an example, I assume, to anyone who might otherwise be tempted to copy Captain Liss's example.'

Croin stared towards the window. Both moons were still in the sky, but the snow-clouds had piled into a massive pall that blotted out all trace of their light. The blizzard made it impossible to see the courtyard, let alone glimpse any illumination that might or might not be burning in the east spire. 'Close the curtain,' Pirane said edgily. 'I feel as though half the world is watching us.'

Croin did as she asked, repressing the temptation to remind her that if Vordegh wished to spy on them a swathe of velvet would hardly serve as a deterrent. As the curtain swished across the window Pirane turned and paced the floor.

'This preposterous instruction will deprive us of almost a tenth of our warrior elite for no valid reason whatever,' she continued. 'I won't sanction it, Croin. I simply *won't* sanction it!'

Croin's seven-fingered hand was still on the curtain. 'We both know how Vordegh is likely to react if the instruction isn't carried out to the letter.'

'Yes.' Pirane stopped pacing for a moment, then resumed again. 'Yes, we do. And we need look no further than this room for one of the candidates he will choose to eradicate as an example to *our* peers.'

'Two, my dear. Two.' Croin saw her surprised reaction to that and his expression grew cynical. 'I was present when Lord Yandros reprimanded Vordegh in the Marble Hall, remember. I was also present at the unsuccessful High Oracular Communion, and at a number of other rites which didn't quite produce the desired effect. The First Magus doesn't enjoy being humiliated, and the fact that you and I have witnessed such humiliations means, I think, that he would prefer to be rid of us both.' He paused, stared down at the table for a few moments, then met her gaze again with a new candour. 'And as matters stand now, Pirane, I think we would be wise to prepare for that eventuality.'

So, Pirane thought, it was in the open at last. She was a little surprised that Croin had been the first of them to voice it; she had always looked on the physician if not exactly as a coward then at least as a highly cautious man, and she had expected him to wait for her to make the first overt move before committing himself. It seemed she had misjudged him.

But how the thing could be done ... that was another matter entirely. Two roads lay open to them in Pirane's view, and both were equally dangerous. To depose Vordegh by nullifying his election to office was out of the question; the only way to remove him was to kill him. But assassination by sorcery would carry an appalling risk, for Vordegh's skills outstripped those of any other magus. And a physical attack had little better prospect of success, for he had his own forms of protection against the mundane as well as the arcane. There was a third option, but Pirane dismissed that from her mind even as she thought of it. Yandros would not intervene. Not even as a favour to a one-time lover, for though his friendship was steadfast, the Chaos lord drew a clear and decisive line at any idea of obligation. It was possible, of course, that he might choose to help her on a whim, as he had helped Savrinor; but, knowing him as she had for many years, Pirane doubted it. No; in this, she and Croin must rely on their own resources.

And, of course, on those colleagues who could be trusted . . .

'I would suggest, Croin,' she said at last, thoughtfully, 'that we devise a small test.'

'A test?' Croin looked at her with interest.

'Mmm. To see exactly where the land lies. Someone, of course, must be punished for the fact that Captain Liss was allowed to escape – that's never been in doubt. But I think we should modify the First Magus's instructions. An execution, yes, but one rider instead of seven. The man they found unconscious in the cellar – Averel told me his name when he reported the matter; I can't recall it now but that's unimportant. He's only a junior in the ranks so he'll be easy enough to replace, and if he's put to death publicly that will provide the salutary lesson Vordegh favours so highly.' She moved back towards the window. 'To send the Chaos riders in pursuit of Captain Liss would be a futile exercise without first discovering his whereabouts, and for that, as you have pointed out, we need to conduct a rite in the Marble Hall.'

'Which we are not permitted to do.'

'Quite. So if we can't recapture Captain Liss, we punish instead the man who allowed him to escape. That, as any rational person will agree, is a perfectly reasonable course of action, and one which ensures the First Magus's principles are upheld.'

A faint, dry smile was playing around the edges of Croin's mouth. 'And if the First Magus thinks otherwise, his attitude will appear . . . irrational.'

'Exactly.' Pirane regarded him slyly. 'We shall learn a very great deal from our colleagues' reactions at that point, I suspect. And it's far safer than risking any direct individual approaches as yet.'

Croin nodded. 'I like the strategy. And of course it will serve as a test for Vordegh into the bargain. After all, he might merely shrug his shoulders and pronounce himself perfectly satisfied by our handling of the incident.' His gaze slid sidelong to her face and his look was sardonic. 'I'm sure you don't believe that any more than I do, but the possibility exists, at least in theory.'

Pirane didn't trouble to comment. 'Well then,' she said, 'if we're agreed, I'll send for Captain Averel and give him his instructions. Noon would be a good time for the execution, I'd say. Before too many of the servants are needed for dining hall duties.'

'Yes. Oh, and Pirane –' as she turned to leave. 'One more matter. Just a small thing, but it might be worth considering now rather than later.'

Pirane pivoted.

'One ally whom I believe we can count on even at this early stage.' Croin inclined his head meaningfully in the direction of the main wing. 'Someone who has very good reason to feel an aversion for the First Magus.'

'Ah . . .' Pirane saw where his thoughts were leading. 'And who also possesses the keenest ears and eyes in the castle.'

'Precisely. He could be extremely valuable in helping us to gauge the temperature of certain waters. And, I suspect, extremely willing.'

There was something vulpine in the look Pirane gave to the physician. 'Yes,' she said. 'Yes. Once this matter is dealt with, I'll speak to him.'

'Discreetly.'

'Naturally. Although there is very little that even we could teach him about discretion.' Pirane's eyes grew speculative. 'Besides, if I know him as well as I think I do, then my visit will come as no great surprise.'

Even Savrinor's reservoir of strategies wasn't enough to keep exhaustion at bay forever, and to Andraia's relief the devices finally ran out. He had been prowling about the castle for most of the night, then shortly after second moonset he had returned, sat down on the couch and almost instantly fallen into a profound and, she prayed, dreamless sleep. Andraia woke a servant to help her carry him to his bed, and told the man to put word out that anyone who dared disturb him in the morning would have her wrath to contend with.

She had hoped that he would sleep on past noon and so be unaware of the unpleasantness outside in the courtyard. News of the public execution had spread swiftly through the castle, and Andraia was having enough trouble with her own feelings on the matter without trying to cope with Savrinor's as well. On one level she couldn't help but be glad that Benetan had escaped, for she was under no illusions about the fate that the First Magus had had in store for him. Nor was she entirely surprised by the fact that the guard was to die for his carelessness; the punishment might be extreme but it was hardly unprecedented. But on another level, the circumstances surrounding Benetan's flight disturbed her deeply.

Benet must have known that this, or something like it,

would happen as a result of his disappearance. Andraia couldn't damn him for that; she was enough of a realist to acknowledge that in his position she wouldn't have hesitated to sacrifice a virtual stranger's life in order to save her own. But in the past, Benetan's standards and principles had been very different to hers. She had often teased him pityingly about what she called his over-active sense of integrity, and he had always been ready to jump fiercely to his own defence. The old Benet wouldn't have allowed one of his own riders to die for his sake; it simply wasn't in his nature. Something had changed him. And though she knew the cause of the change, the thought of how deep it might have gone disturbed Andraia greatly.

She had resolved not to watch the execution, but as noon approached she found herself beset by a grimly mesmeric curiosity that drew her unwillingly but compellingly to the window. There was little to see as yet; a few servants had gathered by some of the lesser doors and one or two higher-ranking secular officials had emerged from the main entrance and were watching from the steps. It had stopped snowing, and a circle had been cleared in the centre of the courtyard, black stone showing through the whiteness. It reminded Andraia sharply of the Chaos Gate's mosaic in the Marble Hall and she turned away, shivering. But after a few moments the compulsion to look crept back and she couldn't resist its pull. More spectators had appeared, spilling into the courtyard, and there were faces at many windows in the east and west wings. It must be almost time . . .

A hand touched her shoulder and with a squeak of shock she turned.

Savrinor had emerged from the bedroom. There were hollow and heavy shadows under his eyes and his face looked gaunt, but he had changed his crumpled clothes for fresh ones and his hair was carefully, immaculately groomed.

He said, 'Forgive me. I didn't mean to startle you.'

Andraia moved to place herself between him and the window. 'You should still be asleep.' Her voice sounded defensive to her own ears.

He shook his head gently. 'There's no need to try to spare me, dear Andraia. I abandoned any pretension to finer feelings a very long time ago.'

Andraia didn't believe that, but she also didn't feel sure enough of her ground to argue with him. 'I hoped you wouldn't wake until later,' she said. 'These occasions aren't pleasant at the best of times, but now . . .'

He smiled thinly. 'Then why are you watching?'

'I wasn't going to. I was only . . .' The lie tailed off and she shrugged helplessly. 'I don't know. Because I couldn't stop myself, I suppose.'

'Any more than anyone could.' Savrinor moved past her and stared down into the courtyard. 'Strange, the fascination that death exerts over the human imagination. How many people do you think are out there now? Fifty? Seventy? Not to mention all the faces at all the windows who, like us, are watching while pretending not to.'

Feeling very uncomfortable, Andraia said, 'I thought you didn't know about it. I hoped you wouldn't find out until it was over.'

'That was a vain hope, I'm afraid. I was informed last night.' Savrinor was still looking at the scene below, intent, like a hawk. Then he said, 'I can't help but pity the poor wretch. He's nothing more than a scapegoat. And I suspect he's being used as a means of testing the water.'

'Testing the water? I don't understand.'

He made a dismissive gesture. 'Ah, it's just a small theory, and I don't yet know if it has any foundation.' He paused, then sighed. 'It's probably better not to think about it. My conscience is already unquiet enough without complicating matters any further.'

She did understand that, for he had told her, and she

slipped an arm through his, pressing against him. 'You were only trying to prevent a greater injustice. You couldn't have known that this would happen.'

'Oh, I did. Or at least I suspected. But I made a conscious choice; I considered Benetan's life more important than that of some junior in the riders' ranks whom I've probably never even set eyes on.' He shrugged. 'It was one or the other of them, after all.'

'And you chose Benet. For my sake.'

'Not entirely. If truth be told, I probably did it for no more noble reason than to spite the First Magus.' He glanced at her. 'My own little form of revenge. Not quite in Vordegh's league, is it?'

'Savrinor, *stop* it.' She shook his arm angrily. 'If you're going to insist on tormenting yourself, then at least find a valid reason! You can't take the blame for the consequences of Benet's escape – all you did was pass a cryptic message to him; you didn't even *see* him! He made his own decision for his own purposes, and you're not responsible for that.' She hesitated, frowned. 'It's his responsibility. His alone.'

Savrinor gleaned a good deal more from her tone, and her expression, than she realized, and it coincided with a few less than pleasant thoughts of his own. Though he was careful not to show it, Benetan's disappearance had been as much of a surprise to him as to her, and for the same reasons. In their different ways they both knew the Chaos rider very well – or had thought they did – and, like Andraia, Savrinor had believed that Benetan's scruples wouldn't allow him to take the advice he was given. He had proffered the advice nonetheless but hadn't expected it to be heeded. In a way, perhaps, it had simply been a means of washing his hands of Benetan and their old friendship; a final clearing of the slate to leave no obligation.

Only, at the last, Benetan had confounded them both.

There was movement in the courtyard suddenly, and a subliminal surge of tension and interest that reached them even at this distance. They looked down. A small party of Chaos riders was emerging from the stable block. Averel walked at their head, his face as white as the surrounding snow. Behind him seven guards – a ceremonial number despite the affair's low key – escorted the condemned man, and in the background the other riders on duty were forming up by the wall as they had been commanded to do.

Savrinor's pale eyes scanned the rest of the courtyard, where the crowd had swelled further, then lingered on the steps of the castle's main entrance. A number of the magi were present, and at their forefront were Pirane and Croin. As he had expected . . .

He looked at Andraia. She was very still and had lost a good deal of her colour, but her expression was calm, almost remote. Quietly, Savrinor slid an arm around her shoulders.

'I know what you're thinking,' he said, 'and I can't answer the question. I don't know what motivated Benetan to do what he did, and at this moment speculation seems like a very futile exercise. I think we have only one choice, Andraia. We must forget about him, and refuse to consider where he might or might not have gone, or whom he might or might not be with.'

She tensed. 'That isn't easy.'

'I know. And I can't escape the fear that in trying to help him I might have made a calamitous mistake. But we must *try*.' Outside, the execution party had taken their places and Averel was being handed a heavy, double-bladed sword. Watching the mixture of bewilderment and helpless determination on the man's face Savrinor surmised that his tenure as the riders' leader wouldn't be a long one. During Benetan's term this kind of thing had never happened, and Savrinor doubted if the old Benetan would have been capable of carrying out the order. The new Benetan, though . . . he was less sure about.

Andraia said suddenly, and in a small voice, 'How will they do it?'

Her tone, and what she said, surprised him, and he looked at her with a sudden new insight. 'You've never seen an execution?'

A shake of the head was the only answer she could give, and his hand squeezed her shoulder slightly. 'Best that you don't look.'

She bit her lower lip. 'You will.'

'That's beside the point. I have to, because I'm required to make a report for the archives.'

'Will it be . . . quick?'

'Oh, yes. But spectacular. Blood tends to fountain from a torso when the head is severed.'

She flinched and, revolted by the comment as he had intended, turned away from the window. It took her a few moments to claw back her poise, and when she did she said, 'Do you think the First Magus is watching?'

'I've no doubt of it.' Savrinor paused. 'But I *do* doubt that it will be enough to satisfy him.'

'What do you mean?'

But he wouldn't answer, only made a negating gesture. This was all a part of his theory and he didn't want to embroil Andraia in it as yet.

Outside, a voice barked out a clipped command. Distance and the glass blurred the words, but Savrinor knew the formalities by heart anyway and a queasy sensation moved in his stomach. Andraia started to turn round –

'No,' he said, and sent a silent prayer to Yandros that Averel's nerve wouldn't fail him at the crucial moment. He had seen that happen once, and the sight of a man still conscious yet with his neck half severed had been very far from pleasant.

Either Yandros heard him or Averel was able to draw

on another kind of reserve, for the whole thing was over very quickly and without drama. Closing his mind's shutters on any other thoughts, Savrinor made mental notes of the details then watched as Averel, his back rigidly erect, walked away in the direction of his quarters while the escort – those who hadn't been given the task of clearing up – fell in behind him. Pirane and Croin had already withdrawn; others were following, and buckets of water were being brought out to wash the flagstones. Doubtless the water would freeze, and the area would be treacherous underfoot for days . . .

Suddenly, Savrinor had a strong conviction that he was going to be sick. He swung away from the window, couldn't respond when Andraia tried to intervene, and all but ran towards the bedroom.

Then stopped. The spasm was fading, passing, and the underlying fear that had triggered it was passing, too. His heart wasn't about to betray him again; there was nothing wrong with him beyond tiredness and hunger. Gods, how long *was* it since he had last eaten? Days . . . he'd been sustaining himself on nothing but wine and drugs since before . . . but he wasn't going to let himself go over all that again. Must pull himself together. *Must.*

He was at the bedchamber door, and gripped the lintel to steady his balance. He sensed rather than heard Andraia behind him, then her hands took a firm grip of his upper arms, like an anchor securing him against the rush of a dangerous tide.

'I'm all right.' He forestalled her anxious question and brought one hand up to close over hers. 'Just light-headed for a moment.' Then he turned his head and kissed her, briefly but with an odd savagery. 'I should eat. That's all that's amiss with me.'

She seized the chance to offer practical help. 'I'll send a servant to the dining hall – no; never mind looking for a servant, I'll go myself. Stay here. I'll not be long.'

She was gone quickly, as though she feared he might raise objections. In truth he would have done no such thing, for he knew that she needed some preoccupation, and preferably a petty one, to stop her mind from dwelling on other, darker subjects. And he, too, would be glad of a few minutes' respite, time to gather his own thoughts and force them into some semblance of coherence.

From sheer habit Savrinor poured himself a glass of wine and took it to the couch by the hearth, where he sat down. The fire was sluggish but he felt too weary to do anything about it. All he wanted was sleep, and his eyelids were beginning to droop when a sound started him back to reality. A light, terse rap at the door . . . Instinct and caution propelled Savrinor to his feet and he was in time to see the latch lifting as his visitor didn't wait for a response. The door opened.

'Madam . . .' The lethargy in Savrinor's mind ebbed sharply as he saw the tall figure of Magus Pirane.

Pirane closed the door and crossed the floor towards him, the hem of her gown whispering over the rugs. Two paces from the couch she stopped and studied the historian carefully. He looked, she thought, extremely ill. But there was no surprise in his expression, and that fitted with her suspicions.

She said, 'Sit down, my dear; there's no need for any formality. I believe you know why I'm here.'

She must have seen Andraia and realized that he was alone . . . Savrinor's eyes grew wary. 'I wouldn't be so presumptuous as to claim that, madam.'

'I'm sure you wouldn't.' Pirane smiled. 'But somehow I doubt that your renowned talent for plaiting disparate threads has suddenly deserted you.' She seated herself elegantly on the couch. 'Perhaps you'll be so kind as to pour me a glass of that wine you're drinking? And then I suggest that we both speak candidly.'

Savrinor's pulse was uncomfortably rapid as he tilted

the wine-flagon. He brought the glass back; as he gave it to her his hand wasn't perfectly steady.

'Sit down,' Pirane said again. He did, and she scrutinized him more thoroughly. 'You're not in good health, Savrinor. How much sleep have you had during the past few days?'

He looked away. 'A few hours, madam. I've – wanted no more.'

'Wanted, perhaps; needed is quite another matter. But I believe I understand your reasons.' Ah yes, that quick narrowing of the eyes; she had struck the target accurately.

'The First Magus is still in the spire,' she continued gently, 'so for the present you and Andraia have nothing to fear from him. However, I don't need to tell you that the hiatus is unlikely to last much longer. And when it does end, you will not be the only ones facing an uncertain future.'

Savrinor's gaze returned to hers and she could see that he was digesting what she had said, and at the same time debating whether or not to match her frankness and speak his mind. Pirane didn't press him but only waited, and after a while he said,

'May I ask you a question, madam?'

'Of course.'

He inclined his head in thanks. 'There are a great many rumours circulating in the castle at the moment about the . . . incident in the Marble Hall. One of those rumours concerns a clash – a confrontation, even – between the First Magus and Lord Yandros's brother, before Lord Yandros arrived.' His throat worked and Pirane saw that his palms were perspiring. 'I didn't witness that, of course. I was . . . unaware of anything at the time.' He paused. 'Nor have I asked Andraia about it; there's no reason why she should be forced to recall unpleasant memories. But I would like to know whether or not the rumour is true.'

Well, Pirane thought, if he wanted to approach the subject in this oblique way, so be it. And it confirmed that the little scrap of information she had deliberately put about on the castle's grapevine had taken root. 'It's perfectly true,' she told him. 'Vordegh made a very serious error of judgement. To begin with, he attempted to justify his actions in the face of the gods' obvious displeasure. That in itself was a grave enough mistake, but it didn't end there. He cast an aspersion on – well, there's no need to go into the details; suffice it to say that he made a remark which was both unwarranted and indiscreet. Lord Yandros's brother took great exception to it, and the issue came to such a head that he was on the verge of killing the First Magus when Yandros intervened.'

Savrinor stared at her, nonplussed. He knew that Vordegh had resented Yandros's censure, and that knowledge was the pivot around which his own fears revolved. But this . . .

'I didn't realize.' He spoke softly. 'I didn't realize that matters had gone so far.'

'They have, Savrinor. And when the First Magus emerges from his self-imposed isolation, I have little doubt that they will go further. Unless, that is, measures are taken to prevent them from doing so.'

He understood now beyond any doubt what Pirane wanted from him, and very carefully he rose from the couch and set his empty glass down on the table.

'I don't believe, madam,' he said, 'that such a step has ever been taken before.'

'Not in this way, no. And even if we do take it now – which in itself isn't yet a certainty – there's no guarantee that we shall succeed.' Her expression altered. 'You comprehend as well as anyone the risks involved. And so I think you understand why we need your assistance at this early stage.'

Savrinor turned and regarded her. 'We, madam?'

'If I were alone in this, my dear, I wouldn't be so foolish as to speak to anyone about it. Not even to you.'

He nodded, and thought: how many others? Croin, for a certainty; he and Pirane were old conspirators. Three, possibly four more of the magi who to his certain knowledge had displeased the First Magus in some small way. And among the more secular echelons? Hard to say as yet, but he could think of a good few likely candidates.

Pirane said quietly, 'All we want from you at present, Savrinor, is an alert ear and a keen eye for the drift of opinion in the castle. Names of those we can trust, and also of those we would do better to avoid.' She paused. 'I know we can rely on you to make your enquiries with absolute discretion.'

Savrinor refilled his glass. He didn't speak.

'In terms of your tally-slate of favours given and received,' Pirane added with faint sardony that, he suspected, was directed as much at herself as at him, 'I don't yet know what I might do to repay this particular debt. But be assured that it *will* be repaid in full.'

Savrinor swung round abruptly. 'I'm not concerned with that, Lady Pirane. My slate no longer exists; I've broken it – metaphorically speaking – and have no intention of seeing it mended. But I must ask one question.'

His tone was fierce, which surprised her and aroused her curiosity. 'Ask it.'

His hand clenched on the glass he was holding and she thought that he might snap the stem. 'Do you – do *we* – have the gods' sanction for this?'

Pirane realized then what really lay at the root of his misgivings. She had overlooked that aspect of Savrinor's character. 'If you are asking,' she said, 'whether Yandros will help us directly, then the answer is no, he will not.' She looked up. 'I know him well enough to say that unequivocally. Yandros doesn't like the First Magus, and I believe that he also doesn't trust him to maintain a sense of proportion and priority. But he will not intervene to remove him, nor to overtly sanction his removal. That simply isn't his way. If it was, he would have allowed his brother to kill Vordegh in the Marble Hall and that would have been a convenient solution for all concerned.'

Savrinor said, 'Then –'

'Wait; I've not finished. As I said, Yandros won't intervene, nor permit any of his brothers to do so. But if *we* should choose to depose the First Magus . . .' She shrugged, then her eyes became intent. 'You've seen for yourself how things stand between Vordegh and the gods, Savrinor; and you also know why Yandros chose to restore your life. Do *you* think we would be going against his will?'

For some time Savrinor held her gaze, his own expression thoughtful. Memories were kindling in his mind, very private and very personal memories. And unless he was deluded – which he didn't believe he was – then the answer was clear.

'No, Magus Pirane,' he said. 'I don't.'

Pirane's look relaxed. 'Then I believe we can rely on you.'

'You can, madam. It will be –' *A pleasure*, he had been about to say. Yes, that was true; but he didn't want to reveal the depth of his feelings even to someone who shared them. Savrinor stared at the contents of his glass. 'It will be a relief.'

CHAPTER IX

'The weather's changing.' Kaldar raised his head like an animal catching a scent. 'Smell it. Wind's backing towards the west, and likely as not that means a thaw.' He made the circle sign with thumb and middle finger, a mark of reverence. 'If it's our Lord Aeoris's doing, I thank him for it!'

Benetan didn't answer immediately. He was watching the changing light over the sea in the distance, trying to judge how long it would be before dusk and then darkness fell. At last he eased a cramped leg, re-focused his eyes and looked for the twentieth time at the weapons sheathed at his belt, checking that they were still in place.

'Snow or rain, it makes little difference,' he said tersely. 'Either will keep the castle scum secure and comfortable indoors. What we *don't* want under any circumstances is a clear, moonlit night.'

Kaldar grimaced. 'All very well for you, Benet. Your coat's a good deal warmer than mine.'

The other man glanced at him, a strange, violent glance. 'Then take it. I don't want the damned thing anyway.' He pulled the black fur from his shoulders and flung it in Kaldar's direction, revealing the Chaos rider's uniform beneath. Then he slid down from his vantage point and back into the shallow gully, free from snow, where they had pitched their makeshift camp. Kaldar watched as he drew his knife and began to prise at something in the rock.

'You'll blunt the blade.'

'Then I'll sharpen it again. Preferably on someone's bones.' A face rose in Benetan's inner vision; he pushed it down, knowing that he couldn't hope to destroy *that* one. At least, not yet . . .

Suddenly he re-sheathed the knife and dropped to a crouch, covering his face with one hand. Kaldar heard the muttered words, an exhortation and a prayer, and he frowned. Since their arrival here at the edge of the mountain foothills, and his first sight of the Star Peninsula half a mile away, a new demon had taken hold of Benetan. He wouldn't talk about it, but something deep-rooted and rabid was driving him to the point where his ferocious commitment to their plan was starting to eclipse Kaldar's own. At first Kaldar had thought it some after-effect of the encounter with Aeoris and the test Benet had undergone; now, though, he was less sure. This was more like a blood-lust, as though the skills trained into him during his years at the castle had suddenly twisted into a new and deadlier form. Benet wanted to kill, and didn't seem to care how or why he did it. And if the craving wasn't brought under control, it was likely to bring disaster on them.

Kaldar cast one more look back at the bulk of the castle standing black and ominous against the heavy sky, then slithered down the rock slope and into the gully.

'Benet.' He stood over the other man. 'Come out of your private Warp for a moment. We need to talk.'

Benetan's hand dropped to his side. 'There's nothing more to say.'

'I think there is. If we go into the castle tonight with this disagreement unresolved, then we might as well lay our heads on a block and invite the magi to cut them from our shoulders.'

Benetan stood up and turned his back. 'There's no disagreement. We both know what we have to do.'

Kaldar sighed exasperatedly. 'But that's just it — I can't trust you not to do *more* than we have to! And if you start trying to settle personal scores' — Benetan made an impatient gesture but Kaldar ignored it — 'then the simple fact is that we'll *fail!* We have three objectives and three only: to take the wand, to perform the ritual and to get Iselia out.'

Benetan turned and looked cynically at him. 'And how do you think we'll achieve those objectives? With a polite request and a courteous thank-you? You're a fool, Kaldar, not a realist. If we're to succeed, there'll be bloodshed. And I mean to be ready for it.'

'You mean to *look* for it!' Kaldar retorted angrily. 'Don't deny it; a child wouldn't believe you! Benet, what in the Seven Hells has been goading you since we got here? Isn't it enough to be doing what we are doing, without looking to create another kind of havoc that will ruin everything?'

Benetan jerked his head aside. 'You don't know what you're talking about.'

'No, I don't, because you stubbornly refuse to tell me! What is it you *want?* Revenge? Because if that's it, then I assure you, your desire can be no greater than mine!'

With an effort Benetan curbed the vicious response he wanted to make. What Kaldar said was true enough. But as yet Kaldar's motive for vengeance was one step removed from reality. He hadn't been in the Marble Hall. He hadn't seen for himself what had been done to Iselia. And he hadn't felt the helpless, ravening bitterness engendered by another kind of betrayal.

Suddenly Benetan knew that he couldn't keep his explosive feelings to himself any longer. Aeoris knew the truth, but Aeoris wasn't present now to ease the fury and the hurt as he had done in the cave. There was no still centre to contain the storm. He *had* to try to explain it to Kaldar. Or a part of it . . . for the rest, the deeper goad, couldn't be said, because there was no way to prepare Kaldar for what he would find when they reached Iselia's cell.

He flexed his right arm, the arm he had thrust into the fire. It was unmarked and undamaged, though he thought that the skin was perhaps a little paler now than on the rest of his body. 'You've never seen any of the Chaos lords, have you?' he said harshly.

The unexpected change of tack threw Kaldar. 'No. Though I hope to great Aeoris that I will before long — under circumstances which they won't like.'

'I've seen them.'

'I know. You told me.'

'Not all of it. Not all of it by any means.' Then Benetan swung round. 'Tell me, Kaldar, what would you do if Iselia — if one of that corrupt litter had a passing inclination for a few hours' pleasure with a mortal woman, and —'

'*What?*' Kaldar's face turned white. '*Are you telling me that —* '

'No. Not Iselia. Andraia.'

Kaldar's demeanour changed rapidly as he realized at last what Benetan really meant. '*Your* woman?' he said.

'Yes. And don't think for a moment she was unwilling; she wasn't.' And because of it, Yandros's brother had persuaded Yandros to intervene in the Marble Hall, and Savrinor's life had been restored while Iselia was promised only further torment. That was the root of Benetan's bitterness. The putrid, cancerous root that made him want to tear out the heart of every human being in the castle because the unhuman beings were beyond his reach . . .

Kaldar uttered a filthy oath. 'That is an *abomination!*' Echoes of his words bounced from the rock around them, then as they faded his expression changed. 'But Benet, I *have* to say this. If you go into the castle meaning to kill her —'

'Oh, no.' Benetan shook his head. 'I've no intention of doing that. They're all tainted with the same evil, and taking it out on Andraia, whatever my personal reasons might be, wouldn't make a whit of difference.'

'Then why —'

'Why the need to spill blood? I don't know.' Calm was

taking hold of him, Benetan realized, in the wake of what he had said. As if he had shriven himself of the venom, unearthed it from the burrow it had dug in his soul. And with its unearthing, cold rationality was starting to return. 'For the sake of achieving something, I suppose, even if it won't give me any real satisfaction.'

Kaldar stared at him. 'Achieving something? Great gods, what do you think we mean to do in the Marble Hall — curl up and sleep?'

'Sorcery's your province, not mine.'

Kaldar's gaze became shrewd. 'Yes; and because it isn't yours, you're looking for another means of striking back at the Chaos lord.' He sighed, shaking his head. 'It's futile, Benet. You can't harm him directly. And if you killed fifty of the human swarm in that castle, or a hundred, or more, do you think Chaos's masters would care? What are mortal lives to them?'

'Nothing,' Benetan said. 'I know.'

'Then stop brooding over what you can't accomplish, and think about what you can.' Abruptly, brittly, Kaldar laughed. 'This is a reversal, isn't it? Remember the night I came to you, soon after Iselia was taken? I was the one who wanted to tear every living soul in the castle apart, and if you hadn't talked some sense into me then, I wouldn't be here to talk some into you now.'

For a few moments a resentful glimmer lingered in Benetan's eyes; then suddenly he relaxed.

'You're right. I'm losing my sense of proportion, and I apologize for it.' A faint smile. 'We've both changed, I suppose.'

'Hardly surprising.'

'No. No, it isn't.'

For a minute or two they were silent. Then Kaldar said, 'How long before the sun sets?'

'An hour; maybe a little more.'

'All right. Then I suggest we eat, and while we do so we

can go over the plan for the final time.' Kaldar started to unstrap his pack. 'We've got to be sure of every last detail. One mistake and we'll both be dead at best before tomorrow morning.'

'You know the ritual?'

'Oh, yes.' And the other sorceries, Kaldar thought; the small but invaluable powers that Aeoris, with his increasing strength, had been able to grant to him and which in a place where sorcery was commonplace would go undetected if used with extreme care.

He pushed a hand into the pack and brought out a small parcel. 'Here. Dried meat-strips. Very old and probably repulsive, but they're all we have.'

'I've survived on worse.' Benetan took a strip and worked it in his hand to soften it, turning and turning. As if it were the hilt of a knife . . . Kaldar watched covertly and was tempted to say something, but made himself check the impulse. Better to let Benet meet his own demons in his own way.

He sat down on the rock and began to eat.

He had sensed this atmosphere once before, and it brought a recent memory to the surface as the two of them eased out from under the deep shadow of the castle's barbican arch. An acute aura of tension that called him back to the bright, cold morning when he had returned from the south, with Kaldar posing as a disaffected scribe. He had found his own riders in a jittery ferment, Savrinor had put an order out to watch for his arrival — and First Magus Vordegh had been planning a new campaign.

Benetan looked up past the ranks of lit windows in the main wing to where the east spire towered against the sky. That evil glow was still shining at the summit, suggesting Vordegh hadn't yet broken his solitary vigil. Possibly that explained the tension, for until the First Magus chose to emerge, no one from the highest to the lowest could know what the next hour might bring. But whatever effect their overlord's absence might be having on the castle-dwellers, it was a circumstance that could only work in his and Kaldar's favour.

The thaw Kaldar predicted hadn't yet begun in earnest, but there were signs. Slush underfoot, icicles dripping, and a sense of impending rain rather than snow in the air. Dropping his gaze again, Benetan scanned the bulk of the castle. No light in Andraia's window. Savrinor tonight, or was she still setting her sights higher than a mere mortal? He pushed down a stab of mingled disgust and anger and forced himself to concentrate on what mattered. The window of his old room was lit; probably Averel had moved in. That was a pity, for it might have had its uses – although there were far safer hiding places. The cellars, for example. And beyond them the stairway that led down through the stack to the beach. At this time of year no one had any reason to use that route, and it would be as good a haven as they could hope to find.

He turned to look at Kaldar, who had stayed back in the shadows. Beyond, the postern gate was closed and barred again – he didn't know what magic Kaldar had used to open it from the far side but, like the magic that had got them across the mainland bridge unseen, it had worked – and with no guard posted after dark they were secure enough while they stayed here. Getting across the courtyard undetected would be more hazardous, but the promise of foul weather was keeping all but the hardiest inside. If they made their way round by the stable block, they could slip through one of the lesser doors and get into the cellar network . . . He fingered the silver Chaos rider's circlet with its half-mask. By a small miracle – or, perhaps, thanks to Aeoris – they had found it in the pass near Kaldar's cave, lying in the snow where Benetan had flung it. He was reluctant to don it again, for he couldn't quite shake off a superstitious fear that its links with the past might somehow infect his mind and undermine his resolve. But it would hide his features, make him anonymous, and that was vital now.

He set the circlet in place and glanced over his shoulder again, trying to ignore the way Kaldar involuntarily flinched at the sight of the mask. 'Ready?'

Kaldar nodded and draped his coat over his head so that his distinctive red hair was hidden. 'Which way?'

'To the right, and keep close to the wall. There's a door beyond the stables. Don't walk too fast, remember – make it look as if we have every right to be here.'

Kaldar smiled sourly. 'I've had more practice than you at that sort of subterfuge. All right; lead the way.'

They moved out from under the arch, slithering on half-melted ice. Benetan feared that the nearer door of the stable block would open as they passed, but it didn't and they were almost level with the second door at the far end when on the edge of his vision's range Benetan glimpsed movement. He turned his head quickly –

The castle's main doors had opened a crack and, framed in the light spilling from inside, a figure was emerging onto the steps. Benetan's mind took in an impression of extraordinary height, a long gown, a glimmer of silver as the illumination touched on skin –

'*Move!*' He hissed the word, at the same moment catching Kaldar's arm and swinging him to the right. They were through the stable entrance in seconds, and Benetan just managed to catch the door before it could slam noisily shut behind them.

He eased the latch back into place, and in the warm, damp gloom Kaldar turned quickly to face him. He hadn't had time to see the figure for himself, and his voice was a sharp whisper as he demanded, 'Who was it?'

'Magus Pirane.'

Kaldar tensed. 'I've met her. She's one of the most dangerous.'

'Yes. And I wouldn't care to gamble on any disguise being proof against her.' Benetan suppressed a shudder. 'For either of us.'

Kaldar let out a whistling breath. 'One close call before we're even forty paces into the castle . . . This isn't going to be easy, Benet.'

Benetan didn't think it worth commenting, but with a gesture indicated for Kaldar to follow him past the ranks of stalls towards the inner door that would admit them to the cellar level. A horse snorted somewhere along the line, making them both start, and Benetan hoped fervently that the sentry was sleeping, as sentries usually did on the night shift. If they were surprised, he would either have to talk his way out of trouble – impossible if the sentry was a man he knew – or kill; and despite his earlier mood, he didn't want it to come to that.

They reached the door without mishap and Benetan eased it open. The steps beyond were pitch dark and he made a mental note to purloin some form of lighting from the store-rooms. Candles would be safest; easy to carry unobtrusively and they could be extinguished in an instant if the need arose. For now, though, he hoped he could rely on his ingrained knowledge of the castle's layout to take them to their destination.

They moved in silence for a while. Benetan's memory seemed to be reliable enough as he negotiated the twists and turns that led them deeper among the foundations. The darkness was claustrophobic and he could sense Kaldar's nervousness, but sound carried unpredictably through these passages and he didn't dare speak any reassuring word. At last, though, there was a faint glimmer of light away to the left and Benetan knew they had reached the wider corridor that led to the store-rooms. The stores were used at all hours and so there was always some illumination down here, however dim, and at the junction of passages they stopped, checking carefully for any sign of movement.

Something rustled a short way off and a small shadow flitted across the floor. Kaldar raised querying eyebrows and Benetan said, 'Rats. Don't worry; they're more frightened of us than we are of them.'

Rats had been a scourge in the northern mines, Kaldar remembered. 'I'm surprised the magi haven't eradicated them. With their power it would be easy enough.'

Benetan shrugged. 'As long as the contaminated food and gnawed furnishings aren't given to them, they won't trouble themselves over something so trivial. We —' He corrected himself. 'The riders sometimes organise a purge, but it doesn't take long for the numbers to build up again.'

Kaldar snorted. 'Someone should introduce felines — the small cats, not those devils that live in the mountains. They'd do the job more efficiently than any human.'

'Horses are the only domestic animals the magi tolerate,' Benetan said. 'Live ones, anyway.' He cast a quick, arid grin over his shoulder. 'Personally, I'm thankful the rats are about. If we have to stay here for any length of time, we'll need something more than meat-strips to eat.'

'Have you ever eaten a rat?'

'Often. One of my sergeants used to catch them when we made camp during sorties. He had his own way of cooking them, and several of us developed a taste for it.'

Kaldar grimaced. 'I've only tried them raw. I wouldn't recommend it.'

Satisfied that the rats were the cellars' only other inhabitants at present, they moved out into the passage and Benetan began to check the store-rooms that lined the walls on both sides. The doors weren't locked, for no servant would risk the punishment meted out to pilferers, and they gathered blankets, candles, enough fuel and kindling to make a small fire, and writing materials so that Benetan could draw a map of the castle's salient areas for Kaldar to memorize. Neither food nor weapons were stored here, and when their supply of water ran out they would have to fill

Kaldar's flasks with snow or, if the thaw came, from the rain-conduits in the courtyard. How long this sojourn would last was a question Benetan didn't want to consider too closely as yet; so much depended on how quickly they could learn all they needed to learn and assess the situation in the castle. And when they had assessed it, everything would depend on their timing . . .

The door to the stairway inside the stack was at the far end of the passage. Benetan unbolted it and they eased through with their spoils.

'Better light one of the candles,' Benetan said, his voice echoing peculiarly in the well. 'The steps start abruptly, and we don't want any broken legs to contend with.'

Kaldar set down his burden. Flint and tinder scraped; a spark caught and one of the candles fluttered into life.

'Gods.' Kaldar looked up at the rock, streaming with damp, above his head, then down into the well's impenetrable murk. Cold air was rising from below, the draught not strong enough to blow the candle out but bone-chilling nonetheless. 'Let's hope we don't have to stay down here for too long. A few days of this place, and –' He broke off and suddenly in the candlelight his eyes glittered uneasily.

'What is it?' Instinctively Benetan's tone dropped to a whisper.

'Voices,' Kaldar whispered back. 'Outside, in the passage.'

Benetan listened and his ears caught a faint murmur. They exchanged a look; Kaldar blew the candle out and they both stood motionless. It was impossible to judge the direction from which the sounds came, but they were drawing closer. Two voices, both male . . .

Cautiously, Benetan eased the door open a crack and peered out. The single, weak torch that illuminated the cellarway still burned, but beyond it the brighter glow of a hand-held lantern was visible as the newcomers approached a turn in the passage. Benetan signalled a warning to Kaldar to remain silent, then flattened himself against the wall, allowing the other man to see past him without the need to open the door any wider.

The voices began to resolve and separate, and now an occasional word was discernible. Benetan heard *tithes* and *in this weather*; the voice was vaguely familiar though he couldn't yet put a name to it. Then the other man spoke. And this was a tone he recognized instantly.

Savrinor? What in the names of all Chaos's demons was *he* doing down here? Savrinor didn't demean himself by grubbing about in cellars; if he wanted anything from the stores he sent a servant to fetch it. Benetan listened harder, trying to catch what the historian was saying . . . and then one word made his skin prickle. He couldn't hear what had gone before, but Savrinor had uttered Andraia's name.

Two shadows loomed on the wall then, and Savrinor and his companion came into view. The other man was taller and some years older, with hair greying at the temples and swept back, and as the lantern illuminated his face Benetan identified him as Qenever, Andraia's father and one of the castle's highest-ranking secular officials. The nature of Savrinor's work brought him into frequent contact with Qenever, Benetan knew, and that also accounted for the reference to Andraia. But it didn't explain this unlikely location.

Savrinor and Qenever had reached the store-rooms now. At the fourth they halted and Savrinor reached to open the door; as it swung back Qenever said, 'Well, we should find everything we both need in here. And as no one will overhear us this far from civilisation, perhaps you'll satisfy my curiosity at last and tell me exactly what's behind this subterfuge?'

The light flared on Savrinor as he glanced at the older man, and Benetan saw that for all his immaculate appearance the historian's face was anaemic and haggard. 'There's little to tell at present,' he replied. They stepped into the store-room. 'And the subterfuge, as you term it, is merely a matter of prudence. You'll agree, I'm sure, that there's no point in –'

The voices were cut off abruptly as the door closed, and Benetan swore under his breath. No point in *what*? Savrinor was involved in some intrigue; that smooth, casual tone had a subtle flavour of deceit which Benetan had learned to detect and beware of. It was unlikely that Qenever had failed to recognise it, but equally unlikely that Savrinor hadn't taken that consideration into account. Something was afoot; something complicated that might – if only it could be unravelled – have a bearing on their own mission.

The two men were gone for several minutes, and as he waited for them to emerge once more, Benetan realized that his right hand was on his knife hilt, clenching and unclenching. Seeing Savrinor had awoken ugly memories and rekindled the anger that had been corroding his mind earlier in the day. Reprisal would give him such *satisfaction*, and he could wish for no better or more private place in which to take it. One strike, across the throat, would be enough to wipe out Yandros's benevolence in the Marble Hall. And unlike Vordegh, Benetan thought, he had justification in plenty.

Fingers closed on his arm and he realized that Kaldar had sensed the impulse in him and was warning him to quell it. With an effort he made his hand relax, fall away from the knife. Speculation was pointless anyway, for Savrinor wasn't alone and Benetan had no particular wish to kill Qenever. But the tension remained, and the hostility, and by the time the store-room door opened again the two forces were like a hot, hard ache in his stomach.

Then Qenever spoke, and what he said drove all other thoughts from Benetan's mind.

'I hope no suspicion still attaches to Andraia?'

Savrinor followed him out into the passage, carrying

what looked like an armful of fresh parchments and pens. 'Certainly not. Although I've not mentioned this matter to her, and I'll appreciate it if you don't do so.'

Qenever watched him shrewdly as he turned to close the door. 'You don't trust her?'

Savrinor swung round. 'On the contrary; I trust her implicitly.' His tone was sharp, with a hint of censure. 'But I see no need for her to become involved in any way. She's been through enough in the past few days.'

'As, I would have thought, have you,' Qenever observed drily.

Savrinor shrugged. 'I'll cope in my own way.'

'For your sake, I sincerely hope so.' They started to walk away, then Qenever added, 'My powers of persuasion, of course, are no match for yours, so what you've asked of me won't be an easy task. Anyone with a modicum of prudence guards their tongue carefully these days, and any potential troublemaker is doubly likely to be cautious. However, I'll do what I can, for what it's worth.'

They were nearly at the turn in the passage and a sudden scrape of a heel on stone masked Savrinor's brief reply. Qenever laughed, though not with any amusement, and moments later the two disappeared and their voices became blurred and indefinable.

As the two sets of footsteps diminished and finally faded altogether, Kaldar uttered a muted whistle. 'Interesting,' he said softly. 'Very interesting . . .'

Benetan stepped back and eased the door shut. His own mind was racing as the possible implications of what they had overheard vied with some very personal and unpleasant thoughts about Savrinor and Andraia. Kaldar opened his tinder-box again and lit three candles, fixing them into crannies in the rough rock walls. Then he turned round, his eyes speculative. 'Savrinor seems to be living up to his reputation for scheming. Who was the other man?'

'Qenever.' Benetan paused. 'He's Andraia's father.'

'Her *father*? Are he and Savrinor good friends?'

'They were little more than colleagues in the past. But Savrinor probably has his own reasons for cultivating Qenever.'

'What reasons?' Kaldar had noted the vicious edge in Benetan's voice.

'If you really want to know, Savrinor seems to be Andraia's first choice for a bedmate at the moment. Or perhaps I should say her second choice.' In the gloom Benetan's eyes glinted with contempt. 'Knowing him, I imagine the idea of having Chaos's leavings adds an extra spice. But I don't want to discuss that, thank you.'

Kaldar studied him sidelong for a moment, then made a pacifying, acquiescent gesture. 'All right, I'm sorry; I didn't mean to pry. Then aside of any personal issues, what do you think might be afoot between Savrinor and Qenever?' He paused. 'And more to the point, what is Savrinor so afraid of?'

That confounded Benetan. 'Afraid?'

'Oh, yes. I sensed it, felt it – I only have the talent in a small way, nothing like Simbrian's abilities, but if the emanation's strong enough I'll recognize it. He's afraid of something. No; that's putting it too lightly. He's *terrified*.' Kaldar stared thoughtfully at the closed door. 'Something's happened here since you left.'

The conversation between Savrinor and Qenever rose again in Benetan's mind. *Subterfuge. Trusting Andraia. Potential troublemakers* . . . It all had the whiff of one thing and one only: divided factions. But divided over what? And on whose behalf were Savrinor and Qenever gathering information?

He said, 'I don't know, Kaldar. It might be a significant thing, or it might be completely trivial; Savrinor's intrigues are so complex that I wouldn't care to hazard either way. But . . .' Instinct prompted him, and he felt inclined to trust it. 'I think it might be in our interests to find out.'

CHAPTER X

Many of the castle's inhabitants liked to take a meal in the early afternoon, and so there were more than two hundred people in the dining hall when Vordegh entered.

His arrival brought silence down on the hall like a solid curtain falling. The diners nearest the doors rose hastily to their feet and bowed; others, further in, craned to see the cause of the sudden upheaval, and the ripple of apprehension spread rapidly.

The First Magus was apparently oblivious to the effect he had provoked. He stalked down the hall, not troubling to acknowledge the obeisances, and his dark eyes scanned the gathering calmly but intently, as though looking for one very precise and specific quarry. His attendant shadows shifted around him, and behind him the silent, willowy figure of Verdice followed, her face cold and haughty.

Four magi were sitting at the table nearest to the vast hearth. Croin was not among them but Pirane was, and as she realized that Vordegh was making towards her she felt tension knot deep within her. But her expression remained serene as she made a formal bow.

'Magus.' Vordegh spoke as though to a total stranger, and Pirane had the peculiar impression that his eyes weren't focusing on her but on a point some way beyond. 'I am given to understand that there has been a deviation from my standing instructions.'

'Indeed, Lord Vordegh?' Pirane shot a vitriolic glance in Verdice's direction.

'Indeed. The Chaos rider's escape from custody does not

please me. And the fact that only one culprit has been punished for the lapse pleases me still less. Perhaps you would care to explain why my orders were not carried out to the letter?'

'Of course, First Magus.' Pirane indicated the table before her. 'Will you grace us by taking wine and food in our company, while I answer your question in full?'

Vordegh looked at the table as though it were Croin's experiment-block. 'I have no need for either, Magus. Only for your explanation.'

Pirane sensed her companions' uneasy chagrin in the wake of that flat statement. They would, she knew, have preferred to leave and thus distance themselves from any confrontation, but Vordegh was so unpredictable that none dared make a move without his express permission. They would stay, they would listen; and now everyone within earshot was paying covert but avid attention. Well and good . . . Provided she herself came through it unscathed – and she believed she would – this encounter could be of great value. 'As you wish, Lord Vordegh.' She made another small but punctiliously respectful bow. 'I made the decision to execute one Chaos rider instead of the requisite seven because I believed that you would not wish their numbers to be reduced by such a factor under the present circumstances. After the heretic girl's confession you gave orders for the riders to stand permanently at full readiness, and I was concerned that such a reduction might make it impossible to obey that order.' She met his gaze. 'I took the decision upon myself in the hope that I could interpret your instructions as you would wish and expect. If I've not done so, I sincerely apologize.'

Vordegh was silent for a few moments, contemplating her words while his brown eyes scanned her face, reading, or so it felt, all that she had not said. At last he shifted his position slightly, causing the shadows around him to flicker and, briefly, darken.

'What steps have been taken to recapture the escaped Chaos rider?'

'As many as have been feasible, my lord. We have scried, and we have also sent out lower-plane entities to search for him.'

'But without success.' Vordegh's tone gave no hint of his mind's temper.

'Not as yet, no.' Pirane hesitated. 'We will need, I think, to use the Marble Hall for a greater working. If Captain Liss went through the Maze, then he could –'

She was interrupted. 'The Marble Hall will not be used until I give sanction. And the Chaos rider warrants no further attention.' Vordegh apparently considered it unnecessary to elaborate on that statement. 'My sole concern is with the apprehension of the red-haired criminal, and in that regard we need do nothing more than wait for him to return for the girl. So, that leaves only the question which I first asked.' He paused for a few moments, studying Pirane's face detachedly. 'In essence, your decision was correct. It would not be in our interests to reduce the riders' strength at present, and new recruits take time to train. However, that does not change the fact that this transgression merits seven forfeits, not merely one.' He glanced briefly around the hall. 'The man executed was responsible for the captain's escape, I understand.'

'Yes, my lord.'

'Then the remaining riders may be exempted in this instance. I shall select six others in their stead.' Vordegh turned again and his gaze lit on a servant who had frozen in the midst of carrying food to a nearby table. A hand gestured negligently. 'That woman.' A second glance; he indicated a handsome, dark-haired young man, son of a high-ranking official, who sat with his mother a short way off. 'That youth.' He turned a little further, considering, then paused – and Pirane saw what he had seen. Andraia was sitting at a table near the window, flanked by two female friends. Pirane hadn't noticed them until now, and with a growing sense of alarm she scanned the crowd for any sign of Savrinor. He didn't appear to be in the hall – but by the First Magus's vindictive reasoning, Andraia might make an acceptable substitute.

Andraia's face had turned a waxen and sickly hue. Even at this distance Pirane could feel the girl's terror like a sword thrusting into her psyche, and she started to move forward, a protest forming on her lips –

Vordegh smiled glacially at Andraia and said, 'The first woman and the third woman at that table.'

One of Andraia's companions fainted; the other could only stare blankly, disbelievingly, as the command sank in. Andraia had risen to her feet, but now she seemed unable to move a muscle.

Vordegh was making his final selections; two people whose identities didn't even register on Pirane's mind. Then he turned to face her once more.

'See to it that they die within the hour, and instruct the historian to witness and record the proceedings for the archives.'

Pirane's silver-tinted face was bloodless. 'Yes, First Magus.' She didn't recognize her own voice.

Silence held like a vice as Vordegh left with Verdice in his wake, and even after the doors had closed behind them no one spoke or moved. Every face in the hall seemed to be turned towards Pirane, every pair of eyes fixed on her, waiting for her to break the thrall.

She couldn't countermand Vordegh's order – and in one sense she didn't want to, for this was the catalyst that she and Croin had been hoping to provoke. But the senseless *waste* of it . . . six useful lives sacrificed at random, simply to exert supremacy and drive home a point. Until this moment she had been haunted by a lingering shred of doubt about her plans, but now that doubt had gone. Vordegh had lost his sanity. And there was only one cure.

She moved suddenly, leaving the table and her rigid companions and sweeping out into the hall's central aisle. All the gazes followed her – then the spell shattered as her voice snapped out with harsh authority.

'*You.*' She had seen one of the higher-ranking servants, a steward, and pointed imperiously to him. 'Find Captain Averel, and tell him to detail an escort of Chaos riders to take charge of the six individuals the First Magus has designated. I also want Master Savrinor summoned to me here, immediately, and –' Her gaze re-focused to the table by the window. Andraia was staring wildly at her, swaying on her feet, hands clenching and unclenching in helpless, inarticulate shock –

Pirane found her voice again. '*And for all the gods' sakes, get that girl out of the hall!*'

Andraia was asleep when Savrinor returned to his apartments a little under two hours later. Physician Revian had been called to her and had administered something that put her beyond the reach of consciousness, if not of dreams. For a few minutes Savrinor stood in the doorway between the two rooms, watching her as she lay in the bed and listening to the rhythm of her breathing. Then he went to his work-table, sat down and wrote a concise, meticulous account of the six further executions which had just taken place in one of the underground rooms adjoining the bathing area. A more practical location than the courtyard; the blood was easier to wash away. Two servants, a secretary's son – Revian was at this moment treating the young man's mother for acute hysteria – and a man in his twenties, who had recently come to the castle from somewhere in the east and had had the potential to join the magi's ranks. And Andraia's two friends. Savrinor had to check the document he had just completed to recall their names, as if his subconscious had already decided to protect itself by erasing them from memory. Not that their names mattered; they were dead now, and – he prayed – in Yandros's care.

He dusted sand over the wet ink and set the paper aside to finish drying. The short afternoon was wearing on, and dull, heavy rain had set in, melting the snow and gurgling drearily in gutters and pipes outside his window. Rain made his bones ache; a sure sign of creeping age. He wanted to go into the other room and lie down beside Andraia, sleep as she was sleeping. But sleep meant dreams. And he had other work yet to do.

He thought it likely that Qenever would come looking for him before long and that Pirane herself wouldn't be far behind. They had agreed, he and Pirane, that provided he wasn't told too much about the true purpose of the exercise, Qenever could be very useful as another gleaner of information, and Savrinor suspected that in the light of this new development he would have a good deal to impart. With Vordegh now ensconced in the spire once more, it would soon be time for the *real* strategy to begin. Strange, Savrinor thought; less than a day ago he had been deeply and, it had seemed, enduringly afraid of the First Magus, but now the fear was fading, leaving a kind of numbness which, while not pleasant, was at least a respite. He hardly cared any more what might or might not become of him. All he wanted was an end to the rule of a man who was making a mockery of everything he had ever believed in.

Another emotion moved him in the aftermath of that thought and he stood up stiffly, went to the window and closed the velvet curtain, shutting out the dismal day. He had lit several branches of candles to enable him to work, but now he wanted no light. Darkness was kindlier, and in darkness the sense of communion with Chaos came with greater ease.

The candles went out, and Savrinor returned to his table. As he sat down and rested his arms on the table top, his elbow knocked a bottle of ink to the floor. The bottle broke and a purplish-black stain spread, though it was hard to make out in the gloom. Savrinor stared at it for a few moments, then looked away. Someone else could clear the mess in the morning, and a rug was easily replaced.

He rested his head on his folded arms and silently, ardently, began to pray to Yandros for guidance and resolve.

Qenever arrived shortly after sunset, waking Savrinor from an ugly half-doze. His private invocation had become mingled with a dream that Physician-Magus Croin was trying to cut his heart out with a broken wine-glass while Yandros was asleep and, this time, wouldn't know what had taken place until it was far too late. Savrinor hid the lurching shock of the dream behind a calm mask and re-lit more candles than were strictly necessary before listening to what Qenever had to tell him. The information was succinct but salient, and after refusing refreshment but expressing his sorrow at the deaths of Andraia's friends, which Savrinor promised to convey to her when she woke, Qenever left. When he had gone, Savrinor drank three glasses of wine – he felt a little squeamish about touching the glass in the wake of the dream, but that spectre faded as the wine went down – and waited for the expected summons.

It was brought shortly before second moonrise by Lua, Andraia's mother, who was also Pirane's lady-in-waiting. The magus required Savrinor to attend her as soon as convenient, she said, as she wished him to carry out some research for her in the castle archives. The phrasing of the message warned Savrinor that Lua knew nothing of what was really afoot, and he gathered up writing materials and prepared to leave. Lua watched him, then asked, 'Is Andraia still sleeping?'

Savrinor paused and looked up. 'Yes. Revian thought it best to give her a strong draught.'

Lua sighed. 'Poor child. And as for those two girls, her

friends . . . truly, Savrinor, I can hardly believe it even now. Such a *wanton* act! What could it possibly *achieve*?'

Savrinor didn't reply. In one sense – the ethical sense – he agreed wholeheartedly with Lua; but on a more pragmatic level he might have given her another answer entirely.

She paced across the room, restless, touching and smoothing her hair with an obsessive little mannerism. 'I wonder if I should stay with Andraia in your absence?' she suggested at last, tentatively. 'Lady Pirane has excused me for the present, and I don't like to think of her waking to find herself alone.' She frowned, then added again, 'Poor child . . .'

'Revian has assured me that she won't stir for some hours yet.' Savrinor had no intention of giving Lua a free hand to explore his private sanctum; and he also suspected that if Andraia were to wake, her mother would not be ideal company for her at present. 'Besides, Magus Pirane is aware of the circumstances. I'm sure she won't detain me for longer than necessary.'

'Well, it's as you wish, of course.' Lua wasn't entirely content but didn't argue. Then her expression relaxed. 'At least I have the comfort of knowing that you are taking good care of her. That reassures me greatly.'

Lua, like Qenever, had never been happy about Andraia's entanglement with Benetan, and had made repeated attempts to persuade her to find a more aristocratic and thus more acceptable lover. This, Savrinor knew, was her way of conveying that she approved of her daughter's new choice, and for some reason the knowledge made him feel exceptionally cynical.

He smiled punctiliously. 'I appreciate the compliment.'

Lua didn't know him well enough to detect the coldness underlying the surface cordiality and she patted his arm, satisfied that she had made her point. 'You'd best go, my dear. Lady Pirane isn't in the best of moods at the moment – it's hardly to be wondered at under the circumstances –

and it probably wouldn't be prudent to keep her waiting.'

She left the apartment with him, and Savrinor took good care to lock the door behind them.

By the time he left Magus Pirane's chambers Savrinor was in no doubt that within the next few days either she, he and a good many others would be dead, or the castle would have a new First Magus. The six executions had been the turning-point. People were disquieted by what seemed a prodigally vicious exercise, and with Vordegh now back in the east spire some were daring to express that disquiet for the first time. It was a small undercurrent as yet, but Pirane and Croin believed that, with a little encouragement, the current could become a flood. And one piece of information which Qenever had passed on to Savrinor struck a new chord in Pirane's fertile mind.

'So the Chaos riders are unhappy in the wake of this?' She touched the tip of her tongue to an upraised finger, musingly. 'How interesting . . . is this widespread, would you say, or simply the stirrings of a small but vociferous element?'

'I have the impression, madam, that the riders are very far from vociferous about it,' Savrinor told her. 'It was their reticence, rather than its opposite, which alerted Qenever in the first place. And it permeates through the ranks, from lowest to highest. Including Captain Averel.'

'Ah, yes; Averel. I really thought that he was going to lose his nerve in the courtyard yesterday.'

'Qenever's impression is that he now regrets having kept it,' Savrinor said. 'He fears that his own men might view his action as a betrayal and despise him for it.'

'And is that fear well founded?'

'No, madam. If anything it's had the opposite effect; there's a good deal of sympathy for Averel in the riders' ranks, and a feeling that he had no choice in the matter.'

'Which of course is true.' Pirane poured more wine for

them both. 'So, they're rallying behind their leader. Not, presumably, through heartfelt loyalty but because they're well aware that if matters had gone askance, any one of them might have been chosen to perform the same disagreeable task on Averel himself. A very noble principle.'

Savrinor masked his expression behind his refilled glass. 'They're only human, madam.'

Pirane gave him a peculiar look, then smiled sardonically. 'So they are. Well, their situation might be manipulated to our advantage.'

For once Savrinor's mind wasn't keeping pace with hers. The wine was strong and, combined with tiredness, was beginning to blur the edges of his thoughts. 'Advantage, madam?' he asked.

'Certainly. The Chaos riders have no occult power of their own, but no one with a modicum of common sense overlooks the value of their physical skills and strength.' Pirane pondered for a few moments. 'What would it take, I wonder, to tilt *that* particular balance in our favour?'

Savrinor began to see where she was leading. 'They are already aware, madam, that but for your intervention seven of their own would have been executed instead of one,' he reminded her. 'And I understand – though I haven't yet been able to confirm it – that the female servant who died at Lord Vordegh's order today was bedding with a junior sergeant in the riders' ranks.'

'*Was* she, now?' The magus flicked him an approving glance. 'Another small maggot to gnaw at the fruit . . . and it all helps to give the six executions a significance which they would not otherwise have had. Distasteful they might have been, but I'm beginning to think they served a useful purpose.'

Lua's bewildered question came back to mind, and Savrinor felt a stab of repugnance at the magus's – and, if he was to be honest, his own – sanguinity. Pirane saw the reaction, and her expression modulated. 'Don't misunderstand me, my dear. I dislike unnecessary deaths just as you do, and I greatly regret what happened today. But if some good can be wrought out of that mindless act, it will be a consolation for us all. Even, I think, for Andraia.' She paused, and her strange, huge eyes suddenly grew very hard. 'You probably don't know exactly what happened in the dining hall. Andraia was sitting at a table with her two friends, and the fact that they *were* her friends was the sole reason why Vordegh chose to add them to his count of victims. It was obvious that his first thought, and his desire, was to choose Andraia herself, and only the fear of flouting our Lord Yandros's warning held him back. However, fear has its limits and vengeance is a powerful force. Had you been there instead of Andraia, I think the temptation might have been too great for Vordegh to resist.'

Savrinor put the back of one hand to his mouth. It was a shocked reflex and, realizing it, he quickly disguised the lapse as a cough. But Pirane saw understanding in his eyes and knew that her point had gone home. If he had been harbouring any doubts, this had dispelled them: even the finest scruples tended to look less appealing when they clashed with the desire to survive.

She rose from her chair, a tacit signal that the interview was at an end. Savrinor hastily stood, too, and Pirane said, 'We shall wait another day or so, I think, to see how far and how deeply the ripples of this affair spread. Continue your investigations, and keep me informed of your progress. Especially as regards the riders.' Her expression became thoughtful once more. 'It's a great pity that the First Magus has nothing planned for them, or at least nothing that we're aware of as yet. One or two of their recent sorties have been a little . . . gratuitous, shall we say, and not entirely to their liking. If they were to be obliged to carry out another such campaign . . .'

'It would need to be at Lord Vordegh's behest, madam,' Savrinor pointed out.

'Yes, it would. And of course we have no influence whatever over his decisions.' But Pirane was smiling, a private and amused smile, and the very slight stress which she had put on the word 'we' didn't escape Savrinor's notice.

Suddenly, as if sensing his curiosity, she looked directly at him. 'Don't try to unravel *all* the threads, my dear. You have your methods, I have mine. We can both be content enough with that.'

It was a gentle but emphatic warning not to probe, and Savrinor acknowledged it with a small bow. 'As you say, lady magus.'

She smiled again, but this time the smile was for him. 'Give my love to Andraia. And the gods watch over you both.'

I pray they will, Savrinor thought as he closed the door behind him.

'I suspect Pirane has something in mind,' Yandros said. 'And if my suspicions are right, she'll have a great deal of support among the rest of the magi.'

He and Tarod were walking on the shore of a lake that glittered under a black sky. Above them, seven vast prisms hung like moons, turning slowly on an invisible but perfectly aligned axis; they cast a strange, chilly light that created shadows across the water's surface.

'I can't say I'm entirely surprised,' Tarod remarked. 'The waters are growing murkier every day, and I've no doubt this new outrage has provoked a good deal of ill-feeling in the castle.'

Yandros glanced at him with mild amusement. 'I'd hardly call seven lives an outrage.'

'Not to us, no. But to the mortals who are directly involved?'

'Mmm. I take your point. Well, certainly it seems that

it's given rise to considerable disquiet, and I don't think Pirane is going to miss the chance to exploit it.'

Tarod wondered just how Yandros had gleaned this piece of information, and he asked, 'Have you spoken directly with her?'

The shadows on the lake surface had begun to dance, forming intricate patterns that had more dimensions than any human eye could have discerned. Yandros watched them for a few moments before replying, 'No. I haven't been back to the mortal world since the small fracas in the Marble Hall. But Pirane performed a private communion ritual tonight, and the message it conveyed was quite explicit. If enough of her peers are in agreement with her, she will act against Vordegh.' He picked a stem from a tall, graceful, rush-like plant growing at the water's edge and twirled it between thumb and fingers. 'And if she succeeds, that will be a very satisfactory resolution.'

Tarod smiled. 'So you'll have what you've desired from the start. An end to Vordegh's rule, but with no intervention from us.'

'Precisely.' Then Yandros's eyes took on a sly glint. 'Or almost none.'

Tarod looked quickly, suspiciously at him. 'You're not telling me that you've changed your mind about the principle of the thing, after all our debating and argument?'

'Oh, no. But there's a world of a difference between acting directly to remove the First Magus and granting a modest and harmless favour to one individual worshipper.' Yandros shrugged. 'A lesser favour, even, than I granted to Savrinor.'

'But one which could affect the greater cause?'

'If a few coincidences fall into place, then it could. But *could* promises nothing and presumes less. In truth, Tarod, I intend only to strike a very small spark, and it will be entirely up to the magi to decide whether or not that spark sets off an explosion.'

'I hope it does.'

'So do I, for Vordegh's behaviour is proving to be far too much of a distraction for all concerned. Until this is resolved, neither we nor the magi can give our full attention to the matter of Aeoris and the human detritus who are working for him. And I'm not prepared to wait much longer for an end to *that* mischief.' He glanced up at the sky, and a quicksilver shiver of energy sang between the prisms, turning them momentarily to a dazzle of jewel colours that reflected in his eyes. 'I'll give Pirane my answer tomorrow night, and I think it would be appropriate to convey it in person. Come with me if you've a mind to.'

The prisms were quiet again, and their light had drained the landscape to a coldly beautiful monochrome. Tarod regarded the tranquil scene for a few moments, considering. Then he said, 'Perhaps I will. I owe a small courtesy to someone in the castle, and this will be as good an opportunity as any to render it.'

Andraia was still sleeping, and Savrinor wanted nothing more than to join her in oblivion. The equation of the hours he had spent awake against those spent asleep during the past few days was one he didn't care to contemplate, and Pirane's strong wine on the heels of the three glasses he had drunk beforehand had affected his faculties. That was rare, and a warning sign. For once, he would heed the warning.

He measured a precise and necessary concoction from his cabinet and swallowed it before carrying the one candle he had lit through to the inner room. Andraia stirred when he climbed into bed beside her; he snuffed the candle out and put one arm around her, soothed by her warmth. She moved again, sensing his presence, and said softly, vaguely, 'Benet . . . ?'

Savrinor shut his own eyes briefly. 'No,' he replied, his voice as quiet as hers.

She tensed as, on an arcane and subliminal level, her half-dreaming mind grasped at some sense of the mistake she had made. Then with a great effort she opened eyes that were heavy with sleep and Physician Revian's draught. The darkness in the room was deep and quiet but she could just make out the pale gleam of Savrinor's hair, and he saw the dim reflection of doubt change to that of recognition. She pressed close to him, and he knew that the memory of her momentary confusion had flitted away and would never return.

'I had a nightmare, Savrinor,' she whispered, the words hazy. 'A terrible nightmare. About Ayla and Serafie . . .'

Ayla and Serafie. Two names on a dismal report for the archives. Two names that had served a greater purpose . . .

'Hush.' Savrinor kissed her hair. 'It was only a dream.' Now, he thought, with the remainder of the night still ahead of them, a lie was kinder. 'Go back to sleep, my love. There's nothing to fear.'

CHAPTER XI

Benetan and Kaldar made their first foray into the castle that night. It was a risk but the risk had to be taken, and they chose, as near as they could judge it, the hour before second moonset. At that time most of the higher-ranking castle-dwellers would be sleeping; a few servants would still be about, but they should be easy enough to avoid if necessary – or, if circumstances were right, to engage in a little gossip.

Servants' gossip, Kaldar said, was the surest way of finding out what was afoot in the castle and how it might affect their own purpose. And although a good many people must by now know the description of the escaped heretic, he had the ability to disguise himself well enough to avoid recognition. It was simple sorcery, but it had the effect of subtly altering the perceptions of anyone he encountered, creating a vague and misleading impression of his face and voice which would quickly slide out of memory and be forgotten. Kaldar would mingle, he would listen, and he would encourage tongues to wag.

With no such ability to camouflage himself, and a better knowledge of the castle's layout, Benetan's plan was to make a covert sortie which he hoped would lead him to Iselia. He prayed to Aeoris that she was being kept in an underground cell as he had been after his own arrest, and not confined in some upper room which would put her out of their reach. And, more fundamentally, he prayed that she was still alive.

He began his search in the area of the cellar complex where he himself had been incarcerated; a maze of narrow tunnels and cramped, bleak chambers, some cluttered with unwanted and probably long-forgotten lumber but the majority left empty. There was no sign of a guard in any of the passages, but that was no sure indication of anything and so he tested door after door, room after room, searching for any sign of life. Time wasn't on his side; he had two hours at most before the first of the day-duty servants began to stir, and though his uniform and mask would be enough to keep most at arm's length, he dared not take chances.

All too soon a nagging instinct warned him that he should return to the hideaway. Having found nothing, Benetan was very loth to abandon his efforts, but caution prevailed and reluctantly he started to retrace his steps, mentally cataloguing the area he had covered. Another wasted day would be frustrating, but there was no help for it. Tomorrow, perhaps, he might take the risk of resuming the search a little earlier.

The candle he was carrying guttered suddenly as a draught disturbed the air. It startled him; he peered into the gloom – and a long shadow moved a little way ahead, at the junction of two tunnels.

Benetan froze instinctively, holding his breath, listening. A footfall . . . he looked frantically over his shoulder but he had left the cellar rooms behind and there was nowhere to hide. No point, either, in snuffing out the candle; whoever was approaching must have seen its glow by now, and to extinguish it would arouse suspicion as well as hampering his eyesight. He would have to brazen this out. *If* he could.

The footfalls were drawing nearer, and on a subconscious level Benetan realized suddenly that there was something furtive about them, as if the newcomer also had no business being down here. That could be to his advantage, and he checked that the silver mask was still firmly in place before, tentatively, taking a step towards the junction. The shadow hesitated – then it moved again, and abruptly a tall, black-clad figure emerged from the tunnel mouth. A hand raised a shaded lantern, then the lantern's shutter slid back, spilling vivid light into the tunnel. A familiar face sprang into clear relief; startled eyes widened, and Lotro said in astonishment, '*Capun Liss!*'

Benetan's heart gave a huge, painful lurch as shock gave way to a confusing clash between relief and dread. He tried desperately to think of something to say, but before he could formulate any response at all, Lotro pre-empted him.

'Capun, what've you come *back* for? There's been a grand dido over you getten out, an' Capun Averel says as your head's forfeit if so as anyone ever d'set eyes on you again! What've you *done* it for?'

Benetan knew he had a choice to make, and no more than a few seconds in which to make it. He had trusted Lotro once before and not been let down, but, if circumstances had changed, to rely on him now might be a fatal mistake. Yet, he thought, what option did he have? Despite his several days' growth of beard Lotro had recognized him instantly, and one word from the young man to anyone else would put an end to everything. He had to trust Lotro a second time. That, or kill him.

Unaware that his free hand was on his knife hilt, he said urgently, 'Lotro, keep your voice down! If we're overheard –'

'There's no one else about, sir. I made sure of that afore I come, and –' Then Lotro stopped as he realized what he had said, and abruptly Benetan caught the significance. *I made sure of that afore I come.* So Lotro, too, had a reason for not wanting to be found here.

Benetan drew breath, and with a silent but profound entreaty to any friendly powers that could conceivably be listening said, 'There isn't time for me to explain everything, Lotro. I *have* to ask you to trust me, as you did before.' He hesitated, watching alertly for any signs of doubt in the young rider. 'I know my return here must seem like an act of madness, but believe me, there's a purpose in it.' He remembered Lotro's stubbornly idealistic reasoning and added, 'A *just* purpose.'

Lotro's eyes lit at the word, and Benetan was surprised to see a strong element of anger in the light. 'If tis just, sir, then you can count on me, certain sure,' he said forcefully. 'After what were done today –'

'What do you mean? What was done?'

The muscles in Lotro's face tightened painfully. 'They killed Ensith, sir. The one we slammed and tied up that night. They said as he was to be executed for letten you 'scape; they made Capun Averel do un and they made us watch.'

Benetan stared at him, appalled. 'Ensith *died* for that? But – but he couldn't have been held to blame!'

Lotro shrugged. 'They blamed en, sir, right or no. And then . . . then First Magus come down from the spire, and . . .' His voice tailed off and he bit his lip.

'And what?' Benetan prompted sharply. 'What else has happened, Lotro? What has the First Magus done?'

Lotro told him, starkly and simply, and when he had heard all there was to hear Benetan felt sick with disgust and impotent fury. Seven people, six of whom had no possible connection with his escape, cold-bloodedly beheaded to slake Vordegh's spite . . . it was an abomination. He hadn't anticipated that such a thing might happen, hadn't even considered the *possibility*.

'Twasn't your fault, sir!' Lotro said suddenly, almost piteously, as he saw the emotions on Benetan's face. 'How could you've known twould lead to this? You couldn't, and no more could I!'

Through the numb shell of shock and grief a hard little spark within Benetan realized what lay behind the young man's heartfelt words. To blame his captain for these deaths would be to blame himself, too, and Lotro's conscience would be unable to carry such a burden. He had to believe that he had done no wrong, and so he had to believe that Benetan's cause was just. It was cold, it was calculating and under the circumstances it was repellent, but Benetan knew he could – and must – use that faith to his advantage.

Loathing himself for it but ruthlessly crushing the feeling, he said, 'Lotro, I don't know what I can say. You're right; I didn't imagine for one moment that my escape would lead to this. But the fact that it did makes my purpose here all the more vital. I need your help again. I need it urgently.'

Lotro's dark eyes narrowed a little. 'You said twas a *just* purpose?'

'Yes. It concerns Iselia.'

The name had an immediate effect; Lotro flinched visibly and pain showed in his eyes.

'You saw her once before,' Benetan said. 'You told me that you were one of those who brought her out of the Marble Hall.'

Lotro swallowed. 'Thass true, sir.'

'So you know where she is now?'

A nod; then Lotro's expression tensed further and he gave Benetan an uneasy look. Slowly and hesitantly, he said: 'I reckon, sir, as there's sunnat you did ought to know. Tis all to do with ... with why I come down here.'

Benetan watched him intently. 'What do you mean?'

'Well, I ... I'm not rightly s'posed to be here-bouts. Not rightly s'posed to be nowhere 'cept in my bed, for I'm on day duty presently. But ... well, sir, I been coming here several nights. To see her, like. And I been thinking that mebbe I could ...'

He was struggling, desperately unsure of whether he dared express what was in his mind. Gently, Benetan said, 'Tell me, Lotro. You've nothing to fear from me.'

163

The youth cast him a look of desperate appeal. 'I been trying to get up courage to kill her, sir.'

'*Kill* her —?' And suddenly Benetan understood. 'Oh . . . oh, yes. An act of kindness. To let her die . . .'

Lotro nodded unhappily. ''Tis what she d'want, sir. Not to suffer no more, not to be . . . the way she is. And I thought I could do that for her, so I got the key to her cell and went there, like . . . but I couldn't do un. Not cold, not that way. I couldn't.' He sighed, rubbing at his eyes with the heel of one hand. 'I went back; I thought mebbe second time twould be easier, but it weren't. Nor third time. I just couldn't *do* un.'

Chill sweat was crawling on Benetan's skin as he realized just how slender the margin of Iselia's escape had been. Lotro thought only to do good, but if his nerve hadn't failed him those good intentions would have led to tragedy.

Yet the abortive attempt to help had triggered another train of thought, and Benetan reached out and laid a hand on the young rider's arm, a gesture of comradeship and understanding. 'Killing someone is never easy, Lotro, and under circumstances like those it's near-on impossible.'

'But *someone* did ought to help her, Capun,' Lotro persisted unhappily.

'I know; I agree.' Benetan met his gaze. 'And it's the reason why I came back.' He smiled, and the smile conveyed a wealth of sympathy. 'You can't end her suffering. But I can.'

'He thinks I mean to kill her.' Benetan crouched over the small fire they had dared to make in the stairwell, warming his chilled hands. 'I didn't disabuse him of the idea; Lotro's loyalties are more than a little confused at the moment and it's better that he isn't aware of the real plan. I told him that I know a way to make it look like a natural death, so no one will be blamed.'

Kaldar was sitting, knees hunched, against the rock wall.

His face was stony and his eyes had a haunted light in them; he nodded curt agreement, then said, 'And you're sure he won't take it into his head to try again himself?'

'Certain. I've lifted the responsibility from his shoulders and all he feels is relief.' Benetan paused, looking at him. 'You know I wouldn't have run that risk, Kaldar.'

'Yes. Yes, I know.' Then Kaldar shivered. 'What is she suffering, Benet? What kind of physical pain, what kind of mental torment?' Suddenly, violently, he sprang to his feet and began to prowl the cramped space between the door and the stairs. 'I can't stop *thinking* about it, *imagining*. It's like something eating at my soul . . .' He expelled breath in a harsh, quick exhalation. 'But I know, I know; thinking about it doesn't help her and it doesn't help us. And tonight, there's nothing either of us can do. But one more day, or two at most, and it'll be different. She'll be safe – or we'll all either be in Vordegh's hands or dead and consigned to the Seven Hells.' His shoulders hunched. 'In which case none of it will matter anyway, because I doubt if there's much to choose between the two fates.'

Benetan looked over his shoulder. 'Kaldar, for the gods' sakes sit down. As you say, there's nothing we can do tonight, so we'd be best advised to find a distraction. Besides, you haven't yet told me what you found during your own exploration.'

Kaldar sighed. 'Yes. Yes, you're right.' He came back to the fire and sat down. 'Very well, then. I'll tell you what I discovered.'

Some two dozen servants, Kaldar said, were still awake and working in the castle's kitchens, clearing the aftermath of the night's meals and at the same time preparing to start the serving of breakfast in a few hours' time. To them Kaldar was just another useful pair of hands, and with helpers in short supply after the First Magus's recent decimations, his presence was accepted without question. And the middle-aged woman with whom he soon fell into conversation had a lively tongue.

It was being whispered throughout the servants' quarters that something was very amiss among the magi. The strongest rumour claimed that they had angered Yandros in some way, and though no one had yet dared to speculate on how the rift came about or even what its nature might be, the story was now too widespread for Kaldar to discount it. Vordegh's brief but dramatic emergence from the east spire had been the only break in a vigil that had lasted since the night in the Marble Hall, and now he was again refusing to communicate with anyone. People believed that he was working on a new stratagem to wipe out the heretics and thus restore the magi to Yandros's favour – and the prospect frightened them. The "lists" of a short while ago had already culled a great many lives from among the servants, and the six arbitrary beheadings of the previous day implied that, should the First Magus require more sacrifices, no one in the castle could consider themselves safe.

'And something else is in the wind,' Kaldar said. 'Not just people's fear of Vordegh but another feeling, underlying it. I couldn't pinpoint it, and the woman I talked with was vague; she'd only overheard a few cryptic remarks. But I have a strong impression that it's something very substantial. And your sly friend Savrinor's involved in it somewhere; deeply involved if I'm any judge. He's said to be ill – the woman told me some garbled tale that at first it was believed you'd tried to kill him, but now they're saying it was a heart seizure – and yet for a sick man he seems to be unconscionably busy. He's about the castle at all hours, talking to a lot of people –'

'Such as Qenever.'

'Precisely. Savrinor never does anything without a good reason, I gather, so stories are flying about what he might

166

be up to. And one of those stories says he's compiling information on who might and who might not be loyal to Chaos.'

Benetan's eyes quickened with interest. 'Loyal? You're saying that there could be secret sympathizers here?'

'*I'm* saying nothing, merely telling you what the latest tattle suggests. But it makes sense. If Savrinor's as dedicated to that demon Yandros as you say he is, who better for Vordegh to use?'

'Oh, no.' Benetan held up a hand. 'No, Kaldar, you're wrong there. Savrinor would be the *last* man Vordegh would turn to.'

Kaldar looked baffled. 'Why?'

Benetan was about to reply when he realized that it would be impossible to explain without telling Kaldar so much more. So much about Savrinor, and Andraïa, and Yandros and his cursed brother . . . and about himself. Back in the mountain pass he had revealed a very small and, in some ways, insignificant part of the story, and though it had made unpleasant telling it had eased a little of the bitterness. Perhaps, then, it was time to reveal the rest of it; break the self-imposed taboo, shatter the ice on the dark well once and for all and reach into its depths.

He said, 'Is there anything to eat?'

'To eat?' Kaldar looked surprised. 'A few more meat-strips. Why?'

'Because there's a lot you don't know as yet.' Benetan unstoppered one of the water-skins, wishing it contained something far stronger. 'And it might take some time to explain.'

Though by morning the rain had at last cleared away and the sun was trying to show its face through the remnants of the cloud, the castle was ominously quiet. Savrinor's keen senses had caught the atmosphere before he left his rooms, and the hush in the corridors and even in the dining-hall when he went to take a sparse meal shortly before noon was very tense.

There were no magi in the hall. In fact there were few diners of any description; the largest party consisted of some half-dozen Chaos riders who had just come off duty and, uncharacteristically, seemed to have very little to say to one another, and the vast chamber felt chill and forbidding. Savrinor ate mechanically, hardly aware of what he had ordered or whether or not it was palatable, and covertly watched the other tables. Everyone seemed to be in an inordinate hurry today, not lingering over their meals, not staying to drink with friends. The memory of Vordegh's presence here and of what he had done was, it seemed, a powerful spectre. Savrinor knew it was also an irrational spectre, for if the First Magus should choose to make another such sortie then the hall was no more likely a venue for it than anywhere else; but despite any amount of logic the undercurrent of dread was infecting him, too, and he had no wish to stay any longer than necessary. He could, of course, have talked to a few people, insinuated into their company in the way he had perfected over the years, asked questions, probed the atmosphere, tested the water. But something in him fought shy of it. Tomorrow, perhaps; but not today. Today, he preferred to leave the dining-hall well alone.

Andraia was with Lua. He had suggested it, aware that in the aftermath of this morning's events she needed the chance to unburden herself in a way that a mother, rather than a lover, was best equipped to deal with. She had woken an hour or so after dawn and, as he had expected, remembered that her "nightmare" was no such thing. Savrinor could only try to comfort her, knowing all the while that she was struggling to keep the worst of her feelings in check, and at last he had sent her — all but ordered her, in fact — to Lua's chamber, insisting that he would be better off alone as he had more than enough work to occupy him until evening.

That was true, for after leaving the hall and investigating one or two more small avenues it became clear to Savrinor that, as Magus Pirane had predicted, the tide of disquiet was starting to rise in earnest. The atmosphere pervading the castle was evidence enough in itself, but a snatch of talk overheard here, and a whiff of rumour there, added enough fuel to confirm it beyond doubt. The danger, however, was that some of the wilder gossip had begun to veer uncomfortably close to the truth. Rumours were abroad of dissension between the magi and the gods, and now those rumours were becoming embroidered into whispers of dissension among the magi themselves. Savrinor hadn't intended to report to Pirane today, but in the light of this he thought it advisable to change his mind. He made the report when his day's investigations were finished and, after a brief interview with the magus, returned to his rooms shortly after sunset. Fewer torches than usual had been lit in the corridors, and although the dining-hall windows were ablaze as ever, the light spilling from them into the courtyard seemed muted and a little grim. Andraia had returned; she seemed better, though still very strained, and she had lit candles and ordered the fire to be made up to a heartening blaze. Wine was set ready, and a servant would bring them food a little later. Savrinor suspected Lua's or possibly even Pirane's hand behind the arrangements, but he wasn't about to complain at being manipulated. A long, quiet evening with nothing clamouring for attention would do them both good.

It all began peaceably enough, and they had finished an excellent meal and were sampling a favourite vintage of wine when the first harbinger of an alert vibrated in Savrinor's marrow. Andraia saw him frown and reached out, catching hold of his hand. 'Savrinor? What is it; is something amiss?'

For a moment he wasn't sure; then: 'No,' he said. 'Not amiss.' For the feeling, the alert, was familiar. A sense that – as he had once put it to Benetan – the castle's bones were shifting. It awoke excitement in him, barely perceptible as yet but welling from somewhere very deep in his mind. He set his glass down on the table, aware that his muscles had tensed and savouring the tension. Too soon, yet, to be sure, but if he was right . . .

Andraia sat upright as he rose, left the couch and crossed the room to the window. 'Savrinor!' She was unnerved now. 'What *is* it?'

He raised a hand, signalling to her to wait. The curtain was drawn; he pulled it aside and looked out.

The last of the clouds had cleared, and with the first moon risen and almost at the full the entire sky was imbued with a diffuse, silver-grey radiance that dimmed the stars. Savrinor scanned the heavens, searching for some tell-tale sign of distortion, or of a colour that didn't quite blend as it should. There was nothing, and he was beginning to think that for once his instinct had let him down, when with no forewarning the far side of the courtyard lit momentarily acid blue as a charge of energy, like earthbound lightning, snapped between the summits of the south and west spires.

Savrinor recoiled, startled, but as he recovered, his skin was tingling with anticipation.

'Andraia.' He didn't look away from the window but held out a hand, beckoning her to his side. 'There's a Warp coming.'

Half on her feet, Andraia froze. 'A Warp?'

Savrinor turned, and she saw that he was surprised. 'You're surely not afraid of Warps?'

'I . . . used to be. When I was a child.' She swallowed. 'It's the sheer *power* of them . . .'

He smiled. 'I know. But that's all a part of their grandeur, isn't it? Pure Chaos – created by Yandros's own hand, and sent to us directly from his realm.'

170

That thought reassured Andraia a little, but she was still reluctant to approach the window. 'I've never watched one before,' she said uneasily.

Savrinor's smile became more gentle. 'Then come and stand with me now. It hasn't begun yet; it's still a long way off and it will be some time before it reaches us. We'll watch it together and give thanks to the gods for it.'

Andraia took a first tentative step towards him and, knowing now that he would be able to soothe her fears, Savrinor turned back to the window once more.

And his body and mind locked rigid as he looked down into the courtyard.

He counted his heartbeats. Two, three, four – it was a meaningless exercise but he *had* to hold on to some sense of solidity and reason, had to convince himself that he wasn't dreaming, imagining –

Then, so fast that she jumped, he spun round. 'Andraia, quickly! Come here – hurry, *quickly!*'

She ran, not knowing what he meant or what he had seen. Savrinor caught her arm as she reached him and spun her to the window at his side. His expression was dazed and he said hoarsely, '*Look.*'

She followed the direction of his stunned gaze . . .

CHAPTER XII

Benetan had wanted to wait until well past second moon-rise before they ventured out, but Kaldar was adamant. Thanks to Lotro they knew now where Iselia was and that her cell was not guarded, and the chances of encountering anyone in that area of the cellars were as remote now as they would be in a few hours' time. He refused to delay any longer – and if Benetan wouldn't accompany him, he said, he would go in search of his wife alone. Benetan gave way, though reluctantly, and they doused the fire and left the stairwell, carrying a candle apiece as they moved quietly away from the store-rooms.

The castle's layout had its peculiarities and drawbacks, and to reach the area they wanted they were compelled to go up to the ground floor and along a minor and little-used passage to another flight of steps that spiralled down into the foundations once more. They were in the passage and almost at the second staircase when suddenly Kaldar stopped and raised his head quickly, alertly. '*Benet* . . .' he hissed.

Benetan, who hadn't seen him halt, looked back. A query formed on his lips but Kaldar shook his head, forestalling him. He was breathing very rapidly, Benetan saw, and the candle in his hand shook slightly.

'I sense something,' Kaldar whispered. 'No –' as Benetan looked in alarm along the passage, 'not in here. Outside.' He swung round, a peculiar, animal tension in the movement. 'We passed a window just now –'

Benetan pointed. 'There, a dozen or so paces back.'

'Douse your candle.' Kaldar snuffed his with a swift pass of one hand. 'I want to see what's out there.'

Benetan was baffled but didn't argue; Kaldar's psychic instinct, he knew, was far stronger than his own. In darkness they retraced their steps, until they reached a small slit of an embrasure. A reflection from the moonlit sky was filtering in, etching Kaldar's silhouette with silver-grey as, cautiously, he looked through the glass.

For a few seconds he saw nothing untoward. The courtyard was deserted, and light from the great hall competed with the glow of the moon to give a disturbing cast to the black flagstones. Then a violent blue flash cracked between two of the spires. Kaldar jumped back, swearing in shock, and Benetan felt hot needles prick the skin at the nape of his neck as he realized what the flash had portended.

'There's a Warp on the way.' Not long ago he would have been aware of it before now, he thought; the reactions trained into him here would have sounded the warning – and the fervour – in his bones. Now, though, he felt only an inward shudder of distaste; at least thus far. 'That's what you're sensing.'

'No.' Kaldar was gripping the stone edging of the embrasure, hands clenched like talons. 'No, it isn't the Warp. Something else. Something more dangerous.'

Benetan moved silently up beside him and his eyes narrowed as he, too, stared at the courtyard. He could see nothing – there had been no more discharges of energy and the sky was still quiet, suggesting that the supernatural storm was a good way off yet. Then the second flash came, a livid, searing crimson, and in the momentary glare Kaldar saw that a small door, at one end of the pillared walkway on the opposite side of the castle, was opening. Two figures emerged – and Kaldar's prescient unease flared into violent alarm.

He jerked away from the window, pushing Benetan aside before he could glimpse anything. For a moment or two he couldn't catch his breath; then it returned with a gasp.

'What's the matter with you?' Benetan demanded. 'What in the Seven Hells is out there?'

'Two men.' Kaldar was recovering his composure; he put a hand to his face and shook his head. 'I don't know what happened; just for an instant something about them rang every warning bell my mind possesses. I thought at first one of them was Vordegh, but it isn't; I've encountered him and I remember him all too well. But these are no ordinary magi.' He glanced towards the window again, uneasily. 'Look for yourself.'

Benetan swung round and stared out. For a moment he couldn't see anyone. But then shadows moved under the stoa, emerged from its shelter, and the moonlight touched on two figures.

'*Great g–* ' He bit his tongue ferociously to stop the unthinking oath before he could complete it.

'You know them?' Kaldar's tone was tense.

Benetan stepped back, trying to force down the blinding, impotent fury that was rising in him. 'It's Yandros and his brother.'

Kaldar moved like a scalded cat, back to the embrasure.

'No!' Benetan said. 'If they see you –'

'They won't. And I want to get a clear look at that demon.' Kaldar was trembling, not with fear but with another emotion, and his blue eyes narrowed to fierce slits as he stared out. 'So that's the form he chooses to take, is it? I've always wondered . . .'

'Come away,' Benetan urged him. 'Don't take the risk, Kaldar! They're not mere magi!'

Kaldar drew back at last. The two Chaos lords were heading towards the castle's main doors; he had seen Yandros raise one hand in a careless gesture, and seen the doors start to swing open in response. 'All right,' he said. 'All right. Now I've seen the face of the creature who is ultimately responsible for Iselia's suffering. That's good enough. I'll remember.'

'Remember the other one, too. There's little to choose between them.'

In the gloom Kaldar couldn't see Benetan's face, but he understood. 'Yes,' he said. 'I will.' A pause, then he gripped the other man's arm and shook it lightly. 'Come on. We've got to find Iselia, and I'm not going to let those two abominations deter me.' He glanced at the window again. 'In fact the further underground we are while they're in the castle, the happier I shall feel.'

They re-lit the candles and continued on their way.

Iselia's prison was in a remote and virtually abandoned part of the cellar complex. Benetan hadn't explored this far the previous night, and as he and Kaldar neared their destination he wondered angrily what manner of twisted reasoning had made her captors choose such a location for her. If further punishment was what Vordegh and Croin had had in mind, this would hardly serve to make any difference. Not if her mind was still the shattered wreck to which her interrogation had reduced it.

Kaldar's eagerness was painful to witness as they drew closer to the cell. He knew, now, most of what had taken place in the Marble Hall, but still Benetan had been unable to tell him the whole truth about Iselia. He should have done; should at least have tried to prepare Kaldar for what he would find. But cowardice had got the better of him, and Kaldar still had the final shock to come.

'Benet!' Kaldar's voice broke into his unhappy thoughts. 'You're lagging. Don't waste *time!*'

Twin blades of guilt and misery twisted in Benetan's stomach. Perhaps the candlelight wouldn't be enough to reveal the worst of it; perhaps Iselia's mind would, after all, have found some relief; a return to sanity or a retreat so far beyond it that nothing would matter any more. But he didn't believe the reassurances even as he tried to hold on to them.

He quickened his pace, and caught up with Kaldar as

he reached the last door in the passage. They both stopped. Silence surrounded them like an invisible, oppressive shroud.

'It's locked . . .' Benetan said unsteadily.

Kaldar laid a hand on the solid, ancient wood of the door. It bore neither handle nor latch, only a keyhole. He smiled. 'That's easily dealt with.' A pause, then he heaved a breath and looked at Benetan directly. 'Listen, Benet, before we go in there's something I want to say. I know what your feelings are for Iselia – no, don't start trying to deny it now; Lord Aeoris saw the truth in your mind, and I saw it too. I just want you to know that . . . I'm sorry.'

'Sorry?' Benetan's face was suddenly taut. He hadn't expected this.

'Yes. Sorry that . . . well, that matters didn't work out more happily for you.' Kaldar uttered an odd little laugh. 'It's easy for me to be magnanimous, I suppose, as I'm the one she finally chose to marry. But I *am* sorry – and I'm grateful to you for doing all you could to keep her safe.'

Benetan turned his head sharply away as he thought of Savrinor and what "keeping her safe" had meant at his hands. Another cruel detail that he hadn't had the courage to relate . . .

'Don't, Kaldar.' His voice was strained. 'I don't want your gratitude.' *For I certainly don't deserve it.* 'Open the door. Let's get this *done*.'

Kaldar regarded him uncertainly for a few moments. Then with a shrug that, to Benetan's relief, suggested he had misinterpreted the reaction, he turned to the door. His eyes closed, and Benetan felt the small flare of power like a wave of heat on his face. A harsh light began to glow over the keyhole, then, clearly audible in the quiet, there came an emphatic *click*.

Kaldar went in first. The room was small and bare but for a feather-stuffed pallet pushed into one corner. On the pallet, wrapped in a dark blanket, a shape lay huddled.

'Iselia?' There was such longing, such ardour and such hope in Kaldar's voice that it was all Benetan could do not to turn and run out of the cell. 'Iselia — my love, my sweet one —'

The shape stirred. Benetan heard a sound like laboured breathing. Then a voice, unrecognizable, hardly human, whispered, 'K . . . Kaldar . . . ?'

Kaldar dropped to his knees beside her. One hand held the candle high while the other took hold of the blanket, lifting it back, drawing it aside. The candle-flame started to quiver violently; shadows jerked madly on the walls, and Kaldar made a shocked, incoherent sound. Then the candle dropped from his fingers, fell, bounced across the floor and went out, and Kaldar collapsed over his wife's ruined body, sobbing as if his soul had been torn in half.

'Benet. She wants to see you.'

Benetan looked up quickly from where he sat on the passage floor, and saw Kaldar standing in the doorway of the cell.

Kaldar's face was colourless and his eyes as hard as quartz, but there was an air of fearsome calm about him. He had done all he could for Iselia. When the first shock was over and his self-control had returned, Benetan had watched him as he used what sorcery he could — or dared — to repair the damage inflicted by the magi. For her body, that was little enough; Chaos's violations could only be erased by a greater power than Kaldar possessed. But he had reached to her mind, seen what was there and coaxed her gently back from the abyss, soothing the screaming tide of memories and terrors and helping her to lock the worst of them away where they could no longer rule her. Benetan had been both moved and awed by what he witnessed, and at last, when a new light had begun slowly but surely to creep back into Iselia's stupefied eyes, he had set down the stump of his candle and, very quietly, left the cell.

Now he rose to his feet. Questions crowded, but only one mattered. 'How is she?'

'She's sane.' A muscle in Kaldar's neck worked. 'At least they didn't succeed in taking *that* from her. I was able to . . . lessen her memories. Weaken them.' He frowned. 'I touched her mind. I saw all the things you couldn't tell me. About the monstrosity Vordegh conjured, and what it did. And about Savrinor.' A pause. 'You knew of that, didn't you?'

Benetan couldn't meet his stare. 'I . . . suspected,' he said.

'And you said nothing to me.'

'How *could* I have done?'

'Yes. Yes, well . . . it seems, anyway, that you didn't know all of it.' Kaldar's gaze focused hard on the wall. 'There was a drug. He gave it to her and she used it to make what he forced her to do . . . bearable. She became addicted; when they tortured her she was suffering from withdrawal, and that made her ordeal even worse.' Suddenly his chest heaved. 'I'm going to kill him. Not now, not this time. But when our gods have their full power I'm going to come back, and then Savrinor will *die*.' Challenge flared in his eyes. 'I want first claim on him, Benet. Do you acknowledge that?'

'Yes,' Benetan said whitely. 'I do.'

'Then there's nothing more to be said.' Kaldar gestured towards the door. 'Go in. Talk to her.'

Iselia was still lying in the folds of her blanket, but immediately Benetan saw the change that Kaldar had wrought. Her face was sunken but serene and her eyes regarded him steadily, clearly. She even tried to smile at him.

'Benet.' Something was still terribly wrong with her voice, something Kaldar hadn't been able to heal. He glimpsed her tongue; black, swollen; and on her neck, where the blanket's edge didn't quite reach, the nacreous stigmata left by her unhuman interrogators were still visible.

She extended a hand from under the blanket and he caught hold of it, seeing as he did so that splinters from the block in the Marble Hall were embedded under her fingernails. He tried to find his voice but couldn't, and her faltering smile showed again. 'Benet. There's little time; you and Kaldar must go soon, or you'll risk being discovered. Kaldar has made me a promise. And I want you to do the same.'

The constriction on Benetan's throat broke at last. 'Anything,' he said. '*Anything*.'

She nodded, though it clearly took an effort. 'Kaldar has . . . told me what happened. In the cave, with . . . with Lord Aeoris.' Her blue eyes closed briefly and she seemed to be drawing strength from the god's name. 'I'm so glad, Benet. Glad you're – one of us now. It's what I'd hoped. It's *right*. And because of it, I – I want you to promise to take me with you when you go back to the Marble Hall. Because, you see, I want to be the one who . . . breaks the wand. Who smashes the Gate.' Suddenly her gaze became unnervingly intense, and Benetan saw an abysmal memory lurking and shifting beneath the surface calm. 'It will be my vengeance, Benet,' she said. '*Mine*. And I want it. I want it above anything else in the world.'

Iselia lay in the darkness, listening to the sound of Kaldar's and Benetan's footsteps growing fainter. They hadn't wanted to leave her behind, but she had insisted that to take her with them now was too dangerous. Now and then someone brought food to her, and if she should be found missing before the plan was ready, it would ruin everything.

Besides, she did not want their company. Solitude was better; she had grown used to solitude now and craved it, for only in solitude could she focus her mind on the one thing that mattered: Aeoris, and the cause. Through all her waking hours – and physical and mental pain made it all but impossible for her to sleep – Iselia made silent and ceaseless invocation to the great lord of Order. Not prayers for herself, for she had no care for or interest in her own future, but for the *cause*, and for the ruin of her enemies.

She was comforted by the promise she had extracted from Kaldar and Benetan. To be the one to break the wand, to hurl it into the portal and into the faces of Chaos's demonic masters; it was the single ambition that fuelled the spark of her will to live, and when she had fulfilled that ambition her fate would have no more meaning. After all, what could lie ahead for her that she could want, now? She had no future with Kaldar. Savrinor had seen to that; seen to it that, however skilled her pretences, she would never again look on the prospect of going to a man's bed without her soul recoiling in repugnance. Besides, she had never truly loved her husband, only his cause, which had become her cause. Nor did she love Benetan; the old affinity they had once shared had died long before she came to the castle and he had been simply a means to an end. And the others; Simbrian, Shammana, Nanithe, all Kaldar's friends on Summer Isle, whom she had never met . . . they were just names, and names meant nothing.

Perhaps, Iselia thought, this coldness within her was not real. She knew she was insane, so perhaps if her insanity could be cured then she would regain the human emotions which had been annihilated. But in her heart – or at least in the place where her heart had been – she didn't believe it. And anyway, it didn't matter. The wand. The cause. Aeoris. There was nothing else. She *wanted* nothing else.

The cellars were silent now. She stared into the darkness, smiling a calm smile as, in her mind, she began to pray again.

*   *   *

With Savrinor beside her it was easier, but still Andraia couldn't entirely banish her instinctive fear as the first signs of the coming Warp swept in from the north. High above the castle wall the shape of the moon was beginning to distort as a massive edge of brooding colours moved slowly, inexorably across the sky. Lightning danced silently but incessantly on the visible horizon and, as she watched, a titanic crimson bolt seared across the heavens, hurling the castle into silhouette against blood-red mayhem. The Warp's voice was audible now, a far-off, thin wailing shot through with eldritch harmonies that seemed to oscillate through every nerve she possessed. Soon, she knew, other sounds would augment that harmony; the roar of unearthly thunder, the howl of incredible, unimaginable Chaotic energies, and, in its way most terrifying of all, the high and triumphant hurricane-shriek as the full power of the storm came howling overhead.

She could feel Savrinor's excitement like a physical charge tingling through her shoulders where his fingers gripped them. His eyes were intent on the heavens, his breathing rapid and shallow. Andraia had seen this strange exhilaration in him before, but this time it was no fruit of narcotic or other stimulant; Savrinor's spirit was responding to the Warp's call and to the gods' presence in the mortal world, and was exulting.

When the knock came, it stilled them both. Andraia's first, fleeting thought was one of animosity; at this moment she wanted no interruption, no intrusion. But then she saw Savrinor's face as he turned to look towards the door, sensed the spark of his sudden intuition. She caught hold of his hand –

The door opened, and Andraia's grasp tightened convulsively as Tarod came into the room.

Savrinor looked at the Chaos lord, hardly able to believe what his eyes and mind were telling him. Then, belatedly, the paralysis that had frozen him snapped and he bowed deeply and reverently.

'Good evening, Savrinor.' Tarod closed the door at his back, smiled at the historian, then looked at the girl beside him. 'Andraia . . .'

Andraia could only stare back fixedly, so shocked that words were beyond her. And a sharp pang went through her as she realized that, tonight, Tarod did not quite have the calm, approachable, almost human mien that he had shown to her at their first and second encounters. There was something very alien about him: she felt a sense of devastating power that hovered at the border of perception, and thought – though she couldn't be sure and a part of her didn't *want* to be sure – that the dimensions of the room had contorted in some subtle way, as though his presence was exerting its own effect on the fabric of his immediate surroundings. This was not the lover she remembered but the being who had been on the brink of annihilating the First Magus in the Marble Hall. The mortal mask he had worn for her was gone, and Andraia quailed inwardly at the memory of her own recklessness.

Tarod suspected what was going through her mind, and his smile modulated a little. 'I'm sorry if my unannounced arrival startled you both,' he said. 'But we have some small business to attend to, and would prefer not to arouse more attention than necessary.' For a moment more his keen gaze lingered on Andraia, until, unnerved, she turned her head aside. Then he looked at Savrinor. 'Yandros wishes to see you, Savrinor. He's with Pirane.'

Savrinor felt as though he were locked into a dream and couldn't wake himself. The gods coming to the mortal world; Tarod seeking him out; Yandros himself summoning him . . . the idea was *impossible* to encompass, and he floundered. 'My lord, I – I hardly know what to – that is, to think that –' He bit the flow of words back, appalled by the certainty that he was making a fool of himself, and gained better control of his tongue. 'Yes. Of course. Of *course.*'

Andraia had found the courage to look round again, and now Tarod returned his gaze to her face. 'The corridors are cold,' he said to Savrinor. 'I'd advise you to fetch a coat.'

Savrinor recognized a tacit message in the words and, knowing what he knew, went into the bedchamber. As the door closed behind him Tarod reached out and touched Andraia's jaw, tilting her head up by a small degree.

She found her voice at last. 'I've never had the chance to thank you. For what you and Lord Yandros did . . .' Her gaze shifted sidelong towards the inner room.

'For Savrinor?' Tarod said gently.

She ventured a small smile. 'For both of us, I think. If he had died, I would have been . . . bereft.' She frowned, as if her own words had taken her by surprise.

There was more, Tarod thought, to the bond between Andraia and Savrinor than either of them was prepared to acknowledge; probably, even, than either of them knew. That pleased him, but he didn't comment, simply said, 'You're not the only one who would have been saddened by Savrinor's loss, Andraia. Contrary to some mortals' beliefs, we *do* value those who are true to Chaos.'

Her smile gained a measure of confidence. 'I don't doubt that for a moment, my lord. But I'm still deeply grateful.'

'Then I acknowledge and appreciate your thanks.' Leaning forward, he laid a hand on her shoulder and kissed her brow lightly. As he did so, lightning spat suddenly and violently across the sky outside and the flash lit the room, etching everything in it with a diamond-hard aura. A howling harmony sang through the stones of the castle, and Andraia saw an after-echo of the lightning's energy flicker across Tarod's face and arms. She shivered and, bizarrely, felt a sense of relief when Savrinor emerged from the bedchamber a few moments later. The historian looked quickly, cautiously at them both, and Tarod, aware of his scrutiny, stepped back.

'Goodbye, Andraia,' he said.

She knew that his choice of words was significant, and lowered her gaze. 'Goodbye, my lord.'

Tarod and Savrinor encountered no one on the way to Pirane's apartments. Yandros, Tarod said, wanted as few people as possible to know of this visit – and least of all, he added, did he want First Magus Vordegh alerted to the gods' presence.

'I trust that won't be a vain hope, sir,' Savrinor ventured. 'Whatever my view of the First Magus in . . . other areas, as a sorcerer and psychic I have nothing but unqualified respect for his abilities, and it's hard to believe that he won't sense something afoot.'

'We made sure that he won't. He neglected to look down from the spire while we were visible in the courtyard, and he isn't aware of our presence now.' Tarod glanced obliquely at him. 'You're still afraid of him, aren't you?'

Savrinor took an unnecessarily deep breath. 'Yes, I am.'

'Why?'

'Because . . .' But how could he say it? For all the upsets of the past few days Vordegh was still Chaos's chosen representative, and Savrinor didn't know if he dared voice what he truly thought to one of Chaos's supreme masters. But then, if what Pirane had told him was true, Tarod had very little respect and a great deal less personal liking for Vordegh . . .

He looked up. Tarod was watching him with an interest which wasn't quite as impersonal as he would have expected, and abruptly Savrinor knew he couldn't dissemble. He said, 'Because I can't convince myself that he will continue to heed Lord Yandros's warning.'

'Ah, yes; of course. The executions, and Andraia's friends.'

The historian was startled. 'You know of that, my lord?'

'Yes, we do. And Yandros doesn't find it amusing.' He paused. 'Do you believe that Vordegh's insane?'

The question was so blunt that it caught Savrinor completely unawares. He stared at Tarod in consternation and received a hard smile in return. 'Don't look so chagrined, Savrinor. I'm hardly likely to damn you for committing the crime of honesty.'

Savrinor expelled air from his lungs. 'You may if you choose, my lord, and I don't forget that fact for a single moment. But my honest answer is . . . yes. I think he is.'

Tarod inclined his head, and briefly a malevolent light suffused the green of his eyes. 'Then,' he said, 'you and I are in agreement.'

As he spoke, a colossal howling erupted from the sky far above the castle, and the floor under Savrinor's feet quaked, almost throwing him off balance. Every window in the passage flared into scorching brilliance, and bolts of light lashed between the walls. Thunder bawled seconds later, sounding like a gargantuan voice laughing, and Tarod glanced appreciatively through an embrasure as they passed. The Warp's bands of ominous colour had blotted out all trace of moons and stars now, and the immense wheel of the storm was slowly beginning to turn. A *crack* of displaced air far out over the sea shook the passage a second time, and a web of lightning shattered the sky.

'Another two hours, I think, before it reaches the coast,' Tarod said.

'Two *hours*?' Savrinor was astonished. 'It's already more powerful than any I've witnessed for a good many years!'

'It will be more powerful than any you've witnessed in your lifetime,' Tarod told him. 'If I recall rightly, it's been a century or more since Yandros created a Warp of this magnitude.'

Excitement moved again in the historian's marrow, mingling uncomfortably yet invigoratingly with an over-powering sense of awe. Yet for all his turmoil an inborn reflex alerted his curiosity, and before caution could inter-vene he said, 'I imagine that he must have his reasons?'

He thought instantly that he shouldn't have had the tem-erity to say it, but Tarod showed no anger, only laughed briefly. 'I imagine he has,' he replied. 'But he'll reveal them to you himself. If he chooses to.'

They reached Pirane's chambers, and within a matter of minutes Savrinor was all but convinced that this entire experience must after all be a dream from which he would be forced, reluctantly, to wake before long. Pirane was not in the outer room, but Yandros was reclining on a fur rug before her fire, his cloak dropped carelessly on a chair and a glass of wine in one hand. His outward appearance was entirely human, but Savrinor, hesitantly approaching, felt the subliminal pulse of a vast, silent energy surrounding him. The curtain of the window was drawn back and it seemed that the turning bands of light reflecting from the sky were pulsing too, in perfect rhythm.

Yandros greeted the historian with a smile and indicated that he should join him. Numbly Savrinor obeyed, and the highest lord of Chaos regarded him for a moment. His feline eyes were grey at present; then their colour shifted to a glittering blue.

'Hand him a glass of wine, Tarod,' Yandros said. 'He looks as though he needs it.'

Savrinor cleared his throat. 'I'm . . . well enough, thank you, Lord Yandros.'

'You look anything but, my friend,' Yandros countered. 'And I'm sure you won't disappoint me by failing to live up to your reputation?' Tarod, masking a smile, was hold-ing out a glass, and Savrinor took it bemusedly. Yandros raised his own in a small salute, his look sardonic.

'A toast to the gods followed by one to the First Magus is the usual protocol, I believe, but under the present circumstances neither seems apposite. So let us say, to allegiance and loyalty.' For a moment his irises turned acidic green; light of the same searing colour blasted across the courtyard outside and the Warp shrieked like a damned soul in the distance.

The wine burned Savrinor's throat but he was grateful for it nonetheless. Tarod, taking some for himself, sat down in one of Pirane's low chairs and hooked a leg over its ornately carved arm. 'Savrinor agrees with us,' he said to his brother without any preamble. 'And despite your clear warning, he's by no means sure that he's safe from any further malice on Vordegh's part.'

'Isn't he, now?' Yandros studied the far wall with hooded eyes. 'That *is* interesting . . . and very much in accordance with Pirane's view.' His gaze flicked to the historian's face. 'You've been conducting a discreet investigation for Pirane over the past day or so, Savrinor. What conclusions have you drawn — what *is* the prevailing mood in the castle?'

With an effort Savrinor held the god's steady, golden gaze. 'Fear, sir,' he said. 'Fear and uncertainty. In the wake of yesterday's events —'

'Yes, I know about that.'

Savrinor nodded. 'People feel that if the First Magus will do such a thing once, he's as likely as not to do it a second time, and with as little warning or — or —'

'Justification?'

'That's not something which I feel qualified to judge, Lord Yandros.'

'You are eminently qualified to judge it, and I think you know that as well as I do.' Yandros's eyes were pewter-coloured now. 'Don't equivocate, Savrinor; there's no need for either tact or caution. People are afraid, are they not, that Vordegh's latest depredations won't stop with a mere six random executions. And *you* are afraid that before long yours will be one of the heads chosen as forfeit?'

Savrinor hesitated a bare moment. Then: 'Yes. That's so.'

Tarod sighed irritably. 'So much turmoil, and all for the sake of one man's petty spite. It's *contemptible.*'

Yandros forestalled any further savage comment with an upraised hand. 'I agree. But it also provides us with firm grounds for taking the steps which we've already discussed.'

Savrinor's expression sharpened abruptly and Yandros saw the reaction before he could hide it. The Chaos lord turned to regard him. 'I see the significance of that hasn't escaped our good historian's notice.'

Savrinor blanched. 'Forgive me – I had no intention of making any presumptions; and your business is none of my concern.'

'Nonetheless, the question's in your mind. So you might as well voice it.'

Something in his light tone alerted Savrinor to the fact that it wouldn't be wise to demur, and he touched his tongue to his lips, trying to moisten them. 'I only wondered if this means that . . . you intend to intervene?'

Yandros's expression grew thoughtful and he considered that for a few moments. At last he said, 'Intervene in what, precisely?'

'In the – the matter of the First Magus.'

'Ah.' Another long pause. Then: 'No, Savrinor, I don't. You of all men should know that it isn't our way to interfere in mortal affairs, or to dictate how our servants conduct their lives. However –' as Savrinor's face fell, 'if I issue a warning I expect it to be taken to heart. And if it is not taken to heart, I shall take steps to remedy the matter.' He smiled serenely. 'Simply to safeguard those to whom I have granted my protection.'

Suddenly Savrinor understood the real reason why Yandros had summoned him here. The god had wanted

188

him to confirm the likelihood that Vordegh would seek a second chance to be rid of him – and he realized now that a very great deal had depended on his answer. For a moment a huge emotion welled in the historian at the thought that he was held so highly in Yandros's affections. But then he looked again at the ever-changing eyes and comprehended his mistake. There was nothing personal in this; nothing whatever. It merely suited Yandros at present to use the boon he had granted in the Marble Hall for a new purpose. Yet although Savrinor should perhaps have felt disappointed, he didn't. Yandros wanted grounds for breaking his own rule; he had provided them and thus performed a service for the gods. That, for him, was reward in plenty.

He said: 'I'm sensible of the honour you do me.'

Yandros smiled, knowing that from Savrinor the words were not merely a well-mannered convention. 'You may leave us now.' He might have added a warning to the effect that their conversation was to remain a private matter, but knew it was unnecessary. 'Goodnight, Savrinor. And thank you.'

Stunned by the thanks, Savrinor rose to his feet and bowed to them both in turn. 'My lords.'

'Remember what I said about the Warp,' Tarod added. 'I imagine you'll enjoy the spectacle. And tell Andraia not to be afraid.'

They exchanged a look which had more than a degree of affinity. Savrinor nodded but didn't speak, and closed the door quietly behind him.

When he had gone Yandros glanced towards the inner door, and moments later Pirane emerged. She had suggested that Savrinor would be unnerved enough by a visit from the gods without her presence to add to his anxieties, but she had heard enough of the conversation to know that all had gone as she had hoped. She took a chair near the hearth and Yandros leaned back against her thigh, one hand playing negligently with a strand of elaborate beading on the skirt of her gown. Outside, the Warp was increasing in violence, the lightning almost continuous and the storm's far off wailing now augmented by the first ear-piercing herald of the hurricane scream. Wind buffeted the castle, shaking the window in its frame, but it wasn't yet the full gale that Yandros had in mind. Circumstances, he thought, would dictate the right moment for that.

'Well, my dear Pirane.' He looked round at the magus and smiled lazily. 'Savrinor has confirmed your doubts, and convinced me that he's not entirely safe from the threat of Vordegh's reprisal.' He took a sip from his glass. 'Normally, of course, whom Vordegh does or doesn't choose to ruin is entirely a matter for his own judgement. But if he goes against my wishes, and persists even when those wishes have been made clear, I am less tolerant.' His eyes burned black, reflecting a violent new charge of power across the heavens. 'I've instructed Vordegh to apply his energies to the matter of the heretics rather than to personal concerns, and I expect to be obeyed. So, to ensure that I *am* obeyed, I think your request for a small reminder of his duty is appropriate.'

Pirane inclined her head. 'Thank you, my lord.'

The formality of her tone amused Yandros but he wasn't in the mood to show it. 'How Vordegh responds to the reminder is for him to decide,' he continued, 'as is any move you and the other magi might contemplate as a result. My only concern is with the present hiatus. It's delaying the resolution of the heretic question, and I don't want that state of affairs to continue. I want Order's ambitions snuffed out. So I will direct a strong hint, shall we say, to the right quarter, and we'll see what develops.'

He set his glass down and stood up with a fluent, economical movement. A cacophony of noise dinned through the room as he reached the window, and the monstrous wheel of the Warp shuddered, twisting the sky. The east spire was clearly visible, a black finger stark against the storm's mad backdrop, and at the summit, the ever-present light burned coldly.

Yandros smiled; then his eyes lost their focus and turned molten silver. Pirane felt a shock of power, and above Yandros's heart a seven-rayed star flared into life, shimmered briefly then vanished.

And in the chilly austerity of the spire's summit room, a thread of thought began to take form in the First Magus's mind.

CHAPTER XIII

The approaching Warp had driven any thought of sleep from the minds and bodies of the Chaos riders. For the experienced men the storm's advent was like a virus infecting their blood as the psychic link forged in them over the years awoke; and even for the newer recruits, those in whom the link hadn't yet formed, the prevailing mood was fiercely contagious. Tension grew rife as the storm increased in intensity and the distant howling began to reverberate through every stone of the castle, and Averel, expecting no order from the magi under the present circumstances, knew that he would be hard-pressed to maintain calm in the ranks. The Warp was calling, demanding a response, and with no outlet for the men's mounting fervour, tempers were beginning to fray as frustration set in.

In the past there had been a simple answer to this problem; among the female servants competition for a Chaos rider's attentions was keen, and more girls could usually be found among the newest of the candidates abducted and brought to the castle in the riders' regular gleanings to make up any shortfall. Now, though, servants were in scant supply, there had been no gleanings since the First Magus's inauguration – and in any case, with feelings running high and bitter after the wanton execution of a junior sergeant's woman, that form of diversion would not have been welcomed by all. So Averel fell back on the methods he knew best, and as the grim aurora in the sky intensified, with the storm's wail now high and shrill on the back of the battering wind, he gave the order for a muster, full regalia, with the promise of a punishment detail for any man who failed to pass inspection. It was little enough to occupy and distract the riders, but it would serve to keep frictions under control until the Warp had passed its climax and swept on southward.

The muster was almost complete when there was a sudden scuffling commotion outside the door of the armoury where the men were gathering, and the duty-sentry rushed in. The sentry was agitated, sweating with something more than the Warp's effect; he looked urgently round for Averel, found him and ran to him.

'Sergeant – I mean, Captain!' Old habits hadn't yet been entirely shaken off. 'Sir, the magi – there's word from –'

'Thank you, sentry, but I'll speak to Captain Averel myself.' Pirane's voice cut succinctly across the garbled message, and the riders snapped to attention as the magus walked in. Pirane noted the response with detached approval, then addressed Averel. 'A private word with you, if you please, Captain. The passage outside will suffice.'

'Madam.' Averel saluted then nodded at the sentry. 'Back to your post.'

The man hurried away and, with a glance over his shoulder warning the riders not to move until he returned to give them permission, Averel followed Pirane outside, closing the door behind them.

'Captain.' In the dimly-lit passage Pirane looked fearsome; she was wearing black tonight, a low-cut gown with a high collar that startlingly accentuated her silver skin. 'I am obliged to tell you that you and your men are about to be ordered out on sortie.'

For a moment's Averel's eyes lit with relief: then he took closer account of Pirane's expression, and her choice of words, and the light abruptly faded. 'Yes, madam,' he said uneasily.

Pirane's lips curved drily. Peasant he might be, but Averel was no fool. 'I'm afraid,' she went on, 'that you may not be entirely happy with what is expected of you tonight;

with the situation as it is, I and the great majority of my colleagues would certainly not have issued the order for an expedition of this kind. However, we have had no say in the matter.' A thunderbolt crashed across the sky above the courtyard and light exploded through a window at the far end of the passage, framing her briefly in a glaring green aura. 'It is a direct command from the First Magus.'

Averel stared at her and momentarily forgot protocol. 'The First Magus? But I thought –'

'You thought he was in the east spire and intending to stay there. So did we all, Captain.' The rancour in Pirane's voice shocked Averel, as did the fact that she was taking no pains to hide her disgust. For a moment it gave the illusion that they were equals, and that confounded him.

'Lord Vordegh demands a full complement,' Pirane said. 'And you are to take the sacrament.'

Averel knew what that meant. They would have no need of their horses tonight; instead, every man would be given the hallucinogenic draught that enabled them to use – and control – their other mounts; the dark, baleful creations of Chaos which, without the drug, could strip an unprotected human mind of its sanity.

He opened his mouth to speak, but at that moment a gargantuan discharge of energy directly overhead smashed all other sound into oblivion. The castle seemed to rock to its foundations, and as the colossal noise died away Averel's ears and mind rang with the aching aftermath.

Pirane's cool eyes met his. 'The Warp is intensifying, Captain, and I think it won't be long before it reaches its full strength. I would strongly advise you not to keep the First Magus waiting.'

Her words brought Averel forcibly to earth and he pulled his mind back onto an even keel. 'Your pardon, Lady Magus. With your permission, I'll ready the men.' He took a step back, then suddenly paused. 'Although if –'

'If?'

Averel swallowed. 'I have no right to ask this, I know, madam, but . . . do you know what's to be expected of us?'

Pirane had anticipated this question, and she waited a few seconds before answering, deliberately giving the impression of hesitancy. At last she spoke.

'Yes, Captain Averel, I do know; and I might as well tell you now, for you'll find it out for yourself soon enough. Lord Vordegh has decided that it is time for the question of the heretics to be resolved once and for all. He believes that the location of their stronghold must be known to sympathizers, but that, as his first edicts failed to uncover them, stronger measures are now needed. The riders will be the instruments of those measures.' She paused. 'The First Magus will personally give you explicit instructions. Your task, in essence, will be to carry out a series of punitive strikes in districts where Lord Vordegh believes information about the heretics has been withheld. These strikes will in effect be a lesson to the populace, to teach them the folly of disobedience to the First Magus's will. You will use any and every means at your disposal to drive the lesson home – and you are to grant no quarter, under any circumstances, to any living soul.'

She had the satisfaction of seeing the expression on Averel's face before, with a nod of aloof farewell, she turned and walked away. His reaction was what she had hoped it would be. And silently, with a hard edge of satisfaction, Pirane gave thanks to Yandros.

'I'm all *right*,' Benetan insisted. His teeth were clenched hard together, distorting his voice, and he pressed his forehead to the stairwell's cold rock wall, fists pushing against the stone as though he wanted to drive a hole through its solidity. 'It'll pass; it'll *pass*. I'm just *hot*.'

Hot, Kaldar thought, was a grotesque understatement, for Benetan's skin was slick with sweat, his hair soaked and his clothes clinging wetly to his body. He had torn off his fur coat and hurled it away; now his shirt hung loose and unfastened and his breath came stertorously, as though there wasn't enough air to pull into his throat. But there was air, and it was bitterly cold, and Kaldar, shivering and watching, knew that Benetan's malaise was no physical illness but something far more hazardous.

'Benet.' He moved towards the other man, reached out and then thought better of it. One touch, even something as innocuous as a hand on his shoulder, and Benetan might lose the control he was struggling to maintain. 'Try to keep calm. Try to fight it. I know it's hard, but –'

'You don't know *anything!*' Benetan interrupted ferociously. On the heels of his words a devastating howl echoed suddenly and violently through the stack, and Kaldar bit his tongue in shock. As the noise subsided he took a grip on his frayed nerves, wishing to Aeoris that they could be anywhere but in this place, where the hollow of the stairwell created an echo chamber that magnified the Warp's noise to horrific proportions. Telling himself he should be thankful that at least they couldn't see the monstrous storm, he said, 'Can't we get away from here? There'll be no one in the cellars with this going on – and it might help if the sound were muffled.'

Benetan shook his head vehemently. 'It wouldn't. *Nothing* will help, unless you're prepared to knock me unconscious and make sure I stay that way until it passes.' Suddenly he pushed himself away from the wall, leaving three damp prints where his face and hands had been pressing. 'Gods, I didn't imagine it would *be* like this, not now! I thought I was *cleansed!*'

'You can't expect to wipe out the effects of twelve years in a few days,' Kaldar reasoned. Another howl sang through the well, accompanied by a shrilling counterpoint at a shockingly high pitch, and his shoulders hunched involuntarily as though to ward off a blow. 'And this one's powerful,' he added, raising his voice to be heard above the yelling echoes. 'More powerful than any we've seen before, I'd say.'

'*Don't tell me that; I don't want to know it!*' But Benetan already knew it, for the Warp was in his marrow and every instinct screamed at him to answer in the way he had answered for twelve years past. He was the Chaos riders' leader and their ways were ingrained in him; he knew better than any and all of them the sheer, atavistic power of the storm's call, for he had been one with the Warps and they had left their mark. Kaldar was right; though he now loathed Chaos and all it stood for, such an influence couldn't be thrown aside as he had thrown aside his coat when the sweating began. And if it didn't end soon, if it didn't pass, he feared that his resistance would crack.

Kaldar was moving back, uncomfortably aware that nothing he said or did was helping matters, when abruptly a new sound mingled with the background tumult of the Warp. It came from somewhere within the castle, at a level not far above their heads – a reverberating clatter, like some large metal object falling or being thrown. And following it, booming down into the stairwell and setting up an ugly vibration in the bones of his ears, the sound of something pounding on iron.

Two spots of livid colour flared high on Benetan's cheeks and his eyes widened. 'Gods, no . . .'

Kaldar had been staring upwards; now his head snapped round in alarm. 'What is it, what's happening?'

Benetan was having difficulty breathing. 'They've taken the sacrament,' he whispered. 'It's a drug – a hallucinogen; it twists the mind and puts you in touch with Chaos . . .'

'Who have taken it? The riders?'

A nod. 'It means they're not using the horses tonight. That noise –' Unconsciously he had counted the boomings; seven, there had been seven. 'There's an iron door at one end of the stables; the riders' leader takes down the bar and knocks seven times, and it opens the way for the other creatures . . .' And they were coming. He could sense them, *feel* them. *Monstrous things of iron and dark, quartz hooves shimmering, cold silver glittering in their eyes, the shadows of great wings rising from their backs . . . Breath like the touch of fire on his face, manes writhing like snakes under his hands; and he could bend them to his will, ride them, direct them, control them . . .*

'I can't keep it at bay . . .' Panic suffused his voice. 'I can't, Kaldar, I'm not strong enough! I've got to –' A convulsion went through him. 'Got to . . . see. At least *see –*'

'Benet!' But Kaldar's shout, and his attempt to block the way out of the stairwell, came too late. Benetan was past him, and in his wake the door into the cellars jolted back on its hinges, smacking Kaldar backwards as he tried to follow. He sprawled, and by the time he had regained his feet and recovered from the momentary dizziness, Benetan was gone.

'*Aeoris!*' It wasn't an imprecation but a plea for help and strength, and Kaldar propelled himself across the floor to where their meagre belongings were stacked against the wall. From his own pack he pulled out a short length of fine rope, once part of a much longer piece that had frayed and broken. It wasn't ideal, but in the absence of a proper binding-cord it would have to do, and quickly he tied three knots in the rope, one at each end and one in the middle. Then he ran out into the cellars and away in pursuit of Benetan.

Benetan had reached the east wing before Kaldar caught up with him. By sheer chance, which later made Kaldar sweat whenever he thought about it, neither had encountered anyone, and the small anteroom off a minor corridor where Kaldar finally cornered his quarry was empty of furnishings, suggesting that they were unlikely to be disturbed.

Benetan was at the room's one window. The sky outside was now a mayhem of appalling colours, and lightning ripped across its face in a ceaseless mesh of silver and crimson and blue as the Warp came screaming towards the coast. Kaldar's own innate terrors were eclipsed by the more urgent fear for both their lives if they were discovered, and against the unholy din he yelled, 'Benet! Come away – for all our gods' sakes, *come away!*'

In the raging lightning Benetan was visible. He had clung to enough sense to be pressed against the wall and would not be seen from the courtyard, but he ignored Kaldar's exhortation. His eyes were wild and hungry and he was clawing at the wall's stonework as though trying to anchor himself to reality. Then, as he too looked towards the window, Kaldar saw what was taking place outside.

He swore with shock and was across the room at a run, catching hold of Benetan's arm and spinning him round.

'Benet, listen to me!' He jerked Benetan's wrist up – Benetan didn't seem to have the will to oppose him – and twisted the knotted rope round it several times, catching the other end tightly in his free hand. With the storm's insanity drumming against his senses he didn't know if he could summon the power he needed, but he hurled all his mental strength into the effort. Something shifted in his mind, faltered, shifted again – then to his intense relief he felt a tingling charge go through him, into his arm and hand, into the rope, imbuing it with a calming, soothing force. Benetan gasped as he felt it; his arm tensed, fist clenching, and for a moment Kaldar feared he would break free. But the sorcery was working, and suddenly the uncontrollable impulse which had pulled Benetan towards the courtyard began to lose its hold. He shut his eyes, and Kaldar could see that reason was returning to him, and with it self-control.

'Benet!' he said. 'Benet, are you all right?'

Benetan's chest heaved and he expelled air violently from his lungs. Then he nodded, his face stark as black light edged with silver shattered through the room. 'I nearly . . .' He swallowed and didn't finish, aware that Kaldar knew very well what he had nearly done. 'It was the sound of it, that shriek . . . it was so hard to resist; and then when I realized what the riders were doing –' He shook his head forcefully as though to clear it, then raised his arm and looked at the cord. 'How did you stop me?'

'It's a basic method. Leave the cord where it is; it'll help protect your mind.' Kaldar looked towards the window and a shudder went through him. 'Seven Hells, I never thought to see this . . .'

Knowing that now he could dare to look without the poison infecting him again, Benetan turned. Against the psychotic sky the castle walls and spires seemed to be twisting into tortuous, impossible contours, as though the world were breaking free of its spatial shackles. The courtyard was a mad arena of milling shapes, and the black and silver figures of men were flowing and merging with something yet darker; malignant, winged forms with eyes that blazed in the storm's furious glare. And blending with the Warp's cacophony Kaldar could hear a screaming, unhuman chorus, savage and triumphant – the voices of the Chaos creatures, hungering to be unleashed.

The steps of the main doorway were visible, though the Warp had turned them to flowing confusion and the great doors behind them were surrounded by a livid and furiously agitating aura. Amid the havoc, a solitary figure was positioned before the doors. Lightning sparked in his dark hair and earthed through his body to scatter away across the courtyard, but he stood unmoving, impassive, watching the scene as calmly as if he were one of Chaos's own gods presiding over their realm. Every fibre of the man radiated cold pleasure, and ugly memories swelled in Kaldar's mind as he recognized Vordegh.

The First Magus raised one hand. It was a slight, almost negligent gesture, but it was answered by a renewed chorus from the monstrous creatures and their riders. A crimson bolt sheared from the summit of the north spire, struck the west spire and ricocheted upwards to join with the howling sky; an instant later the voice of the Warp rose higher, louder, swelling to a mind-splitting roar – and from a buffeting gale the wind suddenly erupted into hurricane force as the full grandeur of the storm came shrieking overhead. Benetan, knowing what to expect, looked quickly in the direction of the castle gates and was in time to see them begin to swing open. Then in the midst of the seething mass of riders and their mounts one masked figure punched his arm skywards. The old affinity stabbed Benetan anew, and hard, as he saw the familiar signal, and he fought against a sudden constriction in his throat, knowing what would follow. Averel – it must be Averel – was shouting at his men, though his voice was inaudible in the storm's uproar. Then the sky tore apart in a white flash; the lightning struck Averel's hand, turning the silver talons of his gauntlet to five tiny infernos, and the tide of the Chaos riders surged towards the gates. Benetan saw the great arch light up suddenly and violently in a flare of whirling colours, as though for one incredible moment the entire force of the Warp was earthing, channelling through it. Beyond the arch he had one brief glimpse of pandemonium – then everything was blotted out by a blinding, deafening explosion of light and noise as the riders erupted from the castle.

For what seemed an age yet must in reality have been only seconds, Benetan was in limbo, every sense obliterated and his mind numb. Then, slowly, the world crawled back and he found himself leaning against the wall for support, his ears ringing and an afterglare dancing giddyingly before his eyes. The world was eerily quiet – either that or the supernatural blast had deafened him – and though lightning still flickered through the room it was sporadic now. He raised his head, saw Kaldar close by; he too seemed to be recovering and they exchanged pallid smiles. Then Kaldar moved back to the window and, cautiously testing his balance, Benetan joined him. The fury of the Warp had gone. The vast bands of colour still marched across the heavens, shot through with intermittent, shivering cross-currents of energy, but there were no more thunderbolts and no more great clamour; only the familiar shrill, piercing shriek like the voice of something unhuman and invisible running high and fast in the sky. The storm had launched the Chaos riders on their way, and they had taken its power with them.

But the courtyard wasn't entirely deserted. Vordegh still stood motionless on the steps, his hair stirring in the wind and his cloak of shadows shifting around him. Kaldar, watching, became aware of the same psychic disquiet that he had felt when Yandros and his brother appeared, but this time with a difference. Again he sensed great evil; but the First Magus's evil had a *human* dimension, for Kaldar perceived a cruelty in him which, whilst it was nothing compared to the pitiless savagery that Yandros and his brothers could inflict if they chose to, was driven and motivated by a sadistic undercurrent that simply didn't exist in the Chaos lords' nature.

He turned away at last and said quietly, 'Whatever he's done tonight, he's well contented with it.' Then he paused, looking keenly at Benetan. 'It's hard to believe you were a part of that for so many years.'

Benetan's eyes became introverted, and when Kaldar saw that he wasn't going to answer he continued, 'How long will the riders be gone, do you think?'

A shrug. 'It's impossible to predict. Anything from a few hours to a few days, depending on the nature of the sortie. It could simply be a gleaning, in which case they'll return before dawn. But I think it's more than that.'

'Why?'

'The strength of the Warp, to begin with. Then the First Magus's presence; I've never known him to watch the riders' departure in person before. And the most significant factor of all is Yandros's visit. This is no regular assignment; there's something else behind it.'

Kaldar was continuing to watch the courtyard. 'If that's true, then they could be away for some time. That could make our task a great deal easier.' He clasped his own upper arms, his posture restive. 'I'll need time to contact Simbrian and ask for whatever help he and Lord Aeoris can give us, and for all we know those demons of Chaos might still be in the castle; so tonight's out of the question. But tomorrow night's another matter. Yandros will be gone by then, and if the riders are still away we couldn't ask for a better opportunity. The one thing we *must* be sure of is the First Magus's whereabouts.'

Vordegh was still on the steps, and no one else had emerged from the castle. Kaldar swung round. 'Damn him, why does he just *stand* there? We need to know where he intends to go; into the castle or back to the spire!'

Benetan suddenly tensed. 'Wait — he's leaving.'

Kaldar darted back to the window and was in time to see Vordegh turn, his shadow-retinue flowing with him, and begin to move. For one wrenching moment he gave the impression that he was about to withdraw through the main doors and into the castle's main wing . . . but then he started down the steps towards them.

'*Back!*' Benetan pushed Kaldar aside and, pressed against the wall, they watched as the First Magus reached the courtyard and glided away, vanishing from their view in the direction of the east spire.

Kaldar expelled breath and tension together. 'Thank Aeoris . . .'

'Come on.' Benetan's mind was working fast, thinking over what Kaldar had said moments earlier and, with the training instilled in him, planning out the bones of a strategy. 'We'd better get back to the stairwell. If we're to make our move tomorrow, we should get a few hours' sleep while we can.'

Kaldar glanced at him. 'Let's hope it won't be the last sleep of our lives.'

'Don't think about it,' Benetan said. 'Not if you want to keep your nerve — and your sanity.'

He headed for the door.

From a window of the unlit council hall Pirane watched Vordegh walk towards the east spire. Her expression was enigmatic, and only when the First Magus had at last disappeared did she turn round.

Amid patterns of light and shadow created by the diminishing Warp, Croin was visible where he sat at the table on its raised dais. Pirane stalked across the hall to join him, the hem of her gown making an odd hissing noise, and sank gracefully onto one of the uncushioned chairs so favoured by the First Magus.

'His instructions to Captain Averel were very precise,' she said. 'And Averel did not like them.'

'Excellent.' Croin's seven-fingered hands were interlaced and he was studying them. Then he smiled. 'I wonder how much of the stratagem was of Vordegh's devising, and how much we owe to Lord Yandros?'

'Oh, it was all Vordegh's own,' Pirane told him. 'Lord Yandros did nothing more than place the idea of a sortie in his mind and provide the Warp for emphasis. As he said, he has no intention of intervening directly.'

'Of course.' Croin nodded, the smile still hovering. 'But even for that small boon, we owe the gods a great debt. I've little doubt that once this mission has been carried out, the Chaos riders will be thoroughly disaffected with the First Magus, and ready to side with anyone who opposes him. And the great majority of our colleagues, I think, will agree with our view that what the riders have been ordered to do is nothing more than a vindictive, vicious and futile exercise that will serve only to turn the populace against us unless something is done to remedy the matter.'

'I'll ensure that the details are known throughout the castle by noon,' Pirane said. 'And I think in the wake of that we can safely make our own attitude known to our colleagues, don't you?'

'I do. In fact —' Then Croin broke off as someone knocked on the council hall door. The two magi exchanged a speculative glance, then Croin said briskly, 'Enter.'

Savrinor came in. In the corridor behind him Pirane glimpsed several other figures, but before she could note any detail Savrinor had closed the door and was approaching the dais. He bowed to them both, then said, 'Madam — my lord. Forgive the intrusion, but something has happened which I think should be brought to your attention.'

Croin, who was fully aware of Savrinor's part in their scheme, looked at the historian with quickening interest, and Pirane said, 'What is it?'

'One of the junior Chaos riders has just been found in the stable,' Savrinor told them. 'He should have ridden out with the sortie, but it seems that his nerve broke when he heard what was to be required of him. He was discovered by one of the grooms; the groom informed a steward, and the steward, fortuitously,' he smiled thinly, 'reported the matter to me.'

'I see.' Pirane's eyes gleamed. 'Where is the rider now?'

'Outside, madam, with two of the servants to guard him. He's not lucid; he witnessed the riders' departure without the protection of the sacrament and the experience has unhinged him. But I thought you might wish to interview him nonetheless.'

Pirane smiled. 'You thought rightly, Savrinor. And I'm

sure Magus Croin can salvage the young man's wits for long enough to serve our purpose.'

Croin nodded assent and gestured towards the doors. 'Bring him to us, Master Savrinor.'

The errant rider was half dragged and half carried in by the two servants, who at a nod from Savrinor deposited him on a wooden settle and departed. A blond-haired youth, still in his teens, with an almost childlike face and body on which the black and silver uniform looked disturbingly out of place. He had, it appeared, attempted to resist capture; a livid bruise was spreading across his forehead where someone had stunned him into submission, and his eyes – an oddly light green – were blank with sickness and shock. He lay passive, helpless, seemingly incapable of comprehending where he was or what was happening to him.

Savrinor's pale eyes focused on the slumped figure. 'He's a very new recruit, I understand.'

'Yes.' Pirane, too, was studying the rider dispassionately. 'I recall him; he was brought to the castle in the gleaning for the First Magus's inauguration. So this would have been his first sortie.' She smiled. 'I can quite see why his courage failed him.'

Croin sat down at one end of the settle and examined the unresisting youth with deft, practised hands. 'No serious physical damage,' he said, 'but his mind . . .' His fingers splayed out across the rider's brow and he closed his eyes for a few moments. 'Mmm. I suspect he won't be entirely sane even when he does recover from the shock. Unless the memories of what he witnessed are entirely expunged, this will leave serious psychic scars. He's been very foolish; if he'd had the sense to take the sacrament he could have saved himself a great deal of trouble.'

'And would have been of no value to us,' Pirane pointed out gently.

Croin's smile was dry. 'Quite. Every storm has its rainbow, it seems.'

The boy was trying now to focus on the faces around him, but with little success. There was, Savrinor thought, something pathetic about his bewilderment, and he was sharply and unexpectedly reminded of the adolescent Benetan when he had first been brought to the castle, an unwilling – no; terrified was a more accurate word – recruit. For a moment, it made him feel just a little uncomfortable.

Then the boy started to cry like the child he was. Savrinor turned away, and Croin stood up.

'The First Magus, of course, would expect us to execute him immediately and without leave of appeal,' he said. 'And doubtless six others into the bargain. But I see no necessity for that; and what the First Magus doesn't know need not concern him.' He glanced cannily at Pirane. 'This could provide the catalyst we need.'

Pirane nodded. 'Especially if the boy's wits can be restored sufficiently for him to tell his sorry tale publicly and in person.' Her mouth pursed speculatively. 'And perhaps we might find ways to emphasize his misfortune a little.'

Croin took her meaning, as, he noted, did Savrinor. 'Well, he'll make no sense in his present condition,' he said. 'But a modicum of work on his mind, perhaps with a few embellishments, should reap a satisfactory harvest, albeit a brief one. And when we have that, I suggest we call our fellow magi to this hall to see and hear the result for themselves.' He glanced at the historian. 'Master Savrinor, I'm sure I don't need to stress the need for discretion, and so I'd appreciate it if you would go personally to my chambers and fetch my bag. Speak to my personal servant; he can be trusted and he'll know what to give you.'

Savrinor looked again at the hapless young rider. It occurred to him that in some ways it might be kinder to execute the boy and have done with it, but he dismissed the thought. Necessity created its own rules, and another life counted for nothing when compared to the good that this night's work could achieve. Besides, sentiment had never been one of his weaknesses. 'Of course, my lord,' he said, and left the hall.

'Two or three days at most,' Yandros said peaceably, 'and the problem will be resolved to everyone's satisfaction.' He rested his elbows on the balustrade of the high gallery he had created, which bore a passing resemblance to the gallery in the castle's great hall, his eyes watching and appreciating the revelries going on below. 'With one notable exception, of course.'

Tarod, who was sitting on the rail and leaning against an ornately carved pillar, followed the progress of a creature made of fire which was weaving an intricate pattern through the seething, colourful throng. Feathers of flame danced above it; other beings sprang to catch them and throw them to one another, and laughter echoed to the vast mirror of the ceiling. Dawn would be breaking on the Star Peninsula, he reflected; and if all had gone as Pirane hoped, then the magi's resolve should by now be firmly set.

'Few tears will be shed in Vordegh's direction when the furore is finally over,' he said.

'Quite.' Yandros smiled wolfishly. 'His funeral should be an interesting affair. I might be tempted to attend and take part in the celebrations.' Pastel smoke was coiling over the scene below them now, carrying with it a sharp, green, aphrodisiac scent. This festivity, like so many that took place in the Chaos realm, had no especial cause or purpose; it had simply begun by sheer chance shortly after Yandros and Tarod returned from the castle. But there seemed to be a particular savour to this gathering; their five brothers were already somewhere in the midst of the revellers and in a minute or two, Yandros decided, he would join them and see what pleasures were to be enjoyed in the throng.

'I think,' he continued, 'that we might leave the magi

entirely to their own devices and set our interest in them aside until this is over. Once a new First Magus is installed we can pick up the threads again; and we'll have plenty to occupy us when that happens, for the matter of Order's stirrings will then take precedence.' He straightened from the rail, stretched his arms. 'In the meantime, though, I suspect we're all a little over-sated with human squabbles and would enjoy a respite.'

A tendril of the pastel smoke had curled over the balustrade now and was drifting languidly along the rail towards them. It shimmered faintly, and something about the shapes it was forming was redolent of fragile faces, slender bodies. Yandros's nostrils flared appreciatively as he caught the scent of it, and he reached out, beckoning. The smoke curled back on itself and glided along his arm, across his shoulder, flowing down the length of his body. The impression of a face grew stronger; vibrant and eerily lovely, pale hair tangling over golden skin, vast, alluring eyes with an unearthly, faraway glow in their depths . . . The succubus slipped free from the shimmering smoke and her arms reached out; Yandros's fingers closed over one pale, delicate hand, staying the creature but implying a promise, and over the bowed head he met Tarod's eyes.

'Let the magi resolve this as they've planned. We need do nothing more, and it will be refreshing to be able to ignore the mortal world for a while. There are other diversions in life, after all, and we've neglected many of them lately.'

A second succubus was forming as the smoke coiled further along the gallery; a lissome shape stretched on the balustrade. There was a sound, very soft yet audible above the tide of festivity below; a gentle *hush* of breathing. Translucent fingers moved, touched Tarod's hair and mouth. He smiled.

'Yes,' he said. 'I think we have.'

CHAPTER XIV

'*The night is silent, but the day brings a flash of lightning. The night is silent, but the day brings a flash of lightning. Hear me and answer. Hear me, Simbrian, and answer!*'

Kaldar repeated the words over and again with feverish urgency, unaware of the shivers that racked him as the bitter salt wind raked across his body. It was hard to concentrate here, with the sea roaring only yards away and the sky racing with tatters of cloud that every few moments hurled squalls against his hunched back; and three times now the fire had almost gone out. But the beach was the only safe place for this work, and he persevered, knowing that he had to break through.

In the lee of the cliff where the vertiginous tower of the castle stack began, Benetan kept uneasy watch on the cave and the stairs. It was only a little after dawn and the chances of anyone venturing down from the castle in this weather were very remote, but caution and frayed nerves kept him alert. After all, he had encountered Savrinor here once, and on a similar day to this. And for all Kaldar's assurances, he believed that it would take only one hint of untoward sorcery to bring someone sniffing on the magi's behalf.

Kaldar gasped suddenly, the sound only just audible above the wind's ramping, and Benetan swung round. Incense-laden smoke ripped away to mingle with spray and he saw Kaldar crouched tautly over the smouldering fire.

'*Simbrian!*' Excitement made Kaldar's tone harsh. '*It's Kaldar!*'

He had forged the link, and quickly Benetan crossed the

shingle to join him. Though he didn't have the psychic insight — or the incense's effect — to enable him to see what Kaldar was seeing, still it seemed to him that the vague contours of a face were forming in the smoke as Simbrian reached from the White Isle to lock his mind with Kaldar's.

'It will be tonight.' Kaldar spoke the words aloud to help their focus, at the same time projecting them mentally across the miles. 'Around first moonset — we can't be more precise. But the Chaos riders are away and Vordegh is still in the spire. There'll be no better chance. We must have all the strength you can lend us!' A long pause then; Simbrian was replying and, unable to know what was passing between them, Benetan paced restlessly back to the cave mouth. A feeling was moving in him which he didn't want to acknowledge yet couldn't deny. He was frightened. As frightened as he had been as a child when the Warps came; as frightened as on the night the Chaos riders had swept through his village and carried him away to the castle. Not because of the practical hazards of their mission, for in his own years with the riders he had faced far greater ordeals and far more spectacular dangers, with an equally slender chance of survival. And whereas in the past he had trusted in the protection of Chaos, tonight he could have faith, justifiably, in the protection of Order, for Aeoris's strength was growing and his shielding influence would be a powerful weapon even here. But for all that, for all it meant and could achieve, the fear was lodged hard and deep in him and wouldn't be shifted. And its cause, its core, was the knowledge that, tonight, he was finally going to break the last threads of the past, and hurl his defiance and his hatred directly in the faces of the gods he had worshipped all his life.

Kaldar was speaking again, but in a whisper that the wind snatched away before Benetan could make out the words. His voice was eager, tense; there were several more exchanges, then at last Kaldar rocked back, shaking his head and running his hands through his hair as though to ground himself back in the real world. The telepathic communication was over, Simbrian was gone.

'Gods . . .' Kaldar couldn't quite co-ordinate his limbs as Benetan helped him to his feet. 'That was more difficult than I'd anticipated. The distractions of this weather . . .' He shook his head again. 'I'm soaked through and half frozen.'

Benetan trod the sullen remnants of the fire out and scattered them to leave no trace that the rising tide wouldn't carry away. 'Is all well on the White Isle?'

'Yes. Though Simbrian told me that he's had reports of new atrocities in the south.' He glanced sidelong, uneasily. 'The Chaos riders are indulging in indiscriminate slaughter – a warning, they call it, to anyone who might be withholding information about us. They're showing no scruples about the methods they use, Simbrian says, and neither he nor Lord Aeoris can do anything to help those who fall foul of them. It's turning uglier, Benet.'

Benetan stared at the sea. 'And turning more people against the magi.'

His tone was coldly indifferent and Kaldar was shocked. 'How can you be so sanguine?' he demanded angrily. 'You're talking as if you were still one of them!'

A day or two ago Benetan would have flared up at that; now, he only shrugged. 'If it sounds that way, it's for a good reason. I *have* to be sanguine, Kaldar. We both have to be, if we want to survive – and if we want our plan to work.' He turned to face the sea, hunching his shoulders defensively. 'What would it achieve if Lord Aeoris tried to stop what the riders are doing? Some lives might be saved, but how long would the respite last? To fight back now would be to expose our hand to Chaos. Lord Aeoris can't afford to do that. *We* have to succeed in our task first, or our entire cause will end in ashes.'

'Simbrian agrees with you.' Kaldar sounded resentful. 'But –'

'But *nothing*. It's the only option that makes sense – and don't harbour the idea that I like it any more than you do, because I don't.' Benetan turned to face him again. 'Unlike you, though, I know the difference between a sound strategy and a noble but ultimately suicidal gesture.'

That, he saw, stung; for in his heart Kaldar knew that what he was saying – and what Simbrian had said – was true. He looked away, his eyes haunted, and Benetan relented.

'Come on.' He moved to Kaldar and laid a hand on his shoulder. 'Brooding achieves nothing, either. There's no point staying here any longer than we have to; let's get back to the cellars.' He paused. 'Will they do what they can to help us tonight?'

Kaldar nodded. It was a tacit surrender of his anger. 'Yes. I just pray it will be enough.'

A heavier gust whipped in from the north-west, setting up moaning echoes through the stack cave. For a moment a shaft of watery sunlight broke through the racing clouds, but it did nothing to alleviate the wind's brutal bite. Benetan shivered.

'So do I,' he said quietly.

The atmosphere had been tense enough during the past few days, but this morning it had swelled to suffocating dimensions that even the dullest-minded of the castle's inhabitants couldn't fail to sense. Savrinor, who had had another sleepless night, felt that he wanted to strike out physically at the air around him, to push it away as if it were a clinging, stifling cocoon. He had tried to keep it from infecting his own territory but even in his rooms the mood was impossible to escape altogether. It shortened his temper, and by the time Andraia woke he was in a barbed and caustic frame of mind. She, however, was not easily cowed as Iselia had been – or appeared to be – and his first acerbic comment provoked an even more pungent response. The clash didn't last, but it surprised Savrinor to realize how close they had veered to a full-scale verbal duel, and how vicious such a duel might have become. He wasn't in the habit of apologizing for his own tongue, but for once he did so, and that caught him unawares too, for the apology led to the need for explanation. Thus far Savrinor had told Andraia nothing of what was afoot among the magi, feeling that the knowledge would only serve to alarm her. But the events of last night had changed the situation radically. She had to know – possibly for the sake of her own safety.

He told her what had taken place in the council hall. For a little over an hour Magus Croin had worked painstakingly on the mind of the young Chaos rider, drawing from him every detail of the terrors that had driven him to risk a death sentence rather than face what his masters expected of him. Croin's methods were ruthless and impersonal, and although the youth suffered no physical pain his obvious mental torment was something that Savrinor found hard to witness.

The story that the magi pieced together was simple enough. The boy was to have ridden with a detachment bound for a certain district in the south, where his own home village was located. And when he heard what he was to do there, his resolve had snapped. Indiscriminate killing, cold-blooded torture, violation, destruction . . . the First Magus had, as Pirane predicted, been very specific in his instructions to Captain Averel, and for the riders' newest recruit the prospect was too abominable to be borne. He wasn't alone in his horror – far from it – but the older riders knew the price of disobedience and had chosen instead to take the drug that would strip away their sense of reality, wipe the fear and disgust from their minds and make them capable of anything. Later memories would be hazy, their focus confined to the ecstasies of the Warp and the ride. But the boy hadn't understood, and, not understanding, was unable to shoulder the burden. So he had hidden in the stable, and when the iron door was unbarred and the riders' mounts summoned out of Chaos, their presence had broken his mind.

Savrinor's last commission of the night was to call on a number of the more senior magi and ask them to attend Pirane and Croin immediately – and covertly – in the council hall. The youth had been crying again, hysterically, when he left, and when his task was complete he returned to his apartments, closed the curtains and sat by the fire in the outer room for several hours, waiting.

The second moon had set when Pirane called to see him. The clandestine meeting was over, and all had gone well. The boy's story had turned the tide beyond doubt, and a strong enough consensus of the magi were now agreed that an early end to Vordegh's reign would be in the best interests of all. A plan had been discussed and agreed on, and they would wait only on the Chaos riders' return before putting it into operation. When they did return, Averel would be interviewed and Croin would unlock the memories which the sacrament would otherwise have blotted from his mind. That, Pirane said, would be enough to ensure his co-operation and that of the men under his command. And their strength, combined with that of the magi, would be a force against which even Vordegh couldn't prevail.

Andraia listened to Savrinor's story, not interrupting once but staring into the newly made-up fire. Only when Savrinor at last paused to pour himself another glass of wine – his fourth – did she speak.

'Lady Pirane says that the First Magus won't be able to stand against such a force. But what does that mean, Savrinor? What exactly do the magi intend to *do*?'

Savrinor set the wine-flagon down and took a sip from his refilled glass. 'They intend,' he said, 'to kill him.'

Andraia's face became very still and for a few moments the tension that permeated the castle seemed to encroach into the room. Then, very quietly, she said, 'Can they?'

'With the riders on their side, Pirane and Croin believe they can.'

'And do you believe it?'

A long pause. 'Yes. I think so. Vordegh's powerful, but he is also mortal.' Something which was all too easy to forget at times, and that too was a part of the First Magus's skill. 'If enough of the magi turn against him, and carry the Chaos riders with them, then Vordegh won't survive their attack.'

'How will they do it? Physically, or . . . ?'

'They'll use sorcerous means if they can. If not,' Savrinor shrugged, pretending to a confidence which he didn't entirely feel, 'there are enough expert swordsmen among the riders to ensure success. He won't destroy them all before they destroy him.'

The implication of his words didn't escape her and she said, 'Then some of his opponents might die?'

'Some of them undoubtedly will. And quite possibly a good many others who aren't even directly involved.' His eyes met hers and there was something very barren in their look. 'We both know what manner of creature Vordegh is. He'll create carnage before he surrenders to anything, let alone to death.'

Andraia was silent for some while, thinking about that, feeling clouds gather in her mind. Eventually she said, 'When will it be?'

Savrinor shook his head. 'I don't know, and I'm not sure that I want to know. Sometime soon after the riders return – that's all Magus Pirane has said.'

There was a further pause. Then Andraia spoke again.

'What happened to the rider, the one who deserted? Is he still alive?'

'Oh, yes. He's still alive.' Though what manner of life

he now had was another matter, for in being forced to re-live his experiences the boy had lost his mind altogether, and even Croin's abilities couldn't patch the shattered pieces back to any form of reason. They would find some simple work for him, Pirane had said; something that would occupy his hands for the year or two of life that he probably had left.

Savrinor realized that he had almost emptied his glass. He was drinking more than was good for him again, and abruptly he reached out and put an arm around Andraia's shoulders. 'When it's over,' he said, 'we might leave the castle for a while. Go south, where the climate's kinder at this time of year. The magi would grant me a leave of absence.'

Andraia looked at him curiously, the Chaos rider forgotten. 'You've never left the Star Peninsula in your life.'

That was true, and Savrinor didn't even know what had prompted him to contemplate doing so now; it was an impulse, a sudden desire to cast off everything that was familiar to him, at least for a while, and exorcise the physical and psychic ache that seemed to have lodged in his marrow. He felt claustrophobic here; that feeling was born of fear, and he wanted to be rid of it.

He looked at Andraia, wondering how he could explain, and saw that there was no need for words. She understood. More than that, she shared his feelings; there was unpleasantness in her past, too, and she wanted to lock it away and begin afresh. A hiatus, a change, a chance to wipe the slate clean . . .

He squeezed her shoulder, but gently. 'You're right,' he said. 'I've never left the Star Peninsula in my life. But there's a first time for everything. And I like to think,' he kissed her, almost playfully though there was still a shadow in his mind which he couldn't quite shake off, 'that I'm not too set in my ways, yet, to scorn the prospect of some new experiences in your company.'

*   *   *

'I can't pinpoint it.' Kaldar shuddered, then his body relaxed as he let his concentration slip at last. '*Something's* stirring, but I can't trace its source or its cause. And I daren't probe any deeper, or I might draw attention to us.'

Benetan rose from his crouched position, wishing he could curb the uneven thumping of his heart. Much of his inner tension had evaporated now that the long wait was at last over, but a different kind of stress had taken its place; the acute and tightly-focused sense of trepidation that he had always felt before a sortie. The hours since their return from the beach had seemed interminable: with no other means of judging the passing of time they had made regular, cautious forays to the castle's ground level, but each time they found to their dismay that the grim daylight still penetrated through a veil of driving rain. At last, though, night had come, the rain ceased and the cloud thinned, then both moons had risen, and finally, on his last exploration, Kaldar reported that the first moon was sinking below the west wall.

But one doubt held them back, for they were certain now that something was afoot in the castle. They had been aware of it all day – the atmosphere it engendered was strong enough to seep even down here among the foundations – and on their ventures to the outside world everything had seemed abnormally, ominously quiet. A sense of *waiting*, such as Benetan had felt before but now profoundly intensified. Yet for all Kaldar's careful psychic investigation, they could learn nothing of its nature.

'At least the riders aren't back yet,' Kaldar said. 'And I'm as sure as I can be that Vordegh's still in the spire.' He got to his feet, the movement quick and tense. 'We can't delay any longer, Benet. We'll have to take the chance, and hope to all our gods that we're not about to clash head-on with something the magi are planning.'

Benetan agreed, crushing down the hard, tight little knot of fear that was trying to gain a hold in the darker recesses of his mind. He knew every stage of their plan, had memorized it and honed it with all the skill his years in the castle had taught him, and now for the third time he began to check that everything they would need was ready. He could still pass well enough as a Chaos rider; his uniform was incomplete, filthy and probably stank by now, but he had concocted a story to cover that. Knife, sword. He would need the one but not, he hoped, the other. The silver circlet and half-mask; whatever happened from here on, this would be the last time he would ever wear it. And a short length of cord, chosen from among the various pieces of rope that Kaldar carried with him. That had a very specific purpose, but he had decided not to think about it unless circumstances should force his hand.

Kaldar, too, was ready. From one of the cellars he had purloined a smock of the kind the servants wore to protect their clothes when carrying out grimier tasks, and with it a roll of cloth large enough to wrap a human form. His only weapon was a short-handled hammer, also from the store-rooms, but he assured Benetan that he'd need nothing more.

Benetan looked around for the last time at the litter of their hideaway. The signs of their presence were obvious – they were even leaving most of their belongings behind – but within another hour or so it wouldn't matter if servants, Chaos riders or the First Magus himself came searching; they would have succeeded and fled, or failed and been captured. In either case, they would have no further need of any baggage.

Kaldar pocketed his tinder-box and two candles, then took a third, lit candle from its niche in the wall. 'All right,' he said tersely. 'We'll walk together to the stairs, then go our separate ways.'

Benetan nodded. 'You've memorized the route to the Marble Hall?'

'I know it as well as I know the lines on my own hand.'

The library was the one great danger, but it was late enough now for it to be deserted, and if it wasn't, Kaldar would assume the role of a new, frightened and bewildered menial who had lost his way on an errand. Unless he should encounter Savrinor alone in the vault, in which case he had the hammer . . .

'Then we'll meet in the corridor that leads to the Hall,' Benetan said. 'And if you're there before me, remember, don't go in — we've no way of knowing whether our presence will be detected the moment we step inside, and if it is, we'll only have a very short time to do what must be done.'

'Don't worry.' Kaldar opened the door and looked carefully out. 'All's quiet. Come on.'

They parted at the stairs, and Kaldar hastened away in the direction of Iselia's cell. Benetan waited until the glimmer of his candle had vanished, then steeled himself for his own part in the plan. He put on the circlet, adjusting it to ensure that his face was well hidden, then straightened and smoothed his tunic as best he could and walked on up the stairs, emerging into the castle's main wing.

It was very quiet. Enough torches burned dismally in their sconces to make the corridors negotiable, but the castle's familiar busy-ness was quite absent. The sense of desertion set the hairs at the nape of Benetan's neck prickling; he ignored the feeling and turned in the direction of the west wing.

Since his return every move he had made in the castle had been furtive and clandestine, and now he had to forcibly remind himself to adopt again the careless arrogance of his former rank. He passed the turning that led to the great hall; no lights there nor any visible shining from the hall itself, though he could hear a distant, muted clattering, suggesting that servants were clearing up in the wake of the evening's activity.

Across the main entrance hall; three more turnings and

then he was climbing a secondary flight of stairs that led to the upper floor and thence through to the west wing. A woman passed him in one of the passages but ducked her head and hurried by without looking at him. His pulse quickening to a painful rate, Benetan walked on.

The corridors of the west wing were unlit, but his eyes were accustomed to near-darkness now and a faint glow from the cloud-hidden second moon filtering in at an occasional window enabled him to see his way well enough. A number of the magi had their apartments here but the First Magus kept himself aloofly apart, and his chambers were isolated in an area of their own. Benetan was approaching that area, perhaps only thirty or forty paces from it, when something moved in the gloom ahead and a figure appeared, coming towards him.

Benetan's body tensed and his right hand went to the hilt of his knife in a quick, instinctive reaction. But the man approaching him was wearing servant's clothes, and as he drew level with a window and the faint light fell on him, Benetan saw that he was also a stranger. Relief filled him; he quelled his thumping heart and gave the man a cursory nod of acknowledgement as he passed, which was returned with a bow.

He had taken three further paces when a voice addressed his back.

'Beg pardon, sir – but do you have business with the First Magus?'

The question brought Benetan to a shocked halt. For a moment a feeling close to panic assailed him; he pulled it ferociously under control and forced himself to turn round.

The servant, who was middle-aged with an oddly-cut thatch of dark hair, was staring at him, his expression hovering between unease and affability. Through the mask, Benetan's grey eyes raked him.

'I don't believe,' he said coldly, hoping to all the lords

of Order that his voice wouldn't falter and betray him, 'that my business is any of your concern.'

'No, sir, no, of course not!' The man bowed nervously. 'Please forgive me, I intended no disrespect! But if you wish to see the First Magus, I thought perhaps I should tell you that he is not in his rooms. I thought to save you trouble, if you were wishing to see Lord Vordegh . . .'

Benetan continued to stare. This, he realized, was an opportunity he hadn't expected; a chance to learn one small but vital fact.

Aloud, he said, 'I see. So as Lord Vordegh retains no servants,' *no, for he had consigned them all to ugly deaths in one of his insane purges,* 'I presume there is no one in his rooms to whom I can entrust a message?'

The servant's expression brightened. 'Oh yes, sir, there is someone, if it's simply a matter of a message. The First Magus's amanuensis; a lady by the name of Verdice.'

Verdice. He had hoped she might be with Vordegh in the spire . . . Benetan's stomach tightened and he found that his fingers were clenching involuntarily. But he had planned for this eventuality and couldn't allow himself to waver now.

He said curtly, 'Then I will speak to her.' The man was hovering as though anxious to perform another good turn; he nodded in a gesture of dismissal. 'I'm obliged to you. You may go.'

As the servant hurried on his way Benetan shut his eyes briefly and took several deep breaths. Great Aeoris, but that had been an unpleasant moment . . . And he wanted to pray to the lord of Order, ask for the strength and resolution that, in the light of what he had just learned, he badly needed now. But he couldn't bring himself to do it. This wasn't a burden he could consign to other shoulders, no matter how powerful those shoulders might be. It was a matter for him alone, and for his conscience. And even if it was destined to haunt his nightmares for as long as he lived, it had to be done.

The black door with its pattern of iron studs that formed the seven-rayed star of Chaos was ahead of him now. Outside it he stopped, steadied his nerve, tried to calm and cool the blood which was burning his veins ... and checked that what he would need was where it should be.

Then he knocked, sharply, twice.

There was no immediate response, and for one heady minute Benetan thought that the servant had been wrong and Verdice was not, after all, in her master's apartments. But then a light footstep sounded on the far side of the door, and moments later it swung open.

The room behind her was unlit, but even in the semi-darkness he recognized Verdice. She stared at him with her customary hauteur, her face with its tell-tale traces of her unhuman origins cold and indifferent. She didn't speak, only raised her fine eyebrows in a wordless query, and confronted with her stare Benetan almost forgot the role he must play.

But then presence of mind came back. He pushed her aside, barging past and into the outer room, and looked wildly around.

'I must see Lord Vordegh! I have news, urgent news, and it's *vital* that he should be told of it!' He swung to face her. 'Where is he?'

Verdice's face was a study in outrage, but her composure was unshaken. 'Lord Vordegh is not here!' she snapped. 'And he has left strict instructions that no one is to enter his private rooms in his absence without *my* express permission! If you have a message for him, you may entrust it to me.' She extended a hand disdainfully, as though expecting him to place something on her palm. 'And then you will kindly leave, Ca—'

The word broke off, and in the same instant they both realized what she had been about to say.

Verdice's chilly eyes narrowed, and it was like watching a predator assessing new prey that had suddenly and unexpectedly moved into its field of view. Her body tensed, and she said in a very soft voice, 'Captain *Liss* . . .'

Benetan didn't have time to think. He didn't know what occult powers Verdice possessed or how swiftly she could use them, and he didn't dare hesitate in case he might find out. He lunged at her, caught her arms and spun her round so that she reeled backwards against him. At the same moment one foot kicked out, smashing the door shut, and with his right hand he whipped the length of cord from his belt and twisted it round her neck. Her head jerked back and she tried to writhe out of his grasp; she was surprisingly strong and his free arm went round her waist, pulling her viciously back. He tightened the cord – it bit into her; an awful, strangulated sound was coming from her throat as she tried to scream, and her hands went to her neck, clawing wildly at the noose and at his face. Her hair was in his mouth and he couldn't spit it away; they rocked and staggered together across the floor, cannoning into something that went over with a splintering crash, though Benetan neither knew nor cared what had been destroyed. She wouldn't give in, she wouldn't *die* – He could sense her mental strength flowing in waves, her will battering against his, and suddenly there was a new note to the feeling; a surge of power, fuelled by hatred and fury and a violent desire to survive. It hit his mind with the impact of a fire-bolt, and he reeled back, taking her with him, their feet tangling in a mad, uncoordinated dance across the uncarpeted floor. Verdice was fighting him with sorcery and she was turning the tables; his hand was weakening, the cord slipping through his fingers. She reached up, jerked at the noose; it slackened and she opened her mouth –

Benetan would never know whether she was about to call up a demon that would explode into the room and annihilate his soul, or simply scream for help. He couldn't think, couldn't reason; he could only react, and in an instant he changed hands, hanging onto the cord with his left while his right snatched his knife from its sheath. The blade gleamed savagely in the glow from the window, and as Verdice began to utter the first shrill sound of her cry, he cut her throat.

Her shriek broke off in a hideous gurgling, and a hot, wet flood cascaded over Benetan's hand and arm as blood erupted from her neck. Verdice thrashed, her eyes starting in their sockets; pure instinct drove her to try to breathe still, but he had put such force into the strike that the knife-blade had severed far more than an artery. A huge convulsion went through her – then she slumped, her entire weight collapsing against Benetan and her head jerking sideways as a fresh fountain of blood spilled over his torso.

He flung her away with an appalled reflex and she hit the floor like a heavy sack. A stain spread, darkening the pale fan of her hair; her mouth was working, eyelids fluttering, but her face was insensate now and she could make no sound. Mesmerized, Benetan stared until she no longer moved. Then, very slowly, he took a pace back. And another. And a third.

The jolt of nausea came suddenly and violently but somehow he kept it down. There was little enough in his stomach. And he couldn't let his control snap. Not now. Not even after this.

Perhaps he had killed a woman before. Perhaps it had happened once or twice or a hundred times on sorties, when the magi's sacrament was in his veins and controlling his mind, and it was simply that, afterwards, he hadn't been able to remember. But whether he had or whether he hadn't, it made no difference now. He had killed Verdice, brutally and in cold blood – *but her blood wasn't cold; it was hot, stinging his skin and soaking his clothes* – and the worst of it, the most terrifying thing of all, was that he felt no horror and no remorse. The sickness had been an animal reaction and was gone now; he could look at the corpse on the floor without any feeling beyond fastidious revulsion. He didn't *care*.

'*Great gods* . . .' In his mind's eye he saw Aeoris's serene face. '*What have I become . . . ?*'

But it didn't matter what he had become. It didn't *matter*. This had been necessary, he had had no other choice. And the night's work was by no means over yet.

His legs felt weak as he entered the second of the apartment's three rooms. The knife was still held loosely in his fingers; he paused to clean it on the curtain that hung at the window and to wipe his hands and face as best he could, and for some twisted reason that small violation of the First Magus's trappings gave him a dark glimmer of pleasure. Now, the inner sanctum. Iselia had told Kaldar what to look for; Kaldar had told him. Besides, he knew what the wand of Chaos looked like. He had seen it, in the Marble Hall, when Vordegh had turned its power on Savrinor and had almost made the fatal mistake of trying to use it against Tarod.

Unless, of course, Vordegh had taken it to the spire. That wasn't likely, for Benetan remembered seeing him stride from the Marble Hall, leaving the wand lying where it fell when Tarod had blasted it out of his hand. Croin, he recalled, had eventually gathered it up and taken it away. So, by all reason, it should be back in its place, here, in the inner sanctum, in the lead-lined box that Iselia had described.

But if it was not . . .

He only just stopped himself from laughing aloud at the thought of what that would mean. The one eventuality to which he and Kaldar and Iselia had no answer. Verdice murdered, the wand out of reach, and about as little chance of their escaping from the castle as of growing wings and flying to freedom. It would be the ultimate joke against

226

them – and one that Yandros would appreciate more than anyone.

Benetan realized that his mind was wandering and he was in danger of becoming just a little hysterical. Shock, nothing more. He could shake it off. He pushed his hair back from his face – it was slick in places, but he ignored that – and moved into the innermost room.

The box was there, as Iselia had said it would be. If Verdice had had a psychic link with Vordegh, as he feared, then it seemed she had died before she was able to invoke it, for nothing challenged him, nothing rose out of the dark to attack him. And no precautions had been taken as a result of Iselia's failed bid; the magi's complacency, it seemed, remained unshaken. It was all so *simple*. The box's repaired lock yielded to his knife, the lid fell back. And the wand was there.

It had a strange feel to it, a little like touching cold glass yet with a slight stickiness which he found repulsive. It was dark, quiescent – his dread that it might awake at his touch and alert the magi to what was afoot receded – and he tucked it carefully into his tunic, where it lodged hard and icy against his ribs.

Verdice lay where she had fallen – strange; knowing what she was, he had almost expected her to have vanished – and he didn't look down as he stepped over her and walked to the outer door. The corridor outside was silent. He would need to go carefully; if he was seen by anyone now, the stains on his clothes and body would damn him instantly. Down to the ground, along the stoa and through the door to the spiral staircase. The library would be empty. It *must* be empty. And Kaldar and Iselia would be waiting.

He closed the First Magus's door at his back and moved silently away towards the nearest stairs.

CHAPTER XV

The rite was familiar, for Simbrian and his fellow sorcerers had performed it once before. But this second time, the circumstances were very different.

They sat in a circle on the crater floor, forty-nine men and women, linked by a fine cord that each clasped with both hands. But instead of the inner ring of seven, led by Simbrian himself, one solitary figure stood motionless at the circle's heart. Aeoris's golden eyes burned with a strange, hard light, and the cord by which his followers' hands and minds were joined shone with a vivid echo of the aura that burned around him.

The sorcerers were silent. Faintly audible beyond the crater's massive rock walls, the sea was booming as a heavy tide sent waves crashing against the great buttresses of the island. But they did not hear it, nor the intermittent, whipping moan of the wind that drove clouds across the sky overhead. Their spirits were linked together, locked together; and Aeoris presided over them all, commanding, controlling, fusing the power that they raised with the power of his own being, to lend Kaldar and Benetan what strength and protection he could for the work they would attempt tonight.

And with another part of his being, Aeoris reached out beyond the dimensions of this world and into another realm, where other presences were poised with an avidness that stabbed through his consciousness like glittering shards of glass. His six brothers, waiting only on the moment when the task would be done, the hope fulfilled, the last barrier broken. Their vitality flowed through him, spilled out from him with an intense power that shivered through the crater. They were one, prepared and ready. And for the first time since Yandros had broken his strength and raised the barriers that banished his influence from the mortal world, Aeoris felt the prospect of triumph burning in him like a fierce, relentless flame.

The first moon had set; the second was waning. Soon, Aeoris knew, it would begin. His mind shifted, focused, honed. Two human souls, on whom so much depended. Across the great distance that separated them, Aeoris sensed the fine and fragile threads of their lives. And a third soul . . . ah, yes; when this was over it would gladden him to heal her mind and her body, and restore her to her rightful place among his own.

He felt, then, a spark of hatred; an ancient and familiar loathing for Chaos and for all it had made of this world through its long, unopposed reign. But change was coming. Tonight, it would truly begin; and though he knew that in beginning it he would reveal his hand at last to his oldest enemy, it no longer mattered, for the alarm would come too late.

With a surge of calm assurance Aeoris turned the shining force of his will towards the castle . . .

It was little short of a miracle, and as he carefully and gently set his burden down and dropped to a crouch before the strange, metallic door, Kaldar offered a fervent prayer of thanks to the gods for his good fortune. Not one living soul, not one shadow of a human presence to endanger them throughout the nerve-racking journey from the cellars. Even the library had been empty and dark. And now they were but a few bare paces from their goal.

He turned his attention to the shape lying beside him on the floor of the narrow and oddly symmetrical passage. Iselia's weight had seemed nothing to him, and she had stayed so still that as he lifted back the folds of cloth that shrouded her he had a sudden irrational terror that he would see her dead face staring up at him. But she was not dead. She smiled at him – and there was a zealous fever in her eyes; a hunger and a yearning and a will that eclipsed all other feelings.

'Kaldar . . .' She disentangled one hand from the cloth and took his in a tight grip. Trying not to be affected by the wasted feel of her fingers he whispered, 'We've done it, love. We're at the Marble Hall.'

Iselia nodded. She had memories of this place, hideous memories, but with a vast effort of will she pushed them away. There was new strength in her, she could feel it; a strength that came not from within but from somewhere beyond her own being. It had begun as Kaldar carried her from the cell and now she could feel it growing. She would have the power to do what would be needed. She would not fail.

'Lord Aeoris is . . . helping us, Kaldar.'

'Yes.' Kaldar, too, had sensed the change in her, and there was an echo of it in his consciousness, an uncanny awareness of his own skill and his own power. Aeoris and Simbrian and their friends must have begun the work they had promised, and an uneasy frisson moved in him as he wondered whether the magi would catch any scent of what was afoot. If they did, it might drastically shorten the time they had to complete their work, and he offered a second, more frantic prayer that Benetan would not be long in arriving.

Iselia stirred again and tried to sit up. He helped her, drawing her against him and not noticing how she flinched at his touch, and she said, 'Kaldar . . . when Benet comes, I . . . I want to walk into the Hall. I can; I know I can.' She licked her lips. 'Last time, I was . . . carried. This time – this time, when I face what is in there, I will *walk*.'

He understood and he said, 'Yes, my love, yes. Whatever you want.'

She nodded. 'You know the ritual?'

'I know it.' *Damn you, Benet, hurry!* He hugged her more tightly to him. 'And we'll stand side by side when I perform it, Iselia. We'll do what must be done together.'

She uttered a broken, husky laugh. 'And, if we must, die together?'

'No! We'll *live*. Don't stop believing that for one moment!'

She looked away and didn't answer, and Kaldar was about to say more when his ears caught the sound of distant, rapid footsteps. Adrenalin quickened in him and he began to rise to his feet, one arm still defensively around Iselia as the other hand went to the hammer tucked in his belt . . .

Benetan appeared, running. Kaldar's hand fell away from the hammer and he started towards the other man — then saw the crimson stains on his clothes, in his hair, smearing his face. His eyes widened in alarm. 'Great gods, what *happened?*'

'I had to kill someone.' Benetan was breathless, the words clipped and harsh. 'Don't ask me about it. I've got the wand; that's all that matters.'

Kaldar was still staring at him. 'Who was it?' he demanded.

'I said don't *ask* me —'

'Not Savrinor?'

'No. Why in the Seven Hells should it have been?' Benetan said irascibly. 'He'll be drugged insensible in his own or someone else's bed by this hour.'

'I only thought —'

'Damn what you thought! If you *have* to know, I've killed the First Magus's servant. In fact I cut her throat, and it wasn't pleasant, and I don't want to dwell on it!'

Iselia raised her head and said sharply, 'Verdice?'

For the first time Benetan became aware of her presence, and in the space of a moment the tight anger went out of him. He looked at her.

'Yes,' he said a little unsteadily. 'Verdice.'

Iselia smiled a very chill smile. 'I'm glad.' And in her eyes Benetan saw none of the revulsion or condemnation that he had feared. Only a strange hunger which, though partly satisfied by what he had told her, was by no means quenched yet.

They helped her to her feet, and the cloth wrappings fell away to reveal the tattered remnants of the dress she had been wearing when she was captured. One of Savrinor's less malignant gifts . . . For a few moments it seemed that her legs wouldn't support her, but then she found co-ordination, cautiously tested her balance – how many days must have passed since she had last been able to stand? – and was steady.

'Yes,' she said. 'Yes. Give me the wand, Benet. Let me take it now.'

He obeyed silently. The wand was stained with Verdice's blood, and that seemed to give Iselia pleasure. She held it tightly in both hands, then slowly turned to face the metallic door and spoke again.

'Open it, Kaldar.'

Kaldar and Benetan exchanged an uneasy glance. Something which neither of them could comprehend was moving in Iselia, driving her. From being the broken and defence-less victim of Vordegh's sorcery she had grown suddenly to a position of strength, almost of command, that over-shadowed them both. She was the prime mover in this undertaking now, and they were both subservient to her will. For a very brief moment Benetan felt a glimmer of the emotions that were alive in her; though in truth emotion had little part in it, for this was something glacial, a hard and immovable core underlying her brittle shell. Such *hatred* – it made his own bitterness against Savrinor, against Vordegh, even against Yandros and his brother, pale by comparison.

She was waiting, staring at the door. Kaldar looked away, touched the door, shut his eyes.

To breach this lock took a little more than the simple sorcery that had unbarred Iselia's cell. A visible aura formed around Kaldar's body as he concentrated his will and drew on the power Aeoris had granted him. Benetan felt a sensation of heat, a rush of cold; for a moment the floor beneath his feet seemed to vibrate as though something had shifted far beneath the castle ... Then light flared violently outwards from the door. Benetan hissed in shock, jerking back and instinctively shielding his eyes. Kaldar swore. Iselia blinked, still staring.

There was a faint *click*. Kaldar touched the door again. And, silently, it swung open.

Pirane raised her head suddenly, aware of a faint but emphatic tingle of disquiet. With nothing specific demanding her time or attention she was reclining before the fire in her apartments, and had summoned several small air elementals to create an entertainment for her. She had been watching their graceful aerial dance, and enjoying the caress of a warm and pleasantly scented breeze, when without warning a new sensation invaded her mind and sounded a sour chord.

The magus sat upright, and at her gesture the elementals paused in their display, hovering above her couch on the borders of the visible spectrum. Quickly, adroitly, Pirane's mind probed the room. Nothing untoward here, and she dismissed her first instinctive conjecture that someone — or rather, more accurately, Vordegh — was attempting to infiltrate her privacy. She doubted, anyway, that the First Magus would resort to such tactics. If he suspected anyone of duplicity he would either confront them in person or, if he was feeling less rational even than usual, launch an all-out psychic attack without a moment's warning. But *something* had disturbed her peace.

The elementals still hovered, but the frisson had broken Pirane's mood and gently, courteously she banished them, adding her thanks. As they flicked back to their own dimension and the breeze gave way to the more mundane warmth of the fire, the magus crossed to the window and lifted back the curtain to look out into the night. Vordegh was still in his eyrie, the green light in the summit window unaltered. Nor was there any sign of the Chaos riders' return, which might have explained the momentary sensation. All was well, it seemed.

She sighed a little irritably. The feeling had passed now, and she suspected that it had simply been a reaction – an overreaction, one might say – to the tensions of the past few days. Little wonder with so much at stake, and it had been over-optimistic of her to think that a simple display by a few low beings would be enough to entertain her and distract her from other thoughts.

There were no lights in the main wing now, save for a very dim illumination emanating from the dining hall; just enough for the servants to do their work. Not even a faint glow in Savrinor's rooms; perhaps the historian had at last had the sense to allow himself a full night's sleep. Pirane gave another sigh, but this time it was gentler. She needed a diversion, something to while away the night hours and put her in a better frame of mind. A meditation, perhaps. If nothing else the discipline would soothe her and stop her from imagining threats where none existed.

She let the curtain fall and stretched, arching her supple back. Then she unbound her hair, cast off her gown and with it the niggling doubt, and moved into the inner room.

'There's no way to judge how much time we might have.' Kaldar looked around him, forcing down the sense of disorientated awe that was trying to get its claws into his mind. 'For all I can judge, Chaos might already be alerted to our presence here; or the door itself might have some link with the magi that warns them of any tampering.' He shivered. 'We'll need to work fast – I only hope and pray that I can concentrate in this damned place!'

They were at the heart of the Marble Hall and the shifting mists were swirling around them like a sea-fog. The colours seemed oddly muted tonight, and Benetan had to fight against an irrational conviction that the change portended some unspecifiable danger. A little way off, vague and ominous and uncannily distorted by the mists' effect, the seven statues of the gods stared down at them; he hadn't dared turn to face them, but Kaldar, who had never seen them before, had stared mesmerized at the colossi until forcibly shaken out of his paralysis.

Though he wouldn't have admitted it to his companions, Benetan had almost lost his nerve as they entered the Hall. Memories of his previous experience here had come back like a physical blow, and he half expected to see Vordegh's tall, shadow-haunted figure waiting for them beside the black wooden block. The block was there – he had looked away from it quickly – but no Vordegh, no Pirane or Croin. Only the black circle that marked the Chaos Gate, quiescent and innocuous now, simply a part of the disturbing mosaic pattern set into the floor. Kaldar, too, had been visibly affected; for all Benetan's careful descriptions nothing could quite prepare him for the reality of the Hall's bizarre dimensions and intimidating atmosphere, and Benetan had sensed his fear as they closed the metallic door behind them and crossed the shimmering space towards their goal. Iselia alone, it seemed, was unmoved. She gazed at the statues, she gazed at the block, and her expression remained enigmatic. Only her eyes burned with quietly ferocious intensity.

Now she turned the wand of Chaos in her hands, stroking it as though it were some dearly-loved possession. She was looking at the circle of the Gate, and she said, 'I'm ready, Kaldar.' A quick, feverish glance in his direction. 'We must begin *now*.'

Kaldar nodded and wetted dry lips as he conjured the words of the ritual into his conscious mind. So brief, and it needed no preparation and no implements – he found it hard to believe that such a simple rite could work, and wanted to pray aloud to Aeoris that his faith wouldn't prove unfounded. But he dared not pray, not here, not yet.

He stepped towards the circle and Benetan took Iselia's arm, steadying her as she followed, though she didn't seem to need or even be aware of his support. On the edge of the circle Kaldar stopped, looked back at them.

'The hammer,' Iselia said.

He handed it to her wordlessly and her fingers closed round the wooden shaft. Then with a very deliberate gesture she shrugged free of Benetan's hand and moved to stand at Kaldar's side. As she looked over her shoulder, her eyes were calm.

'Stay back, Benet. This is for us to do.'

He retreated several paces, his heart pounding painfully under his ribs. Kaldar and Iselia hesitated a bare moment, then they stepped together into the black circle. For perhaps five seconds there was utter silence, utter stillness. Then, quietly but with a strange, intimidating authority, Kaldar began to speak. 'Hear me, O you princes. Hear me, you creators and contenders, you lords of Life and Death, you lords of Air and Earth and Fire and Water and Time and Space.' The words were gathered up by the mists, which sang back in a strange, unearthly harmony that seemed to pile echo upon echo upon echo. Benetan felt as though he was hearing them with his marrow rather than with his mind.

'I am of you and yet not of you; I am flesh and yet I am spirit.' A dark, eerie radiance was forming around Kaldar's figure, draining colour from his vivid hair and turning it the shade of tarnished brass. 'And I speak with the sanction granted to the legions who have stood before me in this place and walked before me on this way.'

There was a sound – felt, not heard, for it was too deep and too subliminal for any physical human sense to discern. A throbbing that began and then hesitated . . .

'I stand before you in this place, and I walk towards you on this way. The way is long but the way is old, and the way is the way of power. I am chosen and I am willing.' Echo upon echo upon echo; the words were merging and melding, flowing together and surging against Benetan's mind in waves as he listened to Kaldar's voice. The dark nimbus was growing stronger, and in Iselia's hands the wand of Chaos began to glow with a chilly, blue-white light . . .

In the west wing, where she lay on her bed, Pirane's trance snapped. She sat up in a single, violent movement –

On the White Isle, a massed shudder went through the minds of the gathered sorcerers, and the cord that linked them glowed suddenly with new vigour. Aeoris's golden eyes began to burn –

And in another realm, something screamed and Yandros felt a prickling of curiosity –

'With the feet that are my flesh I tread between dimensions, and I shall speak the way. With the hand that is my flesh I reach out across the abyss, and I shall speak the way. With the eyes that are the windows of my soul I look from world into world, and I shall speak the way.' Kaldar's breathing was stertorous and rapid. Bands of shadow began to move slowly, grimly along the shaft of the wand . . .

Tarod had moved to join his brother. 'They're opening the Gate?'

237

'Yes.' Yandros's eyes were strangely still, their colour suspended in a bizarre blend between silver and bronze. 'But who is performing the rite . . . ?'

'The locks of time are shattered and the bars of space are burned to ashes! Come, you creators – I will walk with you on the way, and I will reach to you on the way, and I will gaze upon you on the way! As it was in the days before me, it shall be again! Hear me – hear me, and let the seal be broken!' Kaldar flung his arms roofwards as the ritual took full hold of his mind, and his voice rose –

The green witchlight in the east spire went out. In darkness, Vordegh rose to his feet as a violent premonition took hold of him. He pivoted towards the door –

'*I speak the way. And the way is open.*'
Kaldar's voice reverberated through the Hall as he uttered the final words of the ritual, and at the same moment Iselia raised the wand high. The livid white light turned black; under Benetan's feet the floor seemed to quiver – then the air above the mosaic distorted violently and a vaster column of black light flared up from the circle. The column started to pulse in a steady, relentless rhythm; the light of the wand took up the pulse, and suddenly, breaching dimensions and vibrating through the Hall, through his bones, through his soul, Benetan felt the deep, subliminal throbbing begin anew, matching the inexorable cadence of the Gate.

Yandros said: 'Something's wrong –'

Benetan had been prepared for a storm of power such as he had seen during his previous ordeal here; the same ferocious display which had heralded the Chaos gods' arrival. But it did not come. Instead, the column of light intensified momentarily; the throbbing paused for the space of a heartbeat – and then the column twisted, inverted, and the portal yawned open. Kaldar had one bare glimpse of Chaos's realm before the sheer, mind-bending shock of the vista sent him recoiling back with a gasp. Iselia's head turned; her eyes were wild, and there was fanatical passion in her voice as she cried, 'Kaldar – get out of the circle, get clear!'

Mind reeling, he obeyed her without thinking, and as he stumbled backwards Benetan saw Iselia's arm come up. For a moment the hammer was silhouetted against a sudden violent flare of light from the Gate –

'Yandros, what –' Tarod's words cut off abruptly, and suddenly their five brothers were with them. Yandros felt the change, felt the warning; his focus flicked to the portal and the vortex –

The hammer sheared down, and Iselia split the wand of Chaos in two.

For one confounding instant the sound of the wand's destruction was a mundanity; a dull splintering, no more significant than the dropping and breaking of a wine-glass. Then . . .

'*Yandros!*' Iselia screamed the Chaos lord's name at the full pitch of her lungs, her voice rising in a screech that tore through the throbbing pulse that now filled the hall. '*Yandros, you demon, you travesty! Show your face to me, if you dare – and take my gift to you!*'

'*Iselia!*' Intuition hit Kaldar and he realized what she meant to do. She had snatched up the two broken pieces of the wand in her hands and she was lunging forward, to the heart of the circle –

Kaldar cried out, '*Iselia, NO* –'

*   *   *

In the skies of Chaos a thunderbolt that could have shattered a world exploded out of nowhere with a bellowing cacophony, and a vast tide of shock and fury erupted into Yandros's mind. Fire roared up around him in a white-hot inferno; he hurled his consciousness towards the Gate, the others joining with him, becoming one –

For an instant Iselia's figure was silhouetted against the Gate, a dazzling aura blazing around her. Then she seemed to fall towards the vortex, arms upraised, hands gripping the broken wand in triumph, and her voice rose to an insane shriek.

'*DAMN YOU! DAMN YOU!*'

'*ISELIA!!*' Kaldar's scream sliced shrilly through hers. He flung himself across the space that separated them, snatching out, grasping, and Benetan was behind him, racing desperately to reach them both. He saw Kaldar's fingers close on Iselia's arm –

The towering column of black light exploded, and a titanic shock-wave detonated up and out from the mosaic circle. A concussion of sound, light and unchained power blasted through the Marble Hall and Benetan was hurled backwards on it like a leaf in a hurricane as it smashed into his senses. In the instant before the blast wiped out sight and hearing he glimpsed Kaldar's body tumbling, flailing across the floor. And Iselia, as black flames burst into life around her –

Then the concussion pulverised his mind –

The thunderbolt shattered out of the Chaos realm and into the mortal world, tearing the sky above the castle in half and screaming overhead in a blaze of crimson fire. The castle quaked as a colossal upheaval ripped through every dimension of its being; a huge static charge cracked between the spires and ricocheted, howling, into the night – within the shaking walls Pirane came blazing from her rooms, yelling the names of her fellow magi. And Vordegh, on the east spire stairs, called power to himself, the power and strength of Chaos –

'*It's too late!!*' Yandros's voice rang tumultuously out over the mayhem ripping through his realm, and seven spears of lightning hurtled upwards into the churning maelstrom as thunder eclipsed all other sound with its pandemonium. Below them, the Gate's vortex was spinning out of control as Chaos's aeon-old command of its power broke down, and suddenly Yandros could feel another energy, inimical, loathsome, detested, cracking through the barriers he had created so long ago.

The great Chaos lord's face contorted with raging malevolence, and with a flick of movement he turned, sending a stunning tremor through the entire dimension. One word was searing in his mind; one name. *Aeoris . . .*

The cord that linked the forty-nine sorcerers on the White Isle was torn suddenly and violently from their hands, and its glittering strands disintegrated as a circle of golden fire seared up, hurling the crater bowl into stunning brilliance. At the centre of the circle Aeoris flung his head back, hair streaming and whipping around his face as a gale blasted out of nowhere, and his right hand came up in a sweeping gesture.

There was a sound like iron shattering, and a glittering white sword with a twelve-foot blade manifested in the lord of Order's grasp. Light poured from it, spilling across the crater and eclipsing the circle of fire, and as the echoes of the deafening noise rolled clashing between the rock walls, Aeoris called out in a voice that resonated with power.

'My brothers, the last shackles are broken! I summon you – *I summon you all!*'

The air shrieked, and a single flash of lightning split the

sky above the bowl. With flawless precision it sheared into the crater and struck the tip of Aeoris's sword with a gargantuan *crack*. Simbrian and his followers reeled back – for an instant everything was blotted out by a blinding radiance; then vision cleared and, shaking, the stunned mortals raised their heads and looked towards the centre of the circle.

Seven figures stood where before there had been one. Each was a perfect mirror of Aeoris; their faces, their hair, the white garments they wore, all were identical. Their pupil-less golden eyes glowed like banked, unearthly fires, and a quiet, calm and utterly steadfast power radiated from them. Simbrian, rising slowly to his knees, felt that power imbuing him, flowing into his veins and, beyond physical dimensions, into his soul.

Then Aeoris swung to face his brothers and the light in his eyes burned hot.

'Our followers have succeeded!' There was a new note in his voice, a hard and violent edge of urgency. 'Yandros has lost his hold on the Gate – we must make our move *now*, and seize it before he can regain control!'

He renewed his grip on the sword; its aura flared ferociously, and in alarm Simbrian called out, 'My lord, what of Kaldar and the others? Have they escaped?'

Aeoris's head turned quickly. 'We can't be sure as yet – Chaos's influence in the castle is still too strong for us to penetrate. We will do what we can for them, but the Gate is the more urgent priority. Rebuild the circle, reforge the link – once they are away from the Star Peninsula, use what power you can to help them.'

The sorcerer opened his mouth to reply, but before he could utter a word Aeoris turned back to his fellow lords. He raised the sword high once more and a sweet, pure sound, pitched almost too high for human hearing, began to emanate from the blade. The sword's aura blazed anew; Simbrian felt a charge of colossal energy flood the crater, echoing through his own body and mind, and for one instant he seemed to glimpse an incredible landscape super-imposed over the surrounding rock; a place of light and power and titanic, unearthly beauty. Then the vision flashed out – and with a sound like a vast door smashing shut, the seven lords of Order vanished from the mortal world.

CHAPTER XVI

'No, Kaldar, no, there's nothing you can do! Don't fight me – just *run!*'

Benetan's voice rebounded in the confined space of the passage that led back to the library, and he wrenched Kaldar's arm round behind his back, forcing him to turn again. Kaldar was struggling like a madman to break free, but he was no match for Benetan's greater strength or warrior's training, and his feet went from under him as Benetan dragged him desperately on towards the door at the passage's end. Kaldar didn't understand yet, for he hadn't seen, hadn't been *able* to see, and nor could he see now the tears that were streaming down Benetan's face as he propelled him at a staggering, lurching pace along the corridor. All Kaldar could do, again and again, was call Iselia's name, shouting, protesting, and Benetan couldn't stop to make him listen, because there wasn't time; and even had there been time, no power in the world could have given him the words at this moment to tell Kaldar what had become of his wife.

The floor was shaking with a series of huge, jolting concussions, as if the entire peninsula were being ravaged by an earthquake. Benetan knew that they would have no more than minutes to reach the courtyard before they ran headlong into the full force and full wrath of the magi. Perhaps less than minutes; perhaps even now there were men on the stairs, in the library, about to fling the door open and confront them –

Kaldar started to fight again, and though Benetan didn't like doing it he knew he had no choice. He hit the other man, once, at a point on the skull where he knew the blow would stun without doing any real damage. Kaldar's legs folded and his body slumped; quickly Benetan heaved him over one shoulder – thankfully Kaldar was lightly built and not too great a weight – and ran on. As he ran he tugged his sword out of its sheath, hoping to Aeoris that he wouldn't have to try to use it with his burden to hamper him. He reached the door, opened it. The library was still dark and empty; offering heartfelt thanks Benetan groped past the tables and benches to the other door and the stairs beyond. Up the first twist of the spiral, the second – Kaldar's body was scraping against the wall but that couldn't be helped; all that mattered was to get out, get away, reach the main gates and the Maze beyond before it was too late.

He ran on, breath sawing, legs aching, towards the top of the flight.

Venom burned in Yandros's eyes, burned in the air, and the vast thunderheads that filled Chaos's sky shuddered with a discharge of abysmal energy. Then suddenly there was darkness, silence. Yandros felt the presence of his brothers, felt the slow, grim but soundless pulse of their forces pent and waiting. His mind snapped away from the mortal world, away from the shattered Gate and the tumult in the castle, to another dimension, and he felt the rising strength of the most deadly and ancient of his enemies.

He swung to face Tarod and the green-haired Chaos lord who stood beside him. 'Go to the castle! The Gate must be brought back under control, and the magi may not have the power to do it.' He felt the quick, angry spark of their compliance, and added, his voice balefully soft, 'Aeoris has had human help in this. Find those humans, and annihilate them.'

His two brothers turned; black and silver and grey-green mingled, then they vanished into darkness. For a moment

Yandros stood motionless and a cold white glare shivered through his hair, lighting his face starkly and echoing in a flickering sheet of unnatural lightning that swept across the mortal world from north to south. Then he pivoted, and his eyes shifted their focus once more, back to the mayhem of the Gate –

Savrinor emerged from his rooms, Andraia on his heels, to find the main wing in uproar. Somewhere on the ground floor a stentorian voice was raised, but words were indistinguishable amid the background hubbub. And the floor was quaking.

Savrinor had been wrenched awake, and out of an unpleasant dream, by a sound that he couldn't identify but which had sent a shock through him to a primal level. For a moment as he sat upright he had felt the panic of blinding terror – then as Andraia also woke and voices started to shout agitatedly in the corridors outside, the terror had vanished and another kind of alarm took its place. Or rather, an intuitive sense of fury ... With a speed that belied his usual languid manner Savrinor was out of bed, snatching up his robe and heading for the outer room as the angry alarm coalesced into an awful premonition.

Doors banged in the distance; outside in the corridor a servant was running past. Savrinor snarled a question at the woman, but his words were drowned by a sudden explosion of noise outside, above the courtyard, and the room behind him lit up shockingly as a gargantuan thunderbolt went screaming across the sky.

'*Yandros!*' Savrinor flinched violently and the servant reeled back with a shriek, colliding with him. Recovering before she did, he snatched her arm in a vicious grip. 'What, by every demon the gods have ever created, is going on?'

The woman shook her head wildly. 'I don't know, sir! I was told only to fetch the magi, any of the magi –'

The sense of premonition surged again, hitting hard. With an oath Savrinor pushed the woman away; as she scuttled from him he swung round and came face to face with Andraia.

'Is it Vordegh?' Her voice was harsh.

'No.' He had no grounds for the certainty, but was certain nonetheless. 'No. Something else.' He caught her arm. 'Come with me, quickly!' He pulled her after him into the passage, heading towards the main staircase. They reached the landing, where a crowd was milling in the entrance hall – Savrinor saw Pirane's tall figure on the stairs, skimming down, her black hair flying like a shawl behind her; Revian and Garvid were running from another part of the main wing, and Croin and Qenever were among the mêlée below –

'Father!' Andraia leaned perilously over the balustrade, waving wildly to catch Qenever's attention as she saw him. 'Father, what's happened?'

Qenever looked up, but before he could respond there was a commotion by the open double doors that led out to the courtyard. The crowd parted like water, and Vordegh swept into the hall.

'*Be silent!*' The First Magus's voice rang out shockingly and the babble ceased on the instant. Motionless, the crowd stared at Vordegh, at the shadows that writhed furiously around him. The First Magus ignored them; his gaze raked upwards to the landing and Andraia shrank back against Savrinor. But Vordegh was uninterested in them. He waited – then from the direction of the west wing Mcnniam, another of the magi, appeared. Menniam's composedly aloof demeanour had been thrown to the winds; he was dishevelled, wild-eyed. And there was blood on his hands.

Vordegh's voice cut through the appalling silence that gripped the hall. He said, ominously, 'Where is my servant?'

Menniam drew a deep breath. 'Verdice has been

murdered, my lord – her throat is cut! And the wand – the wand of Chaos – has gone!'

Savrinor felt Andraia's ribs heave and he laid a finger on her mouth in warning, pulling her back from the banister rail and out of sight of the hall. As they stumbled against the wall her hands came up to clutch at his shoulders and she stared frenziedly at him. 'Savrinor, they can't – they surely can't have –'

He didn't know and couldn't answer, but the premonition in him had swelled to something far worse and the thought slammed through his mind with bitter savagery: *I should have left well alone – I should have been content to let the magi send Benetan Liss to perdition!*

But even if he could have articulated that to Andraia – which was impossible – the First Magus spoke again, and instantly Savrinor forgot all else.

'You.' He couldn't see whom Vordegh was addressing but could imagine his pointing hand, and the implacable calm in the First Magus's voice sent a shudder through him. 'Take six other magi and go immediately to the Marble Hall!'

There was a flurry of movement; daring to look again, Savrinor saw that Croin and Garvid were among those obeying the order, and Menniam was hurrying to join them. Vordegh swung towards one of the senior stewards.

'I will have every cranny scoured for the perpetrators of this infamy! Summon all servants, wake those Chaos riders who are still in the castle, and inform them that I will kill any man who is not about the search within three minutes.' Rapidly the crowd began to disperse; Vordegh turned again. 'And you,' this to Pirane, who had stood frozen at the foot of the stairs since his arrival, 'make preparations to recall the riders who are on sortie, and await my message.' Pirane hesitated, and he added intimidatingly, 'Don't waste time, Magus!'

For a moment it seemed that Pirane would speak, but

then she thought better of it. A curt nod expressed her acquiescence, and she whirled round and away back up the stairs.

Vordegh cast a ferocious glare at the last of the departing throng. The shadows around him flared with dire energy, then abruptly he turned and strode back in the direction of the main doors.

In the darkness of the courtyard Benetan was just another shadow amid the general confusion as he dragged Kaldar desperately towards the main gates. People were emerging from the castle at a run, and sounds of incoherent voices echoed from the entrance hall, but no one shouted a challenge to him and he had almost reached the arch of the great gateway when Kaldar came to and started to struggle. It threw Benetan off balance and they fell together into the arch's huge shadow, hitting the ground with painful force.

'Iselia –' Kaldar tried to scrabble to his feet, hands groping and flailing.

'There's nothing we can do for her!' Benetan grabbed a handful of his shirt and hauled him upright, then turned quickly away at the sight of his face. *He hadn't realized, there hadn't been time to look clearly and see* – He forced himself to turn back again. 'Either you go back in there alone and die, or you come with me! *Do you understand?*'

Whether or not Kaldar did understand was impossible to judge; he only moaned and cried out Iselia's name again. Then suddenly a voice bawled from the darkness.

'Who's there? Identify yourself!'

Rapid footsteps approached, and Benetan heard the sound of a blade scraping free of its scabbard as he glimpsed an indistinct figure running towards them. He had less than a second to react, and a trained response came to the fore as he recognized the voice.

'Pareye? Seven Hells, man, what do you think you're

doing? Haven't you heard the order? Get to the Marble Hall!'

The figure slithered to a confused halt and Benetan knew that for the moment at least the gamble had paid off; habit was reacting before logic in the Chaos rider's mind and the significance of Benetan's identity hadn't yet dawned. 'The Marble Hall, sir –? '

'That's what I said! You're not deaf, are you? Don't you – oh, gods damn it all, hasn't your sergeant told you what's happened? The escaped heretic has got back into the castle, and the magi want every man in the Marble Hall, *now!*'

'Yes, Captain L –' The rider started to salute – then stopped, and his voice changed. 'Captain *Liss?*'

Aeoris help me, Benetan thought. He pushed Kaldar aside and his right hand renewed its grip on his sword-hilt. 'It's all right, Pareye. I'll explain everything later. Just do as you're –' He got no further, for suddenly Pareye was lunging at him. Steel glinted; he had a momentary glimpse of the man's face, and brought his own blade up fast to block the attack. Pareye wasn't one of the best but Benetan couldn't afford simply to disarm him; that would be too great a risk. Feet and body moved instinctively; his arm twisted, the sword moving with it in a trick that his old weaponsmaster had taught him more than a decade ago –

He heard a sick grunt, but there was no other sound as the Chaos rider fell. That was the great advantage of that particular method; they didn't have a chance to raise an alarm . . .

'Benet!' Kaldar's hand grabbed at him, making him jump like a shot hare. 'Benet, what's happening? I can't *see!*'

I've just killed someone who didn't deserve it. But Benetan kept the thought to himself. He shoved the sword back into its sheath then put a hand to his throat – thank Aeoris, the amulet was still there – and swung Kaldar round, pushing him deeper into the arch's shadows. No one on the gates at this hour. If they could just reach the postern –

Suddenly Kaldar yelled, 'There's something coming, I can sense it! Benet —'

'Move, Yandros blast you, *move!*' Benetan too had felt the deadly foreboding flick across his mind, and habit made him invoke the Chaos lord's name without realizing it as he propelled Kaldar at a stumbling run before him. He couldn't *see* under here; couldn't see a damned thing — his outstretched hand hit stone, tearing the skin from his knuckles, and he fumbled along the wall until his fingers felt wood. The main gates —

'Come *on!*' He yanked roughly at Kaldar, his voice grating breathlessly. *They might have only seconds before the magi closed the Maze, and a hideous power was swelling behind them in the courtyard —*

He found the postern and scrabbled at the bolt, wrenching it back. As the small door swung open there was a drum of footsteps and a voice shouted something in which the word *gates* was clearly audible. Benetan swore afresh and bundled Kaldar through ahead of him. Lightning flashed luridly across the sky as they emerged onto the stack, showing a momentary, stunning glimpse of the mountains in the distance, and Benetan's mind snatched hold of that image. The two peaks, the pass, the cave — Kaldar's retreat — it was the only haven he could visualize in this frantic, panicking moment and there was no time to find anything better. He could see the faint, tell-tale shimmer of the Maze's boundary in the dark ahead and he raced towards it, dragging Kaldar alongside. *The pass, the cave* — He grasped hold of the amulet, hurling all the will he could summon into the visualization. Three more paces, two, one — and the world burst into splintering mayhem as with a huge, buffeting impact the Maze snatched them away.

Another massive discharge spat between all four of the spires, and suddenly the castle was lit up by a ferocious green-white glare as Tarod and his brother appeared in the courtyard. Vordegh emerged onto the steps at the same moment but Tarod ignored him; something else had skimmed across his consciousness as he manifested, and he swung round towards the barbican arch. Thought and intent fused, and a ricochet of raw power snapped across the courtyard to the gates and beyond.

Tarod felt the power strike the Maze, but knew at the same instant that it had come too late. Their quarry had vanished through the gateway; this attack would not touch them. But he knew now who they were, and for a bare second he stood still, his eyes alight with unholy ferocity. Then abruptly he turned again to face the steps and Vordegh.

'My lords!' The First Magus made no obeisance; this was no time for protocol. 'The wand of Chaos has —'

'*The wand is barely a part of it!*' Tarod's voice smashed furiously through the words, and disgust surged in him — disgust for the First Magus's petty obsessions which had led to this calamitous lapse of vigilance, and for his own and his brothers' carelessness in allowing themselves to be distracted. With an effort he controlled the urge to blast Vordegh out of his path and, channelling his anger into a single, savage look, swept towards the main doorway. His black hair roiled over his shoulders and fused with the wilder darkness cloaking him, and an acid aura ignited around him. At the foot of the steps he paused and looked back at Vordegh.

'Go to the Marble Hall.' His voice raked through the charged atmosphere. 'Rally your colleagues; use whatever means you can — if you can — to stabilize the Gate!' Vordegh bowed his head and hastened away without a word, and Tarod looked at his brother. This time when he spoke the words were soft. He said, 'Find them.'

A disquieting light shifted around the other Chaos lord. He nodded, then turned to focus his lethal eyes on the barbican as Tarod took the steps three at a time and stalked towards the doors.

Inside the castle, Pirane had reached the top of the stairs. She glanced to one side, saw the historian and called his name sharply.

'Madam!' Gesturing to Andraia to stay back, Savrinor ran across the landing to join the magus, and in a rapid undertone Pirane said, 'Savrinor, in this emergency all else is in abeyance – you understand me?'

He did, and nodded. 'Madam, if the wand of Chaos has been stolen, does it mean that –'

From below them a voice cut arctically across his. 'It means, Savrinor, that the Chaos Gate has been shattered!'

They swung round. Tarod had entered the empty hall below and stood staring up at them. Savrinor looked at his face, at the flaring aura, and froze, knowing with an innate certainty that anyone who made one wrong move in the Chaos lord's presence now would not live to make another. Then Pirane bowed her head; hastily Savrinor too made an obeisance. Tarod's gaze seared the hall and every torch within his sight went out. Then he turned his attention to the upper floor. The force of his scrutiny was like an ice-cold north wind as his unhuman senses touched the First Magus's chambers and confirmed the truth, and he returned his attention to the two rigidly motionless mortals on the landing.

'Pirane.' The malevolence in his eyes modulated fractionally as he looked at the magus. 'Vordegh has instructed you to call back the Chaos riders?'

'Yes, my lord,' Pirane said unsteadily.

'Ignore that instruction for the present. You may have need of them elsewhere.'

She nodded, swallowed. 'My lord, you said that the Chaos Gate . . .' Her voice faltered.

'The First Magus's wand has been destroyed, and with it our control of the Gate.' Tarod's aura pulsed with an echo of the turbulence behind his words. 'Your heretics have succeeded this time, it appears – this is Order's doing!'

Pirane uttered a shocked oath; Savrinor felt something within him wither and turn poisonous. But before either of them could articulate their reactions, Tarod spoke again.

'Pirane, join the other magi in the Marble Hall.' His gaze shifted briefly to the historian and he added ferociously, 'Your account of this, Savrinor, will make dire reading!'

He headed for the doors, Pirane quickly following. The courtyard was empty; for all Vordegh's orders, no one dared to venture outside in the wake of the gods' arrival. On the steps Tarod's brother turned to meet him, a grim light flaring in his hair and eyes.

'You've found them?' Tarod's voice was terse, and the other Chaos lord nodded.

'Oh yes, I've found them.'

Pirane had hesitated, but at a curt nod from Tarod she moved quickly away towards the stoa and the door to the spiral stairs. As she disappeared, Tarod attuned his mind to what his brother had discovered. So their quarry had fled to the northern mountains ... he could sense the power that had enabled them to escape discovery in the castle, but though that power was inimical and repugnant to his nature, its shield was so weak that he could crush it with a single thought. His eyes narrowed; the shield shattered. At his side his brother uttered a soft, cold laugh, but the sound had no trace of humour. This was not a moment for levity.

They exchanged another glance. Then their thoughts merged –

'*Aeoris! Aeoris, lord of light! Aeoris, high lord of Order!*' Benetan's frantic voice battled with the howl of the wind and he raised his half-frozen face to the sky, striving with all the will he possessed to project his call through the miasma of physical limitations and away, far away, into another dimension. His body was shaking with cold and with the sickness engendered by their flight through the Maze, and Kaldar was a dead weight on his arms as he tried to hold him upright. But he *had* to persevere.

'Aeoris, *hear me! Aeoris, hear me!*' Frustration seethed, but even as he shouted the plea again he knew it was useless. He simply hadn't the ability, hadn't the *power*. And Kaldar, who might have succeeded where he was doomed to fail, was in no condition to help him.

He had been such a *fool*. The Maze could have carried them to any part of the world; one moment's pause, one moment's forethought and he could have visualized a destination far, far away to the south; maybe even the White Isle itself. Reason might argue that there had been no time to pause, but at this moment he didn't give a curse for reason. All he knew was that he had made a terrible mistake, and because of it they were trapped.

It wasn't snowing in the mountains tonight, but the existing drifts made the pass deadly and the wind was funnelling between the towering rock walls with the hard ferocity of steel. Ahead, the way was blocked by a solid wall of snow and ice, where a perilous overhang had crashed down from somewhere high above. And Benetan couldn't remember where the cave had been; whether the pass before it twisted to the left or to the right, whether the sanctuary lay somewhere behind them or beyond the white wall that choked the track.

Peering desperately into the darkness for any sign of a familiar landmark, Benetan fought the twin horrors of sickness and grief as he recalled the last moments before he had fled from the Marble Hall, dragging Kaldar willy-nilly with him. Kaldar had been screaming at him to help Iselia, carry her, *do something*, but Benetan had seen what Kaldar could not see and knew that no power in or beyond this world could do anything for her now. A blackened shell, a charred husk; not just her life extinguished but her very soul. And she had known. In the seconds before she stepped into the portal, she had known, and she had welcomed her fate. That was the most hideous fact of all, the fact he couldn't assimilate or understand. She had been minutes away from freedom; Aeoris would have healed her and erased the memories of all she had suffered, and she had had the promise of a new beginning. But instead of grasping at that promise she had deliberately chosen to die. It made no *sense*. And Benetan couldn't even grieve, not yet, for the immediacy of their own peril was holding all emotion at bay. Grief was there – he knew it was there, and he knew what it would do to him once he was capable of giving it rein. But now, there was only a core of black emptiness in his soul. And as for Kaldar – had he realized the truth, or had shock put him beyond the reach of understanding? At this moment it hardly mattered, but later –

Later. Something grim and bleak took hold of Benetan's mind as he realized suddenly the stupidity of that thought. Unless he could succeed in projecting his call to Aeoris, and quickly, there would be no *later* for either of them. Something would come looking for them before long; something sent by the magi or, worse, by Yandros. And when it did, they would be cornered. Like the rats in the castle cellars.

But at least the rats had faced nothing worse than death . . .

He had to find shelter. Not a hiding place – that would be futile – but something, anything, that would shield them from the wind. And he had to bring Kaldar round, make him understand their peril. For something *would* come. And without Kaldar's help, without his ability to alert the forces of Order far away in the south, they would have no defence and no hope.

In the crater on the White Isle, Simbrian's fellow sorcerers had re-formed the circle of power. The golden cord was gone, but a thin blue tongue of light burned along their arms, channelling through their linked hands, and a wall of cold fire blazed up around the figure of Simbrian himself, who stood alone in the middle of the ring.

Simbrian's eyes were shut, and images were skimming across his inner vision in wild disorder as his mind caught glimpses of what was taking place beyond the physical dimension. He saw the faces of Aeoris and his brothers, their eyes searing like infernos and blinding spears in each of their hands, merging, becoming one – and he saw the churning madness of Chaos's fury, with a spinning black vortex at its heart. He felt emotions – rage, pride, terror, confusion, hatred – and then suddenly in the midst of it all there was another image, tiny, fleeting but clear. Two human figures, impossibly distant, moving –

Aeoris, lord of light – The words flicked through Simbrian's consciousness and were gone, and his eyes snapped open. *Two figures – only two! One of their number had failed to escape . . . but who?*

Simbrian drew breath and strove to pull his mind into focus, under the command of his will. *Kaldar!* Every shred of strength he possessed went into the mental call. *Kaldar!*

His companions sensed his urgency; he felt their minds snatch hold of his cry and amplify it. But it wasn't enough. He couldn't reach the two fugitives. And then in the psychic maelstrom he felt something else stirring; something vast, dark, monstrous. Horror swamped Simbrian's consciousness as he saw and recognized its nature, and he rallied his mind again for a last, desperate effort, a final warning –

In the unearthly non-dimension into which he and his brothers had moved to prepare their attack, Aeoris felt the shard of energy that was Simbrian's frantic call. For an instant the shaft of blazing fire that their mingled wills had become quivered and lost a thread of its cohesion, and the greatest lord of Order tensed, his mind shifting rapidly into another perspective.

Two escaped; and Chaos pursuing them – It would be the work of a moment to reach towards them and pull them out of the mountain pass to safety, but even as the thought occurred Aeoris dismissed it. A moment could be all that Yandros would need to grasp back the advantage. That Aeoris intended to avoid at all costs; and besides, it would be more effective – and more satisfying – to deal with matters in another way entirely.

A savage smile flickered across the lord of Order's face. His brothers sensed it, matched it. The single will of their intent honed again, tautened again, fused again. And the blinding spear of light began to blaze with a new purpose.

CHAPTER XVII

Something cut across Yandros's mind, snapping his attention from the shuddering Gate. With a swift movement his head came up, and suspicion flared as he sensed a change; a movement in another dimension, shifting furtively and quickly between planes. Reaching out towards the mortal world . . .

Ferocious energy flicked into focus in Yandros's mind as he realized suddenly what was afoot. With a violence that ripped apart his surroundings and distorted Chaos's fabric into torturously shrieking frenzy, he hurled a compulsion that was both warning and command towards his brothers in the castle –

Tarod felt the violent echo of Yandros's imperative, and the dark nucleus of shadow that had begun to build in the courtyard collapsed and vanished. The other Chaos lord tensed, and his aura burned more intensely as he too responded to the alarm.

Tarod said, 'The Gate – '

As one they turned, their human quarry forgotten. Across the courtyard was the pillared stoa and the door to the spiral stairway; at a look from Tarod the door jolted open, and two shadows darted across the flagstones, vanishing between the pillars.

Any mortal unlucky enough to be on the stairs or in the library at that moment would have been swept aside and obliterated as the two passed, but the way was empty and seconds later the vault's inner door slammed behind Tarod and his brother as they entered the sloping corridor that led to the Marble Hall. The magi were at the far end of the corridor, gathered outside the Hall but keeping their distance from the metallic door, which was glowing with a fearsome radiance as though it had turned white-hot. Pirane, on the edge of the group, saw the newcomers and came swiftly to meet them.

'My lords, we can't enter the Hall! The First Magus attempted to go through the door, but –'

Tarod interrupted her sharply. 'What happened to him?'

'He's safe, but not unscathed. My lords, the Gate is –'

'We know.' Tarod moved past her; the magi stood aside and he approached Vordegh.

The First Magus, in his colleagues' midst, was on his feet but shaking violently; his garments appeared to be soaked and burned at one and the same time, and veins of livid light danced and skittered over his body, the residue of a power that was slowly fading. Where his left hand should have been, a taloned, bird-like claw clenched and quivered convulsively. Tarod understood instantly the nature and intensity of the power that had attacked him. No mortal agency could control anything of that magnitude, and Vordegh must have been aware of it – madman he might be, Tarod thought, but his courage couldn't be denied.

Vordegh turned his head as the Chaos lords reached him. The forces loose in the Hall had ravaged his face; one side was seared and burned, while the other was encrusted with nacreous scales, the beginnings of a ghastly metamorphosis. But his eyes as he returned Tarod's gaze were icily steady. 'I tried to enter the Hall, my lord,' he said. His voice was unpleasantly distorted by the power's warping effect. 'I tried to control it –'

'It's beyond any human ability,' Tarod told him. 'Keep your colleagues back; we must deal with this ourselves.' Briefly he touched the First Magus's face, then his arm; the scales vanished and the talon flowed back into the form of a human hand, and Vordegh's dark eyes took on a tinge of surprise, as though he hadn't expected Tarod to trouble himself over such a trifling matter. Tarod returned a hard-edged and faintly sardonic smile, then, ignoring the radiation that engulfed his arm as he reached out, opened the glowing door.

He and his brother entered the Hall and roiling darkness met them, shot through with a clashing frenzy of elemental power. Fire and water seethed, battling and colliding; the pressure of a vast mass crushed down, warping the marble pillars, buckling the mosaic floor. The shriek of a rabid wind battered against Tarod's senses, and amid the maelstrom was a derangement of voices; insane laughter, mindless yelling, wild sobbing and, steady and relentless above the babble, a gargantuan and continuous howling. They moved into the pandemonium, and at their backs the door swung shut with a noise that sent echoes tumbling through the Marble Hall. Fire roared at them, water surged, and the Hall's dimensions twisted into hideous illusions. Tarod felt the elemental forces flowing through him, changing his form; he ignored the mutations, and the violent distortion of perspectives, and moved towards the heart of the Hall where the tower of black light burned and raged ungovernably.

Yandros! The call breached dimensions into Chaos's own realm as he sought Yandros's mind. Then suddenly there was the surge of a new presence, a glittering wall of energy bearing down and breaking through the violence. The churning darkness shook with a glare like sheet lightning; he heard his brother's cry of fury as a savagely hostile force pummelled through the Marble Hall –

'*Now!*' Aeoris's voice rang out, and the wall of darkness began to crack apart as the spear of Order's energy clove towards its heart. Light howled through the cracks; they split wider, tearing into chasms as the wall started to crumble. Fire exploded from the spear, a blaze of radiance that blotted out all else, and implacably Aeoris cried, 'Strike – strike, my brothers, *and take what is rightfully ours!*'

Yandros saw the Gate's vortex beginning to deform, beginning to invert; saw the spear of white light penetrating towards its core, and his voice seared to the two minds in the Marble Hall.

'*Seal the Gate! Seal it, before it's too late!*'

The command shattered into Tarod's consciousness, but as he and his kinsman tried to obey, the wall of alien power hammered through the Hall again. The howling, yelling voices collapsed into discord, and through the discord a single high, clear note began to rise.

'*Aeoris!*' Tarod's warning was all but drowned as the shimmering note gained in volume and pitch, shaking the Hall, ripping the darkness apart. '*Fight him! Drive him back!*'

Their minds merged, doubling strength and intensity. They felt the Gate, a whirlwind careening out of control, and they felt Order's presence reaching towards it, grasping, claiming –

Their power snared the portal, the border between dimensions. Together, they chained their minds with Yandros's – then elemental havoc imploded in the Hall as the full impact of the forces unleashed by the Gate bore down on them and channelled through them. They felt Yandros take hold of the rampaging energy, felt it sweep past and out and away into the Gate, felt the tower of black light tottering, disintegrating, breaking the spear of Aeoris' hold –

Aeoris screamed a furious imprecation as the huge backlash of the implosion ripped between worlds. The vortex was collapsing, he couldn't maintain his grasp –

A clap of noise that would have irreparably deafened any human listener smashed through the Marble Hall.

Then Tarod raised a hand — and instantly the sound cut off into stunning silence.

The Marble Hall was still. Pastel mists shifted between the slender pillars and swirled gently over the floor, creating strange and beautiful illusions. Behind Tarod and his brother the seven statues showed dim and immense, their outlines vague in the shifting light. And at their feet, the black circle that marked the Gate was nothing but an inert part of the mosaic pattern.

Tarod raised his head and his green eyes scanned through the Hall and beyond it, seeking any trace of the portal. There was nothing. The seal was complete, and the Gate was gone.

Fury began to rise in him; a fury so immense that he knew even his mind's boundaries weren't enough to contain it. *Aeoris* — he had broken free from the shackles that had held him; he had forced the shattering of Chaos's strongest link with the mortal world. And behind Aeoris, sheltering now in the cesspit of his protection, were the human traitors who had thus far escaped retribution.

He swung round, and a bolt of crimson fire cracked across the Hall as some tiny fragment of his rage found an outlet. Then, with his brother at his heels, he stalked towards the door.

At first, in the wake of Tarod and Pirane's departure, Savrinor's mind had been paralysed. Every muscle and nerve in his body seemed to be out of control and he could only stare blindly down at the deserted entrance hall, unable to move, unable to think. Then abruptly the paralysis had snapped. He knew little of the facts, understood less; but suddenly that didn't matter, for instinct had taken over and his brain was working at fever pitch again.

Taking a fierce hold on Andraia's arm and ignoring her protest, he pulled her back to his chambers at a run. There was no time for explanations, even if he could have found the words; intuition was goading him and there was room for nothing else. He didn't know what he could do, how either of them might be of *use* – if the gods did have work for them, Tarod hadn't paused to leave any instructions. But he couldn't be a passive observer, not in this. There had to be *something*.

Reaching his apartment, he propelled Andraia inside and went through to the bedroom, where he flung off his robe and started to put on more practical clothing. She followed him, and suddenly her voice cut through his churning thoughts.

'Savrinor. Do you believe it was Benet?'

Savrinor looked up, taken unawares by the question, and a coldly detached segment of his mind which still seemed to be functioning against heavy odds found an instant to appreciate and approve the sharply-honed edge of her thoughts. Most women would be too busy at this moment railing at his cavalier treatment to think beyond their own petty grievances; they would be demanding apologies, insisting on explanations, wasting more time – but that wasn't Andraia's way. Knowing that, and knowing too that there was no need to even try to contain his fury, he made no attempt to prevent his answer to her question from showing in his eyes as he countered harshly, 'What do *you* believe?'

She turned away, aware that their thoughts ran parallel, and Savrinor uttered a clipped, aggressive laugh. 'We must give him the benefit of the doubt, of course. Keep a sense of proportion; make no assumptions and no accusations. A man is innocent until and unless his guilt is proven.' He wrenched the previous day's shirt over his head, tearing the silk but not noticing, or not caring. 'After all, isn't that what the entire furore of the past few days has been *about*?' Savagely he flicked his hair free of the shirt-collar, snatched up a belt, buckled it and strode past her into the outer room, to his cabinet. The cabinet doors smacked open;

264

Andraia heard glass smash as a bottle fell from one of the shelves, and she emerged from the bedchamber in time to see Savrinor mixing something in a small cup.

'I should have had the wit to realize.' His voice was ferocious. 'I've had more than forty years to learn the lesson; I should have enough sense by now to know that people are filth and that the human soul is unfailingly perfidious!' He picked up a wine flagon and threw some of its contents into the potion. 'I should have left him to Vordegh's mercies – no, damn Vordegh; I should have killed him with my own hands! But oh, no; not me, not the devious Savrinor. That wasn't *subtle* enough; it didn't fit with my personal scheme, my personal code, my thrice-damned *slate!*'

'You broke the slate,' Andraia said sharply.

He turned his head and looked challengingly at her. 'Did I? I doubt it. Oh, I know very well what I said to you that night, and have said to a few other people since then; but you should also know by now that I'm the most adept liar in the castle when it suits my purposes. That's all part of my reputation, isn't it? That, and my precious slate. Debts of honour and points of principle. Only I seem to be alone in my belief that these things *matter!*'

He put the cup to his mouth, swallowed the contents in one. The taste was vile and he realized instantly that in his agitation his concentration had slipped and the dose of Moonwrack was twice what it should have been. Not that he cared; with no prospect of sleep in the foreseeable future, he would need all the help his body could tolerate.

'Honour and principle . . . there's not a spark of *either* in this benighted world!' He slammed the cup down on the table and swung round, towards the door – then stopped.

'I'm sorry.' Another feeling was fighting to break through the rage. He wouldn't have called it rationality,

265

but at least it had a sane element. 'I have no right to vent my malignance on you.'

'Oh, you have,' Andraia said bitterly. 'But for me, you'd have left Benet to face what he brought upon himself. And rightly so.'

'If I implied that at any time, I was lying yet again. My reasons were entirely selfish, as they always are: it simply gratified me to undo a little of what Iselia had been able to achieve. So my anger is none of your concern.' Savrinor pushed one hand distractedly through his hair and Andraia saw that the hand was shaking. 'It's directed entirely at myself, and I shall have the common courtesy to keep it to myself from now on.' He started towards the door. 'I must go. If anyone wants to know where I am, tell them to ask the gods.'

For the first time since their liaison had begun he didn't kiss her, didn't offer a salute of any kind, but simply left the room. Andraia heard his footsteps, sharp and rapid, diminishing in the direction of the stairs, and she clutched her own upper arms, struggling to quell the emotions that were building up inside her. Emotions of rage and of hatred for a traitor. She knew the truth as well as Savrinor did, and the fact that neither of them had been willing to speak the ultimately damning words made no difference. Benetan had betrayed them all. The gods. The magi, who had granted him the privilege to become what he was. His friends. And, petty and vain though it might be, what hurt more deeply than anything was his betrayal of her and of what they had once been to each other.

Well, that would die now. She would crush and kill it, as Savrinor had killed his own feelings for Iselia. It would be hard for her, as she knew it had been hard for him, but she could find the same solace that he had found in a greater and deeper loyalty – loyalty to Chaos.

On the heels of the thought, she heard a sound begin to rise in the courtyard. For a moment it sounded like distant voices, whispering . . . then it shifted subtly into another timbre, another dimension, and she realized that her first impression had been very, very wrong . . .

Andraia felt the hair at her nape rise; and suddenly beneath her feet the floor began to quiver with a huge, rhythmic pulse. Outside, beyond the window, a terrible glow was shivering into life . . .

She turned, ran for the inner room, and began to search feverishly for her clothes.

Savrinor reached the courtyard moments after the two Chaos lords had returned from the Marble Hall. And as he emerged from the main doors, he was in time to witness their work. His heart crashed against his ribs in shock, and he recoiled back into the shelter of the doorway, jerking his head aside, too stunned to look again. He could hear it moving. A rustling, whispering sound, almost gentle, like rain falling on grass. Its shadow – but no, *it* was the shadow, a void, an impossible darkness – spread over the courtyard like a vast, soft wing, and that shadow blotted out the walls, the spires, the sky, the world. Breathtaking cold washed over Savrinor and he clenched his teeth against the power of it, sensing its enormity, knowing how easily and how surely it could crush his soul.

Then, like a voice in a dream, reaching his ears across a seemingly infinite distance, he heard Tarod speak.

'Fetch them, dark one. Carry them to the Seven Hells.'

The pulsing began again; the slow, subliminal and perfectly rhythmic heartbeat of Chaos. It caught hold of Savrinor's psyche, calling him, pulling him; slowly, unable to resist the call, he uncovered his eyes and looked towards the courtyard again.

He had one clear glimpse of the creature from Chaos in its entirety. Of the proud, alien head etched against the sky like a window onto nothing; of the single, glacial star, impossibly vast yet impossibly remote, that was its eye. Of its *power* . . .

There was no display, no crack of energy, no sudden and violent vanishing. The being faded, slowly, like a nightmare drifting away at the moment of waking. As it faded, silence gripped the courtyard; a silence that nothing in the world could have impelled Savrinor to break. A gust of wind blew across his face, a chill and capricious snap out of the north, but still he stood motionless, refusing even to turn his head aside lest the smallest movement should crack the thrall. Wildly, in the way that trivial and irrational matters sometimes seemed important at such moments, he wondered if Andraia was looking out, if she had seen, if she was afraid —

Tarod turned and looked directly at the historian. He smiled coldly, cruelly, and Savrinor's heart lurched again with the knowledge of how few mortals had ever witnessed such a smile. It was an extreme, and terrifying, privilege.

Then the being was gone.

Benetan was manoeuvring into the cleft behind the rock outcrop when Kaldar moaned suddenly and started to writhe. Benetan's arms and hands were too numbed to hold him; he felt the weight slide away and they both collapsed into the snow.

'Kaldar!' Benetan struggled to his knees, spitting ice. 'Kaldar, keep still, don't try to fight me!'

'I can't see . . .' Kaldar's hands clutched at him. 'Benet, I can't *see* anything! Where are we?' Then he put his fingers to his own face, touching cheek, nose, eyes, and his voice rose harshly. '*What's happened to me?*'

The idea of trying to explain anything under their present circumstances made Benetan want to laugh hysterically. With an effort he quelled it and said breathlessly, 'It happened when the Chaos Gate exploded. You caught the blast.' Then, trying to dredge up at least a spark of common humanity, he added, 'How bad's the pain?'

'Nnnh.' Kaldar shook his head. 'It doesn't hurt. Too

268

cold to hurt. For the gods' sakes, Benet, where *are* we?'

'In the mountains. But I can't find your cave.'

For a few moments Kaldar breathed harshly, rapidly. Then he said: 'The Gate blinded me, it burned out my eyes. Didn't it?' Benetan didn't answer and his voice rose angrily, 'Don't try to pretend – I'm not a child to be placated! *Tell me!*'

'Yes,' Benetan said. 'It burned out your eyes. But Kaldar, Lord Aeoris will –'

He didn't finish, for Kaldar uttered an appalling laugh. 'Lord Aeoris can't afford to spare attention for us now – he has Chaos to contend with!' Suddenly, convulsively, he jerked into a sitting position, throwing off Benetan's attempt to restrain him. 'You said we're not in the cave. Where, then?'

'The pass. There's an outcrop, with a cleft in it – it's out of the wind at least. But a snowfall's blocked the way ahead of us. Kaldar, Chaos will send something after us. I've tried to call to Lord Aeoris for help, but I haven't the talent, I can't make him hear me. You've *got* to help me!'

Kaldar shivered violently. 'I can't.' His teeth were chattering. 'No fire, no incense. Unless –'

The words died away. Suddenly Kaldar was very still.

'What is it?' A new kind of chill struck through Benetan's bones.

'I don't know. But I can sense a change.' Kaldar turned his head as though to look at the other man, a reflexive habit. 'Can't you feel it?'

'No . . .' But Benetan's heart was starting to pound.

'Something's coming . . .' Kaldar's hand groped up. 'Benet, help me up. Help me to stand.'

Benetan hauled him upright. Clutching his arms for support, Kaldar turned his head slowly, his innermost senses probing, feeling, searching. Then –

'Oh, gods . . .' There was terror in his voice.

'What? What is it?' Benetan railed silently at his own uselessness. 'Kaldar, *what's coming?*'

In the crater, Simbrian cried out, 'Ah, no! *Kaldar! Kaldar, I can't reach you!*' And suddenly he knew that they had only seconds, only moments, before what was bearing down on their friends engulfed and annihilated them –

'*LORD AEORIS!*' His cry ripped physically from his throat, ripped between dimensions, seeking the great lord of Order. '*LORD AEORIS, HELP THEM! IF YOU LOVE THEM, HELP THEM NOW!!*'

Kaldar was gasping, his breath sawing like a drowning man as his psyche told him what his eyes could not – but Benetan couldn't respond. He was at the edge of the outcrop, and his mind and body were immobilized as he stared in awe at what was flowing slowly, silently towards them through the pass. *Darkness* – but never in his life had he seen or imagined darkness like it. It was a vortex of utter absence, total nothingness, and as it moved it seemed that all in its path did not merely vanish but . . . ceased. Ceased to exist; ceased ever to have existed. It was negation, obliteration; a force so far beyond death that he couldn't assimilate any conception of what it could do, what it *would* do, to a human soul.

And under the ground beneath him, in the rocks around him, even in the air that he struggled to breathe, he could feel a grim, malevolent throbbing.

'Benet . . .' Kaldar's voice cracked suddenly from his throat. He could feel the thing, feel it approaching, and he knew on a level far beyond Benetan's reach what it was capable of doing. 'Benet, your knife . . . for our sweet gods' sakes, draw your knife! *Kill us both!*'

Simbrian's desperate call penetrated the screaming inferno of Aeoris's rage and frustration, and lightning smashed

between the white thunderheads that cloaked the lord of
Order as his attention was snatched to the mortal world.

'. . . *IF YOU LOVE THEM, HELP THEM NOW* . . .'
For a split second Aeoris's fury focused savagely on Simbrian, on Kaldar, on all of them, for their presumption.
The Gate had been snatched from his grasp, his intent had
been thwarted – in the face of that their petty human
travails were *nothing*, and he wanted to strike at
them, scourge their arrogance, teach them an indelible
lesson –

Then the fury flashed away as a fearsomely calm reasoning took over the lord of Order's mind. Oh yes, there was
hatred in him; a hatred so great that it could goad him
to destroy without thinking, without pausing. But it
had one focus and one alone. The being, the demon, the
ancient enemy who had confounded him in his bid for
supremacy . . .

He saw what was moving through the mountains
towards the fugitives, saw the hands and the minds that
manipulated it, saw their cold intent, and abruptly a new
feeling moved in him. The Gate was beyond Order's reach
now – but its destruction had still served his purpose, for
it had tilted the balance of power. For the first time in an
aeon, Order and Chaos faced one another on equal terms.
It was not enough, not yet; and Aeoris knew well that the
tide could all too easily turn again. But the first and greatest
change had come; and it would be a trifling but piquant
pleasure to add another small twist to Yandros's discomfiture.

The dark harbinger was close to its prey now. Aeoris
sensed the bleakness of its mindless hunger, and felt the
rising terror of the two mortals in its path. On the White
Isle, Simbrian and his fellows were striving to mass psychic
power; but the god knew that their strength was too slight
for such a task. His head turned; around him the clouds
rolled into new forms, and in the human realm thunder

grumbled high and far out over the sea beyond the White Isle. Aeoris's right hand flexed; then the fingers curled –

'*Benet, don't waver! Do it! Do it now!*'

Benetan had pulled the knife from its sheath but his hand was paralysed. He could kill Kaldar, he knew he could; this imperative was enough to smash down every standard and every ethic – but his hand wouldn't *move*. The thrall of the demon had him in a grip he couldn't break; his mind was crippled, his body frozen, and all he could do was stare at the encroaching darkness and await the fate it promised.

Kaldar cried out again and his hand groped wildly, trying to find and grasp the knife. By sheer chance his fingers locked on Benetan's wrist; he pulled, wrenching the other man off balance – and as Benetan staggered backwards the snow under him suddenly erupted in a white blast. He was flung off his feet, cannoning into Kaldar – and the jolt broke the demon's spell, shattering its hold on him and bringing instinct and reflex back in a fearsome rush. He rolled, his body twisting to bring him back upright in one fluent movement, and flinging the knife aside he wrenched his sword from its scabbard. *This would be faster, cleaner, surer – thwart them at the last; cleave Kaldar's head from his shoulders and then reverse the blade and drive it through his own heart* – Two-handed, he swung the weapon up –

And out of nowhere another blade, twice his own height, blazing with light and with no hand to hold it, swept across his sword's path and shattered it in two.

In the castle courtyard, the backlash of Aeoris's violent intervention ricocheted into the minds of the two Chaos lords. They felt the thrust of an inimical force smashing the link between them and their quarry, ripping the prey from the hunter's reach. In the pass, Benetan yelled in shock as the broken sword was torn from his hand and went spinning away. He glimpsed the darkness recoiling, heard a high, shrieking note that seemed to split his skull in half –

And the world exploded in a white-hot blast.

'*Aeoris!*' The shout tore simultaneously from Benetan's throat and from Simbrian's as in an eruption of light the two figures were hurled into the middle of the circle. Kaldar sprawled, stunned, on the crater floor, while Benetan, by a miracle still on his feet, keeled towards Simbrian, who had the wit to catch him before he fell.

'Benetan!' The sorcerer's powerful hands gripped the younger man's shoulders. 'Benetan, it's all right, you're safe, you –' Then the words cut off as he looked wildly around. 'Iselia – great gods, where's Iselia, where *is* she?'

Benetan was struggling to speak but shock had torn away his breath and he could only fall to his knees, doubled over and gasping. The circle was breaking up as people ran to help Kaldar; Simbrian opened his mouth again, wanting to shout the question, shake Benetan, wring an answer from him – but before he could do anything, another voice cut across the rising babble.

'Get them into a cave!' Sheet lightning rattled between the crater walls and a sound like a vast door slamming echoed through the bowl as Aeoris materialized. The lord of Order's face was a savage mask, eyes burning molten gold, and his white cloak billowed around him like a cloud-bank as he stalked towards his human followers. In his right hand, the glittering sword glared with a lethal radiance.

'There's no time for questions or answers,' Aeoris said harshly. 'Carry Kaldar to shelter, *quickly!*' He sensed what was coming, sensed the rising swell of Yandros's rage, and vehemently he cast the knowledge into Simbrian's mind to emphasize his warning. The sorcerer's dark eyes widened, hardened; then he hauled Benetan upright and propelled

273

him towards the bowl's edge and the cave network beyond.

'Help them!' His voice rang across the bowl. 'Get them under cover, and take shelter yourselves!'

The small human tide began to move more rapidly as his companions sensed the urgency in the command. Aeoris raised his head and looked up; for an instant a fearsome tension swelled in the crater as the lord of Order's mind reached out beyond the world's limitations, to another plane . . .

Wreathed in shadow at the heart of his realm, Yandros held and honed the slow, pulsing violence of his wrath. It was contained, it was controlled . . . but it filled him with a titanic and voracious hunger that every last fragment of his being longed to assuage. A hunger for vengeance. A hunger for devastation. A hunger for *reprisal*.

A hand, skeletal, graceful, the skin deathly white, appeared from the deep, shifting darkness that cloaked Yandros's figure, and his long fingers curved with dire grace. Chaos responded; he felt its dimensions shift and alter around him, moulding form and function in compliance with his will. He felt potential become reality; felt it cohere and begin to take on life. And he felt the loathing rise like a black wall . . .

Aeoris called out; a word, a single command. Cold light flared; and his brothers were with him. His head turned; Simbrian, looking back, felt an imminent premonition –

CHAPTER XVIII

Yandros gave no warning. The Warp simply exploded out of the clear night sky, smashing through dimensions and howling into existence above the crater. Simbrian heard a colossal gale roaring from nowhere towards them, then the entire island shook as the wind struck it. Rocks and debris twisted into the air, crashing against the walls; high above their heads a vast slab of the crater's fabric cracked, split away and plummeted down, spinning towards Aeoris –

The lord of Order looked up. Light seared around him, and those humans who hadn't yet reached the safety of the caves flung themselves aside as a stunning discharge of power cracked from the sword in his hand. The falling slab twisted in mid-air then shattered in a blinding eruption that lit the crater like a midsummer dawn. Simbrian had barely regained his feet before a second huge force pummelled him back, pounding his senses as an insane tangle of lightning sheared out of the Warp's heart. He saw its myriad bolts hurtling groundwards, felt the onslaught of their lethal energy, and he yelled wordlessly, furiously, a cry that was both protest and warning, knowing that against this his strength and skill were worth less than nothing. The Warp's gargantuan voice dinned in his ears; people were screaming, and he swung round, yelling over the insane din for them to run, get *clear!* The lords of Order were at the centre of the bowl now, white fire blazing around them. Simbrian thought he heard Aeoris's voice rising above the mayhem, then suddenly seven spears of light flared towards the crater rim. They collided, coalesced, and as the Warp hurled a second charge of lightning groundwards, the light flowered outwards –

'Ah, *no!*' Yandros twisted about, and suddenly the pandemonium that his realm had become was stilled. The highest Chaos lord transmuted his form, and his eyes, narrow and balefully dark in a face lit by the fires of his hair, stared broodingly through the seething murk and into the mortal world.

There was no *point* in this. It was nothing more than a waste of time and strength; retaliation without forethought. And that had never been Yandros's way.

His thoughts sent a shudder through all Chaos's dimensions and he turned his head, studying the currents and patterns that moved and clashed uneasily around him. What he saw made his expression turn cruelly malign. This was an impasse. A deadlock between two antagonists whose powers were suddenly and unexpectedly on a par. And though at present the clash between them had its focus in the human world, that state of affairs would not last. With a memory that reached back beyond any mortal concept of time, Yandros recalled other ages and other conflicts in the unremitting war between himself and Aeoris, and knew that, although mortals might play their own part in the battles to come, the greater game would take place on another plane and in quite another form. He might destroy whatever human forces Order rallied to their cause; Aeoris in his turn might wreak havoc among Chaos's own faithful. But that counted for nothing. When the true contest began, the human worshippers of both powers would be obliged to look to their own salvation, for they would have no meaning.

Yandros touched his own breast, and a cold star materialized over his heart. Like Order's human followers, and like the Warp he had sent to their fortress island, it had no true relevance; it was simply a gesture to implant a modicum of fear into gullible mortal hearts and make some think twice before dancing to Order's tune. Let Aeoris enjoy this hiatus. While it lasted, he and his own brothers had other matters to attend to.

His expression modulated to quiet, deadly contempt. And slowly, implacably, the star began to pulse.

The Warp's disappearance was as sudden and violent as its advent, and in the aftermath Simbrian could only stand numbed while his senses tried to assimilate the new shock. But as wild turmoil gave way to an eerie calm, he sensed something else, something new. He looked up –

Both moons had set and the sky overhead was a black void. But above the crater, poised over its exact heart, a single star hung. Seven spears of light radiated from it, pulsing in a steady, rhythmic flux. The symbol of Chaos . . .

Then the thrall broke and reality snapped back. He saw human faces, indistinct in the darkness, shocked, striving to recover their wits. Someone swore, then stifled the oath. He looked about for Nanithe –

'Simbrian.' Aeoris's voice impinged urgently and the sorcerer turned. The lord of Order was approaching him, eyes burning, hair glittering with an unnatural light. 'We've little time to waste,' Aeoris said without preamble. 'This first attack may have been short-lived, but Yandros won't stay his hand for long.'

'Stay his hand?' Simbrian was dismayed. 'I thought you destroyed the Warp, my lord!'

'We can have no direct effect on any creation of Chaos – nor they on any creation of ours, though that's worth little to us as yet. No; this was simply a brief test, and I don't doubt that Yandros has other experiments in store.' The lord of Order glanced speculatively towards the cave network. 'For all that Kaldar and Benetan achieved, we haven't gained the advantage that we had hoped. Yandros and his brothers sealed the Gate before we could seize control of it and we've lost the one chance we had to cripple Chaos at an early stage.' He smiled at Simbrian, but the smile was hard and humourless. 'You and your people have risked a great deal to come this far, Simbrian. But the risks you must run now will make those early achievements pale by comparison. You must prepare to face the full might of Chaos – and I don't think I need explain to you what that could mean.'

There was a vibration in the rock floor now, matching the pulse of the star overhead. It made Simbrian feel queasy, but he thrust the feeling down. 'No, my lord, you don't.' Then he matched Aeoris's smile. 'But having come this far I'm not about to turn back, and I believe that when I say that, I speak for us all.' He glanced towards the caves. 'Even for Benetan Liss.'

'Ah, yes; Benetan.' The molten light in Aeoris's eyes modulated. 'While this hiatus lasts we must speak to him and hear his story.' He turned towards the caves, indicating that Simbrian should accompany him. As they started across the bowl floor the sorcerer said, 'I doubt that it'll be happy news, my lord. Iselia . . .' He hesitated, then forced himself to voice it. 'She's dead. She must be, or Benetan and Kaldar would have tried to save her even at the cost of their own lives.'

Aeoris glanced at him, his expression mingling compassion with something harder. 'Yes,' he said. 'They would.'

Simbrian closed his eyes. 'May her soul find peace . . .'

Aeoris was aware that Iselia's soul – or whatever remained of it – could have little hope of that, but he kept the thought to himself and walked on in silence.

The star overhead seemed to be pulsing more brightly, but its influence could not touch the sense of calm and stillness that had descended on the island. With an effort Simbrian set his emotions aside. Grief must be held in abeyance; there were more urgent issues to be resolved. And, cruel and senseless though Iselia's death might be, it added a poignant edge to their cause. And gave an extra dimension to the prospect of revenge.

The seven-rayed star flowered silently into being above the castle, and its pulsing glare sent shadows skittering across the flagstones of the courtyard. Then a sharp sound broke the silence, as though a pane of glass had cracked cleanly in two, and Yandros stepped out of a hard-edged angle of darkness near the central fountain. A disturbing light burned around the greatest Chaos lord; it gave his hair a molten quality. And his eyes were black windows onto nothing. Yandros spared the briefest of glances for Savrinor before looking at his two brothers. 'Aeoris took them?' His voice was composed but glacial.

Tarod inclined his head, and Yandros's shoulders lifted in a shrug. 'It's of no consequence. They're insignificant now that they've done their work, and vengeance serves no worthwhile purpose.' Silver glittered in the black. 'Your action in the Marble Hall was timely. We may be forced to meet Aeoris on equal terms in the wake of this, but at least he hasn't succeeded in his bid for ascendancy.' He turned, his gaze raking the dark courtyard. 'Where are our faithful? Cowering in safety, for fear of the punishment we might inflict on them?' The green-haired Chaos lord uttered a cynical bark of a laugh, and Yandros's lip curled. 'Yes, well; perhaps that's not entirely surprising. But their inadequacy has been well matched by our complacency . . . under other circumstances, I might have found amusement in the irony of such a combination. As matters stand, though, the joke has little to commend it.'

'The Marble Hall is quiet,' Tarod said. 'Vordegh and the other magi are awaiting our – or your – command.'

'They'll find little comfort in what I have to say to them. But all right; we might as well get the thing done rather than procrastinate.' Yandros started to turn towards the stoa, then glanced back over his shoulder. 'Savrinor.'

Rigid on the steps, Savrinor made a quick obeisance. 'My lord?'

Yandros gave him a harsh smile. 'You seem to have a stronger stomach than the majority of your peers, historian. Come with us to the Hall. You'll have a good deal to recount for the archives after tonight.'

Savrinor bowed again. 'Yes, Lord Yandros.'

He followed the three across the courtyard, his mind reeling with shock, awe and impotent dread. Down the spiral stairs, through the library and on towards the Marble Hall; a familiar route, and it awoke a clash of recent and ugly memories. There was a sullen, uneasy glow in the narrow passage that sloped down to the Hall, but the metallic door no longer glared white-hot. It stood half open; at a glance from Yandros it jerked fully back on its hinges, and they walked into the Hall's misty reaches.

The magi were waiting, gathered by the seven statues. Yandros acknowledged their obeisances with a nod, then turned to the black mosaic circle that marked – or had marked – the Chaos Gate. Briefly his focus shifted to another dimension and he satisfied himself that the seal was complete. Then his gaze returned to the physical plane and to something else, faintly discernible in the mist, that lay on the floor a short way from the black circle. Something incongruous, anomalous.

He walked slowly towards the object and looked down. Then his mouth curved in a faint, bleak smile. The shape was barely recognizable as human, for the forces the heretics had let loose here had wrought damage enough, and the elemental mayhem that followed had taken a further toll. All that remained to distinguish her was one uncharred lock of blonde hair. Yandros found that he could take no satisfaction from the nature of her fate. She had not mattered enough for her destruction to give him any solace, and he felt only faint distaste mingled with a glimmer of pity for the naivety of her blind zeal.

He looked over his shoulder and raised one hand, beckoning. 'Savrinor. A small detail, but I think it's as well you should see it for yourself.'

Savrinor approached, looked at the remains of the body . . . and was suddenly very still.

'Presumably she was killed by the Gate's implosion,' Yandros said detachedly. 'Or our friends would have taken her with them.'

Savrinor continued to stare down. 'I wish they had, my lord.' His voice was hard, peculiarly controlled. 'A wounded companion would have hampered them, and –' Suddenly he didn't seem able to say any more.

'And allowed my brothers to intercept them before they reached the Maze, thus ridding us of three instead of merely one. Quite. But it hardly matters now.' Yandros paused, then looked astutely at the historian. 'I imagine her death was quick enough to be relatively painless. Does that disappoint you?'

Savrinor wanted to say yes, but knew it would be a lie. What lay on the floor would have sickened him under any circumstances; he had no stomach for brutality of this order. But to remember her living face and body as he did; to recall his old feelings . . . for all the contempt and hatred that had replaced those feelings, such a level of vindictiveness was beyond his capability.

He expelled air from his lungs with a harsh sound. 'No, my lord.' He dared to meet Yandros's gaze. 'Forgive me.'

Yandros smiled, thinly but, Savrinor realized, with understanding. 'From you,' the Chaos lord said, 'I expected nothing less. But don't squander yourself in grieving for her. She was never worth it.'

Savrinor closed his eyes and nodded. 'I know that.'

To his shock then Yandros laid a hand briefly on his

shoulder before turning away and moving back to where the magi were waiting.

'Vordegh.' The Chaos lord's tone and demeanour changed as he addressed the First Magus, and Vordegh stepped forward. For the first time in many days his attendant shroud of shadows was absent. He looked at Yandros, and his eyes seemed to be having some difficulty in focusing.

'There is no point,' Yandros said banefully, 'in dwelling in detail on the mistakes and deficiencies which have led us to this pass. What's done is done, and even I haven't the power to change it.' An unnatural and potentially lethal fire flickered in his hair. 'I will say only that our present predicament has come about as a result of a profitless and ill-advised preoccupation with petty concerns, and I will leave you to draw your own conclusions as to my underlying meaning.'

Far beneath the Marble Hall's floor a subliminal pulsing began, and it seemed to echo in a malignant aura that lit suddenly around Yandros's figure. 'For what cold comfort it may be to any of you,' he continued, 'I hold myself entirely to blame. I was unwise enough to trust in my mortal avatars. I trusted them to maintain Chaos's rule of this world and all within it, and even when I saw that trivial distractions were diverting them from the true threat, I trusted them to recognize and rectify their folly without the need for anything more stringent than a mild warning. That, as I have belatedly realized, was a mistake.'

He turned, started to pace across the floor. The mists cast echoes of his footfalls back to his motionless listeners. 'But it is easy – all too easy – to gain wisdom along with hindsight. Your pettiness, our laxness; it makes no difference now which was to blame, and I am not interested in debating the matter. The *facts* are what count. And the *facts* are that Aeoris and his aberrant brood have broken free from the shackles with which we bound them centuries ago, and are making a bid to gain supremacy in this world. How they broke those shackles is, again, irrelevant. But they have already struck one drastic blow against us, by depriving us of the means to crush their ambitions before they can take form. They have forced us to seal – and thus effectively destroy – the Chaos Gate.'

Savrinor felt as though a cold knife had been thrust through him, and though on some extraneous level his chronicler's eyes and ears were aware of the magi's consternation, he couldn't take their reactions in or afford them any meaning. Yandros had stopped and turned to face his listeners again, and with an appalling and disorientating sense of unreality Savrinor listened as he told them, concisely and acidly, what the three heretics had achieved. The wand broken, Chaos's link with the Gate destroyed. But for Yandros's last-minute command to smash the portal and thus seal the Gate for good, the demons of Order would have gained control of it. And control of the Gate was the key to invincible power in this world. That thought made the historian feel sick to the pit of his soul.

'Our strongest link with you is broken,' the Chaos lord said, 'and Aeoris is mustering his forces to challenge our rule in this dimension. With the Gate at our disposal it would have been the work of a moment to smash his ambitions, send him crawling back to his own realm and consign every last one of his followers to the Seven Hells. But the Gate is gone, and with it our dominance of this world. We have no choice but to meet Aeoris's challenge on equal terms.'

Silence held the Marble Hall in a strangling grip. Yandros listened to the silence for a few moments, then continued.

'The lords of Order are no more capable of destroying us than we are of destroying them.' His eyes flared venomously. 'If that were the case, we would have wiped them from the face of the cosmos a very long time ago. Nor is

Aeoris interested in destroying us. His ambitions lie in this world – he and his brothers want to oust us and take our places as humanity's sole gods.' Savrinor uttered an involuntary oath at that, and Yandros flicked him a bitter smile. 'Our good historian is clearly well aware of what *that* would mean. But Aeoris's success or failure will not be determined entirely by us. A great deal will depend on *you*. For while Aeoris challenges our sway, his human forces will challenge yours, and with the Gate gone you will no longer be able to call directly on power from our realm. You must rely on your own resources to meet and counter them.

'I make no claim to know the magnitude of the threat they pose to you. All I know beyond doubt is that your survival will depend entirely on whether your powers are great enough to oppose the powers of those who have pledged themselves to Order. That, again, is something I cannot predict – though I trust I don't need to emphasize that it would be unwise in the extreme to underestimate adversaries who have already succeeded in calling Aeoris and his scum back to this world, whilst hiding their work and their intentions from all scrutiny.' Yandros's eyes, which had been glittering purple, turned to a metallic shade, and his look became caustic. 'Much will also depend on whether you are still able to inspire and command the loyalty of the people you rule. And in that regard, I anticipate that you will reap the harvest you have sown.'

The silence seemed to draw more tightly on the Hall, closing in like a suffocating curtain ... or, Savrinor thought with a deep inward shudder, like a shroud to wrap the dead. Then Yandros looked again at Vordegh.

'With that in mind, First Magus,' he said, 'I have one final question to resolve. The question of whether or not you are fit to continue in your office.'

A wave of prickling cold swept over Savrinor as he took in the clear implication in Yandros's words. Yandros was staring at Vordegh, his eyes level and penetrating and thoughtful, and though the First Magus held the gaze he didn't dare move or speak. Savrinor watched Yandros with equal trepidation, and as he did so he became horribly aware of something else, something he had been striving to avoid, stirring in his mind. In his conscience . . .

At last Yandros blinked and broke the contact. He had made his assessment, and though he was far from happy with what he had gleaned it had brought him to a decision.

'I see no viable option,' he said coldly. 'I may dislike you, Vordegh, and I may find much to despise in your attitudes and preoccupations. But I can't deny or even fault your abilities. So I charge you to *use* those abilities, to one end and one alone – the destruction of Order's mortal forces, and the preservation of Chaos's rule. You can expect no direct help from my realm; I and my brothers will have Aeoris himself to contend with. You will have only your own wits and your own skills to aid you, and they must be enough.' Then his tone changed, dropping all pretence to moderation, and he added, 'Don't betray my trust in you this time. For if you do, I promise that you'll pay a harder price at my hands than you could ever do at Aeoris's.'

His eyes, dull crimson now, held steady on Vordegh's face. Very slowly the First Magus bowed his head.

'I understand what you say, Lord Yandros.' He made no declarations, no pledges, and nor did Yandros expect them. He had made his point; Vordegh knew the consequences of failure.

'I have nothing more to say.' Yandros's gaze flicked briefly across the immobile figures of the other magi. 'To any of you. Do what must be done; obey your First Magus, and use any and every means to put a stop to this evil.' He paused. 'And may Fate answer your prayers – for I no longer can!'

He turned his back on them and walked slowly towards

the black circle where the Chaos Gate had been. Reaching it, he looked back over his shoulder and some silent and private communication passed between him and his two brothers. Then Yandros made a brief, careless and, Savrinor thought, weary gesture. There was a whisper of sound, and only the mists remained where he had stood. Savrinor felt the cold knife stabbing again, and this time an invisible hand was twisting it. He should have spoken. He should have taken the chance, overcome his fears and found the courage to shrive himself. If Yandros had damned him for his insolence in daring to speak, what would it have mattered? To leave what was in his heart unspoken was worse. But now the chance had gone . . .

Then the paralysis that had clamped down on the Hall broke as Tarod turned to face the magi.

'It's nearly dawn.' He spoke quietly, but the words cut through the silence. 'And I don't doubt that you have a great deal to do – as have we. You have our permission to leave.'

Aware that the words were a thinly veiled command, Vordegh responded with a slight but meticulously respectful bow. 'My lords.' His tone gave no clue whatever to his thoughts; he glanced at his colleagues, a look that bade them all to follow him, and walked towards the door of the Marble Hall.

Savrinor didn't want to leave but knew he had no choice. His chance had come and gone and he could find no pretext for remaining here. Once, he glanced sidelong at Tarod with a half-formed hope – or possibly dread – of catching his eye, but Tarod wasn't looking at him, and repressing an uneasy sigh Savrinor moved on after the magi.

The silent procession filed through the sloping passage, through the unlit and deserted library and up the spiral stairs. Savrinor looked back several times but there was no sign of the two Chaos lords. The magi emerged into the courtyard and Vordegh stalked towards the main wing, the others behind him. But Savrinor hung back. There was a hint of chill light above the castle's east wall, draining the night and imparting a dead quality to everything it touched, and suddenly the feelings which he had been trying to suppress came to the surface in an unexpected and painful surge.

He stopped walking and leaned against one of the pillars of the stoa, turning his face from the dawn glow as though from a searching, accusing eye, and guilt and fear washed over him in a sick wave. What had he said to Andraia about honour, about integrity and loyalty and all the other high-minded trappings of his supposed principles? It was a joke, a hollow sham. Another convenient lie to silence a conscience which by all rights should have goaded him to walk off the edge of the stack. But he'd taken the coward's way – well, he thought cynically, he ought to know that way well enough by now – and had done nothing. And now it was too late.

The magi had disappeared through the main doors, leaving the courtyard empty. Savrinor put a hand to his face and found that his skin was wet with perspiration despite the cold. The Moonwrack; it *had* been too strong, it was breaking up his sense of orientation, making him feel as though the entire castle was revolving around him. He was starting to lose his grip on reality. But he couldn't use that as yet another excuse. There had been too many excuses. *Too many*.

Behind him, a voice spoke his name.

Savrinor jerked round, his hand falling away, and found himself face to face with Tarod.

'You look ill, Savrinor.' Green eyes regarded him, and Savrinor shut his own eyes briefly against a rush of nausea as the castle walls seemed to lurch and topple inwards. He was vaguely aware of the other Chaos lord moving silently away across the courtyard, and he forced himself to say pallidly, 'Thank you, my lord, but I – I'm well enough.'

Tarod studied the historian's dead-white face and drew his own conclusions. But he only said, 'As you wish. I don't doubt you're the better judge of such a thing,' and started to turn away. And as he did so, the dam which Savrinor had been struggling to maintain broke.

'My lord . . .'

Ah yes, there *was* something. Tarod had sensed it in the Marble Hall, a cancer eating at Savrinor's mind which he had been too afraid to voice. It was probably as well that he hadn't voiced it then; for all Yandros's apparent calm Tarod knew his great brother well enough to be aware of how he would have reacted to any distraction or appeal. But Yandros was no longer here. And however trivial the matter might be, Tarod felt inclined to clear the air.

He had paused and was looking at Savrinor again. 'Does it goad you so deeply?'

A nod. Savrinor's palms were slick, and though he wanted to straighten and stand upright, he wasn't sure that he could. He put his hands against the pillar, steadying himself, trying to dispel the sweat.

'My lord, not long ago the First Magus accused me of . . . being a traitor to Chaos.'

Tarod smiled thinly. 'We haven't forgotten that incident.'

'No. No, of course not. And but for your intervention, I'd –' He made a hapless gesture, knowing that no words were adequate. 'But now, Lord Tarod, I have to tell you that . . . the First Magus was right. I *have* betrayed Chaos. But for a deed of mine – and it was a deliberate act, a conscious choice – the heretics couldn't have succeeded in their task.'

Great gods, he'd said it at last. The worm had been prised out of the core, the serpent's nest was exposed. Savrinor had shut his eyes again but he could feel Tarod's

288

gaze on him. It was, or so he imagined, a little like being burned alive.

Then Tarod spoke again. His voice was very composed, very quiet. But there was an edge to it.

He said, 'What was the deed?'

The words came, simply, starkly, and Savrinor told him all that he had thought and all that he had done, from the night when Andraia had witnessed Iselia's secret meeting with Kaldar and Benetan, to the moment when, believing – or wanting to believe – that Benetan could still be redeemed, he had sent the message urging him to save his own skin. When he finished, Tarod was silent for several seconds that seemed to Savrinor like an eternity. In the quiet, the restless murmur of the sea was audible. And the dawn light was growing harsher.

At last, Tarod said, 'You have surprised me, Savrinor.'

Savrinor stared at the black flagstones. He didn't answer.

'You think of what you've done as a betrayal,' Tarod went on. 'But I would give it a different name. That name is freedom of choice.'

Savrinor looked up, unnerved. 'Freedom of choice . . . ?'

Tarod sighed. 'Surely you, of all mortals, understand one of the fundamental principles of Chaos? Your decision was your own, made in good faith because you believed it was for the best, and the fact that you were wrong in your judgement doesn't change that.'

'But –' Savrinor began.

'No. There are no caveats. You didn't act against Chaos; nothing was further from your mind. You're not perfect, but we don't expect perfection.' His mouth curved acidly. 'That's one of the prime differences between us and the lords of Order. We'll take reprisals for treachery, but we don't punish mistakes. If we did, Vordegh and a good few others would by now be in the Seven Hells – and that's to say nothing of our own errors in this unhappy affair.' Then Tarod paused and his expression became harder. 'What is it you want, Savrinor? Forgiveness? Absolution? You won't receive it, for there's nothing to absolve.'

Savrinor drew an unsteady breath. 'But if my actions led to the Chaos Gate's destruction –'

'It's possible that they did. But neither you nor I nor Yandros will ever know for certain, and as we can't undo the heretics' work the question has no relevance. It happened; it's done; and we don't hold you to blame. That's the only comfort I'm prepared to give you, and it should be enough. If you want to continue to torment yourself, that's your privilege; but in my opinion your remorse would be an unworthy indulgence.'

Savrinor felt as if his heart had turned to lead inside him. He nodded miserably ... then abruptly Tarod relented a little.

'You also seem to have forgotten that when you *did* learn the truth about your protégée, it was only your prompt action that enabled the magi to apprehend her. So perhaps, on your slate, the one deed might cancel out the other?'

Momentarily an image of the charred corpse in the Marble Hall flitted across Savrinor's inner eye, and nausea clutched at him again. He forced it down.

'I understand, my lord.' He blinked rapidly, trying to clear his vision. 'And I'll ... think hard on what you've said.'

'Not for too long, I hope,' Tarod said drily. 'Contemplation is a luxury you'll be ill able to afford in the days ahead.'

'Yes ...' Savrinor's face, already ashen, blanched further.

'Then clear your mind of it, Savrinor, and have done. If your conscience still plagues you, exorcize it in working to defeat Order's threat. That, with your devotion and allegiance, is the sum of what we want from you.' For a further moment the Chaos lord's gaze lingered on

Savrinor's face, then abruptly a deeper shadow rippled through the darkness that cloaked him. 'I bid you goodnight, my friend. And let us both hope for good fortune.'

He turned, moved away. The last remnants of night were now shrinking back to the castle walls, but briefly it seemed that another kind of blackness closed in as Tarod reached the fountain where his brother waited. The dark shifted; their forms seemed to merge; and Savrinor was alone in the courtyard.

CHAPTER XIX

The column of black cloud above the castle spread and shattered into a lattice of darkness shot through with shuddering light, and thunder echoed over the sea as the supernatural messengers departed on their mission. The four spires sang with an answering fusillade of energy that rivalled the rising sun, and in the council hall the cold aura that had been flaring around the figure of Vordegh on the high dais sank to a sullen flicker and faded.

The First Magus's composed brown eyes focused on the hall's windows for a few moments as he watched the messengers flick into the void between dimensions and vanish. Then he turned his attention to the tense, silent magi who waited below the dais.

'The Chaos riders will return within the hour.' His voice swept the quiet smoothly aside. He sounded impossibly calm. 'Has my instruction to summon all castle-dwellers to the great hall been carried out?'

Croin, who by default had spoken for his colleagues since the gods' departure, inclined his head. 'It has, First Magus.'

'Then I will address them now.' Vordegh started to step down from the dais, then paused. 'And tell the historian that I expect every word of what I have to say to be recorded.'

Savrinor, Croin knew, was already in the great hall with two co-opted assistants, so he only nodded acknowledgement as Vordegh stalked past him and away towards the doors. Pirane was trying to catch the physician's eye, but Croin affected not to notice until Vordegh was out of sight and the other magi had started to flow out of the hall in his wake. Then, with the appearance of casualness, he moved to her side.

Pirane spoke under her breath. 'Do you think we can trust him?'

Croin watched the door speculatively. The shadows that shrouded Vordegh, absent in the Marble Hall, had returned, and he didn't care to speculate on what that omen could mean.

'I don't see that we have a choice,' he replied, and added, trying to take comfort from the thought, 'Besides, Lord Yandros has placed faith in him.'

But Pirane shook her head. 'No, Croin, he has not. His decision to leave the reins of power in Vordegh's hands was a necessary expedient, because he knows that we can't afford to lose a sorcerer of his skill now. Lord Yandros would have been happier to remove him.'

Croin looked sidelong at her. 'You believe that?'

'I *know* it. We must be vigilant. Our plans may be in abeyance in this emergency, but if there is any sign of trouble we must still be ready to take action.' Her vast eyes darkened. 'And this time we won't have any help from the gods.'

Croin twisted a ring on his index finger. For Vordegh to persist with his personal manias in the midst of such a crisis as this would be beyond insanity . . . but, like Pirane, he couldn't entirely rule out the possibility.

'I hope and pray it won't come to that.'

Pirane was still gazing at the doors. 'As do I,' she said softly.

Savrinor was only a short way from where Andraia stood near the great hall's empty hearth, but since her arrival he hadn't acknowledged her presence save for an initial quick and strangely intense glance and an effort at a reassuring smile which didn't convince. For all his immaculate appearance — fresh clothing with an elegant black velvet coat that displayed not the smallest mark – he was back on the knife-edge; and now it had an extra dimension, a private darkness which he could barely hold at bay. Andraia could see it in his eyes, and also in the faces and responses of his two assistants, who were clearly finding it very difficult to keep on the right side of his vituperative tongue. She had also seen him surreptitiously slip something from his coat pocket and swallow it; the gods alone knew what drug it was this time but his hand had been shaking as he took it.

In truth, Andraia felt little better herself. From the moment when Savrinor had left his rooms to join Tarod and his brother in the courtyard she had been beset by a tangle of emotions in which dread and anger took the upper hand turn by turn. She knew, now, what had happened and what the heretics had achieved, and her initial bitter fury at the magnitude of Benetan's treachery had deepened to a banked but powerful furnace of hatred. And overlying the furnace was a white-hot layer of clenching fear that had no tangible form but which held her in a grip as sure as death.

Suddenly there was a stirring by the main doors. Heads turned in the airless press of the crowd, and Andraia's heart lurched under her ribs as the packed throng shuffled back, creating an aisle for the First Magus.

Vordegh stepped up onto the small dais opposite the hearth, where the chair in which he had sat during his inauguration festivities, and which had remained empty ever since, was waiting for him. But he disdained the chair, and turned instead to face the gathering.

'I will speak briefly, and I expect everyone present to pay close attention.' No preamble, no embellishment; his words simply cut into the silence like a honed blade. 'I have commands to issue. And the penalty for any who fail to carry out those commands in the days to come will be annihilation . . .'

*   *   *

Set faces, hard eyes; and the scent of fear was like a cloying psychic perfume in the air as the crowd began to move out of the great hall. Not a fear engendered by what they had heard, Savrinor thought, but the sharper, more immediate terror of what the coming days would – or could – mean for each individual in the castle. For the First Magus had made one fact clear above all else: that any means which were necessary or expedient to meet and crush the threat of Order's mortal forces would be used, without hesitation and without compunction. What that meant in precise terms possibly even Vordegh didn't know yet, but recent events were all too fresh in everyone's minds to allow them to take any comfort from his words.

Savrinor fingered the graphite stylus in his hand and wished that the dispersing throng would move faster. Until the press cleared a little he was trapped in this corner, and he felt hot, light-headed and distracted. Maintaining concentration during Vordegh's address had been hard and he wasn't sure that he had accurately recorded every word. Looking at his papers now, the shorthand code swam before his eyes and made little sense. If anything was incomplete, he only hoped that his assistants had proved less ineffectual than appearances suggested and would fill in any gaps. If they had failed him, he thought, he would have them both flayed . . .

The crowd was beginning to thin out at last and he turned, ignoring a brief but unpleasant rush of giddiness, and started towards the doors. He had taken four paces when a voice called,

'Historian.'

From the dais, Vordegh was beckoning him. The lights in the hall seemed to dip and flare momentarily and Savrinor's heart started to pound. But the summons couldn't be ignored, and he forged his way against the tide of people towards the First Magus.

Vordegh stared down at him coldly. 'See that copies of

the statement I have made are posted about the castle within two hours. You will then prepare a list of all males of appropriate age and fitness to serve as auxiliaries under the command of the Chaos riders.' One edge of Vordegh's mouth curved with faint but explicit contempt. 'You will not be expected to include yourself in that list. In addition I will require a complete and accurate record of all the castle's other inhabitants, detailing names, ages, ranks and functions. Bring both lists to me in the council hall by noon.'

'My lord.' His surroundings were beginning to look distinctly unreal and, not trusting himself to execute a more formal bow, Savrinor inclined his head.

'The Chaos riders will be returning shortly, and they will have candidates for assignment and preparation. Other magi will undoubtedly find further uses for your services, so you will ensure that you are available at all times from now on.' Vordegh paused, then added with a sting, 'And I would strongly suggest that you make some attempt to curb your more immoderate habits, historian. I have clearly stated the penalty for failure, and I assure you that it will be exacted.'

'Yes, my lord.' Savrinor's skin prickled and he shut his eyes.

'Get about your business.'

'Sir.' Savrinor turned on his heel and walked away.

Andraia was waiting for him by the doors. She took one look at his face and steered him out into the corridor and away towards the main stairs. 'What did the First Magus say to you?' she asked urgently.

He shook his head. 'Nothing untoward. Simply instructions.' He stopped, looked back. 'Damn it, where are those two maladroit fools I brought here with me –?'

'If you mean your clerks, I told them to begin their work while they await your further directions,' Andraia interrupted. 'Which in themselves can wait until you have *rested*, Savrinor.'

'Oh, no.' He started to walk on again, aware that she was holding his arm to steady him and that he needed it. 'No. There'll be no rest. I have too much work to do.'

Her expression grew obstinate. 'Even Vordegh can't expect –'

'It has nothing to do with Vordegh.' Though that wasn't entirely true. 'I won't sleep – I *can't* sleep – until this threat, this evil, has been wiped *out!*'

This, Andraia suspected, was linked with the personal darkness she had seen in him, and she tried to probe. 'Savrinor, what happened in the Marble Hall? Did someone say –?' But he caught her eye with a peculiarly introverted and angry look, and the rest of the sentence died unspoken as she realized that she'd get no answers. She might be persistent, but Savrinor was as immovable as a stone wall when the mood took him, and this was one such time.

She sighed. 'At least you can maintain your strength. Eat, and –'

He cut that off with a scathing laugh, knowing that food would curdle in his stomach. There were other ways to stay awake and alert and he fully intended to use them. Whatever the price, it was better than the one he would pay if he failed to match up to the standards Vordegh demanded.

They had reached the entrance hall now. The main doors stood open and there was some turmoil outside. Savrinor paused to look, and saw that the courtyard was full of people; figures in black driving and chivvying a small sea of milling humanity. The Chaos riders had finally returned and had brought their latest cull with them. Well over a hundred this time by the look of it, and yet another chore to add to his agenda . . .

He said something under his breath, then added, 'I must find Magus Pirane. She'll want to oversee the gleaning.' He pivoted, ignoring Andraia's protest; but as he started back towards the dining-hall, Croin appeared among the still-emerging throng.

'Master Savrinor.' Croin crooked a finger as he intercepted the historian, then nodded towards the courtyard. 'I will inform Pirane of the riders' return. You had best concentrate on your commission for the First Magus.'

Savrinor exhaled in relief. 'Thank you, sir.' He started to turn again, but Croin forestalled him. 'One thing more, Savrinor.' He drew Savrinor aside and spoke quietly. 'You know that other matters are now in abeyance. But the salient word is *abeyance*, and so we wish you to remain alert.' A swift, covert glance back at the hall. 'If things should begin to go awry again, then even in the present circumstances it might prove necessary to reconsider our position. You appreciate my meaning?'

Oh, gods, Savrinor thought desolately, *not even now. Not even after all this* ... Aloud, he said, 'Yes, Magus Croin. I understand perfectly.'

'Good; good.' Croin paused, studying his face. 'In the meantime, if you find the exertions ahead take too great a toll you may consult me for anything you need.' He smiled with a measure of dry sympathy. 'Lord Vordegh might recommend temperance as a paradigm, but it isn't always possible to live up to his ideals.'

Savrinor nodded. 'Thank you, my lord. I'll bear that in mind.' His pale eyes held the physician's gaze for another moment and in their depths was acute and desperate weariness. 'As I'll also bear in mind the ... other matter.'

He walked away to rejoin Andraia.

Benetan stared at Aeoris, his face a study in shock, disbelief and bewilderment. 'My lord ... you can't mean that. You surely *can't!*'

The lord of Order gazed back at him. 'Oh, but I do, Benetan, and my reasoning is simple. You alone of all Order's faithful are qualified for such a role. You have the training, the experience, the insight. We could make no better choice.'

'But my training was at the magi's hands! At the castle, under the aegis of Chaos! This – this is –'

'It's a military duty. In that sense there is no difference.'

Benetan protested despairingly, 'But there *is*, my lord! To lead *your* mortal army, to command and control Order's human forces –'

'As you once commanded and controlled Chaos's.'

'I did, yes, but . . .' How could he explain the grotesque incongruity of it? He wasn't fit for such a commission. He was still defiled by his years as a Chaos rider; years which had instilled in him a cold-blooded inurement to horror, to cruelty, to barbarism. Despite the safeguards, the drugs and trances which silenced conscience and blunted memory, he could still recall enough of his own past exploits to feel shamed and sickened. And now Aeoris wanted him to take up his former role again, though this time as Order's champion. He couldn't do it. It would be an obscenity.

Struggling to find a way to make the god understand, he said helplessly, 'My lord, I'm sensible of the honour you do me in asking this. But I can't take on the responsibility. I *can't*. You see, I – I'm too afraid of what it might mean. What it might do.'

'Do?' Aeoris queried mildly.

'Yes. In battle, in the heat of action. The way the magi train their warriors, it's – it makes no allowance for reason. For sanity. They – we – become something other than human, and once that experience is instilled it's impossible to forget or suppress. It's . . .'

'A bloodlust?'

'In a sense, yes.' Benetan nodded miserably and stared down at his own feet. 'But far colder, and far worse. It's pitiless. And it can't be tempered until the thirst it arouses has been slaked.'

There was silence. Behind him, in the close confines of the small cave where the three of them were sitting, Benetan sensed Simbrian watching him and could hardly bear to imagine what the sorcerer must be thinking. He hadn't wanted to make this confession, reveal so much of that dark part of himself which he had come to loathe. But with Aeoris it was impossible to lie.

At last the god spoke. 'Yet,' he said, almost gently, 'for all your scruples you still crave vengeance.' Benetan looked up quickly, and Aeoris continued, 'On the man who despoiled and then betrayed Iselia. On the magi who tortured her past the brink of sanity. On the lord of Chaos whose careless attentions turned your own lover against you.'

Benetan's brow had creased into a tight frown of pain and anger. 'Yes,' he said unsteadily. 'That's true.'

'Then you must know,' Aeoris said, 'that that is the reason why I want you to lead my army now. And in leading it, to be nothing more – and nothing less – than the warrior that your former masters made you. Fire must be fought with fire. However deep our compassion, however high our ideals, there can be no quarter for those who oppose us. Our followers need you, Benetan. They need your skills, they need your leadership and they need your example. Above all they need that cold sanguinity which you so hate within yourself, to harden their own resolve.'

Benetan stood up and paced across the floor. He couldn't assimilate this. Not yet. All his assumptions and expectations were twisting about, being turned on their heads, and the idea that the contamination – as he now saw it – which the magi had instilled in him should be to Order's advantage had shaken him to the core.

Yet in a hideous way it made sense. *Fire must be fought with fire.* Aeoris was right. Kindness, mercy, integrity, all the virtues he had come to associate with Order's cause, would be worth nothing when the real conflict began, for noble principle was a blunt and useless weapon with which to meet the dark power of Chaos.

Again there were faces in his inner vision. Savrinor, the immaculate, sly-eyed deviant. Andraia, corrupted by his influence and by the wanton caprice of Yandros's brother. Yandros himself, aloof, callous, malevolent. Vordegh, who had put Iselia to torture. And the face of Iselia; her image leading a long procession of strangers and innocents who had died because of Chaos's whims and the brutality of those who upheld its rule. Yes, he wanted vengeance. For them. For himself. For *her*. And for Kaldar, who now was – but he put that thought away, not wanting to add yet another thread to the tangle in his mind.

Aeoris and Simbrian were both watching him. He pulled air into his lungs, expelled it, inhaled more. If he could taste the vengeance he longed for, if he could claw back something of what he had lost, then would it matter how it was achieved? *There can be no quarter for those who oppose us.* Chaos would give none; that was a certainty. No doubt they anticipated that their ruthlessness would give them an advantage; that Order's human forces would baulk at matching their savagery. There could be pleasure in showing them that they were very, very wrong ... and a sweet irony in the fact that the lesson would be taught by one of their own.

He started to say, 'If –' then stopped. There were no ifs save one. *If* he was committed to this cause, he would do what Aeoris wanted of him, because Aeoris wanted it. That was the nature, and the burden, of faith.

The god was waiting patiently, composedly. Benetan met his gaze.

'Will they accept me as their leader, my lord? Knowing what I once was?'

'They will accept and welcome you, Benetan. Because Simbrian and I will be at your side.'

Yes; he could see that it was true. With Aeoris's blessing

on him no one would doubt his integrity; indeed, his presence would be a symbol, almost a talisman. The renegade, the dweller in darkness who had seen the light. Chaos's servant, defying his old allegiance for the sake of justice. Aeoris knew the potency of such a talisman and the power it could wield over the mortal mind. He had not, Benetan thought, been chosen for his skills alone.

An arid smile caught at the corners of his mouth and he looked down at his own grimy, tattered uniform. 'Then if you truly want me to do this, Lord Aeoris,' he said, 'you will have everything I can give. I can't promise to succeed in the task you set me, but if I fail it won't be through lack of dedication. I'll use my skills to the utmost of my ability.'

'As you used them in the past?'

'Yes, if it proves necessary – or unavoidable.' Benetan met Aeoris's gaze with an odd, hard look. 'And I wouldn't care to speculate which of the two is more likely.'

The colour of Aeoris's eyes deepened momentarily. 'Neither would I, my friend. But in the pursuit of victory, it hardly matters.'

'Very well, then. Very well.' Benetan put a hand to his face; suddenly, ridiculously, he wanted to laugh as he felt old, familiar responses coming back into his mind. Plans, strategies, ideas, exigencies; the practical thoughts and preoccupations of the efficient commander. 'It won't be easy,' he said, and was a little taken aback by the sudden brisk note in his own voice. 'They'll be raw, undisciplined; little better than a rabble, in fact. Whereas the Chaos riders are an effective and well co-ordinated force.' He looked up again. 'How many will I have, to begin with?'

Aeoris glanced at Simbrian, who replied, 'Less than a hundred; that will mean all those from Summer Isle who won't be needed in our sorcerous work and who have some knowledge of fighting, however small. But as we move north, those numbers will grow rapidly.'

'Yes.' Benetan was beginning to see the picture. 'I understand. Then what I will need – *do* need, as quickly as possible – is some ten or twelve sound individuals who have a grasp of the basics and can learn quickly to take and interpret orders.' Ten or twelve Averels, he thought; and suppressed a small worm of discomfort as he remembered that Averel was an enemy now.

'There are probably four here on the White Isle already,' Simbrian told him.

'Then I'd like to see them as soon as possible.' Benetan was pacing again, restlessly, then stopped and glanced at Aeoris. 'If time is of the essence?'

'It is, Captain Liss.' Aeoris's use of his old title was deliberate, and accompanied by a faint smile. 'This island and Summer Isle are effectively impregnable; Yandros and the magi know that to attempt an attack on either would be futile. But the mainland is a very different matter – the moment we raise our banner there the full forces of Chaos, human and otherwise, will move against us. And the longer we delay, the longer the magi will have to plan and prepare their assault.' He paused. 'It gives you little leeway, I know, but I want you to make what you can of the four men Simbrian assigns to you by midnight tonight.'

'Midnight . . .' Benetan's eyebrows went up. 'Very well, my lord. I'll do my best.'

'I ask nothing more.' Aeoris took a step towards the cave entrance, gesturing to Simbrian to follow him. 'We'll send the four men to you here, and leave you to begin formulating your plans. And Benetan . . .'

Benetan looked up. His eyes seemed to be focusing on another plane. 'My lord?'

'Thank you.' Aeoris's faint golden aura pulsed once, then he turned and walked out of the cave with Simbrian behind him.

The crater bowl was deserted; most of Simbrian's followers were sleeping after the exertions of the past few days, and those who were awake were occupied in another of the caves, preparing food for later in the day. Aeoris's six brothers were no longer on the island – Simbrian hadn't presumed to ask about their activities – and but for the muffled roar of the sea the atmosphere was quiet, almost peaceful. Simbrian knew, however, that the peace was an illusion, and as he and Aeoris emerged onto the ledge he glanced uneasily skywards. The seven-rayed star of Chaos still hung motionless above the crater, rivalling the sun with its slow, inexorable pulse of cold light. Shadows flared across the rock floor and walls in rhythm with the pulsing, and the sorcerer said, 'It may be no more than an empty display, my lord, but it will intimidate a good many people who might otherwise have rallied to our cause.' He repressed a shudder of revulsion. 'They won't be able to shake off the feeling that Chaos is constantly watching them.'

Aeoris watched the star's cadence speculatively. 'Which probably isn't so far from the truth,' he replied. 'But there are ways in which we might turn its presence to our advantage – as we have turned Benetan Liss's.'

Simbrian glanced briefly back towards the cave. 'I didn't think he'd agree so readily.'

'He has a very powerful motive.'

'Vengeance?'

'As you say, vengeance; and the fact that it's driven by grief gives it an extreme impetus as well as lending him strength.'

'But it's a cold strength, my lord.' The sorcerer sighed. 'I saw it in him when he told us what happened at the castle. Iselia must have suffered beyond any mortal ability to imagine, and we both know that Benetan loved her, perhaps as much as Kaldar did. Yet he told the tale as though it had no power to touch him. And now, he doesn't grieve for her. He *can't*.'

'Oh, he can and does. But something in him has given

the grief another form, less overt but as powerful as any tears or railing.' Aeoris regarded him obliquely. 'By a wry twist of fortune it's the same quality that enabled Benetan to make what he did of his life at the Star Peninsula. There's a core to that young man, Simbrian, that is a rare quality in any mortal, and I think it will be his saving grace now.'

'I understand you, my lord, and agree. Yet Benetan has paid a very hard price for his strength. It saddens me to see that something within him has died.'

Aeoris nodded. 'It has, yes. But one day that part of himself might well rekindle and live again. Benetan knows that, and it's a prospect that gives him hope.' He paused. 'I could rekindle it for him. But it's better – as he would say, were I to offer him the boon – that he finds it for himself.'

They had reached the centre of the bowl now. Simbrian gazed for a few moments at the veins of colour in the rock strata beneath his feet; then, very quietly, he said, 'I only wish I could believe that the same might happen to Kaldar.'

They were both silent for a time, their thoughts moving along parallel paths. Kaldar was at this moment lying in another of the caves, under a spell of sleep cast on him by Aeoris to lock his mind away, for a while, from nightmare. It was the only kindness Kaldar had allowed the god to do for him; that, and the small benevolence of healing the wounds in his arms. How and where he had got hold of the knife no one knew, but he had cut one wrist with it and was trying to slash the other before he was discovered, and it had taken two men to hold him down while Shammana applied a tourniquet to his arm and tried to stem the bleeding. When Aeoris arrived Kaldar had calmed, but it was an unwilling surrender, made only because he knew he had no choice. And when the deep gashes had been touched and had vanished, and Aeoris had turned his attention to Kaldar's eyes, Kaldar had rebelled, snatching his head aside and uttering a harsh '*No!*' He would not be healed of that, he said. He didn't want to see again. Never again, *never again*. And no words of Shammana's, of Nanithe's, of Simbrian's, even of Aeoris's, could sway him. He might acknowledge that to die was a coward's way, that it was not what Iselia would have wanted him to do. But he would not allow his sight to be restored. His world had gone dark, and he refused to accept the light again.

'Kaldar, like Benetan, must find his own way,' Aeoris said pensively. 'I can't force the choice on him, Simbrian; no power has the right to do that.'

Simbrian thought of the anguish and hate that now burned in Kaldar's aura. Kaldar, he believed, would never be able to come to terms with the fact that Iselia had willingly chosen death when the Chaos Gate was shattered. It was a terrible and bewildering betrayal of all his hopes and dreams for their future – dreams which he had believed she shared – and the knowledge of how deep and how savage her psychic wounds must have been was almost impossible for him to bear. Healing of a kind might come in time, but until and unless it did, Kaldar was locked in a private hell from which he would allow nothing and no one to free him.

Aeoris said, 'The only solace that we can give Kaldar now is to succeed in our purpose. My brothers will return soon, and when they do, our preparations will be complete.' He looked at the sky again, and at the star's fluctuating light that seemed to make a travesty of the bright winter day. 'I've waited a very long time for this reckoning with Yandros, and I don't intend to delay any further. At midnight, it will begin – and by dawn we will be on the mainland.'

Simbrian held his gaze. 'All of us, my lord?'

'All of us. Our friends here and on Summer Isle, our followers in the far south; and when we arrive there will be many, many more waiting to join us and form the nucleus of our legion.' Aeoris's eyes narrowed slightly and their colour deepened to a hot furnace-gold. 'Then, my friend, you'll have work enough to compensate for every last drop of frustration – as will we all.'

CHAPTER XX

Savrinor took one look at what was manifesting in the courtyard and shut the curtain, issuing a scorching reprimand to one of the younger clerks who had dared to glance up in curiosity. They would all see more than enough of the results of the magi's work before this was over; there was no time now for gawking, and as he paced back across the room he trenchantly repeated his earlier warning that Lord Vordegh's threats would be nothing to the punishments he would inflict on anyone who failed to meet the standards and schedules he had allotted. Five faces looked fearfully at him then five heads bent once more to their work, and reaching the far side of the room Savrinor frowned into one of the tinted mirrors that hung on the wall before turning and pacing back again. His mind raced as he mentally counted off the tasks already completed. The text of Vordegh's address transcribed and posted up; the lists of castle inhabitants prepared and delivered; now the record of the riders' new cull almost complete, saving mistakes or accidents. Eight clerks pressed into his service; five here, the other three in the library rooting out more records. The moment they returned he would have to start personally on the drug inventories wanted by Croin and Revian; couldn't leave that to subordinates, the cross-referencing was too complex. Then there was the news the Chaos riders had brought back from the south. Where in all the different realms of damnation was Averel? He couldn't afford to lose *time*; had to have those details *quickly*, or his perilously-balanced organization would be thrown out of kilter and everything would start to cave in . . .

When the knock came he snapped out, 'Enter!' so sharply that one of his assistants started and dropped her pen. Averel came in, took in the activity with surprised chagrin, then made a belated salute.

'I'm sorry, Master Savrinor.' Averel's face was drawn with strain and his eyes red-rimmed from exhaustion. He hadn't bathed or shaved or changed his uniform, and there was a long, untreated scratch which looked as if it had been inflicted by fingernails down one cheek. 'I'd have been here earlier, but Magus Pirane sent further instructions about the auxiliaries we're to have, and I had to see to –'

'Never mind that.' Savrinor gestured impatiently towards a chair. 'Sit down, Captain, before you fall down. And drink something.' He poured a glass of wine and held it out; if Averel preferred beer he would simply have to live with his disappointment. And another glass for himself; he'd lost count now of how many he had had but it didn't seem to be making any difference. 'I want details, succinct but salient, of the trouble you encountered in the south.' He took another chair, snatched up stylus and paper, and his pale eyes met the Chaos rider's relentlessly. 'Well?'

To give Averel his due, he was as succinct and salient as Savrinor could have wished. What he had to tell was little enough in itself, but Savrinor saw immediately that the deeper implications could well be another matter. The riders had begun to carry out Lord Vordegh's instructions – Averel faltered here, his face paling and flushing by turns, until Savrinor curtly informed him that he was well aware of what those instructions were – and one or two detachments had met with trouble, for some of their victims – Savrinor's word for them; he saw no point whatever in being delicate about it – had resisted. Nothing too extreme, and certainly nothing that the riders weren't able to crush easily, but Averel was worried.

At this point Savrinor's shrewd eyes narrowed. 'In what

way, Captain? Worried simply because the trouble happened, or because the nature of the sortie itself is plaguing your conscience?'

Averel looked unhappily at the poised stylus. Unlike Benetan he had very little experience of Savrinor, and, aware of the historian's rank and influence, felt out of his depth and more than a little vulnerable. Seeing his dilemma, Savrinor's mouth twitched in a hard smile and he pointedly set the stylus aside.

'I'm not committing every word you say to paper, Captain Averel. Only the key facts. And it will make my life considerably easier, and thus try my temper considerably less, if you can bring yourself to speak your mind without fear of the consequences.'

Averel flushed again. 'Yes, sir. Well . . . I won't hide the fact that a lot of the men weren't happy about the instructions we'd been given. It all seemed very . . .'

'Gratuitous?'

Averel nodded. 'That's probably the best word for it, sir.'

'It probably is; which is why I chose it.' But Savrinor's heart wasn't in the sarcasm. 'So we're agreed on that, at least. But whatever the nature of your commissions in the past, barring the occasional isolated incident the peasantry haven't dared even to think of rebellion. This time, though, they did.'

'It was just a few outbreaks –' Averel began.

'And those confined to the far south; yes, so you've told me.' Savrinor checked his notes. 'But the question I ask is, why? What prompted those particular people, in those particular demesnes, to overcome their fear of the Chaos riders and attempt to defy them?'

Averel looked extremely unhappy. 'As to that, Master Savrinor, I wouldn't like to hazard –'

Savrinor interrupted irritably. 'Come now, Captain. Your men were *there*.' He looked up, a challenge and a warning in his eyes. 'If there's anything you haven't yet told me, or any rumours flying which you're reluctant to repeat, I strongly advise you to rectify that now.'

So at last he got at the whole truth. It wasn't a certainty, Averel was anxious to stress, but some of his men *had* heard rumours. About visions. Visions which had visited certain people in certain districts, telling them of an imminent uprising, an army of human and supernatural allies who rendered no allegiance to Chaos; who were, in fact, sworn to challenge and overthrow the gods. And that army, so the rumours claimed, was led by Aeoris of Order . . .

Averel was in some travail by the time Savrinor had extracted all the information he had to give; he still seemed to cling to the fear that by repeating the rumours he would in some arcane way be held responsible for them. Normally Savrinor would have been indifferent to his discomfort and would have left him, to use the riders' vernacular, to simmer in his own sweat. But for reasons which he had neither the time nor the inclination to fathom, he felt moved to reassure Averel that he had nothing to fear from his revelations, and that they contained nothing that wasn't already only too well known to the magi.

Averel hadn't yet seen the text of the First Magus's address, so at last Savrinor dismissed him with a strong recommendation to read it for himself without any further delay. And, he added with a corrosive tinge in his voice, to prepare himself and his men to go without ease, without comfort, without sleep, without any of the small essentials that made life tolerable, and be ready for anything at a moment's notice.

When Averel had at last gone, Savrinor stood for a few moments listening to the faint but steady scratching of the clerks' pens against the room's quiet backdrop. The noise set his teeth on edge; he wanted to round on them, shout at them, strike out, not with any malice but simply to relieve the strain. But for the little it would achieve the effort wasn't worthwhile. And he still had work to do.

He swung round to his own table, sat down and quickly and capably put his notes of the interview with Averel into more coherent form. One copy would have to suffice for now; sand over the paper, set it aside for a minute to dry more thoroughly . . . on his feet once more he went to the window, hacked back the curtain, stared out. The daylight was starting to fade and there were the beginnings of a bloody sunset over the coast, staining the sky. Courtyard empty now, the things Menniam had conjured gone to whatever destination Vordegh had ordained. The far south, probably, to instil the fear of the gods into that part of the populace who were nearest to Order's corrupt nest of vipers and thus easier prey for their contamination. They would be expecting something from Chaos; what they would get instead would shock them, for Menniam had a gruesome imagination and the blood-energies from twenty-one of the riders' new cull would lend his creations a particularly drastic form of reality. Croin had Revian to help him with that; doubtless they were both still in the Marble Hall, and would soon be sending for servants to clear the aftermath of their work away.

Yandros, he felt sick . . . Savrinor thrust the sensation down, knowing he couldn't afford to be squeamish now of all times. Blot out imagination, blot out stray thoughts; blot out anything that wasn't directly and pragmatically connected with this emergency. He left the window and went to his cupboard, quelling the feeling of resentment that he should have had to accommodate his little army of scribes in his own sanctum. But then Andraia wasn't here and he couldn't look forward to the prospect of any sleep, so what did his privacy matter?

He sensed the clerks' surreptitious gazes on him as he opened the cupboard and mixed what he needed. Let them think what they would; seeing the truth was hardly likely to make his dissolute reputation any worse than it already was, and if they thought this would result in any slackening of the standards he demanded, they would soon be disabused of that notion. Moonwrack – a double dose again; he'd soon learn to get over the initial side-effects and he needed the extra stimulus. And two other substances, carefully chosen to combine a sharpening of wits with the ability to focus his thoughts only where he wanted them. The concoction went down, and he snatched up the new document. He couldn't face the prospect of taking it in person to Vordegh; Magus Pirane would understand and she would see that the matter was properly dealt with. Menniam and the other magi would have some new challenges for their creativity in the wake of it. And Andraia was in Pirane's apartments, helping Lua with her duties; might have a chance to speak briefly with her and try to apologize for this mayhem . . .

At the door he turned and said sharply, 'I'll not be long. If your three colleagues return before I do, tell them to leave their documents for my attention, and stack them in the order given on my list. And I'll put a knife through the hand of anyone who meddles with anything in my absence.'

The door slammed ferociously behind him.

Pirane's interpretation of Averel's news was very much in accord with Savrinor's, and she took the report immediately to the First Magus. Vordegh was in his own chambers, alone, and the rooms were pulsating with a suffocating sense of occult energy that seemed to focus and magnify the energies building up in the castle. It was, Pirane thought cautiously, an encouraging sign; almost for the first time since his inauguration Vordegh was working in unity with his colleagues, using his own powers to feed theirs; and the magnitude of the power he could command was a sharp and sobering reminder of his value to them in this crisis. Yandros might have gambled on the First

Magus's sanity, but if the gamble paid off it could be the saving of them all.

Vordegh's response to the document was swift and efficient. The reports of trouble were centred on four specific areas in the far south; one magus, with a strong detachment of Chaos riders, would be enough to deal with it. He sent for Menniam and Averel; within a matter of minutes both had been given their instructions and Menniam was making preparations to conjure a citadel while Averel rounded up the least exhausted of his men and readied them for departure. There would be no sacrament this time, but Revian had returned from the Marble Hall, and from Savrinor's hasty inventory ordered the administering of a lesser but still highly effective potion to ensure that the riders wouldn't falter in their task. Averel himself wasn't to accompany the riders; Menniam would act as their commander and the captain was required for another mission. A second cull, and with it a further salutary warning to any who might think to join Order's cause. Averel was to carry out the assignment swiftly and ruthlessly, and Vordegh himself would provide a sorcerous emphasis.

Averel's troop left through the Maze an hour after sunset; Menniam departed with the other riders a little later. The first moon hadn't yet risen but the patchily clouded sky glared with the light of the seven-rayed star pulsing like a vast, cold heart overhead. The star was visible across the entire world and it was the only thing that gave Savrinor any comfort as he and his assistants worked on, for there was an ache in his marrow and a sickness in his stomach that no drugs seemed able to banish, and he couldn't keep food down, and there was no end to travail in sight and no hope of an end, and he had quarrelled viciously with Andraia, and though he didn't fear being unable to stay awake, for it wouldn't happen, he *craved* sleep.

Equilibrium was becoming hard to maintain for other

reasons, too, for the atmosphere in the castle was by now at a saturating pitch of tension as the magi concentrated their skills on the raising of power. Vordegh had no intention of fixing on a strategy to meet Order's threat until the nature and movement of Aeoris's forces became clearer, but neither did he intend to remain passive in the meantime. Pirane and several others had begun an investigation on the astral planes to root out as many of Order's secrets as they could, and while awaiting the results of their scrying Vordegh and the rest of the magi planned to ensure that the stirrings of trouble in the south wouldn't be repeated in other districts. Hence Averel's second cull; unable now to draw Chaos's power through the Gate to amplify their work, they needed another source of energy to feed and control the entities they conjured and sent out into the world. Menniam's creations had been only a beginning; more than sixty of the terrified horde brought back by the riders on their first sortie had served their purpose now, and in the Marble Hall Croin still practised his art. When Savrinor made a brief sortie to the library for yet more records he could feel the psychic stench of death from the Hall reaching grimly and tangibly into the vault, and was all too glad to complete his business and leave as quickly as possible.

Shortly before second moonrise there was a hiatus of sorts. Averel's party had returned and the second cull of frightened captives had been listed, assessed and assigned, but the first wave of entities conjured and sent out by the magi would, in Vordegh's view, suffice to put fear into the world at large. The First Magus saw no value in expending more power than necessary; there would be other uses for the new cull, and Croin's and Revian's skills would not be required for the time being.

As the second moon appeared above the castle wall and began to climb on its arc, the flood of demands on Savrinor abated and finally slowed to a trickle. Nothing remained that needed immediate attention, so he discharged his flagging subordinates – though with a warning that the respite would not last long and they could expect to be recalled at a moment's notice. When they had filed gratefully out of the door he sat motionless at his desk, subliminally conscious of the castle's ambience but no longer trying to interpret it. The sick anguish that had beset him earlier had waned a little, though he felt physically at a dangerously low ebb. Dared he sleep for a while? Or if he did, would waking be impossible should some emergency arise within the next few hours? Savrinor scrubbed at his sore eyes and realized that he couldn't make a clear-cut decision. Exhaustion had carried him into a kind of mental limbo; perhaps he should take warning from that and let his body's protests be the arbiter. Just lie down on his bed and allow the world – or at least his part in it – to *stop* for a while . . .

The thought collapsed as someone knocked at his door.

'Come.' Savrinor was too tired to feel anger and his voice simply sounded resigned. The door opened, and he looked up to see Andraia on the threshold.

She hesitated, and for one bizarre moment Savrinor had an impression that she was viewing him as an unpredictable wild animal which might either lick her hand or bite it off. He recalled the circumstances of their clash; it had been over nothing, simply a case of extreme tension in both of them looking for an outlet, and with no one else present to make them preserve decorum and thus keep their tempers in check, the whole thing had escalated out of control. Now Andraia looked haggard and her eyes were red-rimmed, and Savrinor felt as though the entire responsibility for the rift had come to rest squarely on his shoulders.

He stood up. 'I didn't mean what I said.' The words were clipped and he couldn't bring himself to look directly at her.

'Neither did I.' She came into the room, shut the door.

'I saw the clerks leave. I was – waiting for them to go.'

His mood blackened again suddenly. 'Gods damn it, what do you mean, *waiting*? You're not a servant, are you? You don't need anyone's permission to –' Then the angry words broke off and he made a cancelling gesture. 'I'm sorry. I'm overtired.'

'You're not alone in that.'

'No. No, of course.' Now he did look at her, but there was still a trace of resentful doubt in his eyes. 'You've been crying.'

Andraia knew very well that Savrinor couldn't abide tearful women and she said sharply, 'Not on your account, I assure you; so there's no need for you to feel guilty.'

'I don't. I only –' But suddenly he couldn't keep the barrier up any longer, and he shoved his chair aside and crossed the room towards her. She met him half way and her arms went round him as she pressed her face against his hair. 'Oh, Savrinor, it was so *stupid* . . .'

'I know. I know.' He drew her close, crushing, almost hurting. 'To fall out now, of all times, when there's so much else at stake . . .' Fingers dug hard into her back. 'I'm glad you're here.'

She uttered a sound half way between a laugh and a sob. 'One of us had to make the first move, and it didn't seem likely to be you.' There was a peculiar little edge of resentment in her voice but he knew she didn't truly mean it as she added, 'Obviously you have considerably more pride than me.'

'And considerably less sense.' He drew back from her at last and looked seriously into her face. 'I'm afraid I can't apologize more elaborately than this, but I'm sorry for what happened. Truly sorry.'

'I know. And so am I.' She continued to regard him for a few moments longer, then frowned. 'You look exhausted. You still haven't slept, have you?'

Savrinor smiled thinly. 'I was thinking of remedying that

317

oversight when you knocked at the door and interrupted me.' He paused. 'You look little better than I do, if truth be told.'

'Thank you.' She gave the words a sardonic but light-hearted emphasis, then her expression sobered. 'I *do* want to sleep, and now that the castle's quieter I think I could. But I don't want to be alone.'

'No,' Savrinor said quietly. 'Neither do I.' He kissed her, though a little tentatively. 'We could try to keep each other's dreams at arm's length. If you're willing . . . ?'

'Yes,' she said. 'I am.'

In the bedroom, Savrinor was too tired to undress. Instead, by the chilly light of the Chaos star glaring in at the window, he sat heavily on the bed and covered his face with both hands as his lips moved in silent prayer. Andraia watched him, her expression introspective, then when the private moment was over and they lay down together she put her arms around him and moved closer. Softly, uneasily, she said, 'I wish I knew what tomorrow will bring.'

He couldn't answer, and didn't want to try.

Lotro was beginning to feel better, but now and then a last kick from the drug's after-effects caught him unawares and he had to sit for a few moments with his head between his knees until the sensation went away. The sergeant had told him that it would be just like the sacrament, but that wasn't true, for this time he remembered everything that had happened, everything he and his fellow riders had done during what Magus Menniam called their 'cleansing' of the district. Awareness hadn't stopped any of them from carrying out their work; Physician Revian's potion had seen to it that once the operation began it would be completed without qualm. But now that it was over and they were at last allowed to rest, Lotro's conscience was eating at him like a hungry predator. Behind them, Menniam's citadel towered against the night; before them, beyond the long shingle strand that seemed to run forever along this coast, the sea kept up a ceaseless, restless and monotonous hiss. This southern ocean was far calmer than the seas around the Star Peninsula, but something about it made Lotro uneasy. Or perhaps it was just the direction his thoughts were taking ... He glanced sidelong at the other riders, some talking in small groups, others simply sitting on the shingle and staring at the incoming waves; then, more cautiously, he looked over his shoulder at the citadel. In the combined light of the second moon and the star of Chaos glaring high overhead, it looked phantasmic and more than a little frightening. The local overlord was there now with Magus Menniam, and the riders had been warned that this respite wouldn't be a long one; the night was only half over and there would be more to do before dawn.

Lotro wished that Captain Averel were here. He would have explained so much, and answered at least some of the questions that his peers were unable and his masters unwilling to answer. But Averel had been sent elsewhere, and Lotro was certain of only one thing: that all this, all the killing, all the terror, all the horrors conjured by the magi and sent howling out with the riders on their raid, had happened because of what Captain Liss had done. Lotro hadn't read the First Magus's declaration and couldn't yet assimilate the enormity of his former commander's crime. But the memory of the last few hours was like a tight, cold knot inside him.

They had made one sweep through a coastal settlement. Rumour was that the people here had been practising sorcery, trying to conjure monstrosities from the demon-realm of Order, and the riders had been commanded to destroy everything they found without compunction. Yet Lotro had seen no sign of sorcery, no trace of any power that could resist or retaliate. He had seen only helpless and petrified victims, men, women and children alike warped by terror and agony, dying by the sword or by the viler methods of Menniam's sorcerous creations. The settlement was gone now, one with the landscape, and nothing lived or moved for three miles around it. And it seemed to Lotro that, no matter what Captain Liss might have done, such a brutal retaliation couldn't be justified. Surely, *surely*, it wasn't what the gods wanted?

He turned his face to the sky and regarded the seven-rayed star with its slow, steady pulse. A little while ago he had prayed to Lord Yandros, as he had always been taught was right to do in times of uncertainty. But for some reason the prayers hadn't comforted him or given him the resolve he hoped for. All he could feel was that something had gone very, very wrong with the world. And he didn't know what to do about it.

A noise to his left alerted him suddenly and snapped the unhappy reverie. Someone swore, shocked, and Lotro looked round in time to see a number of the other riders getting hastily to their feet. They were looking out to sea, and reflexively he too scrambled upright, turning to face southwards.

Far away, on the horizon or possibly even beyond it, he saw a glare of light . . .

'What in the gods' names –' Someone started to ask the question but cut it off unfinished. One of the horses whinnied uneasily, then abruptly their sergeant was striding down the line, his voice breaking the suspense that held them. 'Someone take word to the magus! *Move!*'

A rider pelted away towards the citadel, but before he could reach it Menniam emerged. Something was perched on his wrist; at first glance it looked like a bird of prey but it was skinless, bizarrely shaped, and its head was that of a tiny horse. The rider dropped back, and Menniam took two paces down the shingle bank before halting and staring, motionless, eyes narrowed.

The light on the horizon was growing brighter, spreading

out and tinting the sky with an eldritch luminescence that almost rivalled the huge, pulsating star overhead. And then, faint but swelling, they all heard a sound like the slow, inexorable rumble of thunder, reaching towards them across the sea . . .

CHAPTER XXI

Shortly before midnight, Aeoris ordered his human followers to leave the crater bowl. Benetan organized the small exodus, and as the procession emerged from the tunnel and began the tricky descent down the steep volcanic slope he kept a sharp eye on his charges, counting heads, checking that no one was in difficulty on the treacherous terrain and trying not to look too often at Kaldar, who walked with Simbrian's and Nanithe's hands to guide him, his face an expressionless mask and the burned sockets of his eyes two hard, dark smudges against his skin's pallor. Since waking from the sleep that Aeoris had cast on him Kaldar hadn't spoken a word to anyone but had merely yielded silently to whatever was required of him. No protests, no conflicts; only an apathy that enclosed and shielded him like a stone wall, as if he had taken a deliberate hold of his own life-spark and snuffed it out. Though he knew the feeling was perverse and a little morbid, in one sense Benetan almost envied him, for sometimes it seemed that Kaldar's desolate numbness just might be preferable to the violent assaults of bitter and furious grief that hammered into his mind whenever he unwittingly relaxed his guard. Yet for all the ugliness of those moments, in truth he wouldn't have traded places. His senses were at least alive; the hurt was proof enough of that. And there was the hope of comfort in revenge.

The procession was nearing the foot of the cone and the ledge that jutted out into the still pool at the end of the sea-inlet. Neither moon was visible beyond the island's towering cliff walls, but the pulsing star of Chaos still hung directly overhead. It cast a ghostly illumination over the scene, draining any semblance of colour from the rock and reflecting coldly on the water's surface and on the masts of Simbrian's ship, riding now at her mooring. The tide was high and the swell heaved sullenly, slapping against the ledge with a dull, heavy sound; Benetan looked away from it and focused his attention instead on the volcano's cone, which rose like a dim apparition behind them. Aeoris was still in the bowl, alone and completing his final preparations; he had told them nothing of his plans but had simply given the order to depart, with no further explanation. Now, as the last stragglers finally reached the ledge and allowed themselves to relax a little, Benetan walked towards Simbrian. Shammana was guiding Kaldar to a place where he could sit down; Benetan took a light hold of the sorcerer's arm and drew him out of their earshot before speaking quietly.

'How long must we wait?'

Simbrian regarded him for a moment, privately noting the hard, wintry cast of his grey eyes, then shook his head. 'Lord Aeoris told me no more than he told you.' He glanced up at the night sky, frowning at the star. 'But I don't think he intends to stay his hand for much longer. He said it would begin at midnight and we'll be on the mainland by dawn.' Now his dark eyes focused speculatively on Benetan's face once more. 'Do you doubt his word?'

'No. No, of course I don't. Though I can't say I know how he intends to achieve it.'

Simbrian uttered a soft laugh. 'Twelve years at the Star Peninsula and you still don't treat such feats as commonplace? You surprise me, Benetan.'

The younger man made a dismissive gesture. 'I know. But during those twelve years I saw only Chaos's ways and means, and Chaos's powers have always been' — he hesitated, smiled thinly and harshly — '*seemed* unsurpassable. I suppose I can't yet fully credit the idea that they can be equalled. Or bettered.'

Simbrian was still watching him. 'Are you afraid?' he asked.

On the verge of a reflexive denial Benetan hesitated as he realized that he neither wanted nor needed to lie. 'Yes,' he said. 'I am. In fact, whenever I consider the prospect of what lies ahead of us, I'm terrified.' Another pause. 'Is that too honest?'

'Not at all,' Simbrian replied. 'Your frankness simply makes it easier for me to admit to my own terror. And I think it's only natural that any mortal with a spark of imagination should feel as we both do. However great our faith and our commitment to the cause might be, there are no certainties in this, and nor will there be until our forces are smashing down the gates of the castle itself.'

'Or until Yandros has consigned us all to the Seven Hells,' Benetan added.

'Or that, yes.'

There was another silence. Then Benetan looked over his shoulder to where Kaldar sat, shoulders hunched, face turned away from the people around him. 'But if it comes to that,' he said, and suddenly there was a note in his voice that sent a sharp chill through Simbrian, 'then I'll make sure that I drag enough of his followers there with me to make it worthwhile.'

Aeoris stood motionless in the middle of the crater floor, hands resting on his own upper arms and his strange eyes focused on a plane far beyond these physical surroundings. In one dimension of his mind he sensed the proximity of his six brothers, who, though they had not yet returned to the island, were still closely linked with him, and a faint, hard smile touched his mouth as he felt their readiness.

Where, he wondered, was Yandros, and what engaged his attention now? Yandros's realm was as inimical to the lords of Order as their own was to Chaos's kind, and Aeoris could not penetrate the veil of its secrets. But he had no doubt that the greatest Chaos lord would be watching, waiting for the challenge, and he would be prepared. So be it. Within the next few minutes, that challenge would be unequivocally issued and the hiatus would end at last.

His hands slid away from his arms and briefly, almost carelessly, Aeoris made a single gesture. Around him the crater walls warped momentarily as though under some massive but invisible impact. Then his mind tightened its hold, and the power began to rise in earnest.

The bowl floor beneath his feet shook as though some titanic stone beast had awakened deep under the island. Aeoris swayed a little, effortlessly maintaining poise, then his mind flicked to his brothers again, sensed the moment, felt the spark and swell of energy as their consciousnesses fused, and he hurled a mental command as sharp and clear and searing as lightning. A white-hot bolt exploded from his right hand towards the ledge and the tunnel beyond it. An unearthly shriek dinned through the bowl, and on its heels came a colossal, cracking groan as thousands of tons of solid rock shifted and lost cohesion. The tunnel mouth split, gaped wide; Aeoris sent the power on and through the passage, cleaving the crater as a sword cleaved flesh, forging through and beyond it –

The bowl shook again with a second and far greater concussion, and the rock floor split from side to side. A wave of heat seared up from the fissure, and Aeoris swung round. His golden eyes flicked their focus back to the mortal world and he swung his arm up once more, this time in a violent, summoning motion.

The crater pulsed again with shocking violence and a huge, ominous rumbling resounded somewhere deep beneath the White Isle as six spears of blinding light sprang into being around him. Flames roared up from under the ground, red tongues that stank of sulphur. And the rumbling was swelling to a roar –

*　　*　　*

Yandros's eyes turned molten as he saw the huge charge of energy take form in the mortal world, but even as the furious impulse to retaliate surged in him a far colder reasoning cut through the instinct and erased it.

His brothers, who by their own differing means were also watching Aeoris's work, turned their attention to him; he knew what they were thinking, and spoke composedly.

'Not yet.' The titanic hall in which he sat carried the echoes of his voice away towards a roof lost in fog and darkness. 'There'll be time enough to respond to this kind of vulgar display without squandering more than minimal attention on it now. I'm more interested in Aeoris's human followers – or perhaps I should say, those who might soon consider *becoming* his followers.' He rose from the bizarre, shifting chair in which he had been sitting, stepped down from the chair's plinth and paced slowly across the floor. 'The bait that Order sets to catch those who waver will no doubt look very tempting to gullible mortal minds. We must see to it that the deterrent is equally persuasive.'

Tarod, who was gazing through a window embrasure with disturbing intensity in his eyes, said quietly, 'A Warp would provide a salutary and effective warning to begin with.'

'So it would. But again, not yet.' Yandros moved to stand beside him and focused his attention on the nightscape, adjusting his consciousness fractionally to view it from Tarod's perspective. 'I see that Vordegh has sent Menniam to meet the first direct challenge. A good choice; he's probably one of the most cold-blooded mortals ever born, and he's also unfalteringly vicious and gifted with an inventiveness that puts mine to shame at times. If any of the magi are capable of driving the fear of Chaos into would-be rebels, Menniam should succeed.'

'And if he doesn't?'

'If he doesn't, then a Warp, as you say, will be a salutary

326

warning.' Suddenly, ferally, Yandros smiled. 'And with one small mutation, it will serve a dual purpose.'

He turned from the window, stalked back towards the chair. 'But,' he said, turning round again as he reached the plinth, 'remember – all of you – that once we make that first move, that first response to Aeoris's challenge, there will be no further respites of any kind. We and our old enemies will be at war, directly and without quarter. And if there is one weakness, one flawed link in the chain of the power we will need to command, it could well bring us down.' His anger was beginning to smoulder again; it showed in the stark contours of his face and in the aura which began slowly to pulse about his figure as the air surrounding him turned black. 'Should that happen, we all know what the ultimate penalty could be. And rather than pay that penalty, I will, if I must, destroy the mortal world and everything it contains!'

'Get them back!' Benetan's voice rang out over the rising tumult from the heart of the White Isle, and he signalled frenziedly to his four hastily-trained lieutenants. 'To the ship – get everyone to the ship! *MOVE!*'

The crater was belching smoke, a churning cloud of darkness that poured up from the broken cone and streamed skywards. The first huge tremor had shaken the cliff walls and hurled half the gathering off their feet; one man had almost pitched from the ledge into the tide-pool, and now there was turmoil as Benetan, Simbrian and a few others who had kept their wits about them started to muster everyone together. Benetan yelled his command again, but suddenly Simbrian shouted to him above the confusion, 'Benetan, wait! Don't take anyone aboard! Lord Aeoris is –'

His words were drowned then by a roar from the crater that slammed against their senses, deafening them. And an instant later the night turned to crimson day as a titanic pillar of fire blasted up from the centre of the cone, obliterating the arctic glare of the seven-rayed star. The entire island quaked and the seaward rush halted as people flailed to keep their balance, staring in awed shock at the crater —

To the accompaniment of a gargantuan rumbling, a shaft of white radiance erupted from the tunnel in the crater wall, challenging the fire, spearing down the flank of the cone towards them. It swept over them; a high, pure note drowned the cacophony and sang through every mind and body, and through eyes that streamed with the pain of the light's brilliance Benetan saw shapes taking form. Then the ground shook again — and suddenly the seven lords of Order were there, standing before the tunnel entrance, around which a spectrum of incredible colours whirled. Seven stunning figures, golden auras blazing about them — and though their forms were human they seemed to Benetan to be vast, gigantic, their dimensions eclipsing their surroundings and dwarfing their watching followers. They had cast off mortal trappings, and were whole.

The seven began to move with a dire grace and purpose that made Benetan feel his heart was being torn out of him. Aeoris was at their head, and with every step he took, the mountain slope before him shifted and twisted and flowed into a new pattern — the steps of a huge staircase, symmetrical and perfect, forming itself from the rock at Aeoris's silent command. Benetan felt his mind reeling as he took in the sheer scale of those stairs; he struggled to assimilate what his senses were telling him but it was incredible, *impossible* —

Aeoris raised a hand and pointed. A compulsion took hold of Benetan, took hold of them all, as though a giant's hands had grasped them; as one every soul turned towards the water —

Silently, eerily, a huge barque was gliding from the maw of the inlet and into the pool. It towered over Simbrian's

328

own craft, and every plank, every spar, every sail and sheet and halyard, was white, glowing with a spectral inner fire that challenged the rising red mayhem from the volcano. No men moved on the decks, no one stood at the rail; the barque was utterly deserted and only a cool, clear light burning at the stern gave any illusion of life. An empty ship, a phantom, yet sliding slowly and steadily towards the jetty with a sure resolve that made Benetan's pulse slow to an excruciating crawl.

Then came a new sound. Sourceless, yet filling the air and swamping the uproar around them, it was the single, summoning note of a horn. Never in his life had Benetan heard such a sound, but even as the shock of it paralysed him, his body responded and he couldn't resist the call. Somewhere in his consciousness – *somewhere; but he couldn't reach it, couldn't comprehend such things* – he was aware of his companions also moving, surging forward with him, surging towards the edge of the jetty, a living tide of people snared in the thrall of the summons. The glare from the pillar of fire now towering into the sky flung wild and livid shadows across rapturous faces, hastening figures; Kaldar was there, and Simbrian and Shammana and Nanithe, and others, blurs in the fire-shot darkness, hastening, running – A gangplank was reaching out from the barque, a dimly shining white path bridging the yawing gulf over black water. His feet were on it, people ahead of him, more behind, and the force in him, the compulsion, sent him stumbling over the divide to arrive breathless and dazed on the phantasmic ship's deck.

And suddenly – *how had it happened? He hadn't seen it happen* – as the last stragglers scrambled on board, Aeoris and his brothers were with them. Their auras still burned, but the breathtaking vastness had gone; they were seven among their followers once more, the masks of humanity restored.

'*Cast off!*' The voice – Simbrian's – jolted Benetan

329

violently back to reason, and he looked up to see that the fire above the crater was turning from crimson to a molten orange shot through with blinding tongues of blue-white. The sky was blotted out by a dense pall that was rapidly spreading outwards in a vast, dark radius; in the smoke's depths ominous lights flickered and danced. And the entire cone of the volcano had begun to shudder ... With a clatter the gangplank was hauled in, and hands grasped the sheets as a moaning rattle from high above heralded the unfurling of the sails. A vast white vision seemed to wash down on Benetan, then he found his own fingers gripping rope as he hauled, with three others, on the main-sail halyard. He didn't know what he was doing, had never crewed a ship before, but it didn't matter, for the energy in him was driving him, powering his instinct, guiding hands and body and brain with a sure skill. He saw Simbrian standing at a great white wheel, saw the wheel turning, then felt the deck heel and swing under his feet as the supernatural barque began to turn. The jetty vanished and massive cliff walls slid past his vision; with no more than a few handspans to spare the vessel's bows cleared the rocks, and with a crack of sound the sails filled as she started to move towards the fissure that would carry her to the open sea.

As the cliffs closed in to either side, Benetan had one final sight of the White Isle's heart. The jetty and the gigantic staircase glowed like pale nacre, and beyond them, high above them, the energies conjured by Aeoris from the dormant core of the volcano belched heavenwards in bellowing mayhem, a column of ravening and unquenchable fire. Then the cone vanished behind the colossal walls and, under the glaring turmoil of the sky, the ship began to gather speed.

They broke out into open water, and as the barque curtsied and then cleaved into the fierce swell of the tide, a thrill shot through Benetan as he saw what awaited them. Six more vessels, every one identical to their own, were sailing towards them out of the east. Under the dangerous sky they were like six shining ghosts – but on each ship's deck, crowding at the rails and staring in eager amazement at the tower of fire above the White Isle, were people.

'Great gods . . .' A voice spoke with soft reverence beside him and a man whose face he recognized but whose name he did not yet know stared across the rapidly shrinking distance between them and the oncoming fleet. 'Our friends . . . all our friends from Summer Isle!'

Their own barque was turning again, going about and falling into line with her approaching sisters. The hair at the back of Benetan's neck prickled suddenly as he sensed another presence behind him, and he turned to see that Aeoris had moved silently to join them.

'To the forces of Chaos who watch us, we will seem a pitifully small force, and one to be easily crushed.' The god spoke quietly and calmly, but there was an underlying note of stern satisfaction. 'They will learn the nature of their mistake soon enough.' Then he raised his voice and called to the sorcerer. 'Simbrian! Leave the wheel – the ship needs no further guidance now, and we have other preparations to make.'

He turned, looked back at the White Isle. For a moment his alien eyes flared with a deep, ferocious light; and a charge of raw energy seemed to impact through the barque from stem to stern. The island answered with a baleful swelling of sound – then the canopy of smoke in the sky shattered into a sheet of fire that stretched from horizon to horizon, and the entire Isle vanished under an inferno of red-hot light as the volcano erupted in a single, immense blast.

For three or four seconds the human watchers on the seven ships heard only a rising roll of thunder, counterpointed by the surging roar of the sea. Then the noise of the explosion smashed into their senses like a wall, and as the shock-wave hit them the world around them seemed to rip apart. For a stunning instant the blaze of the volcano was eclipsed by a blinding white flash – then, flowing out of the fabric of air and sea, cracking the barrier between dimensions, a host of phantasmic forms streamed into the mortal world. Wild images assailed Benetan; a storm of wings, fire-red in the glare from the White Isle; vast, graceful yet dramatically alien bodies cleaving the water, surging alongside the seven ships in a churning wash of foam – and a sound that rivalled even the roar of the volcano; high, clear, pure, as the supernatural legion, Order's own demons, gave voice like an unearthly choir.

Aeoris, standing now at the barque's prow with Simbrian beside him, gazed towards the north-west and the invisible mainland.

'Yandros's human allies know of our coming and are preparing to meet us,' he said. 'Vordegh has sent only one magus to orchestrate our downfall, but the test will still be rigorous. Are you prepared?'

'I am, my lord.' Simbrian's eyes had a strange new intensity; behind their darkness a compelling power was beginning to awaken.

Aeoris nodded. 'Then it is time for you to take your proper place. When this battle begins, I and my brothers must face Yandros and his kin – and from that moment on, our mortal forces will be in your hands.' He turned his head to regard the sorcerer. 'There can be no room for compassion in this, Simbrian. Give no quarter. And stop at nothing.'

Simbrian's answering nod was barely perceptible but still conveyed a chill emphasis. 'I understand you, Lord Aeoris. And I mean to do exactly as you say.'

The entire sky seemed to be on fire from horizon to horizon, and sparks were flying from the hooves of Lotro's horse as it hurtled along the shingle bar. Lotro was crouched over the animal's neck, one hand gripping its mane while the other lashed its neck with the looped reins; in the red-shot darkness the other riders and their mounts were a confused blur around him, and he could hear their sergeant, on his huge iron-grey gelding, yelling demented encouragement as the raiding party headed towards the citadel at breakneck speed.

At the village eight miles away Lotro had snatched one adult and two children, clubbing them down and then hauling them unconscious over his saddle-bow. Their bodies jolted and swayed before him now like limp, half-filled sacks, and another Lotro, his real, human self, would have been appalled by what he had done. But that Lotro no longer existed, for the acrid sting of the raw and violent drug that he had been given an hour ago was still in his throat; his eyes, red-rimmed, were streaming with its effects but a fire that rivalled the fire in the sky was ricocheting through his brain, distorting the night and turning the entire world into something out of a wild dream.

The citadel was visible ahead of them now. He could hear a high, piercing shriek emanating from it, a sound inaudible to his physical senses but slamming into his psyche, and with a sudden, unnatural energy he screamed an answer to the towering silhouette. An aura was blazing around the citadel, black light in which impossible shapes writhed; and the aura's shimmering boundary reflected twisted images from the sea like a vast, dark mirror. Lotro flung a rapid glance towards the ocean and saw the reality of the reflections; seven pale phantasms, moving fast in the darkness, seeming to skim over the water's surface like gigantic and spectral birds. The blazing sky stained their whiteness, turning the towering sails to gore — and in the ships' wakes it seemed that the sea and the air were boiling, as though something gargantuan moved with them out of the south. The fleet was less than two miles from shore now and, goaded by the drug, blind hatred filled Lotro. He yelled again, a wordless imprecation, then suddenly the sergeant bellowed a command and the horses were slewing to a halt, stones hurtling in all directions as their skidding hooves dug into the shingle.

Lotro was out of the saddle in one frenzied movement and dragging his captives down. Their bodies landed with a dull thud and lay motionless, and then Magus Menniam was striding from the citadel towards them. Menniam's dark hair was soaked with sweat and his hands and forearms seemed to be glowing; behind him something black moved, flowing across the shingle, and even above the stamp and whinny of milling horses Lotro heard the sound of guttural, unhuman breathing.

'Get them into the citadel!' The sergeant was bawling orders again and riders were stumbling up the beach towards the towering spectre at the top of the beach-bank. Menniam, ignoring the frenetic activity, stared unwaveringly out to sea, and the slithering creation at his back quivered impatiently. Lotro felt the mindless pull of its hunger like a waking nightmare in his mind but he ignored the call of it and started to heave the first of his victims in the others' wake. Over the shingle, into the engulfing aura of the citadel; the great door stood open, a deep spectrum of colours pulsing and agitating around it, and inside – but Lotro averted his head, refusing to look at what waited inside, refusing to acknowledge the stench of darkness and corruption or the harsh, avid sounds of unnatural life stirring and moving beyond the portal. *The power must be raised, the entities must be fed.* The sergeant's order, drummed into them all, ran through his brain like a litany. And there was only one source of energy, only one means of sustenance, and it wasn't wrong, it wasn't, it wasn't –

Back down the beach at a run, sweat pouring now and congealing like ice over his skin. The first victim gone, no point thinking about his fate, *mustn't* think about it. Now the children. He snatched up the first, turned back towards the citadel — but suddenly, shocking him, the gory arena of the night lit up as a spear of lightning cracked the sky in half. Thunder roared on the lightning's heels, and as its echoes rolled across the heavens Menniam's voice rang out, augmented by a charge of furious psychic energy.

'There's no more time! Leave them where they lie, and get to your horses!'

The magus's tone wrenched every rider to instant obedience, and Lotro was suddenly and violently caught up in the new urgency, running, finding his horse, swinging himself into the saddle as his cohorts milled around him. Overhead there was another flash and thunderous roar that set the horses dancing and shrieking with wild excitement, and as his own mount reared and swung around Lotro saw the seven white ships bearing down on the shore, their sails towering spectrally against the howling sky. And around them, all around them, surging through the sea, beating through the air, came a legion of forms that changed their shape with every moment, and the entire mass of them was spreading out, filling Lotro's vision —

From the shingle bank a sound erupted; a piercing, deafening shriek as the power building up in the citadel reached a pitch and began to flow out from the black walls. Menniam was a gaunt silhouette lit savagely by a sudden glare as energy spat between the citadel's dark towers; then the shrieking rose like the voice of a Warp, climbing dizzily up the scale and ripping the air apart. The Chaos riders screamed their own answer, an ululating howl that rang out in crazed counterpoint. Then Menniam flung his arms skyward and a force like a thunderbolt exploded from the heart of the citadel, smashing into every one of his followers' minds —

The fleet came surging to the beach, and the dark tide of the Chaos riders charged to meet them as Menniam's creations poured from the citadel in their wake. Lotro had a bare few seconds to try — and fail — to make sense of anything before the two powers collided with a fury that turned the world around him to pandemonium. Then he was fighting as he had never fought before in his life, for human figures were pouring from the ships onto the beach, and they were armed, and they weren't afraid, and they were attacking the riders with the ferocious savagery of the possessed. Above their heads the supernatural legions clashed with a frenzy that mirrored the mortal battle below, and the shrieking of the citadel was challenged now by a stronger, purer note that rang and resounded in Lotro's ears.

And, incredibly, the tide was starting to turn against them.

At first Lotro was blind to it, for he needed all his energy, skill and attention simply to stay alive amid the forest of clashing weapons and yelling voices and struggling bodies. But someone — or something — was retaliating against Menniam's supernatural onslaughts. Someone — or something — was challenging the magus and outmatching him. And suddenly, shocking him so violently that he lost his hold on the reins and had to cling to his horse's mane to stay in the saddle, Lotro glimpsed three figures, mounted on white, spectral horses, in the midst of the uproar. One — but the young rider couldn't look, couldn't *bear* to look at the flying silver hair, the burning golden eyes, the sheer *power* that radiated from Aeoris's glittering form. And anyway he was not the cause of the shock, and nor was the second man, built like a bear and with his hands upraised and bolts of lethal, blue-white energy cracking between his fingers. It was the third man, with his black hair and black clothes and the sword that seemed to be on fire clutched in both his hands as he gave voice to a wild, savage battle-cry — a cry so familiar that it seared Lotro's mind to the core.

Lotro twisted in the saddle and yelled his sergeant's

name, gesturing frantically. But the sergeant had already seen, and was mustering those men nearest to him – *but their numbers were fewer, and there were dead horses on the shingle, and black-clothed figures lying motionless, trampled* – and gathering them to attack the trio.

Lotro had one more glimpse of Benetan, and in that moment he knew he was looking at a stranger and a madman. Then from the citadel came a new sound, shockingly urgent, driving a sudden, violent imperative into his mind. A shout went up from the invading horde, a cry of ecstatic triumph, and Lotro's horse reared, hooves skidding as it twisted about –

From behind them, over the shingle bank, a second force was sweeping down on the fight. Gathered by Aeoris's brothers from the further villages and settlements which the Chaos riders hadn't ravaged, they were a spontaneous, untrained but zealous company of men, women and even children, driven by fear and fury to which hope had added a new and compelling impetus. And leading them were six shining warriors, each one a perfect twin to the white-haired, molten-eyed figure at Benetan Liss's side.

Menniam screamed a word that was both an imprecation and a command to the monstrosities he had conjured. The citadel shook; from its portal something erupted like a black torrent, spiralling into the air, twisting, contorting, turning to meet the new threat –

The six lords of Order raised their hands and lightning spat down out of the burning sky. It struck the dark tornado, and the citadel seemed to blast apart as the power Mcnniam had raised recoiled and smashed back on its source. Lotro felt the shock-wave coming in the moment before it struck and, propelled by pure instinct, he flung himself out of his horse's saddle, diving for the ground. Then it hit; he saw a blur of churning hooves, flying bodies, heard his mount screaming, glimpsed Menniam's figure writhing in a storm of unnatural fire. Without knowing it his hand was clamped on the amulet at his throat, Chaos's talisman, his only hope of escape, and trained reflex snapped an image into his mind of the castle, the stack, the surging northern sea. He felt the Maze's power coming at him and had time only for one last, incoherent thought *– that this wasn't possible, it couldn't be happening –* before the world exploded out of existence.

CHAPTER XXII

The Maze flung four survivors from Menniam's force back onto the castle stack an hour before dawn broke over the Star Peninsula. Two of the riders, badly injured, lost consciousness in the shock of the transfer, another had lost so much blood that he was incapable of standing; only Lotro was relatively unscathed, and he was taken immediately to Magus Pirane.

Lotro's report, though fragmented and garbled, was enough to make grim hearing, and as soon as she had all the details that the dazed young Chaos rider could give, Pirane sent him to Revian for medical attention and went in person to Vordegh's apartments. Her interview with the First Magus was brief – and when she left, her face was like a stone mask. Vordegh's reaction to the news had been calm, and his orders clear and specific. As Pirane departed he was writing meticulously on a single sheet of paper. And Pirane felt dread taking deep root in her soul.

She found a servant – in the present circumstances few of the remaining castle servants had any chance to sleep – and dispatched him with a cryptic message to Physician-Magus Croin. Then she headed for the main wing.

Andraia was wrested out of sleep by a hand shaking her shoulder, and in the unearthly light from the seven-rayed star above the castle she opened her eyes to see Pirane bending over the bed.

'Wake Savrinor.' Pirane's voice was chilling, and reflexively Andraia slid free of the confused tangle that her own and Savrinor's bodies had become as they slept. The historian stirred and murmured something unintelligible then sank back into his dreams again, and Andraia sat foggily upright before turning to look at him. Exhaustion lined his face and she started instinctively to protest in an urgent whisper.

'Madam, he's barely rested for the past —'

The magus cut across her before she could say any more. 'The little he's had will have to suffice. Wake him.'

In her entire life Andraia had never known Pirane to use such a tone to her before, and it sent a shaft of fear into her marrow. Turning, she grasped Savrinor's shoulder as Pirane had grasped hers, and squeezed it. 'Savrinor! Savrinor, wake up . . .'

It was a small mercy, Pirane thought, that he had gone to his bed fully clothed; under the circumstances any wasted moments could be disastrous. Waking came hard though, and what she saw in Savrinor's eyes as his consciousness connected with reality stirred something akin to pity in her.

She quelled it and said curtly, 'Four Chaos riders have returned from the south. They're the only survivors of Menniam's party.'

Savrinor sat up with a convulsive movement, his senses snapping into sharp focus. 'The only —'

'Order's forces attacked them; Menniam's citadel was destroyed and Menniam himself killed.' There was far more to the story but this was not the moment to reveal it. Pirane paused momentarily, then added, 'I've just taken the riders' report to the First Magus, and his response is the reason why I'm here. I need to speak with you, and quickly.' Savrinor started to get out of bed, then briefly froze as a savage physical reaction stabbed through him. Pirane said quickly, 'Savrinor. Are you fit for this?'

He nodded, found his voice with an effort. 'Yes, madam.' And thought: *I must be fit; to be anything less would be a betrayal of the gods* . . . The miasma was losing its grip on him; he tried to shake the last of it off. 'I'll be myself in just a moment . . .'

'Madam.' Andraia had started to put on one of Savrinor's robes but paused. 'Savrinor is exhausted –'

'Exhaustion is preferable to the alternative he'll face if anything goes awry now, Andraia – and the same applies to you.' Pirane glanced at the robe. 'Take that off and get fully dressed, *quickly*.' Andraia hesitated and the magus added sharply, 'Before the First Magus arrives here!'

Andraia's eyes widened in alarm. As she flung the robe off and reached for her clothes, Pirane turned to the historian again and said, 'Do you need wine? Or something else?'

He did, but in this emergency it would have to wait. 'I'll be well enough, madam.' Nausea lurched somewhere below the pit of his stomach but it was too familiar now to worry him beyond a relatively meaningless point. Hastily he started to comb his fingers through his hair, then looked up at her. 'What does Lord Vordegh want with me?'

Pirane noted the undercurrent of fear in his voice. 'He has work for you,' she said. 'He's compiling a list – another list, and entirely of his own creation this time. More lives to raise power. But there is a magus among their numbers.'

An appalling shadow moved in Savrinor's eyes. 'A *magus* –'

'Quite. A woman whose . . . recreational interests, shall we say, do not meet with Lord Vordegh's approval.' Andraia had pulled on her gown and shoes now, and kicked the rest of her clothes out of sight under the bed; a swift, expressive movement of Pirane's eyes gave her a clear message and she left the room, closing the door behind her.

Pirane returned her attention to Savrinor. 'We feared this, and Yandros feared it, too. He gave Vordegh one final chance for the sake of his skill, but it seems now that the dangers outweigh the advantages. I believe we will be forced to return to the plan that was proposed before this crisis began. The First Magus must be deposed.'

Savrinor nodded. The nausea was gaining an unpleasantly strong hold on him. 'Madam, is there any hope that the gods might –'

She cut him off before he could say more. 'They can and will do nothing to help us now. They have a greater predicament to occupy their attention, and so we must take matters entirely into our own hands.'

'At a time like this –'

'Quite. But there's no help for it. If we leave Vordegh to go his way unchecked, he will bring disaster on us all.'

A nod. 'What do you want from me, madam?'

'Spread the word and give the warning,' Pirane said. 'Firstly to those magi who endorse us, then to Qenever and a few other key allies, and lastly –' She made a rapid mental calculation; Averel hadn't yet returned from his latest sortie and there was no time to wait for him. 'And lastly, find out how many Chaos riders are likely to support our cause. We will need them.' She didn't add that subtlety and subterfuge were vital; Savrinor of all people knew precisely how to employ both.

'I must leave.' She started towards the outer room and Savrinor followed her, hoping to all the gods that he could stay on his feet. Andraia was waiting. Her face was blanched and there was terror in her eyes, but she had lit a number of candles and spread some papers on Savrinor's table, making it look as though the historian had been working. The magus flicked her a glance of approval then said to Savrinor, 'Don't fear for Andraia – she'll be under my protection from now on. Go to your desk. You've spent the past three hours preparing a new inventory for Magus Croin; make a good pretence of it. Andraia, come with me.'

Andraia hurried out into the corridor, but before following her Pirane turned and looked back. Savrinor had already slid into his chair, and the magus spoke tersely and quietly so that Andraia would not overhear.

'One more thing you should know – Benetan Liss is leading Order's army. One of his own men saw him at the demon Aeoris's side.'

She didn't wait for a response but shut the door fiercely behind her.

Pirane and Andraia came face to face with Vordegh in the corridor. Andraia shrank back, staring down at the floor and trying to stop her muscles from trembling, and Pirane made a quick but respectfully formal bow.

'Magus.' Vordegh seemed to stare through her. 'The historian is in his rooms?'

'He is, sir. I found him working on an inventory for Magus Croin, and I have informed him that –'

Her words were cut short. 'The physician must look for assistance elsewhere.' Vordegh started towards Savrinor's door, then stopped again. 'Why was that woman in the historian's rooms?' Andraia prayed silently that her legs wouldn't give way beneath her and heard, as though from an enormous distance, Pirane's calm reply.

'She was not, First Magus; I brought her with me. I need someone to assist me, and Andraia is proving invaluable.'

Vordegh turned his head to give Andraia a long, inhumanly mild stare. Then he said, 'That is acceptable for the present. If the situation changes, you will be informed.'

Pirane was well aware that she had probably just saved both Andraia's life and Savrinor's, and she hoped fervently that Andraia would never realize it. Her skin crawling, she said, 'Yes, Lord Vordegh,' and steered the girl hastily away as Vordegh walked unannounced into Savrinor's apartment.

'My lord.' Savrinor snapped to his feet as the First Magus entered, praying Vordegh wouldn't notice the fact that he had to hold on to the table's edge to maintain his balance.

'You are working for Magus Croin.' Not a question but

a statement. 'That will cease. I have other tasks for you.'

'Sir.' Savrinor watched surreptitiously as Vordegh paced slowly across the room. The First Magus's dark gaze rested on the cabinet and seemed to see through its ornate wooden doors to the shelves and their contents. Then he looked towards the bedroom, through the half-open door to the rumpled bed, and Savrinor's eyes shut as his mind projected a brief, desperate and futile plea to the gods who could no longer listen.

But though he noted small details and drew his own conclusions, Vordegh had no immediate interest in Savrinor's personal activities. He dropped a single sheet of paper onto the table. 'Your instructions are clearly written. Carry them out immediately. If you are dilatory, you know the price you will pay.'

Savrinor did, and bowed wordlessly. He didn't raise his head as the First Magus stalked from the room, but as soon as the tall figure had vanished he moved rapidly to the door, closed it and leaned against it, shutting his eyes tightly. Sweat prickled sharply as it broke out on his face and hands. *Sweet Yandros,* he thought, *that was the narrowest of margins . . .* In the wake of that came a harsh resurgence of the nausea, but he knew how to deal with it and, gathering his wits and what little was left of his energy, went to his cabinet and mixed what he needed. It wouldn't be wise to drink too much while this particular cocktail was in his bloodstream or the later consequences could be serious, so he resisted the temptation to pour himself a very large glass of wine, and picked up the document that the First Magus had left.

He read it, hesitated, then read it a second time, certain that his mind must be malfunctioning. But it wasn't. He wasn't mistaken, hadn't misinterpreted. Vordegh's instructions were, as he had said, perfectly clear. And beneath the instructions was the list of those who were to be detained and prepared for the death that Vordegh would give them

344

in the pursuit of raising power. A magus. Well, he had known about that, though Pirane's forewarning didn't entirely annul the shock of seeing the name plainly written. But it wasn't the name itself, nor any of the others, that brought the slow, cold, cramping ache rising from the pit of his stomach. It was the reason Vordegh gave for his choices, the reason inscribed in stark words at the top of the page.

Traitors to Chaos. The phrase brought a sick revival of memories which Savrinor had been trying to put out of his mind since his own ordeal in the Marble Hall. Glib and hollow words to justify the unjustifiable and twist the truth to suit Vordegh's personal agenda. The rationale was such a blatant fallacy that to trouble with it at all seemed an act of madness in itself. These people had committed no crime. There was no whiff of heresy here. Yet the old aberration had come back like a cyclical plague, and at a time when every fibre in him should have been dedicated to combating the threat of Order's demons, Vordegh was instead giving free rein to the demons within his own warped mind. Trivial spites, petty vendettas, imagined grievances. A new and lethal game to be played out within the castle's walls while the true enemy spread corruption through the world . . .

A foul oath which he hadn't used since he was young enough to be impressed by obscenities came to Savrinor's tongue. He wanted to scream it to the room, to the entire castle and all that lay beyond it; vent the bleak fury that burned in him like acid. But a cold streak of reason told him that there would be no relief in such a gesture, and instead he laid the paper down, turned, walked to a side table where a wine-flagon stood. This was a particularly exquisite vintage, subtle and refined and rare. Savrinor picked the flagon up, fought back an impulse to hurl it at the wall, and filled a glass which he then drained. The wine seemed to taste of nothing. He refilled the glass, drank

345

again. The gods – or Croin – knew what it would do to him on top of the drugs; five minutes ago he had cared, but now everything had changed. Let the combination poison him, let it stop his heart again or let it merely take ten or twenty or thirty years off the span of his life; what did it matter? He was going to die anyway. They all were; for the magi were faced with an impossible choice. If they concentrated their power against Vordegh, they would have no resources left to fight Order's threat. Yet if Vordegh continued to live and rule, Order's demons would need only to wait and watch and smile as his insanity completed their work for them. For a moment the logic of his thoughts seemed to stand stark and unarguable in Savrinor's mind. But then, unbidden, something else stirred. Memory of his last encounter with the gods; in particular the meeting with Tarod in the courtyard and the Chaos lord's trenchant words on the subject of self-pity. Was he indulging in self-pity now? He wasn't that weak. Surely, *surely* he hadn't sunk that far. Pirane had not despaired. She had entrusted him with a task, and while there was still breath in him, and faith in him, he must summon the will to carry that task out. For if he couldn't, then his existence was worth nothing.

Seven Hells, the wine was having a shocking effect . . . Savrinor fought it, knowing that it was nothing he hadn't learned to cope with over the years of wanton indulgence that lay scattered behind him like . . . but simile eluded him. Faith. That was the key, the one spark that kept the flame alive. He hadn't lost his faith. Wouldn't lose it; *couldn't* lose it; the ability to give up simply wasn't in him. Faith in the gods. Faith in what was *right*.

The walls of the room seemed to surge in on him then recede, fast, inducing a horrible sense of vulnerability as though he were about to pitch off the edge of the stack and fall down, down to the sea a thousand feet below. Savrinor gripped the table's edge with one hand while the other snatched up the flagon again and poured a third glass, spilling a fair amount onto the floor. From long experience he knew the tactic would work, even if the later results proved drastic. Run the gauntlet, get through the disorientation and emerge on the other side. It would restore his strength for long enough for this nightmare to be resolved.

He drained the glass, felt his mind beginning to clear, and even if the clarity had a frail and glacial edge to it he was used to that and could cope.

He left the apartment ten minutes later. The flagon in his room was empty, and his appearance was immaculate and composed and calm. Only his eyes gave away the truth. But no one he met would trouble – or dare – to look too closely. And if they did, what they saw would be something better to forget.

Yandros's feline eyes were slits of dark fire as he stood beside Tarod and watched the relentless progress of the force that moved northward across the face of the mortal world. Their numbers were no surprise to him, though he suspected that they might cause some consternation to the magi when the first reliable reports reached the Star Peninsula. And he felt a twist of bitter irony as he contemplated the degree to which his own human servants – and one servant in particular – had succeeded in turning the tide of human feeling against the powers that had ordained the pattern of their lives for so long.

'They're a rabble.' There was no particular venom in his voice; he sounded, Tarod thought, almost detached. 'But more and more are joining them with each hour that passes.' He moved slightly, restlessly. 'And still the magi do nothing.'

Tarod turned his head. In the darkness of Chaos that cloaked them both his face looked as if it had been carved out of ice. 'The ease with which Menniam and his detachment were destroyed has forced them to re-think their strategy. For all your warnings, they didn't expect Order's sorcerers to wield such power.'

'Nor to have their gods' – Yandros gave the word a twist of exquisite contempt – 'riding at the rabble's head.' He sighed sharply. 'Nonetheless this inaction disturbs me, for I can't help but wonder if there's more behind it than meets the eye.'

Tarod looked quickly at him. 'Vordegh?'

'Vordegh. With the Gate shattered and our link broken it's impossible to read the atmosphere in the castle, but I fear that the final chance I gave him to redeem himself might have been a grave mistake.'

'I could find out easily enough,' Tarod said. 'A brief visit to the mortal world –'

'No.' Yandros interrupted him, one hand making a negating gesture. 'That's precisely the kind of opportunity Aeoris is waiting for. A division of our numbers, a lapse in concentration. Any distraction to take our attention even for a moment, and he'll end this charade he's playing and make his move on this plane.' His fingers flexed, curled. 'I'm tired of this impasse, Tarod. Even if the magi aren't yet ready to meet Order's human forces, I think the time has come for us to take a more direct hand. And if that prompts Aeoris to action, so be it.'

Tarod understood the tacit implication, and the same thought was moving disquietingly in his own mind. With Aeoris's shackles broken and his full power restored, the lords of Chaos and Order were evenly matched – which meant that the final outcome of this conflict was likely to rest in human hands. If the magi couldn't be trusted to play their part, then to goad Aeoris now would carry a high degree of risk.

He glanced again at his brother. 'You're sure about your decision?'

'I'm far from sure about it.' Then Yandros smiled his

familiar, vulpine smile, his eyes echoing it with a glint of hard-edged humour. 'But patience has never been one of my greatest virtues, has it? I grow bored too easily. And I'm bored now – bored with waiting. Let's get this over.'

One hand made a brief movement and the vision of the army on the mortal plane faded. Yandros turned and stared into the shifting clouds that shrouded most of the Chaos realm at this moment. Then he smiled again.

'I recall your suggesting that a Warp would be a salutary and effective warning to begin with,' he said. 'I agree . . . though, as I said at the time, I will make one small change.' His look grew speculative. Just a slight mutation in the nature of the great storms – and the irony of it appealed greatly to his sense of the absurd, for he would do nothing more than give solid foundation to a superstition that had been rife among the ignorant for generations. The belief that to be caught in a Warp without shelter was to court something far worse than death; that the storms had the power to carry a man out of the world and destroy him, body and soul. It had never been true, as all who were genuinely devoted to Chaos knew perfectly well. Simply another legend, a fable created by the undiscerning human imagination. Now though, fable would become reality. There was no malice involved in Yandros's decision; malice was a human trait and one he scorned. But it would serve Chaos's purpose, for Aeoris would realize the danger and would not yet risk tarnishing the zeal of his followers by doing nothing to protect them. A distraction. And with luck, it would tilt the balance of advantage in Chaos's favour.

His left hand moved slowly, gracefully, the fingers tracing a flowing pattern. From the heart of the dimension a sound began to rise, faint as yet but growing stronger. A thin, high-pitched wailing, like an unearthly choir of lost souls . . .

Tarod saw the first flickering light as the spectrum of

349

the Warp began to manifest, and smiled as he understood what Yandros had done. Then they both turned their attention to the mortal world . . .

Each time he surveyed the scene Benetan had to remind himself forcibly that he wasn't dreaming. They must already number nearly a thousand; men, women and children, every one of them marching under the banner – metaphorical at first but now, as fervour grew, literal too – of Order. Untrained they might be, undisciplined and utterly inexperienced. But theirs was a dedication that outstripped that of any formal army ever conceived. And the numbers were growing fast. Fifty had joined them during the past hour, thirty-five in the hour before that; small beer in themselves, but each was a tributary to swell the river into a torrent. Aeoris's six brothers were moving across the land, spreading the word, bringing the faithful to increase their ever-growing ranks. And the word was spreading wider still as the psychic summons that Simbrian and the other sorcerers had sent out before their departure from the coast ran like a forest fire through the rebel network. News had reached them now of a great stirring to the north, a second army marching towards them, gathering followers in their wake as they cut a ferocious swathe through all attempts to stop their progress. By sunset the two forces would meet and unite. And this was only the beginning.

For the fiftieth time Benetan turned in the saddle of his strange, pale horse to scan the human and supernatural legion spreading like a tide in his wake. From a distance, he thought, they must present an awe-inspiring sight. At their head Aeoris rode alone on another of the tall, graceful and shining mounts that he had summoned from his own realm, his silver hair flowing in the wind and seeming to mingle with the wing of his white cloak. An aura burned hotly around him, and above his head a single tongue of fire burned steadily, a beacon visible to every eye in the great crowd. Behind the lord of Order the rebels' three human figureheads rode in line abreast; Simbrian in the centre with Benetan and Kaldar flanking him. Kaldar, his mount attached to Simbrian's by a leading-rein, had set his face unwaveringly towards the north; still he had not spoken a word since leaving the White Isle, and his pallor and empty eye-sockets gave him the look of a fleshless corpse. But to the growing horde that followed them he was a living symbol of triumph in adversity, and the surge of rage and sympathy that his presence engendered added a powerful dimension to their cause.

Benetan's presence, too, had had a compelling effect, for to his uneasy surprise – and as Aeoris had predicted – he had been rapturously welcomed as a hero. His role in the destruction of the Chaos Gate was only a small part of it; the greater triumph, in the minds of those who flocked to Order's call, was the fact that the Chaos riders' own commander had renounced his human and supernal masters and devoted his life and soul to Aeoris.

The populace was rising. The rebellion had truly begun. Yet still Chaos, either in the form of its gods or the magi who served them, had made no move . . .

Benetan turned from his survey and looked ahead once more. The daylight had a nightmarish quality, for though the sky was cloudless the westering sun was obscured by a vast and slow-moving shadow in which banked fires of crimson and gold flickered distantly and ominously. The shadow – an unearthly legacy from the eruption on the White Isle – had moved with them since dawn, when the first clash had been won and the long northward trek began. It filled the sky behind and above them and now it was encroaching slowly but relentlessly towards the pulsing star of Chaos that still glared just north of the meridian. The star's light glittered on a thousand makeshift weapons; on fifty crude but defiantly fluttering banners adorned with the circle and lightning-flash sigil of Order; on the shining forms of a hundred beings from their gods' realm and it seemed to reflect harshly in Aeoris's pupilless eyes as he sat in the saddle of his own steadily striding mount and gazed ahead at the landscape unfolding before them.

Somewhere at the heart of the throng a group of men were singing. Benetan recognized the song as a campfire favourite among the Chaos riders when they were on sortie, and for a moment it gave him an unpleasant frisson. But then he reminded himself that for the most part the Chaos riders were no different, in essence, to the army he led now. Circumstance might change a man's outlook, but the fundaments of his nature stayed the same whatever his fealty. That lesson had come home hard to Benetan this morning, after the fight, when he had been able to put a name to every black-clad figure lying dead on the shingle . . .

He scrubbed a hand rapidly over his eyes, dismissing the memory with a reflex that his years in the castle had taught him to invoke at will. Friends or strangers, it was irrelevant. Chaos's allies were his enemies and there was no room for regret or compassion. He had been trained to give no quarter, and the training was standing him in good stead now.

The singing faded and a cheer went up, followed by raucous laughter. Benetan didn't know what was being celebrated but he called back to one of his new lieutenants, an easterner who in appearance reminded him uncomfortably of Savrinor but had nonetheless a good military mind.

'Tervis – I'll tolerate high spirits, but not at the expense of vigilance! Check all's well and remind them of the priorities. And if they're passing beer around, confiscate it.'

Tervis signalled acquiescence and moved towards the noisy group, and Benetan turned again to find Simbrian watching him.

The sorcerer smiled. 'Can a good commander never relax?'

352

The corners of Benetan's mouth flicked, but with little humour. 'Not if he wants to keep his own and his men's skins intact.' He nodded towards the pulsing star ahead of them. 'That's a constant reminder, and for all their hatred of Chaos the vast majority of our followers have little true idea of the power those devils at the castle can command. We've had just one small victory, but on the strength of it some are starting to believe that the war is already won. I don't want that idea to get out of hand.'

'Or the celebrations to begin too early. I quite take your point.' Privately Simbrian was coming to have a very high opinion of Benetan, and he decided to air the thought that had been troubling him for some while. 'In truth, Benet, I don't like the ease with which we seem to be advancing. We've encountered no resistance so far.' He glanced around him. 'It's easy enough to see why the overlords and their kind are keeping out of our path; with Lord Aeoris at our head no man in his right mind is going to issue a challenge. But Chaos itself is another matter. The magi — and their masters — are too quiet. And I can't believe that the destruction of one citadel had anything to do with it.'

'It didn't,' Benetan agreed emphatically. 'Citadels are small sorcery by the castle's standards, and for all his seniority Menniam's demise won't have weakened them. I think they're waiting.'

'For what?'

A shrug. 'Your guess is probably better than mine. Word from Yandros?'

'That's possible. But with the Chaos Gate gone, who knows how matters stand between Yandros and the magi now? Besides,' Simbrian looked at the star, 'from what I gather of his nature, Yandros won't trouble to wait until his mortal servants are ready. There's something in the wind. I feel it, and I don't like it.'

Benetan didn't reply, and when Simbrian glanced at him

again he saw that the younger man's posture was suddenly tense.

He said: 'Benet?'

No response. But a muscle was working in Benetan's throat and he seemed to be having difficulty in focusing his eyes. Simbrian started to speak again, but suddenly a hand came up sharply, forestalling him.

'*Listen!*' Benetan's voice was hoarse. 'Can you hear anything untoward?'

Simbrian couldn't. But then he saw that Aeoris had turned his head and his golden eyes were fixed on Benetan's face. Intuition struck the sorcerer, and rapidly he flicked his concentration from the earthly plane to search a less tangible dimension.

'Great gods –' The oath was out before he could stem it, and Benetan's head snapped round.

'It's a Warp.' And his bones were answering its call; he could feel the pull of it, the enticement, the giddying seduction of its monstrous power. But there was something else. Something *wrong* . . .

The first high, thin wail sounded out of the north, and on the far horizon ahead of them there was a cataclysmic shudder of baleful light. The seven-rayed star fluctuated then flared blindingly, and a grim shadow swept down from the sky and over the company, clashing with the pall that marched in their wake. Eerie harmonies resonated through Benetan's blood and seemed to penetrate to the core of his being; he shivered violently, fighting their call. Then he saw the sky starting to change, the bands of dark, sinister colour forming and staining the heavens as the monstrous storm began to break through from the realm of Chaos.

A second shiver went through him and with it a wave of sickness that made him sway in the saddle. Something bumped against his mount's shoulder; a hand grasped his arm and, as though from a huge distance, he heard Simbrian's voice.

'Benet! Benet, are you all right?'

'Nn . . .' Benetan shook his head violently to clear it, teeth clenching. 'Not me – it's the Warp; it's –' The third shiver was the most savage of all; then – 'My lord!' Startling Simbrian, Benetan suddenly spurred his horse forward to draw level with Aeoris. 'My lord, this is no ordinary Warp! Something's happened – something has *changed!*'

Aeoris swung round and jerked his own mount to a halt. Behind their leaders the ragged horde began to falter to a confused standstill; voices went up in query or chagrin and sharp orders from the lieutenants echoed above the Warp's distant but increasing noise.

'Lord Aeoris!' Benetan's face was white and his words hectic as he felt the nature of the change that had taken place in the supernatural storm. 'Yandros has –'

But Aeoris already knew what Yandros had done. His mount wheeled around, rearing, and his voice cut across Benetan's like a whiplash. 'Simbrian! Protect our people!' He flung one arm up and a net of white lightning cracked from his hand, shearing outwards into a spitting blaze. Simbrian's mind snatched at the power, grasping it, manipulating it; Benetan saw Kaldar tense violently and felt the psychic impact of other minds joining in as Order's sorcerers realized what was afoot. There was sudden turbulence in the throng, curses and imprecations and cries of warning; Benetan yelled at his subordinates to maintain ranks, keep them *calm*, but alarm was threatening to turn into panic as ingrained superstitions flared to life.

Then a horse slewed out of the confusion and Tervis galloped towards him. 'Sir!' Tervis gestured wildly ahead. 'To the north!'

Benetan looked. In the distance, visible against the vague, green-brown sweep of the plain, a large mass was moving. The northern army – their friends, their comrades, heading to meet them – and in the instant that he saw them

Benetan knew with a sure, hideous instinct what was about to happen.

His eyes widened, and the warning tore from his throat in a frantic yell. '*My lord —* '

CHAPTER XXIII

His cry was hurled into oblivion as the Warp blasted through dimensions and into the mortal world. The entire landscape seemed to twist and invert; Benetan saw the sky shattering under a tumult of wheeling colours, heard the storm's rising howl like the voice of damnation erupting across the heavens, ripping through his senses. Then a blinding glare exploded over his field of vision, and seven thunderbolts seared screaming into the mayhem as Aeoris and his brothers hurled an answering onslaught at the Warp's heart.

As the storm broke, the great mass of the northern army had halted in disarray, and now on the plain ahead there was pandemonium. A wave of monstrous darkness and another of blinding light hurtled from opposite horizons, and for an instant it seemed that the northerners would be smashed and obliterated between the two. But then the racket of the Warp was eclipsed by another sound; a high, pure shriek that assaulted far more than the physical senses. Above Benetan's head the crackling lightning which Simbrian had chained pulsed into a net of fire that whirled like a vast, protective web above the heads of the marching columns — and Chaos's two encroaching waves recoiled with a thunderous noise as the inimical forces met head-on. The shriek was answered by an abysmal baying sound from the sky, and suddenly Benetan swung round in his saddle and started yelling orders to his own men. The impetus came from somewhere beyond him, snapping the reflex of his old training into life, and the psychic charge of it went through the ranks like a firestorm. The army began to move, faster, faster, goaded by Benetan's imperative to meet and join with their northern comrades and become one force, one power, one entity. High above their heads the roar and tumult of the clashing supernatural legions had turned the sky to a maelstrom of shrieking insanity, but the human host was sweeping onward unchecked –

Then to the north-west a vortex exploded into being, black light that shattered the landscape around it to fragments. The boom of a colossal shock-wave hit the two approaching multitudes like a wall, and out of the vortex dark shapes were erupting, a tidal wave of form and energy surging towards them. Benetan knew instantly what was coming and his voice rose again, hoarse with the desperation to make himself heard above the frenzy.

'*The Chaos riders!*' And a kind of madness, a loathing such as he had never known and which his mind could barely encompass, filled him as the image of Iselia's charred corpse rose like a dark banner in his mind. '*Destroy them – DESTROY THEM!*'

Reason had gone and Lotro knew only that he and his fellow riders had burst out of the Maze into mayhem. A hundred questions but no answers: why had they been sent, what were they to do, why had he been put in charge of a detachment, why were more than three quarters of their number untrained and unfledged – his mind was reeling with exhaustion and confusion and the giddying nausea of the sacrament, and the creature of Chaos under him was like a living, screaming nightmare, power and steel and thunder, barely in control. Only a few stark facts stood out like lightning-flashes in a storm; the order to muster had come directly from the First Magus and had encompassed every rider from highest to lowest; but another magus had changed the order at the last moment and some had stayed behind; Captain Averel had stayed behind, and

Master Savrinor was with him, and there were rumours hurtling that something had gone wrong –

But there was no chance now to unravel the tangle of thought and terrified speculation, for the world had become a crazed arena and he was leading his comrades into the heart of it, into a pitched battle of men and demons and gargantuan, discordant forces, and his own life and the lives of many others would depend on his actions in the next few minutes, and the gods couldn't help him, and he didn't even know if he trusted in any gods any more, because everything had gone so hideously *wrong* –

Overhead, the sky resounded to a renewed onslaught. Something vast and grim was rising on the northern horizon, a tower of whirling darkness more than a mile high. It swayed like a titanic serpent before toppling towards land, and the Warp howled in greedy response as the darkness sheared down towards the mass of Order's followers. Lotro heard his own voice yelling, but there were no words, only inchoate sounds; sounds of fury and bloodlust and terror and hunger, because the magi's drug was blazing in him and he knew only that men were going to DIE –

Savrinor stumbled through the castle corridors, trying not to ask himself how much longer his legs would continue to support him. An elemental could have been sent; the magus overseeing the scryers in the council hall had told him so; but no such courier could convey what he had to say this time. He *had* to find Pirane in person.

Three hundred brought in from the gleanings and more than a hundred sacrificed in the past hour. No time even to take them to the Marble Hall; the bloody work was being done in the courtyard now, and the energy released by the slaughter was a savage, palpitating force staining the air. But it was making no difference, and for all Vordegh's ferocious and intransigent will it *could* make no difference, because it was happening too late. Reports coming in by the minute, carried by any and every kind of unhuman messenger; he had seen them in the hall, he had heard what they had to tell. A legion of heretics wiped from the face of the world by Yandros's power, but the monstrosities of Order were retaliating, and the cream of the Chaos riders were reduced to ash, and the demon Aeoris was calling more and more and more humans to rally under his banner, moving inexorably towards the castle while nothing was done to stem his progress –

Savrinor broke the train of thought, smashed it, and quickened his pace through the unlit and empty corridors. Where in all of damnation *was* everybody? But the question answered itself, for he knew that those who still survived amid Vordegh's predations – the lucky few, he thought with a cynical inward wrench – were too occupied amid this waking nightmare to be roaming the corridors. No lights, no servants, he couldn't see where he was going except in the brief moments when a glare of light crackled between the spires and lit the entire castle, and he felt so *ill* – Then a shape moved quickly from the gloom of a side passage, and Savrinor collided with Averel.

'Sir!' Averel recovered his balance and snapped a salute, but it was perfunctory. He looked half dead with exhaustion; earlier Savrinor might have sympathized but that ability was far beyond him now.

'Sir, I must find Magus Pirane!' Averel said breathlessly. 'Thirty riders have come back through the Maze, but they say they're the only –'

'I know what they say!' Savrinor snapped. 'We've had the same intelligence from other sources.'

'But sir, there were more than two hundred in that force!'

'Most of whom were conscripted auxiliaries, untrained, untried and probably worse than useless!' The historian rounded on him and focused a savage gaze on his face.

'They're carrion, Captain, and so are the mainstay of the regular riders! If you have two dozen trained and fit men left under your command you can count yourself lucky – and in the light of the First Magus's new orders, I doubt if you'll even have that bare few for long!'

Averel stared back at him. 'What are you saying, sir? What has –'

The historian cut short his questions with a ferocious, impatient gesture. 'I'm taking the news to Magus Pirane now.' *That and a good deal more*, he appended silently, crushing the piece of paper he gripped in one hand. 'If you want to see her on your own account, you'd best come with me.'

Stark-faced, Averel fell into rapid step beside him. There were unholy sounds in the courtyard but Savrinor didn't spare so much as a glance towards the outside world. He knew only too well what was taking place; a further hundred souls awaiting slaughter, and only a minimal force of armed men to keep them under control as panic set in . . . Bolts of energy were now snapping between the summits of the south and west spires every few seconds, hurling gaunt shadows in through the windows, and once the entire corridor was lit by a flash so gargantuan that it blinded them both for several seconds, as a backlash from the distant Warp in the south punched between dimensions and through the entire castle. They passed a servant, running and sobbing with his face a blank, idiot mask of shock; Averel started to call out but thought better of it and they hurried on.

Pirane was in her chambers. The magus's face looked haggard and the outer room was tingling with the after-effects of magical energy expended; it made Savrinor's ears sing and he shook his head like an animal. As Averel made another tense, exhausted salute the historian crossed to Pirane's table and slapped the paper he carried down on its surface.

'Madam.' No courtesies, no apologies for the sudden intrusion; this was too urgent. 'You must see this!'

Pirane reached for the paper. 'Is there more news from the south?'

'Yes, madam, and it's grave. The demon Aeoris has destroyed the force sent against him. His army is continuing the march northward, and the commoners are flocking to Order's banner like rats to a grain-store. Their numbers are growing by the thousand, and unless the First Magus —'

Pirane interrupted him sharply. 'Where is Vordegh?'

'In the Marble Hall. That —' Savrinor caught his breath, coughed violently. 'That's why I'm here, madam. Lord Vordegh has issued a new order.'

The magus's face grew still and tense. 'What order?' she demanded. 'What has happened?'

'A change of tactic.' Savrinor signed meaningfully with his eyes in Averel's direction and, understanding, Pirane looked at the paper.

'*Great gods . . .*' Reflexively she crushed the sheet as Savrinor had done earlier. 'He can't seriously think that this will —' Then, remembering Averel, she bit the rest of the sentence back and swung round. 'Captain, this is a matter of the utmost urgency! Magus Croin is in the courtyard. Find him, and ask him to attend me here *immediately.*'

Averel, who had been listening but failing to make any sense of the exchange, saluted and left, seeming glad to escape from the room. Pirane looked at Savrinor.

'I don't need to ask if you've read this.' His expression confirmed it, and she nodded. 'It's nothing short of utter insanity, Savrinor! To claim that our enemies' cause is being fuelled by traitors in the castle, and to order *trials* in the midst of this crisis — sweet Yandros, how did we come to elect such a twisted madman to rule over us?' Body tense, she started to move across the room again but Savrinor forestalled her.

'Madam . . .'

She looked angrily at him, though her anger had another focus entirely. 'What is it?'

'I'm afraid for Andraia.'

Pirane stared at him. 'Is her name on Vordegh's list?'

'No. But if the list is composed of people against whom Lord Vordegh has some personal grudge –'

'Then it will only be a matter of time before Andraia's name is added. I take your point. And your name, and mine, and doubtless a good many others who as yet have no notion that they've offended the First Magus in any way.' Pirane's mouth set savagely. 'While we, diverted by this mockery, allow the forces of Order to move ever closer to our gates – great Yandros, if Vordegh is so bent on destruction he needs only wait another few days and Aeoris's filthy brood will do his work *for* him!' Outside, another flicker of light spat between the south and west spires, illuminating her face with a brief, grim radiance, and her eyes took on a hard focus. 'We must take matters into our own hands, while there are still enough of us left alive to do it. Savrinor, how many from the gleaning are –' then she stopped as she saw that the historian was leaning against the table, gripping its edge as though his life depended on it. 'Savrinor?'

'I'll be . . . all right in a moment, madam.' But it wasn't true; nausea and cramp and a feeling of devastating weakness had hit him so suddenly and completely that he knew he would be unable to combat it this time. Slick, chill sweat soaked him, and the room seemed to be shrinking in, the light dimming, the walls and ceiling becoming night-marishly claustrophobic . . .

Pirane said, 'Enough, Savrinor.' For a moment she had wondered if his heart was about to fail him a second time, but it wasn't that; the malaise had a far simpler cause, and one she had overlooked. 'You need to sleep,' she told him. 'Don't argue with me, and don't protest that your drugs will restore your vitality. There's a limit to the damage you can permit, and you're too valuable a player to be eliminated from the game by exhaustion at this crucial stage. I am telling you to sleep, and you will obey me.' She gestured towards the door to her inner chamber. 'Andraia is resting there at my order. Join her.'

The historian started to say weakly, 'Madam, I can't –' but realized that she was right. He *had* to sleep. Even if it meant exchanging one kind of nightmare for another.

He moved slowly, carefully away from the table and across the room. Pirane watched him go, her expression unreadable. Then she snatched up a small piece of iron ore that lay on the table and made a rapid gesture over it. An odd, dark radiance flickered in the room; the piece of ore moved in her hand and distorted briefly and Pirane sensed the presence of the earth elemental she had summoned.

She spoke to the entity in the staccato, guttural tongue of its kind. Her instructions were succinct, and when she finished speaking she felt the iron flare hot and then cold, a sign of the elemental's compliance. The creatures of earth were slower than those of the air, but accuracy and reliability were what mattered now. Pirane set the now quiescent ore down and poured herself a glass of strong wine; then, hearing quick and familiar footsteps in the corridor, poured a second and handed it to Croin as, without knocking, he entered the apartment.

Croin took the glass and drank a third of its contents almost without noticing it. His eyes were fixed searchingly on Pirane's face. 'Well?'

'Savrinor has just come from the First Magus,' Pirane told him. 'Vordegh has new instructions for us.' She indicated the paper and Croin picked it up, scanned it, then raised his gaze to her once more.

'*Trials* . . . ?' Incredulity made his voice harsh.

'Quite. Add to that the summary execution of any

surviving Chaos rider deemed to have "lapsed in his duty" — in other words, to have suffered defeat — and we might as well fling open our gates and surrender to our enemies without any further delay! We gambled, Croin, and the gamble has failed. I see no other choice than to kill Vordegh.'

Croin hesitated a bare moment, then nodded. 'How, and when?'

'Before we consider that, I think there are more urgent matters at hand.' Briefly she outlined the latest news from the south, and had the bleak satisfaction of seeing Croin's look become stark. 'I've sent an elemental to sample the feel of the land where the armies are and gauge the situation with greater accuracy; but I've few doubts that the reports are exaggerated. The Chaos riders, or what's left of them, are in complete disarray, and if we strengthen their numbers with more human auxiliaries we'll be wasting resources that could be put to better use. Besides,' she added cynically, 'according to reports, a good many of the new conscripts who failed to return didn't die but deserted to the enemy.'

Croin's lip curled in a look that matched hers. 'With their numbers already so large that will make little difference . . . but I agree; we must do what needs to be done, and Vordegh's sanction can be damned.' He glanced at the paper again. 'As for the new orders?'

'We ignore them,' Pirane said adamantly. 'There must be no more deaths that don't serve a useful purpose in crushing this uprising. And that, now, must be our sole aim. For if we fail –' She didn't finish the sentence, knowing it was unnecessary.

Croin nodded again. 'That,' he said quietly, 'is what daunts me, Pirane. For I fear it may already be too late.'

Benetan said: 'Leave that one.'

Tervis, the lieutenant from the east, lowered the hand

holding the knife and looked at his commander in some surprise. 'But sir, he's too badly wounded to —'

'I know. But leave him.'

Tervis was baffled. To him the man lying on the ground between them was just one more among the mass of sprawled bodies, and one glance had told him that, though still alive, he was past saving. But the lieutenant had learned enough in the past few days not to question a command, so he merely shrugged and moved on to look for more survivors.

Benetan stared down at the Chaos rider. They had counted the numbers of their fallen enemies and the toll was more than encouraging; given the riders' abilities, it was a staggering triumph. Many had lost their lives in the fighting; some killed in straightforward combat, others caught up in the wild clashes between their own side's sorcery and the unearthly monstrosities conjured by the magi and sent out through the Maze in the riders' wake. Of the wounded, those who were relatively unscathed were being bound and taken to the central arena of the camp, where Aeoris would decide on their fates. The god intended to keep at least a few survivors to be paraded as captives during their northward progress. Their presence, he said, would give a tangible and useful focus to the violent tide of feeling against Chaos and all it stood for. And if some proved genuinely eager to change allegiance, and passed the tests Aeoris would impose, then a place would be found for them among Order's ranks. For those who refused or failed the test and had no other value the remedy would be drastic, but, as the god had pointed out, a swift knife across the throat was a relatively humane end — and there would be no shortage of volunteers to carry out the executions.

Some, though, were too seriously injured to be given a choice. There was a strong argument for leaving them on the battlefield to die in their own time, but Simbrian had vetoed that, and Tervis and two others with strong stomachs had been given the task of putting them out of their misery. Benetan had overseen the work with a grim detachment that unnerved his lieutenants. It occurred to him that he should have found it far from easy to deal in this way with men who had once been his comrades; but the feeling, though vaguely discomfiting, was too remote to have any meaning. This, though, was something different, and unexpectedly it had stirred his conscience to a degree that he couldn't ignore.

He dropped to a crouch beside the fallen man. A slight stirring of the body, a clenching and unclenching of the fingers, showed that the rider was conscious; though whether or not he would be lucid was another matter. The left side of his face was charred from a sorcerous fire-bolt and he had taken more than a dozen serious sword cuts, including the one that had bitten deep into his stomach and would, within a few more minutes, kill him. In the frigid dawn light the growing pool of his blood looked black and unwholesome, starkly contrasting with his drained, deathly white skin. Impossible to know how much pain he was feeling; or perhaps shock and the rapidly ebbing tide of life had numbed him to it? Benetan didn't know, and it was too late to be concerned with such a question. But for all his cold indifference, he felt he had to say something. Had to *do* something. Just this once.

Carefully he reached out and turned the rider onto his back. Blood pumped anew but that couldn't be helped; if it sped the end it would, anyway, be a kindness. Bracing one arm behind the young man's shoulders Benetan raised him to a semi-sitting position, ignoring the stains on his own clothing as he took the weight of the torso, and said, 'Lotro.'

Lotro's one good eyelid flickered and strained open. The eye beneath was a mass of broken blood-vessels, but he

367

could still see enough to recognize the face looking into his.

'C...Capun Liss...' A spasm; he hissed sharply and bit his lip with bloodstained teeth. 'Got any ... w ... w ...'

Benetan knew what he wanted and held the flask he carried to the colourless lips. Lotro couldn't swallow properly; a tiny amount went down but he coughed it back again moments later, mingled with red foam.

'I di'nt want to fight you, Capun ...' The voice was weak and unsteady. 'Di'nt want that ... it d'feel *wrong* to me. An' when they said – they said –' He coughed again, horribly.

'It's all right.' Benetan found himself stroking the young man's brow, as if that could give him some ease or comfort. Foolish, stupid, pointless thing to do ... he snatched his hand away. 'I understand.'

Lotro made an extraordinary sound that, Benetan realized, was the closest he could come to a laugh. 'Well, I'm glad for that, sir, f-for ... for tis more'n I do ... Don't unnerstand nothing o' this ... it d'make no *sense*. But we had to ride out. *Had* to. Was no choice ...'

'I know; I know. And I'm only sorry that ...' But he didn't know what he was trying to say and there was no point in pursuing it. Words were hollow and meaningless; only practicalities could be of any use to Lotro now, and Benetan put his hand to his belt again. 'I've something better than water. Something stronger.' He proffered a smaller flask and the young rider attempted a smile.

'Cann't say as I'd ... refuse it, Capun. Th-thank you kindly ...'

It was a strong spirit and, like the water, Lotro couldn't keep it down, but the taste and the heat of it in his mouth brought a grimace of appreciation. He said something about his home village which Benetan didn't catch, then another remark in which he seemed to confuse his sister with his grandfather; then: 'Tis funny, sir. By rights I reckon I should . . . should be hurting, like. But I cann't seem to feel nothing. Cann't seem to feel nothing at all.' Benetan didn't speak and Lotro frowned, looking suddenly childlike. 'One thing, sir. Just one. An' if I could have a bit more of that drink . . .'

Benetan gave it to him, and haltingly he continued. 'All through, all through the fighting, like . . . I kep' thinking of what Master S . . .Savrinor said to me that time. About justice. You said it too, sir. I remembered that. Kep' asking myself.' With what was now a tremendous effort he raised his gaze to Benetan's face. 'It's for the right, ent it, Capun Liss? What you're doing. 'Gainst the magi. It *is* for the right?'

Benetan opened his mouth to answer. But before the words came he heard a small, rattling hiss and saw Lotro's eyes change. Intelligence was suddenly erased, existence suddenly absent. The young man still stared at him, but life and soul had gone.

Benetan lowered the corpse to the ground and stayed motionless, looking at Lotro's face. Suddenly, for the first time since the night's mayhem ended, something inside him *hurt*, and he wanted to grasp Lotro by the shoulders again and berate him for a fool, for not changing allegiance while he could, for *dying* –

Then, behind him, a flat voice spoke his name. Sharply Benetan turned, and saw a white horse, its coat nacreous in the half-light, standing a few paces away. In the saddle was Kaldar.

'Benetan,' Kaldar said again. At a mental command the horse – which was no mortal animal but a creation of Order – moved a step closer, and Kaldar leaned forward. His features were indistinct, and for an unnerving moment Benetan fancied that the empty eye-sockets could see him. He shook the illusion off with a shudder, at the same time trying not to ask himself how Kaldar could sense where he was and who was before him with such uncanny accuracy, and said brusquely, 'What is it?'

Kaldar didn't answer the question. 'Succouring the minions of Chaos,' he said. 'It should not be done. They should be left to die alone. They should be left to rot alone.'

Despite his pity for Kaldar a worm of revulsion moved in Benetan's gut. 'This was personal,' he said, with a growing edge to his voice. 'And none of your concern.'

Someone else was approaching them on foot, but neither man paid him any heed. 'It is the concern of all when one of our faithful harbours friends among our enemies,' Kaldar said harshly. 'They must all die.'

'He's dead now.' Benetan's eyes flashed angry resentment. 'He lasted only a few minutes, and I don't doubt he was in pain almost to the end. So you can be satisfied, Kaldar.' He saw Kaldar respond with a strange, cruel smile and added savagely, 'Damn you, leave me to do my work in my own way! If you've nothing better to occupy you than —'

'Benet.' The warning voice stopped him in mid-sentence and Simbrian laid a hand on his arm. 'We've enough to occupy us without quarrelling amongst ourselves.'

Benetan had started at the sorcerer's arrival; for a moment he seemed about to reply furiously, then his shoulders lost their tension and he let out a sharp breath. Kaldar, though, turned his sightless eyes in Simbrian's direction and said bitterly, 'There should be no mercy. There should be no exceptions! To comfort the minions of Chaos is something that should not be *tolerated!*'

Simbrian reached out to touch the neck of Kaldar's mount, which flinched away, disturbed by its master's state of mind. 'Kaldar, don't upset yourself. I've no doubt Benet has good reason for what he does, and Lord Aeoris would surely agree that —'

He stopped as, with a savage jerk on the reins, Kaldar swung the horse out of his reach. He said something to it in a harsh tone and it turned and carried him away back towards the heart of the camp.

Simbrian watched him go. 'I had hoped for some easing of his soul in the wake of our success,' he said. 'But I think the hope was unfounded.'

Benetan didn't reply, only continued to stare after the departing horse, and the sorcerer sighed. 'Benet, unbend. It wasn't personal; Kaldar can't help the way he is, and we must make allowance for him.'

He was right, and Benetan acknowledged it with a cancelling gesture that, though still on the edge of anger, was also a tacit apology. With an effort he forced aside the bitter disgust he felt, telling himself it was unworthy. He should feel sympathy, not hostility, for Kaldar now had only one purpose left to live for. All his energy – all his *being* – was devoted to one thing and one alone: revenge, fuelled by a religious fervour that made even Simbrian's pale by comparison. For half the night, almost since the fighting ended, Kaldar had patrolled the camp, a mute and alienated figure on the horse that, through telepathic command, was his eyes. He asked no questions, gave no answers to any asked of him, and on the rare occasions when he spoke at all he had begun to adopt a strange, impersonal mode of speech that blocked anyone's efforts at worthwhile communication. But with his remaining senses, honed by some inner force to a level beyond any normal capacity, he absorbed all that he could not see, and savoured it. He was in pain, Benetan knew; both physical and mental. But he seemed almost to relish his own suffering, as if in some twisted way it comforted him.

Benetan scrubbed one hand across his face, trying to push away his tangled feelings, then saw that Simbrian was staring down at Lotro's body.

'He was a friend of yours?' the sorcerer asked quietly.

Benetan shrugged. 'I wouldn't put it so strongly.' Irrationally, he wanted to make light of the whole thing now. 'But he was a good man. Honest and honourable, and that's rare enough at the castle. And I owed him a debt. I couldn't just leave him to be despatched without . . . well, you know what I mean.'

'Yes. Yes, I do.'

'Though for what help I was able to be to him, I might as well have let him get it over with more quickly.' Then Benetan sighed, a sharp, almost exasperated sound. 'There's no point dwelling on it.' He looked up and his eyes were hardened, resolute. 'You were searching for me, Simbrian?'

It was an implicit plea to change the subject as quickly as possible, and, understanding, Simbrian let the matter of Lotro drop and gave Benetan his message; that Aeoris wished to see him. As they began to walk back towards the centre of their makeshift camp, where a small forest of banners was now visible in the breaking dawn, the sorcerer said, 'Lord Aeoris has tested the integrity of those who have asked to join us, and the news is encouraging. Nearly fifty conscripts have proved themselves; they were all forced into Chaos's service and were too terrified to resist.'

'Conscripts?' Benetan grimaced. 'Gods, the magi must be desperate if they need to reinforce the riders' numbers in that way! Any junior sergeant knows that such men are worse than useless.'

'Quite – and that, of course, can only bode well for us.' Simbrian looked up at the pulsing web that hung high over the plain as though some celestial fisherman had cast an immense net across the sky, then smiled with stern satisfaction. 'Apparently the Chaos riders are no longer taking culls from the villages, and in districts where the people are starting to rise against their overlords there has been no reprisal from the castle. It seems they no longer have the resources to cope.'

'Or are afraid to use them . . . How widespread *is* the unrest?'

'I would say that by now it's almost complete. And of course, with each act of rebellion that incurs no punishment, confidence among the people grows.' Simbrian paused. 'There are a few less pleasant reports of brutality among our own followers, and that's something I dislike intensely; but with their new-found freedom I suppose some excess is inevitable. What matters is that the magi have no hope of containing such a widespread insurrection, and they must know it. Lord Aeoris believes that they won't try but will concentrate their attention on us.'

'I'm not afraid of that,' Benetan said. 'We have both the physical and the occult strength to be more than a match for them, as we've already learned.'

Simbrian, however, shook his head. 'I'm not so sure. The magi haven't reached their limits yet – yes, I'm aware that you've seen what they're capable of at closer quarters than any of us, but speaking as a sorcerer I assure you that, even without the Chaos Gate to help them, what we've faced so far is by no means the full extent of their powers. And then we have Yandros to consider.' He hunched his shoulders against a sudden bitter little gust of wind. 'The Warps are now a deadly threat. And we've had word of three more large forces heading this way and intending to join us.'

'I see your point. Chaos won't ignore that – Yandros could send another Warp and wipe out our allies in their thousands before they have any chance of reaching us.'

'Exactly. That, I think, is why Lord Aeoris has new instructions for you.'

'New instructions?' Benetan's eyes narrowed then, as on a level which he was barely aware of he felt a sudden stirring of intuition. 'What is it, Simbrian? What's about to happen?'

They had almost reached the centre of the camp. Under a large group of banners a body of men were raising their voices in a victory chant, and the strains of another stirring song echoed from somewhere further away. Their army numbered in the thousands now ... but the eager tension of this milling mass was dwarfed by a greater, deeper tension that charged the atmosphere like the uneasy lull before a vast thunderstorm. Among the throng of humanity were forms and faces that were not human; and beneath the shining, pulsating net of power that protected them all, strange, intangible shapes moved and sang and whispered as they flowed constantly between the mortal dimension and another, unimaginable realm. Simbrian gazed about him, his dark eyes intent and seeming to mirror an echo of the unearthly energy that quivered in the air.

'I'm not sure,' he said softly, 'and I wouldn't presume to think that I could speak for our gods. But I feel that we may find ourselves facing our final encounter at the Star Peninsula far sooner than we had thought.'

CHAPTER XXIV

The ritual was to begin at sunset. The delay was unwelcome, especially as new reports carried from the south by elemental messengers suggested that Order's army was already on the move again, but Pirane and Croin decided that the risk should be taken. Darkness would add power to the work that was to be done, and on a mundane level it would also allow more time for the necessary preparations to be made.

The planning of the rite had signalled a clandestine but emphatic shift in the state of affairs within the castle's walls. Pirane and Croin were now effectively giving orders to their colleagues, and the orders were accepted without question. Vordegh had not emerged from the Marble Hall, and speculation was rife as to what he might or might not be doing there. One whisper even hinted at the possibility that Yandros had returned to the mortal world for long enough to annihilate the First Magus and consign his deranged soul to the Seven Hells, leaving only an empty husk lying on the Hall's mosaic floor. But such rumours were based on hope, not likelihood; and this was no time to put them to the test by investigating. While Vordegh remained where he was, he would also remain in ignorance of the changed plans. His newest order had been consigned to the fire in Pirane's chambers, and with it – in the minds of the magi – his remaining claim to office. When the moment was forced on them they would do what had to be done; but henceforth, whether Vordegh was alive or dead, authority rested in the hands of Pirane and Croin.

Though the knowledge wasn't voiced aloud, every castle-dweller knew that this power-raising would be not only the greatest but also, of necessity, the last. After the conflagration on the plains there were too few Chaos riders left alive, let alone fit, to be spared for the gleaning of further captives for sacrifice – and besides, as Aeoris's supernatural avatars spread word of Order's advance and growing strength, the people of the villages and demesnes were losing the ingrained fear that had kept them submissive for so long. News had reached the castle of more than two dozen overlords' fortresses stormed by inflamed mobs, and, unlike the incident which Benetan had witnessed some time ago, these insurrections had succeeded. The magi could spare neither the time nor the power to help; no citadels were sent, no creatures from Chaos were summoned to annihilate the rebels. The overlords, their households and those of their militia who stayed loyal, died. And in market squares and on the breached walls of invaded strongholds, banners painted with the circle-and-lightning-flash emblem of Order's cause had begun to rise like huge, exotic flowers. The tide was turning, flowing faster and more powerfully with every hour. And if this final bid by the magi to stem the flow should fail, then their sway would be broken beyond repair.

Then in the middle of the morning Savrinor and Andraia were woken by Qenever, who had come in search of Pirane.

Pirane was at this moment in the council hall with the other senior magi, and so Savrinor was the first to hear the new report. Order's growing army was indeed moving – but far faster than anyone had anticipated. Theirs was no normal march as had been expected, but a wild and unhumanly swift sweep northwards that was bearing the great force like a living rip-tide across the face of the world. More and more devotees were joining them – the message told of Aeoris's powers transporting entire new detachments as instantaneously as through the Maze – and if their present rate of advance continued unchecked, they would reach the Star Peninsula within two days.

Grey-faced, and racked by a sense of bone-deep cold that nothing seemed able to expel, Savrinor took in the news. In truth it had come as no real surprise; whatever might be pretended for the sake of morale, anyone in the castle with the slightest insight knew by now that Order's power and intention would be focused on one objective, and they would waste no time in seeking to achieve it.

He wetted his lips, and when he spoke his voice sounded alien, as if it belonged to someone else. Or as if he was dreaming this entire episode ... 'Presumably the First Magus hasn't yet heard the report?'

'No,' Qenever said. 'As far as anyone knows, he's still in the Marble Hall. And pray Yandros he stays there.'

'Amen to that ... I'll go the council hall immediately, and alert Magus Pirane.' He swung round. 'Andraia — you'd best return to our rooms.'

Andraia said, 'I can't simply sit there doing nothing! If there's some work I could –'

But Savrinor was too distracted to listen; he was already heading for the outer door, and as it slammed behind him Qenever smiled thinly and without humour. 'There'll be little sense to be had from Savrinor for the foreseeable future,' he told her. 'Or, for that matter, from anyone in the castle, if this report isn't exaggerated.'

Her face grew taut. '*Is* it exaggerated, do you think?'

'We can but hope. But I doubt it.'

'And if this army reaches the Peninsula ... what then?'

Qenever considered for a few moments. Then he said quietly, '*If* Order's followers reach the Peninsula, they'll have one goal and one only: to take the castle and overthrow the magi. If they succeed, then, quite simply, we will all die.' A pause while he subjected her to a hard and thoughtful look. 'You know who their human commander is, don't you?'

'Yes.' Andraia clipped the word.

'Mmm. And I don't doubt you're wise enough to realize that even you can expect no clemency from him.'

'I wouldn't want it,' she said savagely.

'I'm glad to hear that.' Qenever had never voiced his true opinion of Benetan Liss in Andraia's hearing and there seemed no point in doing so now. So all he added was, 'I'm no swordsman, as you know. But if the worst came to the worst, and we were forced to fight, it would give me great satisfaction if I could kill him.'

Andraia flicked him a ghost of a smile. 'Not as great as the satisfaction it would give me.' But her voice quavered as she said it, and when she turned her head away the movement was just a little too quick.

Qenever regarded her tense, rigid back for a moment or two, then sighed. 'Well, it's a prospect that needn't concern us, provided the magi's ritual goes according to plan.'

'Pray it does.'

'Indeed. For if not . . .' But he didn't finish the sentence. Andraia knew the facts well enough, and the shadow that he felt hanging over them all in his mind was closing in, making him suddenly very reluctant to dwell on the subject. Without quite knowing why Qenever abruptly crossed the room, laid his hands on his daughter's shoulders and kissed the bright crown of her hair. 'I must go. Take care, my dear. Tell Savrinor to look after you.'

'More likely I'll be looking after him.' Her voice caught and she tried to disguise it with a cough. 'Perhaps I'll see you later.'

Qenever didn't answer but left her standing by the window. Her eyes were full of tears, and he had seen it, and she knew he had seen. She didn't know why she was crying, and didn't want to know. Better to dismiss it as a momentary weakness and ignore the lapse. Better not to think about it. Better not to think about *anything*.

*   *   *

The magi's response to Savrinor's message was swift and decisive. In the light of this news they could no longer afford the luxury of waiting for nightfall – the ritual must be carried out immediately. And within an hour they were ready to begin.

Unnatural shadows filled the courtyard, defying reason and the clear sky; overhead the seven-rayed star still pulsed out its slow, unremitting rhythm, but it seemed fainter and more tenebrous, as though its energy were being sapped by some competing power. Then there was movement at the castle's main entrance, and the double doors at the top of the steps opened to admit the magi to the courtyard. Pirane emerged first, with Croin a pace behind her and the rest following in twos and threes. Every magus in the castle was present, and in contrast to accustomed procedure there was no ceremony and no formality ... save for the fact that they were naked; a gesture which marked the extreme gravity of this event. The magi intended to hold nothing in reserve, but to give all they possessed – their power, their will, their very souls – to the work that lay before them.

Pirane halted on the steps. Outwardly she had the look of sanguine assurance, but as she took in the deepeningly malevolent atmosphere the thoughts behind the mask of her face were heavy with apprehension. This was their last hope, the final endeavour; if it failed, there would be nothing left – and the consequences of that were unthinkable.

With an effort she focused her attention on the work that lay ahead. Nearly two hundred captives had been herded into the courtyard and now stood as motionless as human statues, while around them a bare handful of Chaos riders paced restlessly, taut with anticipation. Croin had cast a thrall to keep these creatures helpless; the drain on resources was undesirable but had to be borne, for the riders could no longer supply the physical might to keep their prisoners docile. Looking at the stark, immobile faces, Pirane felt a surge of searing contempt at the knowledge that, but for a quirk of chance, these fools might by now have joined the mass marching brazenly towards the Star Peninsula, beguiled into believing that they might face a better future under the rigid, stagnating regime of Order. Each one an ignorant fool; each one a traitor to the gods ... disgust glittered cruelly in her eyes and she turned to Croin.

'If we are all ready, my friend ...'

The ever-present mists of the Marble Hall had grown dense as a winter fog, shifting sluggishly, heavily among the pillars like a dark and oily sea. In what was thought to be the Hall's centre, where a black mosaic circle marked – or had marked – the Chaos Gate, a shape barely visible in the gloom lay rigid and unmoving, arms outspread as though staked to the ground. And the only sound that broke the silence was the harsh, regular and savagely controlled hiss of Vordegh's breathing.

The First Magus's eyes were open, focused towards the Hall's invisible ceiling; what he saw, however, was nothing that had or ever could have any existence in the physical world. Every few minutes his body would rack with a violent convulsion as he absorbed a renewed onslaught from the denizens of the high astral planes through which his mind was forging. But he welcomed the pain they inflicted, fed on it, grew stronger from it. Through pain, he would prevail. Through endurance, he would triumph. And when he reached his goal ... ah, that resolution ran in him like a litany: *when I reach that dimension beyond the seven astral planes, in which the fabric of time and space have their origin, I will hold in my grasp more than any mortal man has ever achieved. Where the gods themselves have failed, I will succeed. The Chaos Gate will thunder into being once more. The shattered link with Chaos will be re-formed. And, as a lesser man might tread an insect underfoot, I will crush the forces that oppose me. The demons of Order. The heretics who have defied my rule to follow them. And the traitors within the walls of my own stronghold* . . .

The ambition inspired him; and if such an ambition was insanity, Vordegh welcomed his madness. He had only to reach out, drive his body and mind to one final excess, one supreme effort –

The shadows that attended him constantly flickered around the black circle, and mingling with the shadows were other forms, born of monstrous imagination, each wearing a face that manifested some part of the First Magus's struggles and desires. Nightmare things, things of power, driven by the hunger to prevail . . .

And yet . . . And yet the final step, the ultimate objective . . . it would not come! He could not reach it . . .

The Hall's mists pulsated with a sudden, shocking disturbance, and Vordegh's body arched frenziedly before collapsing to the floor again. *So close – so close! And yet –*

His mouth opened and he screamed a single word. The name of Yandros, his ultimate liege, echoing through the Hall in a long-drawn howl. But there was no love in the cry; and no dedication as of a mortal man to his deity. Instead, it was a challenge to the lords of Chaos – the challenge of one who had come to think himself their equal; possibly even their rival. The challenge of one determined to triumph over all opposition, no matter what the cost. The challenge of a madman who had passed beyond redemption.

Even Pirane, who had lived far longer than most, could not remember a time when the magi had acted in such concord. It was as though they were not merely of one mind but also of one body, one will, one *soul*. And as the power they conjured began to gain strength and momentum, her doubts and fears were giving way to a slow yet certain rise of hope.

The captives were aware of what was taking place, and their massed faces in the courtyard's increasing gloom reflected the terror they felt; but Croin's thrall still held them helpless and mute. If kindness had been in her at this moment, Pirane might have spared a moment to pity them: did they but know it, their suffering – at least in the mortal world – would be brief, for in order to feed power of the order required today, their deaths must be instantaneous. One single charge of energy, to snatch the souls of these victims and sacrifice them to the force that would strike a swathe of pure devastation through their enemies' ranks and consign their mass of humanity to oblivion. Order's sorcerers might be a force to be reckoned with – Pirane knew, now, that their abilities had been sorely underestimated – but against this, they would have no defence.

And if, as she prayed, the gods were aware of what was afoot, then the magi's attack would be augmented by an onslaught from Chaos itself. An onslaught that would destroy Order's ambitions once and for all.

Like seven birds of prey on a high peak above burning turmoil, Yandros and his brothers kept silent watch. Violent storm-currents flickered and cracked between them, igniting the air into brief but ferocious bursts of fire, but there was, as yet, no need for further communication. They knew the numbers of their enemies. They followed the movement of the growing army, and of the ever-increasing tributaries that streamed to join it. And they were aware of the magi's activity and intention. When the moment came, when the full power was raised and the single, deadly strike prepared, then at last Chaos would break its hiatus and enter the arena directly.

Tarod's concentration was focused on the seven spears of light that, to his unhuman eyes, betrayed the locations of Aeoris and his brothers in the mortal world. Contrary to expectations the lords of Order had not retaliated when the first attack was launched against them, but had been content only to protect their human followers from the havoc of the Warp. That had given Chaos an unforeseen respite – and, as Yandros had said, a welcome advantage. He had still refused Tarod permission to return to the castle and put a final end to the matter of the First Magus, but he had relaxed his vigilance for long enough to concentrate some attention on the magi, and what he learned had satisfied him. Vordegh's hours were numbered, and the working now building towards its climax in the courtyard would serve Chaos's interests very well. When the magi attacked Order's human forces, Yandros would augment their onslaught with another of his own – but he would ignore the mortal battle and strike directly at the lords of Order. Aeoris and his brothers would have a plain choice: to help their human followers and thus risk their own ruin at Chaos's hands, or to defend themselves and leave the great army to cope with the magi's attack as best it could. Either way, Chaos would gain the advantage. Or so Tarod had believed, until the small disturbance began to nag at the back of his mind . . .

He glanced between the banks of tumbling thunderclouds to where his great brother stood motionless. Yandros's eyes were intent as he sensed the growing power of the magi's ritual. But there was an edge to his demeanour, a sudden sharp undercurrent of disquiet that the link between them brought abruptly into focus.

And Tarod knew with a sure instinct that something was wrong . . .

White light flickered around Aeoris's figure and flared across the crimson glow of the sky. It lit a sea of human forms, moving in controlled formation and with indomitable will and purpose as the great army swept onwards. Other, stranger shapes towered among the ranks, and the

383

crack of great wings made a rhythm like a huge drumbeat which shook the air and echoed over the plain.

More and yet more and yet more; mortal or supernatural, no one could count their numbers now. To Benetan, riding the crest of the vast tide, it was like living a wild dream, and the excitement that infused him was far greater than anything the magi's sacraments had ever created. And still there had been no move from the powers of Chaos.

But Simbrian, whose mind was attuned to a subtler plane, had felt the beginnings of a change. Aeoris had given no word as yet, but the sorcerer knew that the seven gods were aware of a shift in the uneasy lull. The hiatus would end soon. It must.

Aeoris turned suddenly and looked at him. The lord of Order's eyes burned darkly, and when he smiled, the smile had a hard edge.

'Rest assured, my friend, the magi *are* preparing,' he said, reading Simbrian's thoughts. 'And when they strike, it will be no mean matter.'

Simbrian looked gravely back. 'I trust we'll be ready to meet it, my lord.'

'I've no doubt that you will. But don't underestimate them. Or Yandros.'

The sorcerer's eyes narrowed. 'You think, then, that –'

He was interrupted. 'I make no assumptions, Simbrian, and no predictions; not where Chaos is concerned. But if the magi's action, whatever it might be, should give Yandros and his brothers the slightest advantage, they will use it. And Chaos *is* stirring; I sense new activity in their realm. Be doubly alert from now on, and pass the same word to your colleagues.'

Simbrian nodded. 'Yes, my lord.'

The rhythm of the seven-rayed star was matched now by a pulsating crimson glare that radiated out from the courtyard and turned the sky gory and grim. Against this background the magi's chanting was like something from the worst of nightmares; the voice, or so it seemed, of a single, unimaginable entity as they uttered their call to the powers they strove to summon. Chilling, sonorous words in an arcane tongue; and the power was rising, coming to them, ready to be fed and controlled and used –

In the Marble Hall a psychic echo of the ritual sent a quivering disturbance through the dark oil of the mists, and the sound of Vordegh's breathing abruptly paused. Slowly, like an animal tensing at the scent of prey, the First Magus rose to a taut crouch, and his eyes, sunken now and with an appalling light glaring in their depths, carefully scanned his surroundings. Other dimensions still impinged on his mind, twisting the messages carried by his senses; but what he gathered and interpreted told him at least a semblance of the truth.

He stood upright with a lithe movement that belied his bulk, and his attendant shadows flowed and agitated around him as they reflected the sudden, disturbing change in his state of mind. The First Magus's lips moved with terrible, controlled precision, and he whispered one word that slid away into the mists:

'Traitors . . .'

The shadows quivered, thickened. Vordegh turned, and began to walk calmly towards the door of the Marble Hall.

Pirane felt as though a fever were raging in her as the chant neared its climax. Tension in the courtyard was nearing an unbearable pitch, and every shred of her mind and body was riveted on the rite and what would follow.

It was coming. She could feel it, a suffocating presence, vast and insensate and ravening, growing stronger with every moment. The last, guttural phrases of the chant began – she was uttering the words now without conscious control or awareness – and her skin began to ache, her hair began to crackle with energy –

A flare of darkness erupted from the direction of the pillared walkway, and a voice rang shockingly over the courtyard, a ferocious accusation that shattered the rhythm of the summoning.

'TRAITORS!'

The chant collapsed into discord. Pirane had time to glimpse Vordegh's figure in the midst of the churning dark, and to see him raise one hand, before a wave of sheer, raw power slammed against her mind. Reeling, she wrenched her senses free from its grip and back under control, then through a daze heard Croin give a desperate, high-pitched cry.

'Fight him! Don't let –'

The rest of his words were drowned by the ear-splitting shriek of energy running amok in the courtyard. Croin's thrall on the prisoners snapped, and there was a sudden, violent upsurge as two hundred souls panicked. The riders were yelling, striving to contain the stampede; the other magi were trying to rally but, still shocked, and torn between the riders' plight and the threat from Vordegh, were thrown into confusion. In the mayhem, Pirane had just one clear thought – if Vordegh wasn't stopped, if they didn't kill him, *now*, then all they had striven for would be smashed to the Seven Hells –

'Croin!' She screamed his name above the tumult. 'We must use our power, turn it against him! HELP ME!'

Croin heard her, and he spun desperately around towards the other magi, calling them to group, to unite their minds and their wills. One of the riders – Pirane thought it was Averel but couldn't be sure – belatedly realized what his masters were trying to do, and yelled for weapons to be turned against the First Magus. But Vordegh had also heard, and his wreath of seething shadows flared anew. A second, stunning wave of power hit Pirane, hurling her off balance; as she fell she saw fire blaze from the First Magus's hand –

*   *   *

Yandros's eyes turned white-hot, and his voice ricocheted through the Chaos realm like the hurricane-scream of a Warp.

'*Ah, no –* '

Thunder howled in answer, and Tarod saw his brother's fury erupt around him like a pillar of fire. A cataclysmic shudder ran through the dimension, shaking the landscape into new distortions. In the mortal world Aeoris sensed the violent change, and his consciousness locked with another realm, readying, poising –

Croin's body exploded in black fire, and the shriek that was the last sound he ever made seemed to tear through Pirane's flesh and bone. Vordegh swung on his heel, pointed again, and two more magi were cut down by a whirling, spitting chain of lightning that annihilated three Chaos riders and a swathe of captives in its path. Scrabbling on all fours across the flagstones Pirane struggled to gather and rally the tatters of her own power, but a renewed wave of energy from Vordegh's mind, intensified by mad hatred, buffeted across the courtyard and sent her sprawling again. And as she started to raise herself she saw the First Magus spread his arms wide –

'*NO!*' Fury hit her like a wall; this was their only hope, their only possible salvation – '*STOP HIM! DON'T LET HIM WRECK WHAT WE HAVE ACHIEVED!!*'

The warning was too late, or Vordegh was simply too powerful. Pirane heard the enormous noise of air being sucked into a vortex, then the louder and more hideous sound of massed voices in one short-lived cry of terror and agony, as the First Magus completed the magi's rite and snatched the life-energy of nearly two hundred human souls. *The sacrifice, their gleaning, the last hope – he was seizing it, destroying it, consigning them all to ruin, and for nothing more than his own vain, demented delusions –*

Pirane opened her mouth and, in a voice deranged by horror and desperation, screamed Yandros's name.

'*Yandros!*' The skies of Chaos roared an echo, and a vast sheet of blinding light ripped the storm-clouds apart. '*We have to stop him!*'

Tarod's and Yandros's eyes met, clashed, across a boiling, howling chasm. There was an instant's pause, then Yandros cried out, 'Go then! Now – and *quickly!*'

Energy cracked between them in a brief but spectacular eruption of flame, and there was a void where Tarod had been standing.

The black, spinning column fed by the souls of the human sacrifices towered skywards, dwarfing the four spires and casting a pall over the entire castle. Pirane could feel its power dragging the strength from her, draining her of life. She couldn't breathe, could barely see; all she knew was that she and the other magi – those whom Vordegh hadn't already slaughtered – were about to die. And there was nothing she could do. It was over; it was done. Their ruin was complete –

Overhead, the seven-rayed star emitted a massive pulse that shook the castle to its foundations. Pirane felt the courtyard lurch under her, saw Vordegh look up in shock. The black column wavered; Vordegh's expression changed to an extraordinary, almost deformed parody of sane comprehension as, with a howl that stormed up and beyond the audible scale and sent a lance of pain through Pirane's head, the whirling darkness turned in on itself and seared back on its source. The power of it struck Vordegh, and the shadows that clothed him were blasted out of existence. The First Magus swayed like a tree in a hurricane, mouth open and eyes bulging; he was trying to scream but no sound came. Then he fell, dropping to the flagstones with a hollow slap that reverberated in sudden, monstrous silence.

Tarod stood under the arch of the main gateway. His figure was indistinct, for black light shrouded him and only his face, razor-edged by shadow, and the furnaces of his eyes, were clearly visible. Pirane saw him. She didn't know whether the other magi had yet seen, and she herself was too stunned to do anything other than stare, still on hands and knees, as very deliberately the Chaos lord walked towards Vordegh's fallen figure.

He wasn't dead. It was incredible, seemingly impossible, that any mortal could have survived such a blast of power, but as Tarod approached, the First Magus stirred and tried to rise. His legs were shattered, but he pulled himself up on his hands, muscles straining under the effort, and met Tarod's polar gaze with a nightmarish blend of haughtiness, confidence and pure dementia.

'I . . .' The word rasped in his throat. 'I have . . . Yandros's sanction . . . I rule. I *rule* . . .'

Tarod halted, stared silently down.

'I am the F . . . the First . . .' Spittle mixed with blood flecked Vordegh's lips and jaw. 'Chosen avatar of . . . of Chaos . . . You cannot deny . . . I am . . .'

'You,' Tarod said quietly and with venomous contempt, 'are nothing.'

He raised his left hand, beckoned to the sky. There was a soft, dank rush of wings and, silhouetted against the glare of the cold star, a shape flowed between dimensions and descended towards the courtyard. Even Pirane turned her head away in startled revulsion as the thing – whether Chaos-born or from some other, unimaginably foul dimension, she would never know and did not want to know – hovered above Vordegh and cast a dire shadow over the scene. Tarod looked at the creature; smiled. Then he reached out, and with one deft movement closed the First Magus's sagging jaw.

'Go silently,' he said. 'We will hear no more from you.'

Vordegh tried to open his mouth; tried to cry out; but

speech – indeed, any sound – was beyond his powers. A wave of hot, wet air fanned across Pirane's face as the monstrosity embraced the First Magus; then it lifted into the air, carrying its burden as though it weighed no more than a feather. For a moment the creature hung over the castle; then a soft, atrocious sigh of satisfaction drifted down and it winged away northwards, silent and relentless as the light in Tarod's eyes.

The Chaos lord looked swiftly around at the courtyard. Every living soul present – and there were few enough of them in the wake of Vordegh's last deranged act – was motionless. Their paralysis had to be broken.

'First Magus!' He snapped the address to Pirane to allay any lingering shred of doubt; all the magi were well aware of Chaos's choice. 'Do what you can.' A rapid yet fearsomely expressive glance at the empty husks of the prisoners, wasted chaff in a barren field. 'Though it will be little enough now.'

'My lord, I –' Pirane began.

He cut her off. 'I must return.' The other surviving magi were rising to their feet; two Chaos riders who had also, miraculously, come through unscathed were gazing at their god with stark, desperate faces, but Tarod had no time to spare for any of them. 'Aeoris must know that –'

He didn't finish, for a high, pure and, to the listening magi, hideous note obliterated his words in a deafening wall of sound. The bowl of the sky seemed to crack in half, and a spear of radiance struck the pulsing star full on.

Tarod spun round in time to see the star detonate and shatter, and at the same instant Yandros's frenzied summons slammed through his consciousness. There was a colossal howl far out to sea; then the sky ruptured into a pandemonium of wheeling colours veined with blinding lightning, and a Warp smashed out of Chaos and into the mortal world.

Pirane saw the Chaos lord's form vanish, felt the impact

of his departure like a whip cutting into her marrow. Despair and panic came surging on its heels but she fought them, mustering her will and straining to be heard above the Warp's tumult and the growing scream of Aeoris's attack on the gods she would serve to her last breath.

'*Raise power! We have nothing to lose now – use any and every means left to you to help our lord Yandros! OR THIS WILL BE THE END OF EVERYTHING!!*'

CHAPTER XXV

The earth beneath them was shaking, and for half a mile to either side of their great mass, clouds of dust boiled like the waves of a vast, foaming sea. If he glanced down, Benetan could see the ground skimming beneath his mount's hooves, passing under him at stunning speed – for time and space were bending to the lords of Order's will, and every step the army took was a mile, and every minute of their progress as good as an hour's travelling. All around them pillars of white lightning sparked between sky and ground, and the thunder of their march was echoed by the growl and boom of the lightning's titanic discharges.

Aeoris was a shining figure before him, the light burning around and above him a beacon to the multitude flowing in his wake. His six brother-gods were still spreading word of the uprising to the remoter demesnes and villages; now and then Benetan glimpsed one or more of them returning briefly to the throng, but only Aeoris was constantly with them –

Then he saw Aeoris tense. The god looked up, as though his senses had caught something undetectable to mortals, and Benetan's mount made a strange, unearthly sound, its nostrils dilating alertly. Aeoris raised his hand, made an urgent, beckoning gesture. A sharp flicker of energy flared across Benetan's vision – and suddenly all seven lords of Order were together at the head of the army.

Benetan wasn't attuned to the sudden change in the psychic atmosphere, but Simbrian was, and the sorcerer's attention snapped instantly to the white-clad figures of the gods.

'Benet, something's afoot . . .'

Benetan opened his mouth to respond, but before he could speak Aeoris turned and looked back. His expression was animated and his voice avid as he called, 'Simbrian! Matters have gone awry at the castle – the magi's plan to attack us has failed! Yandros is – *ahh!*' His last words turned to a startling cry of exultation, echoed by an eerie, ululating yell from the throats of his brothers.

'My lord, what –' Simbrian began to shout, but Aeoris cut across him.

'There is no more time for words! Simbrian, Benetan – you know what you must do!'

A huge, buffeting gale-blast hit them, and the seven lords of Order vanished. Benetan's mount reared, Simbrian's was prancing wildly, and from the legion of Order's creatures that ran and flew with them a sudden formidable noise began to rise –

'Benet!' Simbrian roared out his name as he understood what Aeoris had meant. 'They're attacking – our gods are attacking Chaos!'

And over the clamour, they heard the single, searing note of Aeoris's first strike. They saw the sky rip open, saw the seven-rayed star blast apart as the spear of light found its mark. A cry went up from the massed ranks behind them, a yell of triumph that rang an answer to the roaring heavens, and Benetan flung a glance over his shoulder to see that the vanguard of their followers were breaking into wild jubilation.

'Calm them!' he yelled to Tervis and the other lieutenants. 'We're not victorious yet – this is just the beginning!'

Even as Tervis acknowledged the warning there was a howling discord overhead and the Warp that was Chaos's counter-attack exploded into being. Ropes of white-hot flames writhed and scourged to earth, and the grassland erupted into a wall of fire ahead and to either side of the army.

'*Simbrian!*' Benetan screamed. But Simbrian had already reacted; arms raised, he was summoning his own powers, and Kaldar's voice joined with his in an eerie, wailing harmony. The fire-wall was surging towards them; at the edge of the great throng people started to scream in terror — then cloud blackened the sky, and with a hissing roar a rainstorm hammered down on the burning land and on the heads of the multitude. Drenched in seconds, and gasping under the downpour, Benetan glimpsed unearthly faces and forms amid the cataclysm as elementals of fire and water clashed and fought for dominance — but the fire was collapsing, and suddenly, at a final cry from Simbrian and Kaldar, flame and rain together were swept away and vanished.

Yet the Warp still advanced, and now the clouds were scattering to smoking, scudding fragments as the huge wheel of the supernatural storm began to turn in the sky. The creatures of Order still running with the army set up a clear and shiveringly harmonic chorus in challenge to the storm's grim voice, and, recalling what Yandros had done to the nature of the Warps, Simbrian was preparing himself to defend their followers when a shout from Benetan snatched his attention.

'Simbrian! Look — *look!*'

High above the Warp, at a mind-numbing distance, a shape was materializing, like a vast thunderhead towering and piling into the atmosphere. Spires and columns rose from it, wreathed in lightning, and with a jolt of shock Benetan recognized in its form a titanic and ominous image of the black castle.

'The magi!' he shouted. 'They must be —'

'No!' Simbrian interrupted him, his voice only just audible above the noise of the Warp. He had swung round in his saddle and now gestured violently westwards. 'Not the magi — this is something else!'

And in the west, like a shining mirage challenging and

defying its dark counterpart, a second citadel was forming in the sky, a glittering vision of towers and turrets haloed in golden light.

'Not the magi!' Simbrian yelled again. 'It's the arena of the true battle, Benet – the battle of the gods!'

Even as Benetan understood, there was a renewed uproar from the Warp, like gargantuan and abysmal laughter. For an instant the entire scene, land and sky and all they contained, distorted – then the ground ahead of the army erupted and split open, hurling rock and debris upwards like an explosion. Darkness roiled from the rupturing chasm, and there was fire in the darkness, and a charnel-house stench borne on a searing wind, as a horde of beings, things of Chaos, the beautiful and the hideous and the impossible, came swarming into the world, shrieking hunger and defiance. Another huge distortion swept over the scene, and in its wake came a swell of lethal energy –

'*To arms!*' Benetan screamed the words without conscious awareness, propelled by the instinct of his own past. He knew these creatures, knew their ways, had ridden among them – he knew what they could and would do! And the Warp was sweeping down on them, a vast scythe that would cut down thousands unless –

'*SIMBRIAN! HELP US!*'

Like a smashing, thundering wall, the Warp hit –

Under the skirl of colours dancing wildly across the sky, the faces of Pirane and her fellow magi were stark with strain. Tendrils of oily light snaked and whipped across the courtyard, and the things they conjured were a seething maelstrom of faces and forms around them. Elementals and other denizens of the lower planes, attracted by sorcery and harnessed to the cause, whirled in crazed dances of their own among the confusion, and on currents of cold silver-grey radiance that arrowed from the castle's four spires and focused their power on the Maze the magi's creations were sent streaming away to join the battle in the south.

And through Pirane's mind rang a foreboding and terrible sense of desperation. More power, and yet more . . . but it wasn't enough, it couldn't be enough, for Vordegh had reduced their numbers to mockery, and there were no souls left with which to call and feed the greater beings that might have saved them . . . Two magi, spared from this work to keep astral watch on Order's forces, had brought dire reports; and the gods were beyond reach; and still the enemy's great army advanced . . .

A thunderbolt shrieked overhead and smashed into the heart of the Warp, which now filled the entire sky from horizon to horizon. Pirane felt the castle shake to its foundations, and she screamed an imprecation against the demons of Order, while from her clawing fingers tongues of fire erupted to form yet another creature, another weapon. *We are doing all we can, but it isn't enough!* And in the halls and rooms and corridors of the castle – was there panic, was there pandemonium? She didn't know and no longer cared. Highest to lowest, they must all fend for themselves; the magi could waste no thought on other mortals now. All she knew was that every sinew in her, physical and mental, was straining to breaking point, and the world was spinning around her, and they must raise more POWER –

Benetan didn't know how many had been annihilated by the Warp, but he couldn't afford to spare them so much as a thought, for now they were in the thick of a fight the like of which neither he nor anyone among them had ever known. Flying bodies, screaming mouths, raking talons and claws and fangs; Chaos's demons were a howling tide crashing against them, and the tide had to be turned, for as it turned so the greater battle between the gods would

396

turn. His sword was a glinting blur in the mayhem, and to either side he could glimpse other swords, and knives and spears and staves, any and every weapon that this vast human mass could wield. His mount's hooves and mane sparked tongues of lightning; as it fought it gave vent to a shrill, high-pitched wail that was echoed by a hundred other eerie cries. And mingling with the cacophony of sound were voices of Simbrian and his fellow sorcerers, fighting not with physical weapons but with sorcery, driving their adversaries back, decimating them, destroying them. High overhead the two citadels – the shining star of Order and the dark thunderhead of Chaos – shimmered and twisted and pulsed, a titanic mirror of the tumult below. Tidal waves of blackness clashed with walls of glittering light in concatenations that seemed to rock the world, and the sky was alive with monstrous colours. Then out of the north a beam of radiance appeared, sweeping across the heavens like a cold spear. Benetan heard a new discord of sound – he flung a glance upward and saw the tumbling, churning company of misshapen things that were riding the spear of light, speeding from the Star Peninsula to join battle with Chaos. Alarm punched through him, he screamed a warning –

From the towering citadel of Aeoris and his brothers, *something* launched itself into the turbulent vault of the sky. Vast wings cracked down with a noise that momentarily drowned all else, and the gigantic avatar arrowed across the path of the oncoming horde. They met; a conflagration blazed like an exploding sun, and the magi's creations shattered to oblivion as the power that impelled them was devastated.

Benetan heard his own voice yelling in triumphant fervour, and all around him others were joining in as they too saw the destruction of the magi's attack. It was an inspiration, a goad; suddenly they were drawing new strength and vigour from an untapped reserve. The tide *was* turning, and Benetan raised his voice again in an exultant rallying cry:

'VICTORY! *VICTORY!*'

The furnace of pure Chaotic energy that Yandros had become was aware of the magi's assault and its dire outcome, and the rage that erupted through his consciousness was intensified by the tearing agony of despair. The Warp bellowed an answer to his fury, but though the great storm now rampaging across the world had slaughtered their human enemies in hundreds, even thousands, it was in vain, for Aeoris was countering each onslaught, and he and his demon brothers were widening that first, brief breach, and with every blow they struck Yandros could feel Chaos's power diminishing. For one short minute, as Tarod dealt finally with Vordegh, he and his brothers had been divided and vulnerable; knowing it, Aeoris had seized his chance and with it the advantage, and now Order's forces had the upper hand.

Great tremors shook land and sea as Yandros's wrath smashed the barriers between dimensions, but though he craved to destroy the mortal world and all within it – *as they could have done, as they should have done* – it was too late, for the power of the lords of Order was too great and the tide of mortal energy too strong. With a frenzy that sent a network of lightning crackling across the heavens Yandros cursed the soul of Vordegh in the Seven Hells where Tarod had consigned him, and cursed his own folly in gambling as he had. The gamble had failed – and now it was too late!

The rage within him rose to a pitch, blazing, gargantuan, overwhelming. He felt the kindred violence of his brothers, a vast, primal tempest, and their essences joined together for one final, desperate assault –

The embattled forces saw it coming, saw the rampart of absolute, devouring darkness burst from the black citadel

398

in the clouds and boil earthwards. The air roared and burned before it; Simbrian yelled to his sorcerers to beware, to muster their powers —

And with a sound that smashed through every boundary, light blazed out across the world.

Benetan uttered an involuntary yell of shock and swung around in his saddle. In the southern sky the turmoil of cloud and smoke and the Warp's lurid colours had been ripped away, and the sun hung at its zenith, a throbbing crimson inferno. Around the glaring corona, seven great stars shone with a steady, inexorable radiance. They lit the entire land like a golden mirage; and as their rays struck the wall of darkness, the darkness recoiled, falling back, disintegrating, collapsing —

There was a terrible cry, a lament of massed, unhuman voices, and suddenly the creatures of Chaos seemed to turn in on themselves. Forms changed and twisted, and like a grotesque river they rose into the air, coalesced together and streaked towards the receding dark.

And high above the earth, among the tatters of the Warp, the black citadel began to quake . . .

Savrinor came down the main staircase, nearly missing his footing several times as his sense of balance failed him. He needed more Moonwrack; he had lost track of how much he was taking now, but he seemed to crave greater and greater amounts just to stay on an even keel. The documents under his arm were like a leaden weight, and he wasn't even sure why he had gathered them, what he meant to do with them. He was simply driven by an instinct, a habit, to keep them _safe_. Not in the library vault; no one could go there now, not while the magi still worked in the courtyard. But somewhere. _Somewhere._

He reached the foot of the stairs, which from the top of the flight had seemed a dizzying drop away, and paused to let his reeling mind clear a little. To his left, the council hall. Two magi there, frantically applying their skills in renewed efforts to learn what was afoot, to discover how matters stood with the gods, to learn *anything* that might aid the castle. To his right, the great dining hall. Qenever had commandeered a handful of bewildered clerks and the hall was now a mustering point for information of any kind. Andraia was with him, helping him, but everyone was losing the battle to convince themselves that the whole exercise was not insanely pointless.

And in the courtyard were the other magi, led by their new First Magus, Pirane. He could hear the sounds of their chanting, mingling with the howl of the Warp, and had glimpsed their work from his window. What he saw chilled him, because by comparison to the rite they had attempted earlier it was so little. Yet now, in the wake of Vordegh's last, ruinous act of madness, it was all they had . . .

The castle felt remarkably calm. *Too* calm – or perhaps, Savrinor told himself, his senses had simply strayed too far over the borders of reality now? A minute or so ago he had heard a woman screaming hysterically from somewhere in the main wing, but he hadn't investigated and doubted that anyone else had troubled themselves either. Perhaps he was dreaming. Perhaps this was a nightmare, and in a little while he would wake and find himself safe in his bed with Andraia beside him.

But the torment in his stomach, in his *soul*, gave the lie to it.

He drew breath, aware on some vague level that his lungs were making a harsh and unhealthy sound, and gathered his wits to move on.

As he took the first step a shriek went up from the courtyard, and the castle shook with a massive tremor. Savrinor reeled against the banisters and, through a daze of shock, dread took hold of him. *What had happened? What was afoot?* Papers forgotten and dropped to flutter where they pleased, he stumbled urgently towards the double doors.

He was half way there when the doors smacked open. Two magi were silhouetted against the insane sky, and between them they supported the swaying figure of Pirane. She couldn't stand unaided; the last of her strength was gone and her face was a gaunt travesty, great eyes sunken, mouth working as she tried feebly to protest.

'*Great gods* –' Savrinor choked the oath out. 'I'll fetch Revian –'

One of the magi interrupted, his expression twisting with bitter intensity. 'Damn Revian! He can do nothing to help her or any of us! Those demons have smashed our sorcery, and with it the Maze – we have no more resources left; we have *failed!*'

As he spoke, there was an instant's psychic warning that hit them all like an icy, clutching hand. Then, stunningly, the sky lit up and a blinding radiance blasted through the entire castle. Shouts of alarm and fear rang from the direction of the dining hall; with a cry Savrinor covered his face with his hands against the glare. And Pirane's voice rose up in an anguished moan as she collapsed to the floor.

'Ah, no! Ah, *NO!*'

They came running; from the hall, from the council chamber, from passages and doorways, a clamour and hubbub of people rushing to see and to understand. Andraia and Qenever appeared; leaving her father Andraia caught hold of Savrinor's hand and they were propelled with the flux to the doors, to the courtyard –

And as the first of the gathering crowd stumbled outside, a dreadful silence fell.

The Warp was gone. The currents of energy streaming from the four spires were gone. In the sky, the sun burned vast and gory. And seven golden stars, like brilliant jewels on a huge, celestial necklace, proclaimed the triumph of the lords of Order.

Savrinor felt Andraia's fingers crush his, and her voice

when finally she broke the thrall of silence was a hoarse, barely audible whisper.

'*Sweet gods . . .* '

Someone laughed hollowly, brokenly, and a tall, elderly and haggard female magus on the steps cast a look almost of pity in Andraia's direction. But Savrinor could not speak; could not outwardly react in any way. All he knew was that his entire body was beginning to tremble, and the trembling bit deep, deep down through flesh and bone and marrow into the core of his being. As he stared at the seven golden stars he felt an emotion so powerful that he thought it would choke him. Hatred – hatred for the heretics and turncoats and traitors who had brought the world to this. Hatred, too, for the ultimate traitor, Vordegh, who had betrayed the gods he was sworn to serve and, in his deranged arrogance, had set himself above the rightful rule of Chaos.

In the centre of the courtyard, by the fountain, a new shadow manifested, darker and deeper than the shadows cast by the blazing stars. Savrinor's heart contracted, missed its pulse with a short, sharp stab of pain . . . and in the heart of the shadow the figure of Yandros took form.

The great Chaos lord's face was a chill, dead-white sculpture, devoid of expression. For a long moment his slanted, feline eyes took in the scene in the courtyard, while their colour changed through crimson, emerald and purple to a cold, ominous grey. No one moved. Then, very quietly, Yandros spoke.

'Where is Pirane?'

From the doorway a voice answered, 'I am here, my lord.'

Heads turned, and people moved aside as Pirane emerged onto the steps. She had recovered enough to walk unaided, but her movements were hesitant and unsteady. She looked old, and worn to the bone.

'First Magus.' A gaunt, bloodless hand reached out from the folds of darkness cloaking Yandros, and Pirane curtsied to one knee. Affection and something resembling sadness glimmered momentarily in Yandros's eyes, then vanished. 'We are defeated. Aeoris and his brood have broken our sway, and we shall have no choice but to concede to them. This castle is now the only stronghold left to us in the mortal world, and when it, too, falls we shall be banished from this dimension, just as we banished the demons of Order long ago.' He paused. 'The castle *will* fall, Pirane. But some of you, at least, might have the chance to be spared Order's retribution. Open these gates of your own free will to Aeoris's human army, and it may be that their commanders will allow some of your number to live.'

Pirane's mouth contorted faintly, a bitter ghost of a smile. 'If matters were reversed, Lord Yandros, I would not be so foolish as they are.'

Yandros returned the smile, giving it a harder edge. 'That is what I thought you would say. But the choice is yours. Unlike Order, we have always granted our followers freedom. That is a principle of Chaos, and the fact that it has led us all to this does nothing to lessen its value.'

Pirane bowed her head. 'I understand you, my lord. But . . .' She took a breath, and drew herself up to her full, formidable height. 'There will be no capitulation. We will stay loyal to the last – and destroy as many of them as we can before we die.'

Silence gripped the courtyard for several seconds. Then Yandros nodded.

'Then you justify my trust in you.' He turned his head, hair glinting acidly in the brazen light, and looked up. 'They will come at first moonrise; I think the idea of attacking at our favoured hour will amuse Aeoris, if he is capable of amusement. You must prepare in whatever way you feel fit.'

'And . . . you, my lord . . . ?'

'Our true power is broken, but until the castle is conquered Aeoris cannot send us into exile. We will repay the compliment of your loyalty, and be with you.'

And the shadow, and Yandros, were gone, leaving only silence and a terrible stillness in the courtyard.

CHAPTER XXVI

Savrinor was sitting at the desk in his outer room when Andraia came searching for him. He didn't look up immediately, but he stopped writing and then, very slowly and deliberately, laid his pen aside.

Andraia didn't speak, only gazed at him. He was immaculate; hair combed, clothes fresh and pristine; as elegant as though he were about to attend some formal celebration in the great hall. But the doors of his drugs cupboard stood open, and on the table beside him were several phials, a glass, an empty wine-flagon . . . and a long-bladed knife.

She stepped forward at last. 'Savrinor . . .'

He did look up then, and his eyes gave away everything.

'I thought,' he said matter-of-factly, 'that it might be as well to get it done with now, rather than wait for one of Order's minions to save me the trouble. But slashed wrists or an overdose of narcotics both seem rather sordid, not to mention cowardly. Besides, I still have work to do.'

She said, '*Work* . . . ?'

'Mmm. Oh, not at the magi's behest; though I like to think they'd appreciate the gesture if they didn't have other matters to occupy them at the moment. The notion is my own. And this,' indicating the document before him with a gesture that almost but not quite bordered on the savage, 'is personal.'

'Savrinor, stop it, *please!*' Andraia crossed the floor and put her arms around his shoulders as her own carefully-maintained mask began to crack. 'Oh, my love. Oh, my love . . .'

For a few moments his own emotions broke through, and he gripped her elbow, turning to press his face against her hair. Then, abruptly, he drew back. 'No, Andraia.' His voice was calm. 'We mustn't give way; not now. To do that would be to give satisfaction to our enemies.' He cupped her jaw with his hands. 'And don't cry. I can't abide tearful women.'

Andraia felt a sharp spark of indignation kindle in her, and, as Savrinor had calculated, it pulled her back from the brink. 'I'm not crying,' she said, and meant it.

'Thank the gods for that. Very well, then: tell me where you've been. What news there is.'

Oh, she could have told him so much, Andraia thought despairingly. Trying and failing to calm her hysterical mother. Discovering that her father was absent from the hall and finding him in his chambers with three women and a very large quantity of wine. Meeting Physician Revian on the stairs and hearing that the kitchen servants had been fighting and one had killed another, but what was the point now in punishing any of them, for it could serve no conceivable purpose. Learning that the backlash of power when Order repelled the magi's last assault had crippled the Maze, and now it could not be used or even closed, so the castle had only its physical defences left . . . 'Does it *matter* what news there is?' she said bitterly. 'Savrinor, there's so little *time*.' She cast a restive glance to the window. The seven stars had gone from the sky now, and the sun was westering, filling the courtyard outside with a familiar, roseate light. Everything looked unnervingly normal. 'It will be dusk soon. Then first moonrise. And then –'

'I know.' Savrinor paused. 'Have you got a weapon?'

'What?'

'I'd strongly advise you to get one. Knife or sword, whichever you feel better equipped to handle. One of the Chaos riders – Kivris, I think his name is; he's acting commander now that Averel's dead – recommends it, especially for the women in the castle.' He shrugged. 'As he said, our enemies are a rabble; and I don't want you to be . . .' Suddenly, unexpectedly, his voice caught, and with a violent movement he got to his feet, chair scraping back, as the self-control that drugs and determination had enabled him to hold on to started to crumble, like a stone wall being breached.

'Damn them! Yandros *damn* them!' He started to cough violently, took a grip on himself, wiped his mouth. 'Forgive me, I . . . just for a moment, it all . . .'

'I know.' Andraia took hold of his hand, squeezed it.

'I have matters to attend to.' He swung back to the table and gathered up the papers stacked there, then paused and looked intently at her. 'Will you help me?'

She nodded, not knowing whether she truly wanted to be in his company, or in someone else's, or in no one's. And she pushed down the thought that had been with her since morning and still ate at her like acid, locking it away where no living soul, least of all Savrinor, would ever find it.

The thought of her one-time lover now become her deadly enemy, Benetan Liss.

The sun's last rays were flaring over the sea when the army's spearhead emerged from the mountain pass and saw the Star Peninsula spread out before them.

Silence fell as the massed ranks assimilated the awe-inspiring vista. Under the sunset the sea had turned blood-red, starkly contrasted by the silhouettes of islets and reefs and the jagged coastline stretching away to east and west. But it was the castle that held every eye and every mind. Darker than the blackest night, the walls and the towering spires seemed to absorb every particle of light that fell on them; the great building stood poised on its stack like a predator, and as he looked at it Benetan felt intensely mixed emotions move within him. This scene was so familiar. He had seen it first as a terrified adolescent, then over the years had grown as accustomed to it as to the sight of his own face in a mirror, and lastly had returned to it as a wanted man in the tragic bid to save Iselia. Though now he loathed the castle and all it stood for, it had a place in his life that could never be erased.

He wondered what Simbrian was thinking. This was the sorcerer's first sight of the magi's stronghold, but his expression showed no surprise and little animation; he simply gazed thoughtfully at the view ahead of him and had no word to say. Beyond him Kaldar on his white horse sat motionless, but his nostrils flared as though at some scent, and his hands on the reins were suddenly white-knuckled with tension. And Aeoris, who had taken human form again to lead them all on this final undertaking, only smiled a cool and contented smile. Then Benetan became aware of the men behind him beginning to shift and murmur as their first rush of awe faded. There was a hunger in them, a growing greed for action and for more besides, and suddenly he was thankful that, this time, he did not have the full might of the entire army to control. Sorcery, Aeoris had said, would be as vital a factor as arms in the conquering of the castle, and he had commanded Benetan to take only a force of two thousand to join the fighting on the physical plane. So, leaving the vaster bulk of their followers to celebrate victory, a company consisting of Simbrian's sorcerers and the best of Benetan's fighting men had continued on the journey northwards, to their ultimate goal.

Still they had travelled at supernatural speed, and still the beings of Order ran and flowed with them. But as they drew nearer and nearer to the castle everyone had experienced a great sense of eerie tranquillity, which in the aftermath of the pandemonium that had gone before seemed like a waking dream. Their triumph was a certainty now; against incredible odds, Order had *succeeded* in its bid to overthrow Chaos; and the realisation brought a strange and almost bewildering feeling of peace.

Nonetheless, the victory had not been bought cheaply. Many of their followers had died; not only among the army's numbers but throughout the land, where Order's devotees – and, for that matter, those still loyal to Chaos – had had no protection from Yandros's last and most violent attack. Benetan grieved for them – but Aeoris said only that their deaths, though regrettable, had served a greater cause, and that should be comfort enough.

The restlessness behind him was increasing now, and Benetan forced himself out of his musing. From here the castle looked oddly vulnerable. No sign of any defences; no sign even of life. The Maze, he knew, could no longer be used, making it impossible for the magi to seal themselves off from the outside world. They could, of course, have destroyed the narrow rock bridge; but that would be no barrier to Aeoris, and they must know it. Yet they would have no intention of capitulating; that he could be sure of. What, then? What did they plan?

Aeoris turned in his saddle and looked back at him. 'They'll be aware of our presence,' he said. 'Prepare your men, Benetan. There will be losses, but we can sustain them.'

Not for the first time Benetan found the god's sanguine attitude discomforting. Enough people had already died . . . must there be yet more, and did they mean so little? But he said nothing, only nodded acquiescence and thrust down the squirming disquiet in his stomach.

The daylight was fading, the sun no more than a furious splinter on the horizon as night approached in a vast, soft wing out of the east. From the supernatural legion an eldritch singing began, a challenge and a promise. And the great bulk of the castle seemed to grow darker still . . .

Aeoris raised his right hand, and at the sign a new tension took hold through the ranks. Then, almost gently, the hand came down, pointing towards the distant stack. Light flowered, and from the tip of the Peninsula a radiant path flowed outwards, eclipsing the rock bridge to form a broad and shining road to the castle's very gates. And like a slow but purposeful river, the company began to advance.

The sensation began deep among the castle's foundations, a steady, ominous throbbing like the pulse of a colossal heart. Every castle-dweller felt it; every one of them knew what it portended. And it was the signal for Pirane to leave her chambers and make her controlled and dignified way to the central staircase.

The entrance hall was thronged with people. At the heart of the gathering stood the magi, and around them were officials, secretaries, Chaos riders, servants . . . the gamut of the castle's inhabitants from highest to lowest. Some, Pirane knew, had come only because they hoped for their masters' protection; but for most this was a silent testimony of allegiance. In the guttering light of torches they formed a bizarre, almost surreal tableau; then as Pirane appeared there was a movement, a turning of heads, and every eye focused on her as, tall and stately and stark in the simple black robe she had chosen, she walked down the stairs.

The crowd parted for her; at the end of the hall two Chaos riders opened the double doors. Dusk flowed in like fog, and Pirane moved out onto the steps of the courtyard. There, a shadow of absolute darkness awaited her; she bowed to it, and said, 'My lords.'

A pinpoint of light flickered in the darkness, a momentary image of a seven-rayed star. Then the shadow melted, and seven figures stood in the courtyard.

Yandros, serene, beautiful, lethal. And behind him, his six brothers. Black hair, like smoke curling. A vision of fire. Silver and green, and eyes that promised insanity. Ice-whiteness, and an eagle's profile. Darkness; profound peace. A silhouette deeper than the furthest reaches of space ... Pirane's mind was flung back to the night of Vordegh's inauguration, when she and so many others had been granted the unparalleled privilege of looking upon the faces of their seven gods. Even in her vilest nightmares she could never have dreamed that she would see them all again under circumstances such as these.

She looked into Yandros's eyes and said: 'They are coming, my lord.'

Yandros smiled, coldly, and a sword burning with black light took form in his hands. 'Then reap a good harvest,' he said. It was the old blessing of the magi to the Chaos riders, but with a new and dire meaning.

Pirane inclined her head, then lifted her gaze to the castle wall and beyond that to the sky. There was a new light rising in the south, where the mountains began. And, faintly but growing stronger and clearer, the sound of a sweet, harmonic and unhuman singing.

The First Magus raised her arms, and began to summon the strength of her will for the very last time ...

By first moonset, it was over ... but at a price which Benetan and many others among Order's followers had not expected to pay.

Four brief hours since the creatures of Aeoris's realm had launched themselves in a shrilling, singing tide against the gates of the castle, augmented by the power of Simbrian and his fellow sorcerers. The magi's retaliation was swift and ferocious, but from the beginning it was clear that they had no true hope of prevailing: their intention, simply and savagely, was to annihilate as many of Order's human forces as possible before the moment of their final downfall. And in that, they had succeeded. How many died in the crossfire of occult carnage before the gate was finally breached, Benetan could not begin to calculate; the magi's powers might be all but exhausted but they still had the ruthless will to fight, and Simbrian and his comrades, themselves beleaguered by the storm of the counter-attack, could spare little help or protection for their warriors. But amid the tumult of yelling and howling, the turmoil of power run amok, the din of monstrous, elemental clashes between Order's demons and the horrors conjured from the castle, there was suddenly a rising shriek of jubilation as the magical defences were sundered and, with a grinding rumble that sent echoes shouting out over the sea, the great gates of the barbican arch began to cave inwards.

They poured through in a bloodthirsty, screaming tide, and the small detachment of Chaos riders who had been struggling to hold the gates by physical force were hacked and trampled to oblivion as the spearhead rushed over them. Benetan, clinging to the mane of his shrieking mount as it bore him into the thick of it, had a frenzied impression of twisted faces, struggling bodies, steel and blood and lightning; a magus, wild-eyed and with one arm charred to the bone, hurled a spearing bolt of energy into the heart of the invaders; fire erupted and men howled in agony, but in a snarling surge of warriors the magus was overwhelmed. And in the midst of it all, their forms flickering and flaring, the seven lords of Order and the seven lords of Chaos added a greater and still deadlier element to the mayhem as they joined battle beside their followers.

But Benetan could spare no time for the gods' conflict, for he was suddenly beset by human attackers; men and women of the castle, armed with swords and knives and blazing torches, knowing him and hating him and thirsting for his blood above all others'. From that moment, as the conflict raged on, he knew nothing but the sheer pandemonium of preserving his own life; it was every man for himself now, no chance to rally, to regroup, to deploy any form of strategy. This was mad, uncontrollable warfare.

But finally, inevitably, the end came. Not in a clear-cut, exultant victory such as future ballads would proclaim, but in a gradual abatement that at last died away into a peculiar and disconcerting hiatus. In a sudden, uncanny silence, Benetan found himself sliding wearily from his mount's back to stand, on unsteady legs, staring around him at the courtyard. The first moon had vanished below the castle wall, but the second moon rode high among a scatter of stars, steeping the scene in cool, dim light.

The death toll was impossible to assimilate, let alone assess. The entire courtyard seemed to be strewn with corpses, allies and enemies indistinguishable. Somewhere near the pillared stoa, a man was moaning. And from the castle's west wing came, bizarrely, a burst of gleeful laughter.

Others, though, *had* survived, and were moving slowly, dazedly about him. Where were the rest? This couldn't be all; surely it couldn't . . . He turned and looked towards the main doors. They stood open, and from inside the castle there was a vivid dance of light and shadow. A figure carrying a burning brand moved in the entrance hall, and moments later one of the great torches in its wall bracket sprang to life. Benetan stumbled towards the steps, climbed them, went in. Feet were sounding overhead on the upper floor; other steps echoed in the direction of the council chamber, and from some distant location came an exultant whoop followed by a hollow thud.

Then a voice spoke to his left, spoke his name, and Benetan turned to see Simbrian.

'You survived . . .' Benetan's voice quavered; he laughed at that, and also at the absurdity of so obvious a statement. 'Thank the gods . . . ' A pause. 'Kaldar?'

'Unscathed, as are most of our sorcerers.' Simbrian frowned as though in pain. 'Our warriors, the ordinary men, took by far the worst of it.'

'They always do,' Benetan said wearily. 'You did all you could to protect them, Simbrian. You're not –' He stopped. He had been going to say, *you're not a god*, but there was a dimension behind that which he didn't want to explore. 'Ah, never mind. We have *some* left alive?'

'Oh yes; many. They're combing the castle, looking for any of its inhabitants who have escaped us. Tervis told them to be thorough.'

'Tervis. He came through it, then . . . I'm glad. And what of the magi?'

'All dead save for one; a woman called Pirane. I understand she is – or was – their new First Magus.'

'*Pirane?* Great gods, then they must have –'

'They overthrew Vordegh, yes. That, I think, is why their first great assault on us went so catastrophically wrong. But even Pirane's no threat now. She's a prisoner, and her powers have been curbed.' Simbrian paused. 'She's under guard in the great hall, and . . . others are with her. Lord Aeoris wants you to join him there.'

Benetan's stomach contracted suddenly. *Others?* Since the attack began he had given no thought to any inhabitants of the castle, but now, abruptly, a rush of thoughts and memories and old resolutions came into his mind. After Iselia's death – though now that seemed a world and an age away – he had promised himself that if the chance ever came, he would have scores to settle here, and one score in particular. Was Savrinor still alive? Knowing the historian as he did, Benetan thought it more than likely; Savrinor was as cunning as a cat, and had an equally feline instinct for self-preservation. He would not have joined the fighting. He would be skulking somewhere, preserving his own skin to the last. For Iselia's sake, in her memory, Benetan wanted to find him . . .

But then the second thought came, and abruptly his thoughts of Savrinor crumbled as he asked himself: *what has become of Andraia?*

'Benet?' Simbrian spoke into the sudden tense silence. 'Did you hear what I said?'

'I . . .' Benetan's face had become haggard. 'Yes, I – I

heard. Forgive me; I was just . . .' *Was her corpse among the litter in the courtyard, in the castle's rooms and corridors?* He thrust the awful mental image away, telling himself that her fate did not and must not matter to him. 'Yes,' he continued in something more akin to his normal voice. 'The great hall. Of course; I'll come.' He shuddered as they walked away together.

By some quirk the pitched battle that had raged through the castle had not touched the dining hall, and now, in an area near the dark and empty hearth, a small, strange gathering had assembled.

Aeoris was present, and Kaldar, and some dozen more of Order's faithful, all from the inner coterie. Pirane had been offered a chair but had scornfully declined it; she stood between two armed men, intimidatingly regal even in defeat, and her eyes burned with bitter contempt.

And before the fireplace, gaunt, formidable, lit by a glacial aura that burned about him like nacre, was Yandros.

Benetan stopped dead as he saw the Chaos lord, and a sharp, ugly sickness rose in his gorge. Yandros saw, and his mouth curved in an exquisitely sardonic smile. Then he turned his unquiet eyes to Aeoris.

'So another puppet comes to dance to his master's tune. Ah, well; if in some obscure way it satisfies your conceits to have Chaos's final capitulation witnessed by such creatures, it's of no significance to me.' A shrug, and a strange, cold ripple seemed to run through the hall.

Simbrian spoke up. 'And your followers, Yandros? Those who survive – they have been loyal to you. Will you not plead for them?'

Kaldar drew in a sharp, angry breath at that, and Benetan realized belatedly that among their number there was no little dissension over the fate of Chaos's surviving faithful. Kaldar, of course, would want revenge; Simbrian, typically, would speak up for leniency. And he himself . . . ? He didn't know.

Abruptly, startling him, Yandros laughed. 'I would not presume to plead or even to speak for my human followers,' the Chaos lord said. 'That, perhaps, is one of the fundamental differences between us and Aeoris's bloodless brood.' He paused, regarding the sorcerer closely. 'It's a great pity that you chose your loyalties as you did, Simbrian. You are an intelligent and talented man, and that's rare enough among mortals. However, your will is your own, to follow as you please. But I would strongly advise you' – a swift, acidly venomous glance in Aeoris's direction – 'to have a care in your dealings with your gods. You may find that the freedom you espouse is not *entirely* what you have been led to believe.'

He turned, then, to face Aeoris fully. 'Let's be done with this tiresome charade. You wish to hear the words; I will say them. I concede defeat, Aeoris of Order. My brothers have already retreated to our own realm; I will follow them, and then you may set the final seal on your triumph. But before I leave, I have one small service to perform.'

He held out his left hand, and Pirane, who had listened intently to the exchanges, moved abruptly towards him. One of her guards made to stop her and Kaldar said sharply, 'What is that treacherous whore –' But Yandros interrupted, and for the first time his voice was savage.

'Quiet your human worms, Aeoris!' His fingers locked with Pirane's, and with a swift movement he turned and kissed her hand. Pirane bowed to him; Yandros's grip on her fingers increased, so that she winced. Then, she smiled . . .

Yandros made one negligent gesture, and black fire erupted around Pirane's figure. Someone yelled, horrified, someone else swore aloud in shock – but Pirane flung her head back, and the strange, almost joyous peal of her laughter rang to the rafters of the great hall.

It took only seconds. Then the fire sank, flickered one

last time, winked out. Yandros gazed at his own hand, still extended and clenched now into a fist. Then, negligently, he opened his fingers, and a scatter of dust drifted to the floor. One flagstone was darkened; but there was nothing else to show where Pirane had stood, and where she had died.

Slowly, calmly, the Chaos lord turned his gaze back to Aeoris. 'Are you content, my old friend?'

Aeoris's mouth set in a harsh, controlled line. 'Go,' he said softly. 'Leave this world in peace.'

'Peace . . .' Yandros repeated the word thoughtfully. 'Ah. We shall see.'

He swung round. For a moment the bright crown of his hair seemed to blaze as though with another kind of flame. Then, without a sound, he was gone.

Stillness hung like smoke in the hall. Aeoris stood motionless, gazing through the hearth before him, through time and space it seemed, into another and, to mortals, unimaginable dimension. Kaldar was breathing harshly, his chest rising and falling; someone laid a hand on his arm in an attempt to soothe him but he flung it savagely off. Simbrian stared at the floor. And Benetan felt as though he were standing on a precipice that might at any moment give way and pitch him into a void.

Chaos, defeated and banished . . . It had seemed an impossible fantasy, a kind of delirium. But it had happened. An end to injustice; an end to tyranny; a new, brave and exhilarating world in which any and every hope and dream was possible. It had *happened* – and he, the predator reformed, Chaos's reaver who had turned against his own kind, had been among its orchestrators.

Why, then, *why*, did he feel as though he had lost his entire world?

Aeoris moved suddenly, breaking the thrall that gripped the company. As the paralysis shattered away, sounds began to impinge from the distance. Shouting, running feet, yelps of delight and relish; the crash of something heavy falling and smashing . . .

'Simbrian. Benetan.' The lord of Order spoke with quiet, absolute authority. 'Some of Chaos's minions still evade the search. Find them, deal with them as you see fit, and restore peace to this place before dawn. Let us be rid, once and for all, of Chaos's taint.'

He left the hall, and Benetan stared after him. *Deal with them as you see fit* . . . 'Simbrian!' Suddenly and urgently he turned to the sorcerer. 'The men – if they find survivors, they'll butcher them!' And there was a face in his inner vision, a memory which, despite the savagery and the bitterness and the vast gulf between them, still *hurt*. Anyone else, *anyone*, and the vengeful groups now running riot through the castle could do as they pleased. But not to her . . . He put a hand to his sheathed sword, and for one moment the pitiless echo of the hunter, the Chaos rider, showed in his eyes.

'I'll have no atrocities here!' He snapped the words out. 'There's been enough barbarity – it must *stop*.' A pause. 'Simbrian, help me!'

'Yes,' Simbrian said. 'Gladly.'

They left the hall together.

CHAPTER XXVII

When he heard the footsteps on the stairs of the library vault, Savrinor thought for a few seconds that his stomach would betray him and he would vomit. *This, then, was the end of it* – but the spasm ebbed, driven perhaps by a reserve of spirit – he wouldn't go so far as to call it courage – that he hadn't even known he possessed.

One man: just one, and by the sound of it a man used to subterfuge. Likely enough that they would send one of their better minions to search this cranny, rather than let the rabble run indiscriminately through it. These archives, after all, were valuable. They could be *used*.

Or could have been . . .

The footsteps had slowed; the intruder was cautious now, not knowing what to expect. That would give him another few seconds; a saving grace. Savrinor looked at the pile of ashes in the middle of the floor, and smiled a particularly private smile. Why did he feel so calm? Perhaps it was the drugs, or perhaps he was in truth as mad as First Magus Vordegh had been; caught up in a personal obsession that eclipsed all other considerations. He had been careful, so very careful; choosing only those documents which would have been precious jewels in the hands of Order's sorcerers, while the rest, the mundane histories and herbals and tithe-records and all the other *tedious* dross of his office remained as pristine as it was worthless.

Oh, and that last paper. His personal testament; his last tribute to the gods he served. It lay now on the table beside him, just beyond the candle-light's reach. They would find it, and he wished them joy of it. Joy, and a worm in the bud of their dreams. For he had told the *truth*.

The footfalls reached the bottom of the spiral stairs and stopped. Savrinor looked up, raising his candle so that its light reached unsteadily to the door. Sweet Yandros, he felt so *ill*. Everything was unreal. Why wasn't he afraid any more?

Then the door eased open . . .

Benetan halted on the threshold and stared at the scene before him. He hadn't expected this. To his mind the library, untouched as yet because few among the hunting parties even knew of its existence, had seemed the obvious refuge for survivors seeking shelter from their conquerors. He had thought, he had hoped — but thought and hope collapsed as he stared into Savrinor's drug-laden eyes.

'*You* . . .' The word cracked from his throat, and in it was a turmoil of emotion.

Savrinor said: 'Dear gods . . .'

Slowly, feeling that he was moving in a peculiar, sluggish and heavy dream, Benetan began to draw his sword. One strike, just one, and this serpent would meet the fate he should have suffered a long, long time ago.

Then, shocking him, Savrinor said in a shaking voice, 'For both our sakes, Benetan, just tell me one thing, and then you can do what you will with me. *Is she alive?*'

Benetan's hand froze as, through all the fury and the hatred and the vengefulness, he felt the raw power of Savrinor's plea. And he couldn't answer it.

'I tried to find her,' the historian went on. 'Gods help me, I *tried*.' In his mind he was running again through the frenzy of corridors, knife in hand but with no conception of how he might use it if he was forced to do so; dodging, evading, searching, seeking . . . 'I don't know where she is!' He sucked air into his lungs. 'Yandros damn you, Benetan Liss, *do you know what's become of her?*'

In that moment, Benetan knew that he couldn't kill

420

Savrinor. Something – and it was so hard to assimilate, so hard to *accept* – bound them together. Not hatred. Not hatred, but love . . .

'I don't know.' His voice sounded to his ears like the voice of a stranger. 'Like you, Savrinor. Like you . . . I don't know where she is.'

He turned; he left the library, and Savrinor, and the ashes of the magi's sorcerous secrets. And none of it, *none* of it mattered any more.

Savrinor stared at the open door and the dark stairwell beyond. On some distant, detached level he was aware of how close his brush with death had been, for Benetan loathed him, and, by his lights now, with every reason. But the knowledge no longer had the power to cow him, or even to move him. And the work which for the past hour had been the focus of his existence suddenly had no more meaning . . .

He uttered an old, terrible oath, and reached to a pocket of his coat. There was a phial there; one he had brought from his rooms and which was, in one sense at least, an ultimate solution. The road to damnation would be paved with pleasure, but was that so bad a thing? After all, there was nothing else left now. Nothing else at all.

But then a spark of an emotion he couldn't name – possibly the last vestiges of the will to survive, and something else besides – kindled in a deep, locked-away part of his mind. Chaos was defeated. His world was gone. But *something* still remained. One hope. Just one . . .

Savrinor slid the phial back into his pocket. With an ingrained reflex he smoothed his hair back, and flicked a smear of ash from his sleeve. Then he set the candle down on the nearest table, to burn out in its own good time, and started towards the stairs.

She was in one of the corridors of the west wing when Benetan found her. The passage was unlit, but an untoward movement, a darker shadow among shadows, gave her away as she shrank from his approaching silhouette. Benetan moved with the swiftness of his training; the tip of his sword clashed startlingly against a parrying knife-blade, and he found himself staring into her hectic green eyes.

'*Andraia!*' Shock, thankfulness, confusion – he couldn't separate one from another, and over all was the giddying relief of finding her alive.

She stared at him. Her hair was a wild tangle, her skirt torn and dirty, and there were other, darker stains on her bodice. She said: 'Benet . . . oh, gods, Benet . . .' But if he had hoped to hear relief in her voice, there was none. She was like an animal, knowing only what she saw before her, feeling only that he was an enemy. The past, and whatever it had once meant to her, was forgotten.

Slowly, carefully, she rose from the crouching position she had taken at his approach, and the hand holding the knife – clumsily, he noted on some distant level – dropped to her side. An odd, feverish colour flamed in her cheeks, and she said, 'Do what your new masters want of you. Get it *over* with.'

He didn't understand. 'What –'

'*Kill me.*' Venom made her voice crack. 'It's what they expect, isn't it? Or . . .' Her hand trembled, and her savagery increased. 'Or are you going to pretend that you still have some feeling for me? That you're *sorry* it has come to this?'

Benetan continued to stare at her, trying and failing to understand the emotions that were coursing through him. He still loved her. Even though they were inimically opposed, even though he had also loved Iselia, and had given his ultimate loyalty to her, he still loved Andraia . . . And suddenly, desperately, he thought: *there could yet be a chance –*

'Andraia!' He threw the sword aside, not caring about

422

the danger from the knife in her hand. 'Andraia, listen to me, please! I don't want you to die – you've got everything to live for, or you could have if you'd only choose it! We – the followers of Order – we're not vengeful,' and he pushed away an image of Kaldar as he said it. 'If you'll come with me –'

She cut across him. 'They killed my father. Butchered him, in the courtyard. I was there. I *saw*.'

'Gods help me, it was a *battle* –'

'I killed someone, too.' She stared almost musingly at the knife, which was pointing towards Benetan's stomach. 'I had a sword, and I stabbed him in the back. The blade went into his heart and I left it there.' Now she looked up again, and there was scorching disgust in her eyes. 'My mother's dead. My friends are dead. And you ask me to come with you, and join your traitorous, murdering – *Yandros!*' Spittle flecked her lips and she wiped it away with her free hand. Then her fingers flexed on the knife hilt. 'I'd like to do to you what I did to that other man. I'd like to *kill* you.'

He watched the knife. 'You hate me that much?'

She frowned. 'No. No, I don't think I do hate you. I did, for a while, but now . . .' She looked at his face searchingly, thoughtfully, then repeated, 'No, I don't hate you now. But I hate what you've done. You betrayed the gods, Benetan, and for that I will never, *never* forgive you.'

He said, 'Andraia, if you'd only try to understand, to see the truth . . .'

'Truth? Oh, no; no, Benet, no.' She drew air harshly into her lungs. 'Do whatever you will to me; either kill me or let me go to my gods – *the* gods – in my own way. But don't insult me by pretending that your *truth* is any less twisted than Vordegh's ever was!'

They looked at each other once more, and Benetan knew then that nothing he could say or do would sway her. The chasm between them was too vast; it could not be bridged. Neither of them was capable of bridging it. He said uneasily, 'What will you do?'

'Does it matter to you?'

It did, but he couldn't bring himself to admit it, and he looked away.

'Let me past, Benetan,' she said. 'I've nothing more to say to you, nor you to me, and what I do or where I go from now on is none of your concern.' She made a move away from the wall. 'Let me go. Or, Yandros help me, I *will* use this knife.'

He stepped back, and with the shreds of her dignity Andraia slid past him.

'Goodbye, Benet.' She turned her back, took a step along the corridor. Her voice was beginning to shake. 'I won't wish you good fortune, for that would be an empty gesture.'

Two more paces, her shoes loud against the quiet. Suddenly Benetan said, 'Savrinor's alive.'

Andraia stopped and he heard the sharp intake of her breath.

'In the library.' *Why, in Aeoris's name, was he telling her this?* 'I saw him there.'

She looked back at him, strangely, curiously, perhaps guessing or sensing something of what had taken place between the two men. And Benetan thought, though he couldn't be sure, that tears glinted in her eyes.

'Then,' she said, 'I will find him.'

She walked away, turned a corner, was lost to sight. Seconds later Benetan heard her footfalls quicken as she began to run.

Dawn broke amid stillness and calm, and as the first rays of the sun filtered through the dining hall's tall windows Simbrian touched Benetan's shoulder to rouse him.

Benetan raised his head from where he had pillowed it

on his folded arms, and his exhausted eyes focused on the sorcerer's face. 'Simbrian . . . gods, have I slept?'

'Only for an hour.' Simbrian smiled at him. 'And it was necessary. You worked well, Benet. The castle's quiet and peace has been restored as Lord Aeoris commanded.'

Benetan pushed back the bench on which he was sitting, and rose to his feet. Every muscle in his body ached. 'Then there's been no further trouble?' he asked.

'None. Even the wine-cellars are untouched; Tervis put reliable men on guard against any looting.' Simbrian sighed. 'We couldn't stop the early excesses, but it was only a savage few who behaved barbarically.'

Benetan nodded. That was always the way; in every basket of apples, as the saying went, there were some which were rotten and threatened to infect the rest. Later, he would deal with those rotten ones, cut them out. That was all part of a commander's duty . . .

'And what of the castle-dwellers?'

'I think most are accounted for. Many tried to hide; there were some skirmishes and . . . well, you know already that the majority of those who were found were killed. Some are doubtless still eluding us, but there's time enough to search them out.'

'Yes. I'll organize that; send the better men. There's no need for any more killing.' He flexed his fingers, which were stiff and sore. 'Where is Lord Aeoris?'

'In the council hall.' Simbrian smiled, his eyes suddenly warming. 'He has sent for others from our number. The women; Shammana and Nanithe will be among them. And other good friends. His brother-gods will join us, and then there's to be a celebration.'

'Of victory?' Suddenly there was a strange edge to Benetan's voice, but the sorcerer shook his head.

'No, my friend, not of victory or of war or of any grandiose triumph. Simply, of the dawning of a new era. And that is something in which we can all rejoice.'

Benetan saw them then, in his mind, in his inner vision. All those who, willingly or otherwise, had had a vital role to play, like the pawns of a gambling game. Vordegh, whose madness had kindled the first true spark of rebellion. Pirane, who had taken Vordegh's place too late. Lotro, who in his innocent quest for justice had unknowingly helped to turn the tide. Iselia, who had fulfilled her promise to the gods and suffered so much for it. Kaldar, surviving but damaged beyond repair. And Savrinor and Andraia . . . where were they, now? Did they find each other, or were they just two more corpses to be counted and given to the pyre that was to mark the final cleansing?

Then one more face formed in his mind's eye. Beautiful, aristocratic, mercurial, unhuman . . . Yandros of Chaos. For centuries a god to be worshipped; now a demon to be reviled. He had no place in this world now. No place at all.

Benetan raised his head and looked at Simbrian, and felt the leaden weight beginning to lift from his heart. It would take time to depart entirely, but no matter. One day, it *would* be gone.

'Something in which we can all rejoice,' he said, repeating the sorcerer's words slowly. 'Pray it's so, my dear friend. Pray it's so.'

The door opened with a click that sounded loud against the muffling quiet in the stairwell, and as it swung back Savrinor saw that the room beyond was furnished only with necessities. A table, a chair, a long, wide couch with cushions and two neatly folded blankets at one end. Nothing more. Gory morning sunlight slanted in through the window, and dust-motes danced in the shafts that pooled on the bare floor. He stood staring at it all, aware with some other, meaningless part of his mind that the climb up the titanic staircase hadn't exhausted him as by rights it should have done. His heart was labouring, yes, but nothing more; the drugs he had newly taken – Moonwrack, and something more – had given him, albeit temporarily, an abnormal strength, and the fact that their influence was also making everything look and feel very unreal didn't seem to signify. After all, wasn't everything unreal now? Everything he had ever known, ever understood, ever believed in? It had all been swept away, and nothing could possibly matter any more.

Behind him Andraia moved. Her hand touched his, tentatively, and he realized that he had been standing meditating as though there was nothing in the world to concern or alarm him. Well, perhaps in truth there wasn't . . . but all the same her touch prompted him to move into the room and look about more closely. Ah, yes; there was another door, all but hidden behind the high-backed bulk of the couch. Very small, very narrow; but beyond it there would be stairs winding up the short distance to the spire's summit. That would be good enough when the time came.

It still seemed to him a miracle that they had found each other. He had been in the west wing, trying to reach his rooms in the hope that she, too, might make her way there, and in a little-used corridor they had simply and unexpectedly come face to face. There had been so much to say, yet neither of them could articulate it; bereft of words they had sought only to evade the armed groups still patrolling the passages searching for survivors. Savrinor was above all else a survivor, and knew the castle's byways better than anyone now left alive. They had come through. And in his room, which had been ransacked and thus was safe, they had talked at last, and the decision had been made. Just one more stealthy foray in the breaking dawn, through corridors now eerily silent and empty. They had encountered no one, friend or enemy. And now they had reached their destination, in the haven of the north spire.

Andraia closed the outer door behind her. A very *final*

sound, Savrinor thought. She too looked at the inner door, but there was no need for either of them to voice the obvious, and to do so would have seemed in poor taste. Then she walked slowly to the south-facing window; Savrinor followed and together they gazed down on the dizzying drop to the courtyard. All was still; the scene looked strangely peaceful. And the world seemed so *quiet*. Only the wind was audible up here, sighing and mourning as it blew in from the sea. It would be easy to imagine that nothing had changed, that this was simply another morning and life within the black walls was continuing as it had always done. Savrinor found the vista almost unbearably macabre and turned his face from it, looking instead at the curve of Andraia's neck, at her shoulder above the begrimed dress; at her skin, at her hair. For a moment it seemed anomalous, even aberrant, that he should be aroused by such things at a time like this; but then he had already thought that carefully through and concluded that it was not. Quite the converse, in truth. It was a last oblation, a final celebration and thanks to the gods of Chaos. Yandros, he believed, would unequivocally approve.

He leaned forward, bowed his head and touched his lips to the hollow between her neck and shoulder, at the same time letting one hand come to rest on the small of her back. Andraia turned towards him and shut her eyes, pressing her cheek against his hair. Softly, she said, 'They must still be searching. How much time do you think we have left, before they reach this far?'

'I don't know. Maybe two hours, maybe three or more. They might not even trouble to make the climb. Starvation would flush us out before long.' He paused. 'There's time enough.'

'Yes.' She nodded; he felt the slight movement of her head. 'Oh, yes.'

Savrinor took the phial he had brought from his coat

pocket. Sunlight caught the glass and made it wink like a tiny, ruby eye; the liquid inside glowed with a peculiar nacre. Andraia looked at it and then at him, a question in her eyes, and he smiled at her in a way that held a very faint echo of the old Savrinor, the sly, feline sybarite. 'It's very strong,' he said. 'I might even say drastic, for it could well be that in my state of health the after-effects could stop my heart. But it seems a little superfluous to worry about that now.'

Andraia almost, but not quite, laughed. 'And me?' she asked. 'Would it harm me, too?'

'Oh, no.'

'What would it do?'

'It would . . . concentrate you. Not just your mind; everything. A very close focus. Like the other phial, the first phial; do you remember? But more so; far more.' He kissed her cheek, savouring the taste of her skin. 'If you want it.'

She hesitated, thinking, then a little to his surprise she shook her head. 'No, Savrinor, I don't think I do want it. I just want to be me, this one last time; me, and nothing more nor less.' She tried to smile but couldn't quite compel the smile to happen. 'Do you understand that?'

He believed he did, and as her arms slid round him he held her close, wishing that he could be like her and forego the craving, the imperative, to heighten his world and his senses in order to find fulfilment. But wishing the impossible served no purpose. Their own different ways; their own different needs. Let it be, he thought. Let it be at that.

He measured the dosage he wanted from the phial and added just a little more; a kind of bravado perhaps. Then he led her to the couch and, as the drug started to catch fire in his brain and body, carefully and meticulously removed her clothing, pausing every now and then to watch and appreciate her for a few moments. Andraia's hands moved over him, gliding, exquisite now that physical awareness was becoming highlighted; suddenly he pressed down on her and bit her shoulder, catching her by surprise and making her cry out. The sound she made pleased him, as did the marks his teeth had left in her flesh. His own clothes had begun to feel intolerably hot and clammy; he stripped them away without ceremony, conscious now of Andraia's fingernails drawing long, stinging lines down the skin of his back and of her body moving against him with increasing fervour. Every nerve in him seemed to ache, and somewhere deep under the ache was a grief that he had no power to exorcize or express. But the drug was taking hold and it allowed him to turn the sorrow aside one final time and be what he had always been, give rein to it, his gift to her in their last sacrament . . .

Andraia saw the look in his heavy-lidded eyes change subtly but potently, and felt the temper of his body change, too. A strange, vital but perilous hunger; the knife-edge again, but this time with a very different emphasis. Then quickly and unexpectedly, like a predator, his hands moved. And his kiss changed to something far less controlled –

'Savrinor –' She snatched her head aside and tensed, shrinking back, suddenly uncertain. Savrinor smiled sensually, and there was a challenge in his look. His hands moved again, swiftly, forcefully, and she gasped.

'You're *hurting* me!'

He caught hold of her hair, looked steadily and almost thoughtfully into her eyes. There was a welling bead of blood on her lip and he could taste its saltiness on his own tongue. Then his narrow hips insinuated between her thighs and he said, very softly, 'Do you care?'

He felt hot to her, an unnatural heat, burning her skin and bringing a kind of pain that was almost too pleasurable to bear. And a part of Andraia that was purely animal, purely impulsive and instinctive, rose up from the night-world of her subconscious mind and overflowed into a giddying surge of desire and need.

'No,' she said. 'No. No.' And her hands reached out and her body arched towards him, calling him to her and welcoming him into her, and, as they began to move together with a desperate urgency, she prayed silently for the hurt and the bliss and the fear and the triumph to combine and coalesce in one last ecstasy on the road to oblivion.

There was nothing left to do or say. It was impossible to judge how much time had passed; such concepts seemed to have no meaning any more. Their bodies and limbs were reluctant to untwine; the couch was comfortable and their shared warmth a balm, and if they closed their eyes it was almost possible to believe that this quiet, very private interlude could be made to last forever.

But forever was an illusion. At last Savrinor slid away from her, and Andraia sighed a small sigh that seemed to express more than any words might have done. Sorrow, reluctance, wistfulness, resignation . . . and even a strange and ambiguous form of contentment. She watched him as he dressed – he took his time, as though trying to stave off what lay ahead – then reached for her own clothes. She fastened his shirt for him; he her bodice for her. Then she combed his hair until it shone, now and then pausing to kiss him in a gentle, almost childlike way that contrasted acutely with their earlier passion.

He said only one word to her, his voice quiet and serious as he stood before her and laid his hands on her waist. 'Ready?'

Andraia nodded and her arms slipped away from his neck and shoulders. They walked hand in hand to the inner door; Savrinor opened it and the stairs twisted before them. Light slanted down the short flight from somewhere above, and a draught of fresh, chilly air wafted against their faces.

Impulsively, incongruously, Andraia wanted to make a joke, but nothing appropriate would come to her and she stayed silent.

Fifteen stairs, that was all, and then the world spread out before them as they emerged onto the summit of the spire. The strength of the wind came as a sharp surprise; Andraia swayed and almost lost her balance before Savrinor's hand and a quick clutch at the carved stonework steadied her. Regaining her composure she shivered, and felt him move more closely against her.

'Are you cold?'

'No.' She made to shake her head but, up here, thought better of it. Then she smiled wryly. 'Not in that sense.'

He uttered a strange semi-laugh. 'Who can say what we'll be in a little while from now? Cold, or hot, or . . . simply oblivious.'

Her green eyes regarded him sidelong, thoughtfully. 'You'd know the answer better than I would, Savrinor.'

It was the first time that she had ever asked him, however obliquely, about his experiences during the minutes before Yandros had restored his life in the Marble Hall. Savrinor thought back – reluctantly even now, though that struck him as a little absurd under the circumstances – then sighed.

'I have no answer, Andraia. Maybe before this,' a brief, damning gesture towards the courtyard encompassed all his feelings, 'I might have felt some certainty. But not now. The gods are no longer a part of this world and I don't know whether they're still even aware of our existence, let alone able to reach out to us. Or, if they can, whether they will.' He turned his head to look more directly at her. 'So, this threshold is as new to me as it is to you.' A pause. 'Does that upset you?'

It did, but to tell him so would have seemed unkind, so Andraia only took hold of his hand and squeezed the fingers. 'An adventure,' she said quietly, her voice barely audible above the ramp of the wind. 'We must look upon it as that.'

There was nothing more to say that seemed worthwhile. A part of Savrinor wanted to ask her so many questions — about herself, the small and almost meaningless things which he had never troubled to find out; about her likes and dislikes, hopes and fears, dreams and ambitions. But though those words wouldn't come, one question had to be asked. Perhaps it was vanity, a need to bolster his own faltering courage, though that was a goad which could all too easily rebound on him. Nonetheless, he voiced it.

'And Benetan,' he said. 'What about him?'

'Ah, Benet.' Unconsciously perhaps, Andraia still used the shortened form of his name. 'He'll prosper in his new role, I've no doubt of that.' Her mouth hardened a little. 'I wish him neither well nor ill of it. That's the sad thing. I don't care enough any more even to hate him.' For a moment her expression was unreadable. Then: 'Let's go to the north side now, Savrinor. I don't want to look at what the castle has become; I want to remember it as it was and as it should be. At night, under the moons. Without this *taint.*'

Savrinor nodded. An ache was beginning beneath his ribs and it was an emphatically physical pain; the drug he had taken was claiming its price, as he had expected. No matter. Time might be running out for him, but what remained would be enough. He would win the race.

Steadying each other, they moved carefully around the narrow catwalk, leaving the courtyard behind, turning towards the endless vista of the northern sea and the edge of the world. The wind took on a chillier bite, and under his hand Savrinor felt Andraia relax.

'Better,' she said, half to herself, and raised her face towards the sky. 'The air tastes clean now.' Then abruptly she turned and focused a clear, brilliant gaze on him. 'Let's not wait any longer.'

433

Her arms slipped round his neck and she leaned towards him. Savrinor's hands took hold of her and when he kissed her it was a lover's kiss, intense yet gentle, offering all he had to give but asking nothing in return. She clung to him briefly, then raised her head and touched his cheek. She wasn't crying. She knew his view of tearful women.

'I love you, Savrinor,' she said. 'I only wish I'd realized it a very long time ago.'

'Perhaps,' he replied softly, 'it doesn't matter. Perhaps there's far more ahead of us than we could ever have hoped to find here.'

She closed her eyes briefly. 'I pray to our lord Yandros that that's true.'

'As do I.'

For a little while they stood unmoving, the wind stirring their hair and clothes. Savrinor offered a silent but profound invocation to the gods of Chaos, knowing that she was doing the same. Then, urged by a mutual but unspoken instinct, they turned and looked down. Sheer, smooth, black stone as the spire fell away and merged with the castle's outer wall. Then the granite of the stack, a thousand feet to the surging, white-capped swell of the sea. The tide was high and the sunlight imbued the water with subtle shades of green and blue and purple. It looked very beautiful.

Savrinor's hand closed suddenly on hers and the grip was intense. He said: 'Stay with me, Andraia. I don't want to be alone.'

He saw the answer to his appeal in her eyes, and the pain in him faded and lost its meaning. No need for any more words; no words, now, that could be relevant. The gods, he was certain, understood.

He gave the briefest of nods. Hand in hand, as one, they stepped forward, over the spire's edge, and felt the vastness take them.

434

EPILOGUE

The library smelled of burned paper, and traces of smoke still drifted and clung among the curving stones of the vault ceiling. Such a waste, such wanton destruction . . . but as he held the document in his hand, Simbrian had suddenly no thought for the ruin wrought by Savrinor's last act of loyalty. For the words written here were coming home to him. The words of a final testament, a final defiance, to which there could be no reply.

The immaculate hand, the graceful script. It said much about the kind of man Savrinor had been. As for the text itself . . . it spoke of a fealty that matched Simbrian's own; unshakeable, enduring, incorruptible. And as he read the last paragraph, above the flourishing signature, Simbrian felt the steady calm within him ebb just a little . . .

'Our gods go into exile; we go to destruction. But we have solace in the certainty that the rigid and stagnant reign of Order cannot endure for all time. Let it take five generations or five thousand, the circle will come about once more. Our gods are patient, but in time the challenge will be issued. Chaos will return.'

A strange, cold breath blew through the vault, and the door creaked gently as though an invisible hand had touched it. Simbrian looked round, and for a few moments stood motionless as a small, uneasy frisson brushed across his psyche. Then, with a small and faintly self-deprecating smile, he laid the paper down. There was no other presence here save his own. No ghosts.

He walked slowly, peaceably from the library, closing the door behind him.

* * *

And in another place, another dimension, estranged and isolated now from the world of mortals, Yandros gazed from a narrow window in a tall, dark tower that stood incongruously alone in the midst of a bleak landscape. The tower and its surroundings were an ironic comment on the events of the recent past and their final outcome, and reflected the Chaos lord's present disposition . . . but in the distance, where the horizon merged indistinctly with a murky sky, pinpoints of light were shifting like restless will-o'-the-wisps, suggesting, to anyone who knew Yandros well, that there was another and altogether more combative dimension to his mood.

Tarod entered the room – which bore a faint resemblance to the spire rooms in the castle of the Star Peninsula – and moved silently across the floor to join his brother. Yandros looked round briefly, then resumed his contemplation of the scene. His eyes, which had matched the colour of the sky, changed abruptly to a strange, dark gold and he said, 'How much time will pass, I wonder, before the seeds of disillusionment are sown and start to take root?'

Tarod smiled reservedly. 'Truly, Yandros, I wouldn't care to hazard. Possibly a mere few years. Or possibly many centuries.'

Yandros turned his head again and gave him a long, assessing look which held more than a trace of cynical amusement. 'Centuries? You have more faith in mortal nature than I have – but then perhaps that's not to be wondered at; you've always been something of a champion of humanity, after all.'

Tarod didn't respond to the remark, and for a small interlude Yandros studied the landscape again, his expression inscrutable. Then, meditatively, he said: 'And that, of course, could stand us in good stead at some time in the future . . .'

A sound, almost but not quite like the restless movement

of wings, sounded from somewhere overhead, and Tarod raised a dark eyebrow queryingly. 'What do you mean?' A pause. 'Do you have some plan in mind?'

Yandros shrugged. 'I wouldn't go so far, yet, as to term it a plan ... let us say rather, a speculation.' He turned once again and suddenly there was a calculating, almost malevolent spark in his eyes; an echo of the assured and sanguine ruler. 'And if it takes your predicted centuries to come about, what does that matter? We are as skilled in the art of patience as we are in many others. We can afford to wait, and we can find amusement enough to occupy ourselves during the waiting. We shall watch, Tarod. We shall see the road that these mortals take under the austere and narrow regime that Aeoris will impose. And when the seeds he has sown bear fruit, and the fruit is ripe, we shall be ready to pluck it from the tree.' Tension flickered through him, a brief but emphatic sting that set thunder bawling dismally in the far distance. 'We of Chaos have always been adaptable to the winds of change, and able to ride and use those winds to our own advantage. And in time we will use them, Tarod. We will challenge the rule that Aeoris has imposed on the mortal world – and you, with your understanding of the human soul, will perhaps be our most powerful weapon.'

'I?'

'Yes.' He stepped away from the window at last and laid a hand on Tarod's arm. There was something conspiratorial in the gesture, something that spoke of a future promise. And, though the knowledge was now beyond the reach of either the historian or the gods he had served until the last, the words that Yandros uttered then echoed Savrinor's last, defiant challenge to his conquerors.

'In time ...' he said softly. 'In time, my brother, the balance will swing again. And Chaos will return.'

THE END

David Eddings

Domes of Fire

Book one of
The Tamuli

PRINCE SPARHAWK AND
THE TROLL-GODS

Queen Ehlana and the Pandion Knight Sir Sparhawk are
married, their kingdom peaceful at last, their union
blessed with a very special daughter named Danae. But
soon trouble sweeps westward from the Tamul Empire to
disrupt not only the living of Eosia but the dead: horrific
armies are being raised from the dust of the long-past Age
of Heroes, threatening the peace won at such cost in
Zemoch.

Prince Sparhawk is called upon to help the Tamuli nations
defeat these ancient horrors. Perhaps the Troll-Gods are
once more loose in the world! With Ehlana and a retinue
of Pandion Knights, Sparhawk will make the hazardous
journey to the Tamul Empire . . . only to discover in fire-
domed Matherion, the incandescent Tamul capital, that
the enemy is already within its gates.

Full of marvels and humour, romance and shrewdness,
above all full of magic, the resources of the epic form are
mined deep by the greatest of modern fantasy writers.

ISBN 0 586 21313 9

David Eddings

The Shining Ones

Book two of
The Tamuli

HAVOC AND WAR

Prince Sparhawk is pledged to fight the enemies of the
Tamul Emperor Sarabian with all the skill and cunning of a
Pandion Knight. Meanwhile his Queen, Ehlana, educates
Sarabian in the art of ruthless statesmanship. Sarabian is
transformed from a mere puppet ruler into a formidable
politician. But still Trolls, vampires, werewolves, zombies,
ghouls and Ogres form a vast conspiracy to take over the
Empire. Most disturbing of all are reported sightings of the
Shining Ones amongst the hordes. These luminous beings
inspire more fear than the rest combined. And Sparhawk
and his companions must resurrect the sacred jewel of the
Troll-Gods to combat them.

The enemies of the Empire know that possession of the
jewel makes Sparhawk as dangerous as any god. But gods
are among his foes. And while Sparhawk defends the far-
flung Tamul Empire, he cannot also protect his beautiful
Queen.

David Eddings, the greatest of modern fantasy writers,
unveils the hidden powers at work in the story of Sparhawk
and the Tamul Empire, an epic for our times.

ISBN 0 586 21316 3

David Eddings

By the world's greatest living fantasist, the Sparhawk books: volumes
one to three of The Elenium and volumes one to three of The Tamuli